PENGUIN BOOKS

THE LONDON PIGEON W

Patrick Neate is the author of two previous novels: *Musungu Jim and the Great Chief Tuloko*, which won a Betty Trask Award, and *Twelve Bar Blues* which won the 2001 Whitbread Novel Award. He divides his time between London and elsewhere.

PATRICK NEATE

THE
LONDON
PIGEON
WARS

PENGUIN BOOKS

PENGUIN BOOKS

Published by the Penguin Group
Penguin Books Ltd, 80 Strand, London WC2R ORL, England
Penguin Group (USA) Inc., 375 Hudson Street, New York, New York 10014, USA
Penguin Books Australia Ltd, 250 Camberwell Road, Camberwell, Victoria 3124, Australia
Penguin Books Canada Ltd, 10 Alcorn Avenue, Toronto, Ontario, Canada M4V 3B2
Penguin Books India (P) Ltd, 11 Community Centre, Panchsheel Park, New Delhi – 110 017, India
Penguin Books (NZ) Ltd, Cnr Rosedale and Airborne Roads, Albany, Auckland, New Zealand
Penguin Books (South Africa) (Pty) Ltd, 24 Sturdee Avenue, Rosebank 2196, South Africa

Penguin Books Ltd, Registered Offices: 80 Strand, London WC2R ORL, England

www.penguin.com

Published by Viking 2003
Published in Penguin Books 2004
1

Copyright © Patrick Neate, 2003
All rights reserved

The moral right of the author has been asserted

Set by Rowland Phototypesetting Ltd, Bury St Edmunds, Suffolk
Printed in England by Clays Ltd, St Ives plc

For my coochie-momma and my oldgeez, who never sold their souls to cynicism nor this city neither.

'The first requisite to happiness is that a man be born in a famous city'
  Euripides

Contents

1
The unilluminable peepnik and the declaration of war

It might have been as much as two months after Trafalgar that the war began. Or as little as two weeks. You want to know the verity? Don't ask a pigeon. My memory fades like an aeroplane's puff into the clouds and I scope that the peepniks don't say 'bird-brained' for nothing.

Gunnersbury likes to claim that hostilities were commenced at the 'battle of Trafalgar' (a battle named after a square named after a battle; isn't that something?). She says this because, accepting all her qualities of leadership and politics, she does like to be at the acorn of it all. An honest pigeon admits we are a vanitarious species and Gunnersbury, with her wholesome white breast and pink toes to die for (even an old bird like me can't help but notice those), is surely the vanitariest. But the verity is that Trafalgar was just a skirmish, a starling-tempered flare-up of pointed beaks and posturing. How can it have been the beginning of a 'war' when, as far as I remember, none of us had heard that word before let alone spoken it? For me, therefore, the 'war' began with its utterance and that was two weeks or two months later with the murder of Brixton23 above the Brixton Tarmac.

Can I illuminate Brixton23 for you? I want to because, even to my bird brain, his good character merits a place in this history and illustrates the tragedy of our conflict.

Ask anybirdy and they'll tell you same as me: Brixton23 was well-liked. Not a bad feather about him; a straight-talking, crow-flying sort of geez. He was a live-and-let-liver who died for taking sides and isn't that a contradiction only civil wars can explain?

When most birds recall him, they talk about a genial, simple-minded soul who liked to spend his summers around the profligate wastebins of the Brockwell Lido where all shapes of peepniks clucked like chickens and strutted like peacocks at the first signs of the sun. He was content like we all were once; the kind of geez who let the sparrows take first pick at a best bit or a bisquit and stood back with a benevolent smile on his beak. He'd say something like, 'Aren't we all birds of god's own sky?' Only I don't remember him speaking, of course.

He was also, by the geography of his roost, just about typical of the In-Out birds (as they came to be known). Caught in the no man's land between the Pigeon Front and us Surbs, he could have joined either side and the other would have had no reason to grumble. But Brixton23 was a real pigeon-fancier and, like a lot of us, he took a wholesome shine to Gunnersbury and I hazard it was that, in the end, that cost him his life (that more than political or religious certainties anyway).

That night we were flying back from a bin raid, keeping low on the Kennington Road to avoid the RPF spotters who could see for miles from their lookouts high above the Thames. We were beaking on about our successful mission. It had been our most daring raid yet: Leicester Square, right in the heart of Pigeon Front territory, their proudest possession. Of course, a raid like that would be impossible now because we'd be clocked before we made it across the river. But, back in those early days, us pigeons (RPF and Surb alike) still struggled to tell one another apart so, with equal measures of planning and luck, we could swoop into an enemy stronghold like it was our god-given right.

We were talking as we flew, reliving the thrill of it, and the night-owl peepniks – minicabbies, drugsters, hermetic sexers and the like – looked up in astonishment when they heard our chattering squawks overhead. Gunnersbury was telling how she swaggered up to that geez Garrick (only Regent's right-wing, for god's sake!) and swiped the niblet right out of his beak. Not just any niblet either but a six-inch squirm that wriggled all the way down to her gizzard. And squirms were a delicacy in the RPF Concrete, even if they were still two-a-penny on our Surb commons.

Gunnersbury was at the apex of our formation as we passed Brixton station and began, with the confidence of proximate Surb territory, to climb high over Acre Lane. I had Gunnersbury's left flank and Sutton9, a crude hulk of a pigeon and typical suburban heartlander, had the right. The rest of our party was made up of the usual suspects: radical, young hotheads (all fly-by-night ideals and high-pitched calls) and older extremists who'd spent their whole lives waiting for a cause like this to follow (though they hadn't known it, of course). Brixton23 was right at the back; our tailguard.

We were just swooping over Sainsbury's when somebirdy – a mangy coochie called Finchley440, I think – spotted the peepniks in the car park below and we had to stop and watch, didn't we? Hovering 200 feet up where any hawkeyed pigeon could see us.

Let me tell you something: before Trafalgar no peepnik ever paid us the blindest bit of notice and I could have flown into the lobby of the Ritz in a top hat and a monocle singing the FTSE 100 at the top of my call and the most attention I'd have got would have been a shower of stale crumbs from the Korean *sous-chef*. But vice versa? These days us pigeons can't resist watching the peepniks. In fact, some coochie-mommas fear for their squibs who'd rather watch the most boring street scene from the comfort of their nest than ever spread their wings. When I was barely out of the egg, I liked nothing more than pussy-teasing or bird-bathing. But times change and I don't want to sound like my oldgeez. Because it's not just the peepniks who say that's something they'll never do.

The action in the car park that night was a real humdinger and we watched transfixed. There were about eight of them (a mixture: sweets and savouries; greysens, blaxens, brownsens and pinxens; even a babchick) and they were hammer-and-tonging it like you wouldn't believe. We couldn't tell exactly what was going on, flying in halfway through as we were, but one of the sweets, a tangled number with limbs like coat-hangers and electricity hair, was wailing almost as high-pitched as a squirm in your beak. And the babchick was crying, too, as only those peepnik babchicks know how.

Then, sudden like a thunderclap, a strapping cue-ball pinxen pulled back from the group and he was holding a shooter; a small, blunt-snouted automatic that was cold and grey against his pinxen skin. One of the others, a blaxen with a penthouse manner, said, 'Goodness me!' even though there was no goodness about it.

'What you want them for?' exclaimed the strapping toter. That's what he said all right though I couldn't peep what 'them' were.

One of the sweets spoke up and, though her voice was strained, she wasn't shitting herself like most of her fellows. 'It's a bank job,' she said.

'A bank job?' the toter exclaimed and he laughed nastily. I knew where that was coming from because this was no typical bunch of streetnik desperadoes. Although you can never say for sure.

I tell you, this was better than the motion flixtures that I sometimes catch through a suburban window. And our raiding party was hovering on the edge of our thermals and we'd clean forgotten about the dangers of the RPF. Come to think of it, now I conjure it in my mindeye, even Brixton23 was watching the action unfold instead of guarding our tails. And didn't that In-Out geez pay for his carelessness?

Picture it rolling out like this. The peepniks were gathered around a car, one of those cash BMWs with mirror polish and tinted bird glass. On one side stood the cue-ball pinxen with his shooter, on the other side were the cowering rest and between them a holdstuff that sat open on the bonnet (though we couldn't see what was inside it). At first, the pinxen (he looked a real thugalicious sort) pointed his shooter at a slouching greysen whose phyzog sang both courage and confusion; like he didn't know quite where he was (in front of a .22 in a car park in Brixton, whether he liked it or not). But then he turned his aim on another nik who detached himself from the pack. This savoury was talking to him. We couldn't hear what he was saying but the smoke of his voice wafted up among us and it smelled like calm.

I stared at this peepnik and I doubletook. He wasn't what you would call a blaxen or a pinxen. He certainly wasn't a greysen and I don't think you could even describe him as a brownsen. I still don't know how I'd illuminate him but, at that time, I'd only seen one such peepnik before; the day of Trafalgar, two weeks (or two months) earlier. Was it the same fellow? Was it the same foodchit with the red and white box that had sparked that first scrimmage?

The cue-ball pinxen was beginning to panic. You could hear it in his strained voice and see it in his movements as he jabbed his shooter towards the strange peepnik like it was an accusatory digit. But the savoury stayed cool and drew unheard clucks of approval from our pigeon posse above, who said things like, 'What a Tom cat!' and 'That nik's frosty!' I didn't say anything because, to be veritas, I was spooked at the sight of him. Looking down at his crown I was filled with a sudden and unexpected foreboding like a blocked gutter in the rain.

In the immediate aftermath of what immediately followed, I attributed my misgivings to what had immediately preceded. But now, with the benefit of a little distance, I know that misgivings have a name. MURRAY. And when a bird says that name, especially a strong-accented Surb coochie with a tasteful vibrato, doesn't it sound as seductive as a mating coo? MURRAY. The Rs can roll for ever in a name like that. MURRAY. Those boundless syllables that stretch out beneath you like a road to the horizon. MURRAY. And disappear behind you to a time before the wars, before Trafalgar, before the Remnant of Content, before the consciousness of consciousness when you were as free as a bird. MURRAY.

I took my eyes off the action for a moment and noticed Brixton23 talking to two pigeons I didn't recognize who must have ghosted into our party from up and out of the Santley Street shadows. He caught my eye and he looked sheeply. 'They're local,' he cooed. '17 and 228.'

Brixton23 didn't get that things were already past neighbourhood. But I don't think any of us did. Not really.

It was at the exact moment that I hissed a warning to Gunnersbury that I caught sight of them; a mass of the Pigeon Front, maybe 200, rising from behind the terraces with Regent himself at their head. The peepniks below were immediately forgotten as the RPFs fanned out around us, all cooing, soft and threatening. Our posse quickly organized ourselves in a tight tail-to-tail unit and only Brixton23 was left out. He looked confused as he floated further away from his comrades. Then one of the 'locals' he'd been calling to nipped his leg with her beak and he yelped in pain.

I can still picture him now as the two birds manoeuvre him further and further away from the safety of our midst; the nervous flutter of his wings and the fear in his amber beads.

Gunnersbury was at our head and she addressed herself directly to Regent (an ugly, magpie-looking geez with dull grey feathers, a mottled breast and a black ring around one eye). I could tell she was scared but, to her credit, that coochie managed to keep the warble in her call.

'You're in our air now, Regent,' she declared. 'You think my spotters haven't already pinned you? There'll be 2,000 Surbs here before you can flap twice. You'd better head back to your dirty eaves in the Concrete where you belong.'

Gunnersbury was right, of course. But we didn't know when the reinforcements would arrive and Regent just chuckled and his RPFs pressed perilously closer. I thought we were roasted for real and Sutton9 began to make bold braggadocio threats. 'Come on, you fucksters, I'll peckchop the lot of you!' That kind of thing.

'Gunnersbury?' It was Brixton23's plaintive call and he'd lost his warble for sure. That poor bird was now surrounded by the Pigeon Front and there was nut all we could do about it.

Suddenly we heard a distant coo and I knew at once that our Surb reinforcements were nearby. There was a clucking of concern among the RPF and I swear I even saw a flash of fear in the twitch of Regent's head.

As soon as she realized that the Pigeon Front would have to retreat, Gunnersbury began to laugh; a low, taunting rumble of a noise. But Regent wasn't going to leave Surb territory empty-beaked and he signalled to Garrick. Those two geezs spread their wings and took a vertical. At first we thought they were flying for cloud cover but then they diverted and dived into their own forces, scattering the RPFs as they flew, homing in on the isolated silhouette of Brixton23.

Nobirdy made a sound, not even the victim himself, as two sharp beaks tore at his wings, breast and feet. We had never seen such a thing and our calls caught in our thinning throats, Surbs and RPFs alike. How can you react to the unimagined horror of a pigeon killing a pigeon? You can't, that's how. And as Brixton23's feathers floated away, up and down on gentle gusts, we found ourselves transfixed by the evil of it all. Soon that gregarious geez wasn't flying any more; he was airbound only by the biting beaks of his attackers. And then, with one final jerk of his head, Regent gashed a huge wound in his chest and pulled away and Brixton23 plummeted like a stone.

Time moves fast for us pigeons. Do you think we (mostly) avoid pussy claws with the mock of flight alone? No. We live in an accelerated world that elongates the anger of even an experienced Tom to retarded-looking movements. So I swear that I watched Brixton23's fall in slowtion, his crumpled carcass plunging to the peepnik world of terra firma. And when his corpse impacted the birdscreen of the cash BMW in the car park below, shattering that glass like a map of Who Owns What, I knew that nothing would be the same again.

Our Surb army was close at our tails now and Gunnersbury flew out of the security of our unit and right up to where Regent hovered. In verity, Regent himself looked shock-stilled at what he had done. But there is no doubting that we were one coo away from an all-out, mass dogfight. Who knows? Maybe such a sky battle would have ended the conflict then and there.

Gunnersbury had just opened her beak when the whip crack of a shooter shot rang out from below. I tell you something, courageous or cowardly, there's nothing so sure to scatter pigeons as a shooter's report and the sky was soon massed with birds flying every which way, searching their bearings, squawking like crows. In a matter of seconds, the RPFs were heading north (I could see Regent and Garrick in their midst) and the Surbs flying south. But I had to hang on for a moment or two longer to ensure that Gunnersbury was safe and I rode the currents, looking every which way. When I found her, I could scope that she'd been confused by the shooter's volume and the coochie was circling no more than twenty feet above the ground. In spite of myself, I glanced at the peepniks below and I couldn't believe what I saw.

I'd assumed that the shooter shot was shot by the cue-ball pinxen; that he'd either been firing at us pigeons (one of whose number had smashed the birdscreen of his car) or, spooked by the falling Brixton23, he'd pumped a startled round into the unilluminable savoury. But, instead, my bird's-eye view picked out the pinxen's corpse spreadeagled on the Tarmac and over him stood that same frosty nik with another shooter in his hand. I couldn't help myself, I just hovered there for a second too long and – I tell you veritably! – the man I call Mishap glanced up and looked me straight in the bead.

The next moment I was gone. With Gunnersbury at my side, I was soaring high over Brixton Hill to Tooting Common and beyond. But I was wishing for eyelids to blink the expression on that savoury's phyzog – innocent and knowing and certain and confused all at once – from my mindeye.

By now, Gunnersbury and I were way behind the others and we stopped on the trusted oak with the hole in its trunk; partly to catch our wind and partly because this was where she'd stashed the Remnant of Content and for some reason that made us feel safe (fly with me and you'll understand). It was mostly, though, to ensure that no RPF wannabes had spotted us separated from the flock and figured to make a name for themselves.

Gunnersbury couldn't keep still, hopping around that branch like a squib in a puddle, and there was a frenzy about her phyzog that filled me with disquiet. Then she fixed me with her bead. 'When you peckchop a squirm,' she began, 'clean down the middle, what are you left with? Are they two squirms that wriggle away or two halves of the same one?'

I said I didn't know and when I looked at her I scoped that she didn't either.

It was on that branch that Gunnersbury said it. 'This is war,' she squawked, her call strained and excitable. And she was right. Because, like it or not, the London Pigeon Wars had begun.

2

Hat semaphore

Freya spent a long time on the invites. They were orange and blue card, each with its own unique sketch of one of her designs on the front and the words 'Hats off to Freya!' written in glittered glue. Inside was 'Come to Freya's launch!' in silver. Below that was written the date and venue and 'Dress code? Hats of course!' in gold. She wondered whether the precious inks and exclamation marks gave the whole thing an appropriate sense of occasion.

She sent the invites to a lot of people she knew and a lot of people she didn't. She invited all the London milliners, buyers and fashion hacks she'd ever heard of. She invited the few friends who'd voiced their doubts to her and the many who'd voiced their doubts to each other. Her use of the word 'friend' was, as it often is, more careless than she realized.

She rented a spacious space above a gastropub in Westbourne Park. It was OK; polished floorboards, tatty armchairs, junk-shop lighting and walls painted a deep, womb purple. Her £200 included the barman too, a fey Eastern European with high cheekbones and expert disdain. She spent the afternoon decorating the room with orange streamers and blue balloons. She fanned out a clutch of her flyers on each table. She'd taken the photograph herself and she didn't like it much but it would have to do. She put a further £200 on the tab. After that her guests would have to buy their own drinks.

The only major problem was the toilets, which smelled of rosewater and urine. There were no locks on the doors, most of the taps didn't work and the seats were covered in a thin film of grime. She asked the manager if he'd sort it out and he said he would. The manager was an Italian mannequin; all sprouting chest hair and greenish shadow. When he talked to her, he stared curiously at her flat chest with a face that said 'they must be in there somewhere'.

Freya was sure he wouldn't do anything about the toilets but she didn't think it mattered much.

She went home to change at six thirty. Her guests were due at eight. She lived in what the rental market euphemistically called a 'studio apartment' just off Ladbroke Grove. It was a bedsit. The living/sleeping area sat four comfortably enough: three on the two mattresses beneath the bay window and one on the wicker chair. The left-hand wall was lined by a clothes rail that bowed beneath the weight of Freya's outfits. The right was given up to all sorts of hooks hanging all sorts of her hats, and a central full-length mirror that she'd surrounded with multicoloured fairylights bought from a market stall. In the middle of the room, a coffeetable supported a portable TV and video, a bonsai tree and a dozen aromatherapy candles. Beneath it were stacks of fashion magazines, catalogues and shoeboxes holding Freya's sketches, materials and salvaged offcuts.

The kitchen was a one-in, one-out affair divided from the rest by the break between floorboards and faded lino tiles. There was a small sink above Formica cupboards that she'd decorated with collages of free postcards and flyers collected from fashionable pubs and bars. The hinges on the baby fridge were repaired with gaffer tape. The two-ringed hob was set into the end of the work surface right next to the concertina door leading to the tiny bathroom. Any carelessly placed saucepan made it hazardous to take a piss.

The hot water was off again so Freya had a cold shower and sang show tunes to steel her courage. From the clothes rail she chose a twenties-style black chiffon dress and her iced nipples stuck out at right angles. She tried using the hairdryer to soften them but it didn't really work. She slipped into her favourite pink sandals, girlish but classy, and dropped her cigarettes, keys and purse into the antique pink handbag that her grandmother had given her. Then she took off her sandals and sat down on the floor. She lit a sandalwood candle and meditated for two minutes but her new mantra was still uncomfortable and it felt like twenty. She'd wanted to calm her nerves but found, instead, that she now had a vague but undeniable headache.

When she put her sandals back on, she promptly turned an ankle on the loose floorboard and a heel snapped off. In the past an accident like this (especially on such a big night) might have reduced her to tears. But she was slowly toughening and she knew that successful businesswomen didn't cry over a broken heel so she considered her alternative footwear options. She settled on a pair of pristine white trainers with vivid pink flashes on the side. They were utterly inappropriate but she was keen to give the handbag an outing and nothing else matched at all. She shrugged at herself in the mirror.

Entrepreneurs can get away with wearing whatever they want, she thought. Especially in this business.

She pinned up her chaotic blonde hair into a shallow pudding that wasn't so much a style as a coping mechanism. She leaned into the mirror and applied a little eyeliner and lipstick that only seemed to accentuate the thinness of her mouth. She wondered if collagen implants were painful. She was sure they were expensive. She tried some foundation but the amount required to cover her natural blush and pale freckles gave her complexion the texture of cement. The woman at the counter had described her skin as 'bone china'. Like the bottom of a favourite teacup, Freya thought as she smudged away all the make-up with a ball of cotton wool.

She was pleased with herself: just about ready with half an hour to spare. Now for the finishing touch. She lifted her latest creation carefully out of its box. If hats were some kind of semaphore (which, in Freya's opinion, they most definitely were), then this one said 'elegance'. A rounded black base fitted comfortably over her piled hair to gently clutch the base of her skull and four pink feathers lay languorously back from the top like sophisticated French courtesans stretching out on a *chaise longue*. It was perfect.

She looked out of her window at the night sky and saw no rainclouds, just stars and pigeons silhouetted against the sky. It would be fine. She caught sight of her reflection in the pane and smiled shyly. She draped her pale-pink wrap with the ethnic brocade trim casually around her shoulders and headed out.

The All Saints Road was early-evening empty. This was always the quietest time of day, before the fashionable restaurants began to fill and after the local kids and crackheads seemed to take an agreed breather in their games and negotiations. Only Jasper and Learie, two of the local drunks, were in the street. Jasper's family, people said, had once owned half of South Kensington and he certainly had that oyster voice even if his wealth was measured only in golden Special Brew. Learie, people said, was a Windrush Jamaican with voodoo skills. But these days he only mastered spirits at £9.99 a litre.

The tramps were arguing over a cigarette butt when Freya passed but they quietened down respectfully at the sight of her. Learie offered an incomprehensible greeting, thick with patois and alcohol. Jasper touched the brim of his battered bowler. 'You look a thousand soup coupons, my dear!' he announced.

Freya stopped and smiled. She was in plenty of time. 'It's my launch tonight,' she said. 'My business.'

'Fabulous!' Jasper said as she offered him a cigarette. She knew he had no idea what she was talking about. At least he was taking an interest.

At that moment Freya felt something land lightly on her head. She waved an irritable hand that glanced off something warm and soft and substantial. The winos were staring at her curiously and she blinked. Then she heard a low coo and a vindictive beak nipped her ear.

In retrospect, Freya was surprised she didn't scream. But she didn't. She just shook her head from side to side and slapped at the bird with her hands and made vague panicking noises under her breath. 'What is it?' she squealed. 'What is it?' Jasper and Learie looked on in drunken puzzlement.

The pigeon was gone in less than a couple of seconds and the three of them watched in silence as it flew away with the hat secure in its talons. It landed on the canopy of a deserted shop front and began to tear at the hat, shredding the pink feathers in an instant. Then it sat back to admire its beak-work. A moment later another pigeon appeared and perched next to the thief, flapping its wings and making bizarre, clucking noises that sounded like a scolding. Reluctantly, the thief nudged what remained of the hat with its head and it dropped into the gutter.

Freya's hand was shaking and she was blinking repeatedly as she gingerly touched her ear. Her fingers came away a little bloody.

Jasper cleared his throat. 'That's not something you see every day,' he said.

'You mind?' Learie helped himself to one of her cigarettes. As he lit it he said, 'Bad magic!' and he began to chuckle. 'Ras claat!'

Freya bit the insides of her cheeks until they hurt. Then she went inside to choose another hat.

As it turned out, it didn't much matter that Freya was half an hour late for her own party. Almost all her guests (those who showed up anyway) still gave her a good head start. When she arrived, there were only three people standing at the bar. Tariq and Emma were already too embroiled in an argument to acknowledge her and Bast looked like he'd already drunk the best part of her first ton.

'All right, darling?'

Bast approached her wearing that leer she'd learned to hate. His hair, dashed blond at the front, fell slickly over one eye and gave his manner a permanent shiftiness. If only he were that interesting. He went for her lips but she deflected him with a cheek that he sloppy-pecked. He fondled her arse proprietorially before she could back away and she wondered, not for the first time, how you finished something that had never started.

'I thought you were going to wear your new creation,' he said.

'I had an accident,' she replied and shyly fingered the wide brim of the substitute.

'Right,' he nodded. She knew he didn't care.

Bast went through his typical rigmarole but – a result of the alcohol, she guessed – it took even longer than usual and he had her cornered for an age. He told her about a new job he was considering. She asked him about the old one, which, of course, he'd lost, which was, of course, 'the best thing that could have happened'. He nodded a bit more. He asked her to remember the old times and she said, 'What? A week?' and he looked crestfallen and protested 'nine days'.

In spite of herself, Freya felt briefly guilty. Then she felt angry with herself for feeling guilty. Then she felt more angry with Bast than ever.

He said things like 'We were good, weren't we?' and she

shrugged. He tried, 'And . . . you know . . . *that* was the best', and she remembered his Barry White mutterings and she felt a little queasy. 'Do you remember the night we met?' he asked and she realized that she didn't. 'The all-night garage,' he added and then she did and she considered that she must have got what she deserved because who else picked up layabouts on a Rizla run at the twenty-four-hour Esso? 'There are some things you can't fight,' Bast concluded and Freya thought this very true and she made her getaway, patting him on the arm and ignoring his protestations.

By now the party was filling up and she hadn't even noticed. She was briefly exhilarated as she took it all in but she couldn't see a single industry face. These were all her friends: people she knew from university or around the neighbourhood, people she knew through people, people who knew people she knew, and some other . . . well . . . people. There were lawyers and accountants and bankers, dot-com whiz-kids and media stereotypes, bad barmen who might one day make good actors and bad TV producers who couldn't run a piss-up in a brewery. There were suits over shelltops, parkas over Prada and Calvin Klein poking out above low-slung Levi's. There was Identikit Ami, the sweet TV presenter who was so uniformly beautiful that she was always mistaken for someone else; there was Nick Jackson, a square-jawed, bespoke-tailored wide boy who was 'something in the City' and talked about himself in the third person ('Well, obviously, at the end of the day, Nick Jackson's going to do what's right for Nick Jackson'); there was Connor who wrote links for daytime telly and wore spectacles as a mark of his intellect and a light beard as a nod to his Irish heritage; there was Lucky who dealt large quantities of grass and small quantities of coke twenty-four seven from the glove compartment of his ageing Jag. And there was Karen – Tom's ex – loving up to her new squeeze, Jared, an impossibly pretty toff and her boss in the mayor's office. Freya suddenly considered that inviting her hadn't been such a good idea (for any of them) and she wondered where Tom was. He was still so gutted it was probably a good job he hadn't pitched.

If you'd hovered above the crowd or flitted between the groups, you'd have heard all sorts of conversations, snatches and anecdotes. People complained about the lack of free drinks and finger snacks. They talked work and play. They exchanged brand names and logos and pop references like kids with Top Trumps or Pokémon cards or pogs. And they looked Freya up and down and shook their heads as if the very sight of her confirmed their worst fears.

'That hat!' one exclaimed.

'She's trying to look eccentric.'

'But she just looks eccentric.'

'There's a difference between trying to look eccentric and succeeding, and just looking eccentric. Know what I mean?'

'Exactly.'

These were twirtysomethings – Tom's expression to span the ages of, say, twenty-seven to thirty-four; the age range in which degrees of wealth, power and happiness significantly diverged for the first time. Among them, there was an elaborate pecking order that would have been best explained as a Venn diagram. Some people picked up the flyers and said 'good roach material' and laughed to themselves. Some people picked up the flyers and told stories about Freya. 'A new business?' they said. 'A shop?' And they ummed and they erred and they concluded, 'Good luck to her. That's what I say.' Some people told stories about other people who were there. And those people told stories about people who weren't. Some people went outside to take cocaine and returned looking queasy and complaining about the state of the toilets.

This party? It was full of successful London people. They

were not all rich or powerful or happy but at least they took the starring roles in the imagined movies of their own lives. They were good at London and knew how to chew on the city like cows on the cud, pick it clean like jackals, gorge on its waste like pigeons. And none of them wore a hat.

Apart from Bast (who didn't count because she'd met him at an all-night garage and spent the following nine days – he said – trying to kick him out of her flat), only four people actually greeted her.

Emma and Tariq came over and Freya didn't know what to do with herself. Emma looked sicker than ever and it was somehow embarrassing. She was so skinny, fading away, and her lank black hair, now badgered grey in places, was middle-parted like cheap curtains, half drawn to reveal gemstone eyes that seemed to be burrowing into her skull. AIDS? Anorexia? ME? It could have been any thoroughly modern disease but all the tests had come back negative. Freya avoided her eye and stared doggedly at Tariq. She was fascinated, not for the first time, by the slight misalignment of his nose. He'd told her once how he'd broken it. A fight at university or something. She couldn't remember. He didn't look like much of a fighter.

Tariq was proposing a toast. 'To Freya,' he proclaimed. 'And thanks for the drink.'

Emma tutted and said, 'Of course, we'd buy you one if we could afford it.'

'Em!' Tariq had that tone in his voice; scolding and pleading all at once.

'Sorry,' Emma tried to fake a chuckle. It didn't work. 'But we can't stay long. We've got to get back for the sitter.'

Tariq shrugged and gave Freya a 'some people' look, which Emma saw (as intended), and they resumed their bickering. Emma may have been sick but it hadn't softened her tongue and Tariq made no allowances. Freya backed away. It was depressing watching her friends' marriage disintegrate. It made her lose faith when she didn't think she had any left to lose. It was like window-dining at the Turkish end of the Edgware Road when romantic smells and exotic names collapsed into all too familiar cynicism and she said to herself, 'They're just glorified chip shops.' It left an empty feeling in her stomach.

The other two? There was Kwesi of course. She reassured herself that he didn't fit in any better with her friends than she did. Then again, they weren't really his friends.

'Dope party,' he said and he hugged her warmly.

'Thanks, K.'

'Creativity's got to stick together, right?' He thrust a flyer of his own into her hand. 'You coming in a couple of weeks?'

'A couple of weeks?'

'My gig.' He looked hurt.

'Of course.'

'Cool, cool,' he said. 'You cool?'

'Sure.'

Kwesi squeezed her hand and smiled and his face, despite his best efforts at creative pain, opened up as ever, as wide as a pop-up book. His eyes and lips were big and wet and glistening. She looked at his flyer. It said 'Per-Verse' in red and purple graffiti lettering. Then, 'Spoken word at the CCC featuring Paul O'Shaughnessy and K with your host MC Wordsworth'.

She'd known Kwesi for four years and she knew he was a poet because he'd said so on their first meeting; a key plot point in the long-winded story of how his dad was threatening to disown him. But she'd never seen him perform. She remembered he'd told her that he'd stop writing on his thirtieth birthday. At the time, this had impressed her as indisputable artistic integrity, quirky but admirable. Now, six months from the big three-zero, it just sounded premature. Success lends weight to all kinds of foolishness. You can float away on failure and never be seen again.

Freya watched him move from group to group, handing out his promotions. People nodded enthusiastically as he talked and they glanced attentively at the leaflets. But when his back was turned, they screwed them into balls and dropped them into ashtrays or on to the floor and they returned to their conversations as if he'd never existed.

'Freya?'

Karen caught her arm. She turned and immediately felt uneasy. They'd been friends once, hadn't they? Real friends with a connection based on more than just Tom. But now they had Tom in common (whatever *that* meant), they no longer had anything in common.

After Tom and Karen split up, he'd made stupid, bitter claims about what had actually happened. He reinvented their history and said things like, 'She gets a new job and we're finished. Go figure', and 'She's making money now, Frey! You see? She's *made* it.' He would light a cigarette and she'd rub his head, feel uncomfortable and contemplate what she didn't dare say. But now? Freya considered that maybe he'd had it right all along. Because, seeing Karen face to face for the first time in months, she had the definite sensation that Karen was looking down on her. She wondered briefly if she was paranoid but concluded she couldn't be. Because she didn't even care.

The fact is, Freya thought, if you're at the bottom then people have to look down on you. Better that than they ignore you altogether.

But it was still no surprise that her connection with Karen was broken.

'Have you seen Tom?' her former friend asked.

'No. I don't think he's here yet.'

Karen was gazing at her fixedly. She looked like she had something important to say but settled for, 'It's a good party.'

'Thanks.'

'I like the balloons. They make it look like a prom. You know. Like a movie. *Pretty In Pink* and you're Molly Ringwald. You've even got the hat.'

'Right.' Freya smiled in spite of herself.

'I'm sure it'll be a success. The business, I mean.'

'I hope so. Thanks.'

Freya felt herself soften a little. Karen frowned, reached beneath the brim of Freya's hat and lightly touched her ear.

'What happened? You're bleeding.'

'It was . . .' Freya was about to tell her about the pigeon but she suddenly felt ridiculous and her cheeks began to flush. If that story got around it would just be ammunition. 'It's nothing,' she said, fetched a tissue from her pink bag and began to dab self-consciously at the sore spot. There was a moment of silence between them. It was an embarrassed kind of silence because they both had their reasons for saying nothing and they each hoped the other couldn't spot them.

'Have you met Jared?'

'Once.'

'I should introduce you properly. You'd like him. Even if he is a posh boy.'

Freya didn't know what to say to that. The 'posh boy' addendum spooked her because she knew it was Karen's way of trying to re-establish the connection; like she'd put on a badge saying 'I'm still one of you'. But it was a feeble effort. Because the class distinction was only one Karen herself would have thought to make anyway. And besides, she wasn't still one of them and, what's more, she didn't want to be and they both knew it.

Eventually Freya said, 'Sure.'

'Later on, then.'

'Sure. Later on.'

Across the room, Freya glimpsed Tom coming in and she felt suddenly guilty. She saw something unknown but very guessable flicker across his face and her heart sank. But it was gone in a flash and Tom was beckoning her over. He looked excited. Freya hadn't seen him so cheerful for ages and she'd forgotten how cute he could look. He was running his hands through his cropped hair in that way of his. No matter how short he cut it, it always looked messy.

'You're late.'

'I know,' he said. 'Sorry. Look . . .' He could barely get the words out, he was so excited. 'I've got . . . I've invited a guest.'

'A woman?' She almost laughed.

'No. Look. You'll never guess who I met today.'

'Who?'

'Guess!'

She wasn't in the mood for guessing. 'I don't know, Tom. Who?'

He was rubbing his hands frantically across his head and his feet were jitterbugging from side to side.

'Murray!' he announced.

'Who's Murray?' Freya was looking at him blankly.

'Murray!' he said. 'You know. *Murray!*'

She suddenly caught on. Of course, she'd never met Murray but this was going to be interesting, wasn't it? She felt herself kindling though she didn't know why.

'*Murray* Murray?' she asked.

'Murray Murray,' Tom confirmed.

'You're joking.'

As if on cue, Murray walked in. Of course he might have been waiting for Tom's signal, but his timing seemed impeccable. There might have been a lull in every conversation at that moment but ... whatever ... the room was silenced nonetheless and all eyes seemed to be turned to the door. Freya caught a single voice behind her (Karen's, she thought), breathy and respectful: 'Murray?'

Freya had heard so much about him in the five years she'd known Tom and Karen but he wasn't at all what she'd expected. He was neither particularly tall nor short, fat nor thin, muscular nor scrawny. He was wearing jeans and a sweatshirt and tatty trainers. For all the stories, his first appearance was unremarkable and disappointing, like a first glimpse of the Trelick Tower. He was smiling broadly. He did have good teeth. And there was the hat, of course: a purple crushed-velvet thing like a collapsed topper that sat – as you say of hats – at a jaunty angle on his head. He looked like that Dr Seuss character. The cat in the hat, she thought.

He was smiling. At her. He looked straight at her, past her, through her, inside her and her guts turned somersaults and she thought, What the fuck is going on?

'I was told I had to wear a hat,' he said.

3

The signs are good

Karen was quizzing Tom but he was hardly listening. She wanted to know 'where the fuck' and 'when the fuck' and 'how the fuck' and lots of other enthusiastic questions with fuck in the middle. But, for all his excitement about Murray, Tom could only muster monosyllables in response. Because him, well, in the first place there was his own question that had been nagging at him from the moment he'd run into Murray in Trafalgar Square that afternoon. And in the second place (and more to the point) he saw this as his latest chance to have the same conversation with Karen that they'd been having for the best part of nine months. And he was *sure* . . . well . . . he *thought* . . . or at least . . . *reckoned* he had something new to say this time. But he also knew that as soon as he broached the subject, he'd adopt that expression (intense and a little pained) and that tone of voice (not far from a whine). He wouldn't be able to help himself and she'd spot it in a flash and hear it in a second and she'd pull *her* face and adopt *her* voice in return. 'Tom,' she'd say, 'please!' And that would be that.

Karen didn't look at him. Not once. She was watching Murray butterfly around the room, her attention rapt. Every now and then she'd say, 'I just can't believe it.' Barely above a whisper. 'I just can't believe it. Murray.'

Tom stared at Murray – he took in his easy smile, the wrinkle of his forehead, the way he licked his lips – and he felt a forgotten jealousy rising in his belly. But this wasn't just any jealousy. Tom realized he was *Murray*-jealous; a unique sensation with a style and substance all of its own that he hadn't felt for years. Not since college. He was jealous of Karen's attention, sure. But that jealousy was familiar and, frankly (or maybe falsely), dealt with, and this was somehow more than that. He'd forgotten how Murray made it all look so easy; the minutiae of human interaction. Those numerous, distinct smiles that, once upon a time, Tom had counted and ordered in his head, those unnoticed flutters of expression, conversation and body language that charm or irritate, anger or amuse; those were Murray's speciality, his currency, his core business. And when Murray turned it on, Tom knew there was no stopping him.

Murray talked to Tariq, of course. But Tariq was flummoxed. He didn't know what to say and he ran one hand self-consciously through his hair that was a decade thinner than the last time they'd met; and the fingers of his other hand drummed on his stomach that was a decade tubbier. That Murray should have walked back into their lives? It beggared belief. Murray was smiling.

'Nice hat,' Tariq stuttered at last.

'It is, isn't it?' Murray said, cheerfully tugging at the brim.

'Where have you been?'

'You know,' Murray shrugged and he turned his smile towards Emma who blinked like she was looking straight at the sun.

'This is my missus,' Tariq said, 'Emma.'

'Hey, Emma.'

She took his hand but she wouldn't meet his eye. She said, 'Sorry. I didn't catch your name.' But she knew who he was all right.

'Murray,' he said.

Tariq told him about his business and Murray said, 'Predictive technology? Damn! You always had your finger on the pulse, china, know what I mean?' Then Tariq told him that he was on the verge of bankruptcy and Murray's expression didn't flicker for an instant. He didn't say anything but he put his hand on Tariq's shoulder in a conspiratorial sort of way. It was a gesture that said, 'You know everything's going to be all right, don't you? So don't worry about it'. But his body language must have been a whole lot more powerful than speech. Because Tariq had said those same words to himself a hundred times and they'd always sounded hollow before.

Tariq told him about their baby, Tommy (after Tom), and Murray shook his head and looked bewildered. He said, 'Shit! A baby? Shit! Congratulations!' as if it were the most amazing thing he'd ever heard; as though babies were a bizarre myth of coitus that Tariq and Emma alone had just proved to be true.

Emma said, 'We should be getting home actually. The sitter will be waiting.'

'You're going?' Murray looked forlornly at Tariq. 'You can't go *now*. I haven't seen you for . . . what? . . . Six years?'

'Ten,' Tariq said.

'Exactly. Ten years.' He turned to Emma. 'You've got to stay for a bit. Anyway, it sounds like you two could use a night out. Both of you.'

Emma smiled. 'Sorry, Murray. But we've got to get the last tube.'

'So get a cab.'

'To be honest, mate . . .' Tariq suddenly looked sheepish and lowered his voice a little. 'Look. To be honest, things are tight right now. A babysitter *and* a cab home's a bit extravagant, know what I mean?'

Murray was staring at him. Tariq blinked. He didn't like talking about his money situation; especially not when he was standing in a room which, to his eye, was full of contemporaries who pissed their cash up the wall like it was going out of fashion. These guys? For them, a tenner was no more than a cheap straw for their gak habits.

Murray dipped into his pocket and pulled out a fat wad of notes. Tariq was alarmed and more embarrassed than ever. 'No!' he began. 'Mate . . .' But Murray was already pressing thirty quid into his hand.

'You remember how many times you helped me out?' Murray asked.

Tariq looked at him. That was true.

'Besides, Tariq, it's only money, for fuck's sake. Who cares? It's your friend Francesca's big night . . .'

'Freya.'

'Whatever. Don't you want to stay for a while? I haven't seen you for, like, a decade. Come on, you're doing me a favour. Emma. Please.'

Tariq turned to look at his wife and he ummed and erred and he said, 'It's just she's not been well.'

But Emma's eyes blazed. 'You're not blaming me.'

So Tariq shrugged and took the cash. 'Thanks, Muz.'

'Good. So just call the sitter and tell her you're going to be late. I bet she'll be glad of the cash. Besides, she's probably got some spotty kid half-naked on your kitchen floor by now . . .' Murray paused. Emma looked alarmed. 'Or not. Just give her a bell and then we can catch up. Properly.'

Tariq took out his mobile and dialled home. He retreated from the noise a little and cupped a hand over his free ear. Murray raised his eyebrows at Emma and grinned. 'So then . . .'

'Tariq has told me a lot about you.'

'Really?' he said. He looked momentarily puzzled and he licked his lips. 'I'm going to get a drink.'

A moment later Tariq turned back to where Murray had just stood with a smile on his face. 'No problem,' he was saying. But Murray was gone.

Murray wandered over to Karen and Tom, who were still hovering on the fringes. They didn't see him coming. As he approached, Karen was saying, 'Come on, Tom! Please!' She sounded exasperated and her expression was strained and irritable.

Murray clapped Tom on the shoulder. 'Tom!' he mimicked. 'Please! How many times have we been over this? What does that say?' He paused and looked between them; a nervous smile flickered on his mouth. 'Oops. Put my foot in it haven't I?' But, seeing him, Karen was too excited to care and she threw her arms around his neck and planted a fat kiss on his cheek. 'Murray!'

'Hey, Kazza.' He squeezed her tight.

He looked at Tom over her shoulder and his expression asked, 'You all right?' Tom shrugged. Murray stood Karen back with his hands on her hips and looked her up and down, taking in her sombre suit, sensible shoes and her hair, which was scraped back in a ponytail. 'Look at you! You're so . . . *decent*!' He was laughing. 'What happened?'

'It's been a long time, Muz,' she said. 'Some of us have grown up.'

'You remember when we first met? You were a right little casual, remember? All pixie-boots and pedal-pushers. And you had that terrible fucking boyfriend. What was his name?'

'Kush.'

'Kush! That's right. What kind of a name is Kush? A horrible little thug. How long did he harass you?'

'I don't know. Like, two years.'

'At least two years. I remember that shit and I'm telling you, Kazza, you were well out of that one.' Murray glanced at Tom. 'Then you hook up with china here and you got into all that hippy shit. What was that about? Fuck! Now look at you. Aren't you the chameleon!'

Karen's smile was fixed in place. 'I grew up.'

Murray couldn't stop laughing. 'Good! I meant it as a compliment. It's good to be a chameleon. From what I've heard, you've got to be a chameleon these days.' He took Karen's hand and lightly squeezed her fingers.

'Pots and kettles, Muz,' she said. 'You always were an arsehole.' Her smile was mobile again.

'Me? Really?' He looked hurt – just for an instant – then it was gone. He turned to Tom. 'So how are you two doing, then?'

Tom dipped his chin a little. 'Murray. I told you. We split up.'

'Yeah?' He stared at Karen, his expression blank. 'Shame.'

There was an uncomfortable silence. Karen looked at Tom as though he'd betrayed a secret. Tom didn't know what that was about. She thinned her lips.

Karen bombarded Murray with questions then. But he laughed them off one by one. What the fuck had happened to him? What do you mean? He'd been around. Where the fuck had he been? Around. What the fuck had he been doing? You know. This, that and the other. Yeah, yeah. A lot of the other. No. He hadn't seen anyone from college. He'd been away a lot. All over. Just fucking around. He wasn't going to disappear again, was he? Of course not. Shit. He didn't exactly *disappear* last time. Did he promise? He promised.

'Who's that guy?' Murray was looking across the room.

'What guy?'

Murray pointed out a floppy-haired beanpole who was staring their way.

'That's Jared,' Tom said. 'Karen's boyfriend.'

Karen's eyes flashed. She suddenly felt embarrassed and angry but she wasn't sure why. She tried to hear bitterness in Tom's voice. But there wasn't any. Maybe that was the problem. For someone who was supposed to be gutted, he sometimes seemed remarkably composed. She felt briefly irritated with Jared too. What business did he have looking their way? Or maybe it was just the situation. Because seeing Murray seemed to turn back the clock, it rewound her to a zestier time and she was suddenly confronted by all kinds of images of things they'd done together (her, Murray and Tom, Tariq too) and her mind was a collage of snapshot moments of laughing faces. She realized that she hadn't thought about Murray for a long time but, now that he was standing next to her, it was like being reminded of a favourite movie that had been gnawing at the back of her mind or tickling her tongue tip for longer than she could remember. For some reason she thought of *The Breakfast Club*, the moment where Bender shows off the cigarette burns on his forearm, and she felt briefly confused, even a little scared. And she couldn't be sure whether she was remembering something about Murray or something about herself. She looked up at Murray curiously but she couldn't figure his expression.

'So you'd better go and see to your man,' Murray said.

'Who?'

He nodded across the room. 'Jared.'

Murray and Tom watched Karen worm her way towards her boyfriend. When she reached him, Jared bent to kiss her cheek but his eyes were still in their direction.

'So what happened?' Murray asked.

'What?'

'You and Karen. What happened?'

Tom shrugged like it was no big deal. 'She got a new job. She made it and got selfish. I was a teacher. I didn't.'

'"As selfishness usually extends to devotion, so devotion usually returns to selfishness."'

'What's that? Shit! You sound exactly like my therapist.'

'A quote. *The Spiritual Self.* I've been reading.'

'*You?* Reading?'

'*You?* A therapist?' Murray stared at him for a moment, eyes sparkling. Then he nodded. 'And this bloke?'

'Jared? He's her boss.'

'Right,' Murray said. 'What does she do?'

'She works for the mayor. A policy advisor. Transport. Something like that.'

'You're joking!'

'I know. A big change, right? You remember her at college? Marching against the Poll Tax, to reclaim the streets, against the Gulf War, to support the miners . . .'

'The miners? I think you've got your dates mixed up, china. The Miners' Strike's, like, ancient history. Your memory's playing tricks on you.'

'Yeah? I could have sworn she marched for the miners.' Tom started to laugh. It was a strange noise, cold and hollow. 'I don't know. There were so many causes I lost track.'

Murray started to join in. But somewhere in the back of his throat, the laugh transformed into a grunt. 'I told you. She's a chameleon.'

He was looking out across the room. If Tom had glanced at him at that moment, he'd have seen his eyes narrow a little. But Tom was lost in his own thoughts. He was replaying the confusions of 'Karen's Boyfriend Kisses My Girlfriend' in his mind's eye and trying to remember how it felt for *him* to kiss her on the cheek and feel her proprietorial hand slide around his waist. Of course he still greeted her with a peck even now. But the gesture had a qualitatively different feel to it. He wondered about that and it made him sad. So he bit hard on his lip and tried to think about something else. What surfaced was the question that had been bugging him since the afternoon and, come to think of it, for years before, on and off.

'Murray . . .' Tom began.

'Who are these fuckers?'

'Sorry?'

Murray kissed his teeth. For some reason he seemed suddenly impatient. 'This lot,' he said. 'These people. Who are they? Which ones am I supposed to like?'

'What?'

'I mean, it's like a code isn't it, china? Shit. I'm out of touch. Who am I supposed to like?'

'I don't know.'

'Like, what about that guy Jared?'

'Don't know,' Tom shrugged. 'I've only met him once or twice. He seems all right. Karen likes him.'

'She's his girlfriend.' Murray smiled broadly and Tom spotted a smidgen of food stuck next to one of his canines. It looked like meat, Tom thought. Chicken, of course. 'So what does she know?'

Watching Murray now, Tom recognized an expression that he hadn't seen in years. But it was still as familiar as the face in the mirror and it provoked familiar tinglings in his fingertips and that tightness in his chest.

'I think it's time I mixed,' Murray said.

'You're not going to . . . are you, Muz?'

'What?'

'Cause trouble. You know. *Murray-fun.*'

It was the spark in Murray's eyes. *That* was the expression. 'Murray-fun? I don't know what you're talking about.' Murray glanced at him and blinked. Very slowly. 'Like Karen said, some of us have grown up. *I*'ve grown up, china. I've changed.'

Murray glided away. Tom considered following him, just in case, but the party was now in full swing and he wasn't feeling sociable. Why should he indulge in idle chatter when he could watch his ex getting lovey with her new man? He was alarmed by the coldness of this thought. He realized his feelings had shifted. Somewhere along the line, the raw pain of losing her had given way to this sardonic ache. He missed the raw pain; it was a lot more wholesome.

He watched Murray plotting his course through the flotsam of the party to the main swell. Maybe he really had changed, because he spotted few of the little signposts that used to identify Murray in full flow. He was talking to that fool Bast who was almost too drunk for verticality. But Murray was listening and nodding and smiling like the most well-mannered socialite and the only signal of any discomfort was the occasional wince at a blast of Bast's breath. He patted Bast on the shoulder and moved on.

Now he was talking to Identikit Ami who looked typically uncomfortable in her inflexible telly armour that cocooned her fragile ego beneath a soon-to-be-silicon breastplate and blonde helmet. Tom knew that vanity was one of Murray's favourite games and he could unwrap it with all the enthusiasm of a kid with a birthday present. Tom realized that, unconsciously, he was holding his breath. But Ami was soon laughing and pouting and flicking her hair, happily indulged by Murray's smile and charm.

Now he was talking to Kwesi and, Tom considered, if any fruit was ripe for some Murray-plucking then it had to be the K-ster with his ridiculous ghetto-chic manner, his good intentions (that were almost as impossible to doubt as they were to take seriously) and the self-importance that had grown in inverse proportion to his achievements. Kwesi was pressing one of his flyers on to Murray. As Murray read it, Kwesi tilted his head a little and set his mouth in a growling sneer (two of his more absurd affectations). Tom bit on his lower lip as he waited for Murray to react. He had become, he realized, a social rubber-necker watching in flat-footed fascination for what happened next. As far as Tom was concerned, the assassination was not in doubt; merely the chosen weapon. Would it be the slice and dice of the sharp tongue? The desiccation (wry and dry)? The acid spit? The nerve pinch? Or maybe the slow burn (that only caught up with its victim on a lonely night some time later and struck with the venom of a whisper)?

Murray carefully folded Kwesi's flyer and slipped it into his back pocket. He looked up and said something. For a moment, Kwesi didn't react – This is it, Tom thought – then his affected sneer dissolved into a bright, open smile. He took Murray's hand and enveloped it in one of those elaborate handshakes that gave Kwesi, in Kwesi's opinion, a hint of the rapper. Murray was smiling too. Maybe he really has changed, Tom thought. And for all his worries about Murray 'causing trouble', he wasn't surprised to find his heart gape at the possibility.

Tom was suddenly quite overwhelmed by sadness and it was an almost physical sensation that had him opening his mouth to scream only to be silenced by another choking gobful of the stuff. His brain was Old Street and the traffic came from all directions. He looked over the heads of the heaving party and he thought about pebbles on the banks of the Thames that abrade each other to bluntness until they can sit one on top of the other, cheek by jowl, uncomfy and awkward but bearable once the numbing kicks in. He remembered Murray when he'd first met him at college: the raw mischief of him, the passion for everything and nothing in particular. He thought about children growing into adults who for one brief second poke their heads from manholes to take a glorious breath of THIS IS ME fresh air only to open their eyes and find themselves nose-to-tread with an articulated's tyre. He scoped the room and he saw the disappointment in the twirtysomething eyes of the likes of Freya and TV Ami and the complacent certainty that played on the twirtysomething faces of Jared, say, or Big-In-Property Jackson. He experienced one of those moments of clarity that catch you unprepared like ice cream on your teeth or the first sight of St Paul's rearing from the city. The disappointed and the smug? It made no difference; they were still all stymied by either side of one equation. One group were prostitutes to their dreams, the others kept dreams as their mistress to be indulged on seedy nights in a Travel Lodge. Hooker or punter, Tom thought, you still fuck like animals beneath the same dirty sheets on the same dirty bed in the same dirty room.

And what about him? Tom considered his dreams and he inevitably stumbled over Karen, whose image was like a corpse lying on the doorstep of his memory (he could step over it but it wasn't the kind of thing he could ignore). Maybe it was seeing Murray or maybe it was his earlier session with the therapist because, for the first time in a long time, he examined the carcass from every conceivable angle but he couldn't avoid the same conclusion. He used to be smug and now he was disappointed. He was a trick turned whore and wasn't that the real shitter?

Seeing Murray was like the breaking wash from a sixty-foot cruiser. It had tossed him up the Thames shore and left him jagged in his new spot. He remembered them all together (him, Murray and Karen, Tariq too) and, in the absence of present hopes, he made the common mistake of recalling old ones that had long since been washed away. Tom found himself longing for the numbness. Is this as good as it gets, he thought?

Tom shook his head vigorously to loosen these bad thoughts a little. He headed for the bar and bought himself a bottled beer. He rolled the cool glass across his forehead a couple of times; like they do in the movies. He noticed Bast at the far end of the bar, asleep on a bar stool, resting his head on an empty pack of Bensons. He said to himself, 'It could be worse.' But it didn't help because he didn't really believe it.

He spotted Murray ensconced with a gang in the middle of the room, all laughing and joking, and he made his way over to join them. He wasn't feeling sociable but perhaps he could lurk around the fringes and at least their banter would save him from himself. Freya was in this group. And Tariq. And Nick Jackson and a few of his bespoke cronies. Karen and Jared were among them too. Generally Tom would have given them a wide orbit but he now had . . . How did he describe it to himself? 'That reckless-misery thing on the go.'

As he approached, Tom realized that Big-In-Property was in full flow and even Murray was standing back. Jackson was puffing on a cigarette and nastily drunk and, egged on by his mates (whom Tom knew only by their nicknames; things like Chalkie, Buzzard and Shithead), he was taking the piss out of Freya in a guileless and vicious way. Karen was shaking her head. Tom knew her well enough to see she was simmering like Brick Lane. Jared was placid but, at the sight of Tom, he rested a big and bony hand on her shoulder. Tariq looked embarrassed and he kept glancing around the room as though he expected someone to come and sort this out at any moment. Freya looked mortified, like a rabbit in headlights, and her face was blotchy flushed. Chalkie, Buzzard, Shithead . . . Murray too . . . they were all sniggering.

'So, Freya,' Big-In-Property was saying, 'let Nick Jackson get this straight. You just went to the bank manager and said you wanted to open a hat shop?'

Freya nodded.

'And you had a business plan?' he went on, his voice

coloured with an effective shade of incredulity. 'Research? Projections? All that kind of thing? Yeah? And he lent you money?'

'That's right.'

'He said . . . what? "Twenty grand? A hat shop? Why the fuck not?" Something like that.'

'No. I . . .'

'So . . . umm . . . did you wear one of your hats to the meeting, then?'

You had to give it to him; Jackson's timing was immaculate, setting up the punchline like a pro.

'Yes,' Freya said, her voice quivering with self-conscious defiance. That was it. Jackson packed up laughing and Chalkie, Buzzard and Shithead joined in. Freya tried to giggle. But the effort died on her lips and, instead, she covered her mouth with one hand and hugged her other arm to her chest as though she were trying to protect herself against a dust storm.

But it was Murray who laughed the loudest and longest. He hooted and guffawed, he threw his head back and cackled, he creased and convulsed, he laughed until he cried and he screeched 'Fuck me! Fuck *me*!' until everyone else was distracted and watching him; Jackson and his mates included. Nobody could say anything. Murray was bent double with his hands on his knees and, every time one of the others opened their mouths, the giggles would come again.

'I . . .' Jackson tried (reverting to the first person for once). Murray cracked up.

'You . . .' Jackson began. More laughter.

It must have been a full minute before Murray finally straightened up but it felt like a lot longer because nobody could even remember what he'd been laughing at. His bizarre hat had fallen low over his eyes and he took a moment to adjust it with both hands so that nobody could see his face.

When he finally dropped his hands, his expression was as blank as a piece of paper.

Jackson pulled irritably on his cigarette. 'You all right, mate?' he said.

'Hilarious,' Murray said flatly.

Tom said, 'Hey, Muz', just trying to catch his attention. But Murray was staring emptily at Jackson. 'You got a spare?' he asked.

Jackson shook his head. He coolly raised the butt to his lips. 'Last one, mate,' he said and he sucked deeply.

'Right,' Murray said.

Jackson started spluttering. Then the splutters turned into a full-blown coughing fit. Now it was Freya's turn to giggle but the laugh froze on her face as Jackson suddenly turned an alarming puce as he fought for breath. Chalkie smacked him on the back but that only seemed to make it worse as his eyes started to bulge and his whole body shook and the coughs turned into retching.

'You all right, china?' Murray said. Nobody knew quite what to do so it was Murray who took control.

'Let's get you outside,' he said, his expression as concerned as Islington. 'Get some fresh air.'

He slung Jackson's arm around his shoulder and began to half carry him towards the door. Tariq offered to help. 'You need a hand?'

'He'll be all right,' Murray said.

As Murray and Jackson stumbled outside, the little group began to splinter. For a moment, Chalkie, Buzzard and Shit-head looked genuinely worried but they were soon nudging each other and saying things like 'Stupid arse' and 'What a pussy!' Freya found herself standing next to Jared. She was upset. 'I wonder what happened,' she said. Jared shrugged. 'I'm sure he'll be all right.' Tom and Karen and Tariq gathered in a little triangle. None of them said a word and they could hardly meet each other's eyes. Tom wondered if the other two were thinking the same as him.

It was ten minutes before Murray and Jackson returned but, by then, everyone had forgotten where they'd gone anyway. It was a total shock, therefore, when the whole party was suddenly silenced by Jackson's screams as he burst into the room. He was holding his face in his hands and he was largely incoherent; although the blood that was splattering his brushed grey lapel and spurting down his white designer shirt left little doubt that it was an ambulance he was after and several people reached for their mobile phones. There was then a brief and ludicrous delay while the would-be Samaritans looked at one another as if to say, 'Are you calling? Or should I?' during which Jackson lay on his back in the middle of the floor and screamed some more. Freya and Karen rushed to kneel next to him and gently coaxed his hands away from his face. At first, with all the blood that fountained from the wound, they couldn't see what had happened. Then, as Karen tried to clean his face with a beer cloth from the bar, she jumped back and yelped in surprise and disgust. The soft bulb of gristle at the end of Jackson's nose was gone. For a relatively small injury, it gave his face an astonishingly bizarre look and produced an equally astonishing quantity of blood.

At that moment, Murray walked in. He was holding his purple felt hat in his hand and it was blood-stained and mucky. He looked agitated as Tom approached him. 'Murray! What the fuck have you done?'

'Me?' Murray exclaimed. 'It was this little fucker!'

He upturned the hat and a limp bundle of feathers and bones dropped heavily to the floor. It was a dead pigeon.

Unsurprisingly, it took a while before anyone was convinced that Jackson had been savaged by a pigeon because, at that time, such an attack was unheard of. But then Freya piped up to recount the theft of her hat and she showed off the peck wound on her ear to the curious. Even Jackson, dosed with a large brandy, a handkerchief pressed to his nose, confirmed the story and made Murray sound like quite a hero for wrestling the pigeon off his face. People were impressed too that Murray had actually killed the bird and the blokes in particular looked at him in a new and admiring way.

Murray shrugged. 'It was just a dirty fucking pigeon,' he said.

By the time the ambulance arrived, the party had inevitably started to disintegrate (because a night gets no higher than a pigeon attack) and Freya's friends began to leave. They thanked her and wished her luck with her business. They nodded at the uniformed ambulance men tending to Jackson and said things like 'Shame about . . . you know' and 'Awful!' and 'What a terrible thing'. But secretly they were still buzzing with the thrill of it and the stories they'd tell on Monday morning about Big-In-Property Jackson and Murray the Pigeon Slayer. Unintentionally, it was Karen who summed it up best. She hugged Freya. 'You throw quite a party,' she said wryly. And she was right.

Freya half-smiled and said, 'Is this what happened in *Pretty In Pink*?'

Karen shook her head. 'This is *Carrie*,' she said. 'Big-In-Property as John Travolta.'

While the ambulance men fussed around Jackson ('Fuck! Don't touch Nick Jackson's fucking nose!'), Murray slunk off to a window and stared out at the night sky and Tom didn't spot him for a minute or two. It was only when the injured property broker was wheeled away (a wheelchair? A bit over the top, Tom thought) that Tom glimpsed his friend's silhouette. Tom was exhilarated although he didn't know why (or at least didn't want to admit why).

'Muz?'

'Yeah.' Murray didn't turn round.

'I wanted to ask you something.'

'Shoot.'

Tom paused. He suddenly realized that the question he'd wanted to ask for god knows how long . . . well . . . he'd never actually organized it into words. And now that he tried to do so, he found it almost impossible. In fact, he wondered whether it was actually a question at all or just a series of thoughts that needed clarification.

'Look,' Tom said. 'Right. You know the last time I saw you at college?'

He was staring at Murray. He could see his eyes reflected in the dark glass. Murray said nothing.

'The last time I saw you . . .' Tom continued. 'Well. What . . . what I mean to say is . . . Well . . . what I said . . . You know I didn't mean it, right? I mean, that's not why we haven't seen you for . . .'

Murray leaned forward and Tom heard him take a sharp breath. 'Fuck!' he hissed. 'Look at that!'

Instinctively Tom pressed his face to the window. The pane was cold against his forehead. It took his eyes a moment or two to adjust to the sombre outside. Then he saw it. Although he didn't know what 'it' was. It looked like a vast black cloak billowing across the purple sky above the rooftops opposite.

'You've got to admire them, china,' Murray said. 'I mean, you've got to fucking admire them.'

'What's that?'

'Pigeons,' Murray whispered. 'The pigeons.'

4 The thing about Murray

The thing about Murray . . . Well . . . how long have you got? He was just someone people talked about and they began their opinions with the words 'The thing about Murray is . . .'

Here are some things about Murray. 'He's basically a wank-uh,' said the gargle-voiced Sloane, allowing that final syllable to die beneath his chinless chin. 'He is a very nice chap,' said the Indian shopkeeper who sold him vacuum-packed chicken roll at nine every morning. 'The thing about him?' said the American tourist. 'He's fine and he knows it.' And she touched her friend's elbow and pointed across Kensington High Street. 'He's attractive in a quirky kind of way,' said the blushing academic. 'He's one of them brothers who thinks he's white just because he passes,' said the president of the London University black caucus. 'He's a fucking wigger,' said the pinking DJ in the Stüssy hoodie and he kissed his teeth in disgust. 'He's not what I expected,' said Freya, the first time she saw him. 'He's just too bright for his own good,' said the nervous boy at the bar and his comrades nodded in agreement. 'He's just not that interesting,' said the nervous boy's friend and the comrades nodded again and they kept talking about him anyway. Sometimes, before she'd met him, when Tom or Karen or Tariq related their hilarious stories, Ami would say, 'The thing is, he just sounds like a bit of an arsehole.' But she'd never seen him in action and she still listened to the stories because she was intrigued.

The thing about Murray was there were lots of things about him – passionate things, extreme things, fundamental things, ephemeral things, contradictory things – and, if you heard people refer to him, the only similarity of tone you might spot (and then only if your ears were pinned right back) was a vague suggestion of regret ... No. Jealousy ... No. Somewhere between the two. And it was a quiet suggestion, like the sound of London in the dead of night when you can close your eyes and take a deep breath and you listen to the silence and you still know exactly where you are.

When people talked about Murray, especially if they weren't Murray fans ('The thing about Murray is I don't actually like him'), they often caught themselves in mid-sentence and said, 'So why are we talking about him, then?' or something similar. But they couldn't help it. Some people managed to hate him, to despise and dismiss him and delude themselves by saying, 'The thing about Murray? I see him for what he is.' But even they couldn't help but care what he thought and what he did and what he would think and do next. Murray was just one of those guys who was in some strange way ubiquitous, monolithic, as unignorable as the Westway. Take Princess Diana or 9/11: when she died or the Twin Towers collapsed everyone ended up having an opinion whether they wanted one or not. Right. Exactly. He was simultaneously as familiar and untold as London itself.

Say Murray's at a house party thrown by one of Tom's teaching colleagues in a Tulse Hill maisonette that's all flat-pack pine and lurid linoleum. The dimmer-switches are low and there's jazz funk on the stereo and Murray's dancing so outrageously that nobody else can get on to the small living-room dancefloor and Tom is mildly embarrassed.

Murray meets a girl. She's probably a plain Jane with no more than a dash of slap and a flowing skirt that signals the luggage on her hips. She's a lurker, hiding on the periphery where her prints match the wallpaper, smoking a nervous cigarette and sipping a glass of Bulgarian red. But Murray? He spots her in an instant and whisks her off to a quiet spot – the corner by the fridge, the balcony or the top stair. Even as she looks at him, she knows she's playing with fire but she's a little tipsy and she tells herself she doesn't care. So she opens up to him about her job as an office manager in Elephant and Castle and the studio flat she's just bought off the Kennington High Road.

'Right,' Murray nods. 'Really? Great!'

From anyone else's mouth, these are just platitudes, conversational staples. But, somehow, Murray imbues them with another quality. You could call it enthusiasm but such a definite term doesn't quite suffice. Because this quality is less tangible; a vibrancy, say, apparently innocent and unironic. Because to look at Murray's expression you'd have thought office management was the eye of the next revolution and a Kennington box quite the most desirable address in the city.

With such a vibe at her back, Plain Jane will tell him everything: her dreams, her fears, her history (potted and re-potted like her cheese plant). If her dad died of bowel cancer at the age of forty-six? Murray finds out in minutes and he nods or shakes his head as appropriate and he wipes his mouth with the back of his hand and holds the movement for one second as though time has to stop still in the presence of such a unique tragedy. Maybe she's a recovering anorexic? She lets that slip too and Murray says he'd never have guessed and he tells her how good she looks and he offers her a sausage roll. Perhaps she's fucking her boss? Murray tuts and rolls his eyes and ticks her off with such sympathy that she thinks she could be talking to her mum (as if she could have ever told her mum such a thing!).

Murray makes her feel like a princess and she goes home on a high and, for once, she doesn't fight the minicab driver over the odd pound. She hasn't noticed that Murray said nothing about himself and she knows nothing about him (because she never asked). She remembers pressing her number into his hand and his enthusiastic acceptance. And she successfully ignores the indisputable certainty that he will never call (because why burst that bubble?).

Some people said that the thing about Murray was he used those he met and then spat them out like hour-old gum. But ask Plain Jane? She wouldn't hear a word against the guy who made her feel like a princess for an hour. Just an hour. One whole hour. Because she knows that in this city you take your heroes wherever you can find them.

Murray is in a Soho nightclub. He's lounging at the bar making easy small talk to the statuesque blonde with a Lycra body and ten-quid-a-pop incandescent orange tan. She feigns little interest at first because she's used to guys trying their luck, even if this charming chancer with the curious complexion (or is it just the light?) is a cut above the average. But watch a little closer. Do you see the way she adjusts her body position, bit by bit, almost imperceptibly opening herself up to this stranger one proud breast at a time?

'I'm with my boyfriend,' she says and Murray nods because he's known all along.

'Which one is he?'

She points him out, probably some body-built strapper with more mirrors than books, and Murray is uncertain and squints as if short-sighted: 'Which one? The bow-legged guy?'

A couple of minutes later, Murray makes his excuses and backs off just as the boyfriend comes over. As the hunk approaches, she notices the slight roll in his gait and his ten-to-two knees for the first time. And no amount of hours in the gym are going to address a flaw like that.

Once, more than ten years ago, Tariq witnessed a comparable scenario play out in the Crown and Two Chairmen. 'The thing about Murray,' he said shaking his head, 'is he's, like, a sprite or a goblin. Something like that.'

Karen didn't agree. She didn't like it when others invested Murray with magical qualities. It scared her. 'He's just having Murray-fun,' she said and that was the phrase they all used after that. 'He's a social terrorist.'

Picture this. Murray joins a gang of blokes around a bar. They could be anyone: South London geezers with expensive designer shirts and a taste for bottled beer, round-the-way Peckham guys with wary manners and gold-toothed smiles, earnest Muswell Hill graduates supping real ale, City slickers with shot veins around their noses and cushion-chewing buttocks, Soho bohos in capacious pants made from technologically crafted parachutes. And Murray can talk and he can listen. He shouts down the loudest big-mouth, he catches group attention with his mumbling tone, he listens, sage and interested, he snipes, he ironizes and he never fails to take centre stage even if he has to move it to the conversational suburbs. Cars? He knows the tread on a factory-fresh Cosworth tyre, the wattage of every JBL bass bin, the economy of a Volvo engine, the acceleration of an MX5, the satirical statement of a Ford Capri. Music? You name it he's got it: the latest white label or import on Greensleeves, Van Morrison's lost album, the Pink Floyd boxed set, DJ Shadow on his iPod. Women? He's fucked them: chip-shop chic, bootie-bouncing garage chicks, wives, mistresses, born-again virgins.

When Karen labelled Murray in the Crown and Two Chairmen, Tom was there too and he joined in the laughter because he liked the idea of 'Murray-fun'. But he couldn't really agree with 'social terrorist'. As a phrase, it sounded like just the thing you'd been looking for but it didn't actually work. Because surely a terrorist has a cause (however ill-conceived).

As far as Tom was concerned, Murray was more of a spurof-the-moment joiner, a passerby who spots the riot-in-waiting and, seeing the opportunity for good looting, chucks the first rubbish bin through the electrical store's window. The way Tom saw it, Murray was a chancer, first and last. And Tom had known Murray longer than anyone.

They met at London Media Tech, a recently upgraded polytechnic in the urban armpit between Farringdon and Barbican. It had started life in the late sixties as a small graduate journalism college on the back of a bequest from Lord Such-and-Such but had gradually expanded its curricula until it achieved full university status, had campuses dotted around the city and taught all subjects to equivalent levels of mediocrity. LMT appealed to all sorts; local kids with ambitions unmatched by their grades, earnest hopefuls from former colonies attracted by the cheap fees and numerous bursaries and provincial public schoolboys who cared about nothing beyond a spell in the big smoke. Mostly it handed out poor-quality degrees to poor-quality students for little more than three years' persistence.

Tom and Murray lived in the same hall of residence through-out their first year but didn't speak until the final term. Before that? Tom doubts Murray even knew who he was. But every-one knew Murray, at least by sight or reputation. By then, there were already all kinds of rumours doing the rounds (about his racial background especially) but the facts were only three. Everyone knew Murray partly because he never pitched up to seminars (which granted him both cachet and, bizarrely, increased recognition), partly because he had only one name, but mostly because he only ate chicken.

He was famous for it. In his first week at LMT, Murray complained to the senior tutor's office that the canteen didn't serve chicken for breakfast. At first they thought he was joking. People often thought Murray was joking. At first.

He made an appointment to see the senior tutor; a liberal anthropologist called Daffyd Jones whose creases were stronger than his backbone. Jones should have seen it coming. After all, it was him who'd let Murray in despite his lack of A levels.

In his admissions interview, Murray had employed an unusual technique. Ignoring the senior tutor's run-of-the-mill questioning, Murray chose instead to launch into a passionate polemic against his reputation, arguing that all the anthropologist's work thus far was blatantly racist in conception. Unsurprisingly, Jones was somewhat taken aback and, further bewildered by this would-be student's uncertain racial status, he found himself glancing at Murray's application form for the tick boxes beneath the heading 'Ethnicity' (because he needed to know what he was dealing with, didn't he?). When he discovered that Murray had ignored the twelve definite alternatives in favour of the thirteenth ('other'), Jones suddenly felt profoundly guilty and convinced of his own prejudice. And it was a slippery slope from there.

Much of Murray's argument seemed to be based on the opening passage of the introduction to Jones's *Africa: A Biography*, which began with the line, 'Africa has long been perceived as the most mysterious of continents.' But he reasoned so cogently, responded with such quick wit and identified the professor's moral funny-bones with such easy precision that, by the end, Jones felt like his entire academic career had been turned on its head.

'You leave me on a sticky wicket, Murray,' Jones had said. 'You cannot expect that I should admit you to LMT only because a failure to do so would further reinforce your allegations in your position as a student of . . . umm . . . "other" ethnicity.'

'Of course not,' Murray replied.

And his acceptance was confirmed the following day.

At the 'chicken appointment', it took Murray less than ten minutes to bamboozle the senior tutor once again. Jones mumbled vaguely about making allowances for Jews or Moslems and the pragmatic need to look after the interests of the many. But Murray questioned the professor's definitions of religion and utilitarianism and espoused powerful arguments in support of the individual and against the tyranny of the majority. He rubbished numerous nutritionist reports with countless historical examples of flawed scientific advice and he quoted the college's constitution, '. . . to endeavour to provide acceptable food in the canteen for all sections of the college community.'

'But, Murray,' Jones complained, as soothingly as possible, 'what section of the college community do you represent?'

'Professor,' Murray chided. 'Don't you remember my LMT application? "Ethnicity", it said. And I said, "other".'

'But other people eat food apart from chicken!'

'Other people? Or *other* people?'

'I'm sorry, Murray. I don't follow.'

'Which other people?'

'Other people.'

'Which other?'

'Well! I don't know I'm sure but . . .'

'Precisely. For the purposes of this college I am other people. And I only eat chicken.'

Thereafter Murray ate chicken for breakfast, lunch and dinner. Grilled, fried, boiled, casserolled, roasted, glazed, braised, barbecued and souped. Shredded, wings, skinned breasts, *à l'orange* (or any other fruit you'd care to mention), Sunday traditional, sweet and sour, Thai-style, thighs, drumsticks and broth. The head chef didn't mind because he liked Murray and he liked the idea that he was helping put one over on the establishment.

Sometimes, in the years after they left LMT when they were still together, Tom and Karen argued about who had introduced Murray to the other. When they had these arguments they both pretended the subject was actually something else.

'It's not *about* who met Murray first,' Karen would sneer (as if that were quite the most ridiculous suggestion). 'It's *about* the fact you always have to be right. What does that say?'

Or Tom spat: 'It doesn't matter who knew Murray when. What matters is the way you want to squabble.'

But they both knew they were lying. Because it *was* about who met Murray first and it did matter. For some reason, they both felt proprietorial of their relationships with Murray, even as those relationships faded into the past.

In the decade after leaving LMT, when Murray was gone from his life, Tom realized that his memories – of his childhood, adolescence and student days – changed. Some dissolved while others were accentuated and his perception of his own character (who he *was*) dissolved and was accentuated accordingly. But his memories of Murray? They remained as crystal clear as a Hyde Park morning (or so he thought). Their meeting, the things they'd done, that final argument; they were like lampposts that illuminated his past and made it somehow comprehensible. Tom knew that Murray's essence (as a chancer) was liquid and changeable but at least the jelly-moulds of Tom's recollection retained their definite and immutable shape. For some reason Tom never explained it to Karen like that (why it was *about* Murray, why it mattered). If he had, she'd have understood.

For the record, Tom met Murray the day before Karen but, for all their arguments and personal significances, this tells you little about them as a couple. More intriguing is that neither of them actually introduced Murray to the other because it was, in fact, Murray who introduced them. If Tom had remembered this when their relationship was evaporating before their eyes in Hanger Lanes of hot air and bad feeling, he'd have felt his stomach yo-yo and cold sweat clam between his shoulderblades. If Karen had remembered this, her eyes would have fired as if this confirmed her every suspicion and she'd have commented: 'What does that say?' But they didn't remember.

Tom met Murray in the small Catholic chaplaincy at LMT. A Catholic chapel in one of London's new universities is an incongruous cubby-hole at the best of times but the stand-in priest (while the resident was under investigation) made it seem downright ridiculous. Father Callaghan, despite the clues of his name, was an ancient cockney with a taste for fire and brimstone. His services were carried out in a fug of incense, confused (and inappropriate) ideas and turgid slabs of Latin that he delivered with the intonation of a bingo caller and the twang of rhyming slang. The way Callaghan saw it, his predecessor (Father Joe, currently under investigation) had surely been corrupted by the devil-may-care (and he *does*) atmosphere of university life. So Callaghan determined to drive out the standards of modern Catholicism: pretty Irish girls with their dwindling consciences, and three-chord, un-musical guitarists with arhythmical tambourines. He was so successful that within a month even the happy clappies (with those bright sweatshirts and spooky fixed smiles) had jumped ship and Sunday mass was attended only by earnest Africans, nervous virgins and the occasional suicidal tendency. And Tom, of course, who was coming towards the end of one of his spells of desperate, panicked Christian faith.

On that particular Sunday, Tom was lost in torpor through-out the service, hugging his boredom around his shoulders like a cosy duvet, and he didn't even notice Murray until the recessional hymn. Then Father Callaghan announced the number and, to Tom's astonishment, launched, unaccompanied and unironic, into the opening verse of a dusty old favourite called 'God Bless Our Pope'. His voice was like a gurgling drain and even the Africans (whose notorious conservatism was stuck somewhere in the mid-nineteenth century) looked at one another, embarrassed. Then, for the chorus, Callaghan's voice was joined by another; a booming baritone behind Tom's left ear that was close enough to make him jump.

Tom swung round to find Murray giving the hymn his all. His eyes were smiling brightly and his spittle flecked Tom's forehead. Murray nodded, respectful and conspiratorial, at Callaghan as the priest processed down the aisle and out of the back of the chapel and Murray was left singing alone.

'God bless our pope!' he chorused.

'God bless our pope!' he enthused.

'God bless our pope!' he howled.

'For heeeee . . .' Enjoying his solo, Murray luxuriated in every word of the last line. 'Issssss . . .' He elongated alternate vowels and consonants like he was stretching toffee. 'Goooooooood!'

Murray closed his hymn book and beamed. The Africans muttered to one another and looked at him disapprovingly. They thought he was joking. The suicidal tendency with ginger hair and sideburns hurried for the door, stumbling noisily over the pews. His face looked stricken, like Murray's voice had carried him over the edge. But Tom? He just stared.

He'd seen Murray before, of course – hanging around the hall, feet up in the TV lounge, relishing six nuggets or a McChicken burger (minus bap and salad) – but he realized he'd never actually looked at him and Murray had certainly never looked back.

At first glance, Murray was utterly unexceptional. He was averagely tall, averagely slim (though it was difficult to tell in his baggy T-shirt and track pants) and his black hair was cropped to a millimetre or two in a way that spoke more laziness than intent. But the more you considered him, the harder it became to pinpoint his looks.

After leaving LMT, when Tom told stories about Murray to those who hadn't met him (like Freya or Kwesi or Identikit Ami), they'd often ask about his appearance to build a mental picture. But, to their frustration, Tom would shrug and say: 'He just looks normal.' Because that was easier than trying to explain something to them that he couldn't explain to himself. There was something about Murray's face . . . His features were even and not especially Plasticine but, any time you chose to stare, he always looked completely different from the time before and you couldn't put your finger on why.

Murray was, of course, a master of expression and occasionally Tom wondered if that had something to do with his curiously shifting looks. Smiles? Where most punters average around five (typically: happy, sad, tolerant, intolerant and indifferent), Murray had as many as the people he met and the circumstances he encountered. But the fact was that the mechanics of Murray's different smiles (or any other expressions, for that matter) appeared identical (and Tom knew because he'd studied them), so the differences had to lie elsewhere. Sometimes Tom hypothesized that the substance of Murray's expressions lay only in the response of their intended. But that couldn't be it. Because when Murray smiled affectionately the next-door room could sunbathe in the warmth and when he looked scornful a whole tube carriage would be chastized. Tom concluded, therefore, that the power and variety of Murray's expressions must be on some different, unknowable level. Like magic.

He suggested this once to Karen and she shook her head and tutted irritably.

'I only said it's *like* magic,' Tom protested.

'It's just a trick,' she said finally. And Tom was left wondering what could be more like magic than a trick.

Apart from his command of expressions, Tom otherwise tried to attribute Murray's inconsistent appearance to the 'whole race thing' (and hadn't they played some games with that? Especially in the Race Card version of Murray-fun). Because Murray was undoubtedly mixed race ... Well ... probably.

He was probably mixed race but which races in what measures was anyone's guess. He was, say, certainly dark-skinned for a white man and light-skinned for an Asian. So what, then? Mediterranean? Sometimes. But not always. His nose was broad and his lips were thick but would you say he was African? Sure. When he chose to be. His eyes were like almonds with a hint of Siam. So there was a dash of Sri Lankan, perhaps? Maybe. If he wanted you to see it. Among numerous other backgrounds, Murray could carry off run-of-the-mill Anglo-Saxon, light-skinned Jamaican, high-caste Indian, Cape coloured, swarthy Mediterranean, even Aboriginal Australian. And just because Tom had never seen him pass as a Scandinavian? Fuck it, he was sure it could be done.

But Murray never changed his accent or body language when assuming a role and somehow that made him all the more plausible. Hanging with posh boys in blazers? Perhaps they assumed his estuary accent and scruffy clothes were an affectation (no different from the pipes they smoked or the cravats at their necks) and they could forgive him that. Or what about closing-time drinks with the South African bar staff? They were impressed by the ease of his London manner-isms but never questioned for a second his upbringing in the Rainbow Nation. So, when Tom considered it, the uncertainty of Murray's racial background was a symptom of his unpinnable looks rather than any explanation. And a decade of thinking about that hadn't illuminated Murray one bit.

'He's good, isn't he, china?'

Those were the first words Murray ever spoke to him.

'What's that?' Tom blinked. His eyes were dry.

'The pope, I mean. He's good. "God bless our pope for he is good." You can't argue with that.' Murray patted his hymn book approvingly, like it contained all the truth in the world.

'Yeah,' Tom said dryly. 'He's great.'

'Fantastic!'

'Amazing!'

'Fantabulous!'

'Perfect!'

'Perfect?' Murray frowned. 'Nobody's perfect.' He held out his hand and Tom accepted. It was warm and dry and unusually small. 'I'm Murray.'

'Tom,' Tom said. 'Tom Dare.'

'Tom Dare? Great name, china! That's a "don't fuck with me" kind of name, huh? A superhero kind of name.'

Murray was still holding his hand and, when Tom tried to take it back, he squeezed it a little before letting go. Tom was embarrassed. 'It's only a name,' he said.

Murray smiled. 'Sure. But it's a start.'

It was exactly twelve years to the day after their first meeting, the day of Freya's launch party, that Tom ran into Murray in Trafalgar Square. Of course Tom didn't notice the symmetry and, if he had, he'd have thought nothing of it. If Murray noticed . . . Well . . . he certainly didn't say anything and you suspect he would have done. Because Murray didn't believe in coincidence.

Tom had taken lunch hour and the first two periods of afternoon school to head into town and see his therapist, a bizarre and wealthy Buddhist called Tejananda (Tom wasn't sure he'd take the recommendation of one of Ami's TV mates again). Afterwards, he dawdled back because he wanted to think and he meandered south of Soho, heading vaguely towards Charing Cross and the Bakerloo Line. He was thinking about Murray and, whatever destiny he tried to attribute to this later, it wasn't a coincidence. Tejananda liked to discuss what he called 'Moments of Truth'. So Tom had been talking about Karen (of course) and this had led, inevitably, to Murray.

Tom was striding across the square, excuse-me-ing his way past the map readers, snackers and smokers who loitered in his path. He ducked behind a gang of Nikon brandishers who were shooting pictures of Trafalgar Square's empty fourth plinth. Only the plinth wasn't empty any more; the enormous lions at each corner were now complemented by a clear cast of an inverted plinth at the square's apex. Tom was briefly confused until he remembered reading about some kind of competition to fill this statue gap. So this one-gag wonder must have been the winner. It seemed utterly appropriate. What with the aftershock of an hour's therapy, Tom was in a reflective (if muddled) state of mind and he thought that the perceived need to fill every gap (even with the representation of a gap) was somehow typical. But typical of what, he wasn't sure.

'Hey! China! Tom Dare! Superhero!'

Someone was shouting at him and Tom lowered his gaze from the plinth to a figure sitting on the step below. Despite the familiarities and his recent thoughts about Murray, he didn't recognize him; not at first. It was only when he came striding over, scattering pigeons, and Tom saw the fried chicken he was munching from a red and white carton that he made the connection. 'Murray?'

'Who else?' Murray said, broad-beaming. He offered Tom the carton. 'Want a piece?'

Tom shook his head and Murray dumped the remainders

of his chicken in a bin. Tom wanted to say something but he was smiling too, wide and happy, and then his smiles turned into a laugh. So Murray beat him to it and Tom remembered that the thing about Murray was he always beat you to it and this made him laugh all the harder.

'Where have you been?' Murray asked.

Of consciousness

Us birds are confused fucksters for sure. While the peepniks divide up their world into there-and-backs, then-and-nows and Tom-Dick-and-Harrys, us birds see everything as a sweep. Or used to, at least. Typically, albeit without the banes and benefits of language, we always called a tree a tree and a foodchit a foodchit; things like that. And, if the last few weeks (or months) have taught me anything it's that more definitions don't necessarily make you understand no better (and they sure make it tricky to know where to take a shit). So don't blame me if this story comes out as wriggly as a squirm that doesn't know its anus from its head.

Ironic that the niks talk of 'pigeonholing', don't you accord? I tell you, that's something to make geezs laugh like the wind in plastic bags. Because peepniks with their penchant for exactitude still don't have no talent for a precise metaphor; not even to describe something that describes them so pinpointedly! Of course I only figure this now because I know that us pigeons live in the instant while the befores and the afters are as various as compass points in the vast expanse of the sky (that triumphs six to four over terra firma for starters). And that's precisely my meaning (if you've got eyes in the back of your head enough to see it).

So what I'm trying to say is an apology. Because I started with the Declaration of War as if it were the start even if I admitted at the very start that it wasn't. But you need to understand that just because it wasn't the start doesn't mean it wasn't the best place to. Peepniks? They tell their stories in terms of beginnings and middles and ends, which is all well and good for babchicks at bedtime but will never illuminate nut all of a narrative tangle (with all the intrigues therein).

Look at it this way, stories are like a glance at the London skyline from suburbia. Like it or not, you can't help seeing over the low-slung homogeny of terraces and semis to the clear silhouettes of sky-scrapers that stand up like niks' middle-finger fuck-yous to the heavens. So your focus is on the view from those peaks in the aspiration that such might illuminate the sprawl below. And a story is just the same; begin from a point that makes sense and maybe the rest will take shape too. It doesn't always work but we'll fly with it for the second; only don't let Gunnersbury hear me beak on like this because all this talk of skyscrapers in the Concrete is not what you might call a respectable Surb perspective.

Check me out! Aren't I quite the peacock (who, for all his fine attire, is still a bird brain nonetheless)? Because, for all my hypoth-esizing, I'm not sure I understand Trafalgar now any better than the day it happened. Let me put it like this; a consideration about consciousness from somebirdy who's still new to its rigours: 'Con-sciousness is a blessing in disguise.' And it's such a good disguise that most of you never even see it for what it is. And that's the verity as sure as my name is Ravenscourt (when, a few weeks – or months – ago, I wasn't conscious of my own self).

I don't recall much about the morning. I was flying in from the west – did I tell you that I'm an In-Outer too? – and I was in the company of all sorts of geezs and coochies. Don't ask me who because I can't remember and that's a fact but I'm hazarding that Gunnersbury must have been among them because we hail from nearby roosts and she was certainly in Trafalgar Square by afternoon.

My recollections are hazy, disjointed, jerking and silent; like those home flixtures that stir up sounds and smells and tastes but little in the way of lucidity. We were perched on Nelson, clocking foodchits among the peepniks below and swooping down occasionally to peck up niblets like a best bit or a bisquit or a crust.

Some recollections nip me like a loving coochie's beak. I know it was windy because I can still feel the breeze beneath my wings and the simple joy of gliding on a current as if it was your friend; your fate even. I know there was food in the air (as well as in the bins) because I can taste the thickness of the atmosphere above all manner of stands and stalls. I know the Square was busy because I can still scope the chaotic movements of the crowds, swirling like paisley with the surges of strong-willed niks, the shuffles of bemused yellowsens and the dawdling of old knackereds or, conversely, babchicks. I know too that I felt foreboding. Although, of course, I didn't have the word for it at the time, its sweet stench still clings to my feathers no matter how often I bird bath.

Picture this: two niks converging from two sides of the Square. At ground level, of course, they're nothing but two more phyzogs in the sea and their trajectories as random as the foolish sparrows who don't know where to spot the next foodchit. But now fly with me to Nelson's feet and enjoy a bird's-eye view and scope the way those two niks cut through the paisley swells like two motor boats on a collision course and you know there's something up.

I peeped it, of course, but I wasn't much into contemplation at the time (none of us pigeons were). Instead the home flixture is freeze-framed in my mind like a picture postcard of my first sight of that unspectacular greysen and the unilluminable nik I like to call Mishap (for fear of the syllables of his proper name). The greysen was deep in thought and he paused for one instant as though track-stopped by a memory. Seeing this, Mishap took a detour and perched beneath the transparent, upturned nothingness where a lion should stand (that's confused a reckless blackbird or two, I can tell you). Then the unilluminable nik stood up and was walking towards the greysen. He was devouring unilluminable stuff on the move with all the voracious relish of a rat with a carcass.

What followed? I couldn't tell you with any exactitude because we were gone, diving towards the Square in a pack. I couldn't tell you who was at our apex either so it's the history of events that informs me it must have been Gunnersbury. But, trust me on this, it's not important because in those days, when a pigeon dived, you dived with them with no more sense of why or who than a babchick accepting a bottle. Gunnersbury? Well . . . the way I scope it these days, I realize that she was not defined by the random choice to dive but by its consequences and how that fact impacts upon your consciousness, consciousness thereof and, indeed, contemplation therefore, is up to you.

Next thing I knew, I was hovering above a rubbish bin as two birds tucked in at exactly the same time. Again, it is only retrospect that names them as Gunnersbury and Regent, the magpie-looking geez who went on to form the Pigeon Front.

For some reason – I don't know why – I scoped for the two niks and spotted them disappearing into the paisley. I have a vague recollection that I wondered how their path might plot from above. I didn't contemplate it but, nonetheless, I figure that still might have been my first tug of consciousness. But I was quickly brought back to the rubbish bin by the sound of a warning coo which, I should explain, was about as fowl-mouthed as us pigeons got at the time.

Gunnersbury and Regent were teetering on the bin rim and fighting over the unilluminable nik's unilluminable stuff, tugging at either side and squawking like two squibs trying out their calls for the first time. This might not sound remarkable to you (especially if you're one of those pretentious 'you are what you eat' fellows who cannot enjoy a meal without the proper manners and accoutrements). But look at it like this: that bin was overflowing with all kinds of delicacies like baps and bisquits and best bits (there was probably even a squirm or two if you had a taste for soul food and were prepared to dig deep). And here were Gunnersbury and Regent scrimmaging over that stuff that comes in a red and white carton. We'd all seen the stuff a thousand times before but none of us ever went near it with its slippery texture and stink like death, so god knows how you illuminate those two pigeons' behaviour. A 'mishap', and that's the verity.

I can still hear their calls as if it were now, the way they seemed to crystallize into words like I was watching the very instant when a stream freezes. Because what was an amorphous flow of communication (despite its indubitable current) suddenly pulled itself apart and reassembled into a distinct structure of indisputable meanings.

'Fuck off! It's mine!' Gunnersbury was squawking. 'Get off me, you ugly fuckster! You want me to peckchop your magpie phyzog?'

And Regent just kept repeating the same phrase, again and again: 'You fucking Surban coochie! You fucking Surban coochie!'

Imagine that! Your first moment with a language (if it was indeed the first) and this is what you hear! When I think of the infinite subtleties of complication and contemplation in what has followed, I am still astonished by the gutter slime of those first words. You might suspect that language derives from the intricacies of co-operation and compromise but I illuminate it like this: cooperation and compromise always have to follow disagreement so maybe the first words of any tongue are always likely to be 'fuck off'.

The rest of us pigeons were there in a flash but I was the very first. I heard other voices saying 'Who are you calling a fuckster?' and 'Go back where you came from!' but I didn't say anything. Maybe I didn't trust my beak to produce such raw meaning because I just butted my head into Regent's breast. Like I knew how to fight! Like any of us did!

I don't know why I automatically sided with Gunnersbury but that's what happened. Perhaps it was because she's such a peachy coochie (and even an old bird like me can't fail to see it) or perhaps it was just because a fight has two sides and I peeped I'd better join one or the other. Gunnersbury figures that I instinctively knew she was one of my own, a fellow Surb, and maybe that's the verity. But the fact is that, since us pigeons factionalized, you'll find honest Surb troopers who hail from the eaves of Westminster and the occasional RPF who once roosted on Mitcham Common. So how do you explain that?

The scrimmage can't have lasted more than a minute (although, like I explained, a minute can be an hour to a pigeon) but I remember clocking the agog phyzogs of the surrounding niks; the quick-fire snapping of the bemused yellowsens and the head-scratching greysens who said things like, 'You don't see that every day.' Then Gunnersbury and Regent both wheeled away at exactly the same instant, each with a trophy in their beak, two scraps of the unilluminable stuff from the red and white box that looked to me like bones from the hulkingest pigeons you ever saw.

Gunnersbury took a vertical and I was on her tail just like that, as though I believed she knew what had just happened and where she was heading. My old wings couldn't keep up but I squawked to her at the top of my call: 'What's that? What's that you've got there?'

I could hear her breathing, thick and fast, and her answer came muffled by the trophy in her beak. 'It's the Remnant of Content,' she called significantly (like *that* meant anything). And then she was gone, high over Leicester Square to Piccadilly and beyond.

I was spooked and I don't mind admitting it. I headed west towards my roost because for the first time it felt like 'home' (with all the emotional frippery attached to that word). I was sure I was being chased although I didn't know who by; perhaps Regent and his cronies or maybe that hulkingest pigeon who'd lost his Remnant of Content. Don't ask me because I'm not suggesting it makes sense. But you can bet I chose to fly low, zigzagging down backstreets parallel to the Bayswater Road. And I wasn't the only one. Oh no! I scoped all kinds of other coochies, geezs and squibs with similar intentions and I realized that, whether they'd actually been in Trafalgar Square or not, the word had already got round (in every sense). They spotted me too but we avoided each other's beady eyes as though we each figured we might chance to look upon the phyzog of our fear. Let me illuminate it like this: I was scared and I was confused and my blood was piston pumping. So obviously that was a cocktail for anger and that's the verity.

By the time I reached Notting Hill, my imagination was running unchecked and I was too anxious to wing another block so I caught my breath beneath the overhang slates of a low terrace. It was cold and damp and miserable under there and I didn't even have a clear view of the sky. But I figured it was the kind of place that no self-respecting geez would stop and, if a squib tried to join me, they'd have felt the point of my beak, no doubt.

I must have perched in that one spot for hours (which felt like years) but it didn't calm my pipping pigeon heart one jot. I was all fired up with madness and fear and hatred and the fact that I couldn't say who I was angry with or scared of or hating only made those sensations run hotter. The old birds (me included) always warn that a pigeon who doesn't clock the sky for too long becomes a moonatic and perhaps that's the acorn of it. Because from my perch, I couldn't scope nut all and my bird brain ran riot with all kinds of imaginings as the daylight goldened and greyed and faded to black and the lampposts began to half-heartedly hum. I could have sat there all night. But I'd have gone crazy, no question.

It was dark when I spotted a sweet below. Come to think of it, I might have seen her since (the night of the Declaration of War, perhaps) with the unilluminable savoury I call Mishap. But I can't be sure because most peepniks look alike to me. She was talking to two streetnik desperadoes (the kind who protect the best bins like they were their own preserve – a thought that would have once seemed ironic, if I'd known the word back then) and she had four feathers on her head that were the colour of a summer-evening sky over a roam-free Surb common. How can I illuminate? Those feathers captivated me and my racing pigeon heart quickened to impossible speeds.

I fluttered out from my hiding place as silent as a breeze and I landed right on that sweet's head. At first she didn't notice but then the confused phyzogs of the streetniks alerted her and she began to shake her head from side to side to throw me off. But I recollect she didn't scream. Riding her movements, I tried to catch her hair in my beak for balance but nipped down on her ear instead. I hadn't meant to do that but the heat of her blood was a thrill. I dug my talons into her headgear and lifted it clean off and I took a forty-five awkwardly away. The hat was so heavy that I had to land on a shop awning just across the street. I don't know what came over me but the sensations of madness and fear and hatred suddenly overwhelmed me and I began to tear and pluck and shred those feathers as though they were the adornments of my most veritably vanitarious foe. I clocked the confused phyzogs of the three peepniks on the pavement below but I only stopped when another bird fluttered down next to me. I had been so consumed in my frenzy that I didn't even hear that pigeon's approach and I was as startled as a starling and I flapped my wings in fright.

It was Gunnersbury. 'For the sake of the heavens,' she said. 'I don't know what the fuck you're doing.' She still held the Remnant of Content in her beak and there was something of the eagle in her eyes.

Later, when we discussed it, Gunnersbury postulated that, in my confusion, I mistook that sweet's headgear for an RPF geez and no wonder I attacked. Maybe. But I'm hazarding that even the mooniest moonatic could tell the difference between a pigeon and four pink feathers on a hat. As for me, I illuminated it to Gunnersbury that I'd thought the feathers could be other trophies of Content (yeah, yeah . . . whatever). So she asked me why I was shredding them and I claimed that I was distraught when I realized my error. But the verity? Honestly, those feathers captivated me like the niks are captivated by a glamorous shop window and I wanted to possess such fine, delicate objects with their subtle colour and touch like duck down. But, when I had them to myself on that awning, I was disarmed by a thought so obvious it drove me to frenzy: what was I, Ravenscourt, a pigeon, to do with four pink feathers; other trophies of Content or not?

Since the 'battle of Trafalgar' (as Gunnersbury likes to call it), the conflict has been illuminated, in reverse chronological order, in terms of personality, hatred, principle, territory, and the Remnants of Content (as snatched by Gunnersbury and Regent). But do our bird brains acknowledge that our reinventions of heroism and villainy and causes to champion and idols to worship have overlaid the verity of a scrimmage over unilluminable stuff dropped into the rubbish by Mishap. As we pigeons squabble over the contents of a dustbin, is there no triumph for the consciousness of consciousness?

6
Because poetry's disappointing

The café in the Clapham Community Centre was packed. Indistinct beats pumped through the sound system and made black coffees shimmer in their cups. Acquaintances parted curtains of cigarette smoke to kiss each other on either cheek. Busy-bee, thirtysomething women with snoods beneath haystack hair fiddled with the microphone, speakers and the building blocks of the stage. Paintings by children from the next-door primary school hung precariously from the walls by peeling inches of masking tape. The linoleum floor was tacky underfoot.

The café was a community facility and, as such, strained to be all things to all people. Signs on the wall read 'No Smoking Before 8 p.m.' in thick red capitals to ensure a clean-air environment for the local kids. But nobody took any notice and the local kids figured it was the best place to stop for a clandestine cigarette on their way home from school. 'I was gasping!' they'd gasp as they sparked their first of the day and lounged on the plastic chairs. Then somebody or other's mother would storm in and drag somebody or other out by the ear and consign ten JPS to the dustbin from where they'd be retrieved by a laughing classmate.

The café sold subsidized tea to the homeless and expensive bottled beer to jobless arty types with furrowed brows; it accepted Luncheon Vouchers for focaccia sandwiches with salad garnish at five quid a throw; it hosted meetings for women's groups and men's groups, mothers and toddlers, pensioners, alcoholics, wine tasters, cheese tasters, the local Magic Circle, the local church, the local junkies. There was once a double-booking by Male Awareness and Women's Refuge which led to three fights and, worse, two couplings.

The crowd in the café tonight was suitably diverse. Kwesi had described it as a 'black night' but, typical for London, that meant no more than a bizarre mixture of ages, races and classes, archetypes and stereotypes. There was a social worker with a bad marriage and a mistress who used to be a client and had persuaded him of his undiscovered talent. There was a student who'd found a new outlet for his creative juices (other than Internet porn), a music teacher who wore his greying hair in a ponytail and still saw a rock star in the mirror and a genius on the page, a cab driver who'd named his kids after the Arsenal back four, a journalist who felt a cut above the rest – because she wrote for a living, didn't she? – and wished the rest would notice. There was a gaggle of ageing wholemeal hippies with opinions by the pound, a pack of Jamaicans with sharp clothes and sharp attitudes, a brood of ethnocentrics (of all races; a state of mind rather than culture) with pouting lips and perfect posture, and a flock of god knows who (well . . . a hat maker, a teacher, an identikit bottle blonde and a tech-stock victim).

This crowd in the café? You wouldn't have thought they had anything in common. But they did. They were all poets. Or wannabe poets. Or friends of poets. Or friends of wannabe poets. Because tonight was Per-Verse, the café's monthly celebration of spoken word.

'These people are united,' said one nose-pierced hippy solemnly. 'By the love of verse.'

But she was wrong and she probably knew as much. Because poetry was merely the banner they sat beneath, the rallying call that had them scurrying from all parts of London. Poetry was the flag run up the mast of the good ship *Disappointment* but it was disappointment that brought them all here; disappointment with themselves or each other, with their fate or fortune. And they expressed this various, shadowy, ineffable but nonetheless undeniable sensation through poetics; in the words themselves or the performance or merely the fact of being there.

Performance poetry is not a meritocracy. Generally the stars of this scene were those who'd hung around it the longest. Sometimes their poetry improved and sometimes it got worse but it didn't much matter since the main thing was that they were the most perennially disappointed. And it was this that had led Kwesi to top the bill at Per-Verse at the CCC and he was revelling in the limelight, moving from group to group, hugging hippies, touching skin, shaking hands and kiss-kissing.

Tom, Tariq, Freya and Ami had taken a table close to the door. None of them had been to Per-Verse before (Kwesi had never topped the bill before) but that wasn't the reason they weren't talking. They were each stuck in the traffic of their own disappointments, eyes straight ahead, brains chugging, like the buses in the jams on the Holloway Road. They fitted right in.

Tom was wondering where Murray and Karen were. And then he wondered why he wondered because Murray was always late (always used to be, anyway) and Karen was probably with him. He didn't know why this thought bothered him so much (because he was past that, wasn't he? At least that's what he told Tejananda) but it did. He glanced at Freya and he felt himself bristle. There was something about the way Freya sipped her juice that wound him up, that nervous look like she was scared she was being watched. Tom twiddled his thumbs beneath the table and chewed on his bottom lip. These days he was irritated by everything Freya did and he knew it wasn't her fault.

Tariq drained the last of his beer and smacked the empty back on the table. It was one of a line of three. He was drinking for England because he'd been fighting with Emma again and had left her at home with the baby. He knew that getting drunk would only make it worse but that, in some unadmitted way, was kind of the point. Freya was smiling at nobody. She felt guilty about her juice that Tariq had bought because she couldn't really afford to buy a round herself and she knew that Tariq, for all his carefree magnanimity, couldn't really afford it either. Two weeks of Freya Franklin Hats and she'd spent more on cappuccino than she'd taken in sales (twelve pounds to eight; four coffees to three hat-pins and a scarf for a fiver). And what was Tom so moody about? It wasn't her fault (whatever *it* was).

Freya turned to Identikit Ami and immediately felt worse. Because Ami always looked so beautiful (albeit in that telly way which meant that, if you stared at her for too long, you might be almost spooked by the symmetry of her features). Feeling Freya's eyes upon her, Ami quickly looked elsewhere and tucked her hair behind her ear. She didn't want any attention because she'd already been stopped three times that day, mistaken first for a VJ from MTV, then that Brit-in-Hollywood actress and finally the girl from the cereal ad with the chimps in pyjamas.

The whole monkey thing had been the most trying. She'd been hanging morosely from a strap in the rush-hour tube on her way to yet another meeting (with fortyish TV producers in outfits at least a decade too young) when she'd felt an arm snake around her shoulder. Spinning round, she'd found herself confronted by a leering, florid businessman with no neck and breath that smelled of milky coffee. She'd been about to knee him in the bollocks when he'd said: 'So what do your little monkeys eat for breakfast?' She'd looked helplessly around the carriage and found that all the other passengers were smiling too.

Now, sitting in the CCC, she considered the accessibility of fame; that the businessman should have felt comfortable hugging her like a favoured goddaughter. And she wasn't even the right woman.

She knew that he must have vaguely recognized her and she felt a little sick as she wondered which cable channels he watched. Perhaps it was her spell anchoring *Surf 'n' Turf* (the ill-fated Internet-gambling show on Tech Television), or her time fronting OBs on the Weather Channel or, worst of all, her stint as the 'croupier in a bustier' on late-night TVX. She'd only agreed to the latter because the company claimed they were trying to move into mainstream programming. She knew that fame was getting cheaper and so was she.

Freya was feeling uncomfortable so she decided to make conversation. She couldn't think of an opening gambit so she turned to Tariq and asked perkily, 'So how's business?' Because that seemed safe enough.

Tom looked up and flashed a glance at her. She didn't get it. Typical.

'Great,' Tariq said. 'Just great.' And he accentuated the final 't' to make sure she understood it was anything but.

Freya frowned. She realized she'd plunged head first into sticky shit. Why hadn't Tom warned her? She knew that Tariq's business was in trouble but she hadn't known how much; largely because she hadn't the first idea what his business was. She cleared her throat: 'That bad?'

Tariq forced out a you-gotta-laugh laugh. 'I sacked my secretary today. I had to explain to her that we were losing six grand a week. She said if we were losing that much then what difference did it make to keep her on. She kind of had a point.'

'Shit,' Tom was empathizing. 'I mean, *shit.*'

'Oh,' Freya said.

Ami looked blank. 'What exactly do you do?' she asked and Freya was pleased.

Tariq tried another of those laughs. 'What do we do? It's a good question, Ames. Are you sure you want to know?'

Ami shrugged. 'Sure.'

'Basically, we've patented a predictive technology that enables pattern modelling of apparently chaotic behaviours, random events and the like via an extremely user-friendly, wysiwyg interface. Sorry. That's "What You See Is What You Get". To be honest, the algorithms involved are nothing special. But what's unique is the interface, the flexibility of the technology and, therefore, the potential business applications.'

Ami looked blank. 'I have no idea what you're talking about.'

'OK. Think of a trend. Say people start buying a particular brand or style of jeans and before you know it those jeans are everywhere. The makers and their competitors will want to understand how those jeans are so successful, right? Generally this involves analysis of advertising and marketing and the collation of material from things like focus groups; but, frankly, that kind of information is always guesswork at best. Our technology, on the other hand, takes as a fundamental premise that there's no such thing as random choice and, through processing countless variables, produces a precise statistical analysis of both the history of the trend to this point and its likely future development. What that means is that if you see some kid buying the jeans in a shop in Croydon, you'll be able to examine his previous behaviours and, what's more, what he's going to buy next. It's like playing god, you know?'

'But that's amazing!' Freya said. She sounded genuinely enthusiastic.

'Oh yeah. It's great.' There was that 't' again. 'Trouble is, I didn't want to go down the venture-capital route and I didn't want a loan; so I fronted thirty per cent and got into bed with one of the dot-com success stories for the rest of the cash. Trouble is, they've just gone tits up and now we're brassic. I lock myself away for a year doing R and D and I look up to find everyone's buggered off. Shall I tell you what it's like? You ever play hide-and-seek at a kids' party? You hide in some cupboard for hours and then, when you think you've won, you come out to find all your little friends have left. And you know what else? They've eaten all the birthday cake.'

'It's still a good idea,' Freya insisted.

'There's no such thing as a good idea if you don't put it into practice.'

'But you'll find more backing.'

'Yeah? Not now. There's no money. Everybody's running scared. Unless you got a spare 150K knocking around?'

'So . . .' Freya had reached a dead end. 'So what are you going to do?'

'Don't know.' Tariq licked his lips. 'Get drunk, I guess. And listen to some poetry.'

Freya began to flick through Tom's paper. She wasn't really interested but it saved her from looking at anyone else. Then a short paragraph on an inside page caught her eye and she marked it with her index finger and exclaimed excitedly. 'The pigeons! It's in the papers!'

None of the others seemed remotely interested but Tom managed to say, 'What pigeons?' He made the question sound slightly pained; like a patient uncle indulging his show-off niece.

'*The* pigeons,' Freya said. 'It says so here. "London's pigeons have become the focus of capital conversation in the last fortnight as numerous reports of erratic behaviour begin to come to light; everything from attacks on pets (and occasionally people) to apparent suicides. A young couple's picnic in fashionable Hoxton . . ."' She started to laugh and stopped reading. 'They say "the last fortnight". That means me and Big-In-Property must have been two of the first!'

'That make you feel special?' Tom said acidly. And he immediately regretted it. Freya looked hurt. What was the matter with him? 'Sorry.'

But the communication (or its lack) that passed between their eyes was quickly broken by Tariq who, for some reason, thought the pigeon story was the funniest thing he'd ever heard and he laughed uproariously and spilled his drink and his belly shook beneath his flimsy T-shirt. He tried to speak but his every word collapsed into a snort and he covered his mouth just in time to catch most of the spraying mucus.

'Sorry!' he gasped at last. 'But that kills me! Even the pigeons are depressed! What the hell have they got to be depressed about? That makes me feel a whole lot better!'

Tariq cracked up again. He threw his head back and laughed so loudly that people on other tables (the ethnocentrics especially) began to stare disapprovingly. Tariq didn't care. If they had a six-month-old baby, a sick wife and six grand of debt every week . . . *then* they could tell him to shut up.

He only stopped laughing when a bubble of air caught in the back of his throat and he started to hiccup instead. Now he felt a little stupid. He ducked his head under the table and tried to drink from his beer bottle upside down. The bubbles went up his nose and he spilled most of it on his shoes. He realized he was pissed. He took a small package of tobacco from his pocket and started to roll a cigarette. He thought the concentration might help his hiccups but the paper kept sticking to his damp fingers and he soon gave up.

The music was lowered a notch or two as Wordsworth, the

host of Per-Verse, took to the stage. He was middle-aged with more than a hint of New Age about him. He wore cowboy boots and tight patchwork trousers in corduroy and denim and various shades of purple. An impossibly shiny red nose poked out from implausibly healthy dreadlocks. His long white fingers wrapped around the microphone but, for a moment, he said nothing. The Jamaicans began to kiss their teeth and the hippies shushed them. The music faded to nothing when Wordsworth pressed his lips to the mic.

'Welcome to Per-Verse,' he whispered. His voice was breathy and cigarette-cracked.

> From me, your host, Wordsworth.
> What are words worth?
> What are words worth?
> Words are worth . . .

He paused portentously. Tariq hiccupped. Tom started to giggle. The hippies shushed them. 'The earth!' Wordsworth concluded. But no one was listening.

The first poet on stage was an old hand called Paul. He was a professional Irishman who swore with a Roddy Doyle accent and made virtue of his disappointment by telling bitter wisecracks in eight-line stanzas, spitting out punchlines that invariably included the phrase 'middle class', delivered with a dismissive sneer. At one point, the ponytailed music teacher laughed at the wrong moment and Paul paused mid-line to call him 'a middle-class fecker'.

He periodically swigged from a half-pint of clear liquid. Either poetry had driven him to alcohol or alcohol to poetry; there was definitely some connection. The hippies admired his tortured genius, the ethnocentrics' pouts ripened a little more with every choice curse, the Jamaicans weren't listening.

The social worker's mistress didn't get what Paul was moaning about, the student would have enjoyed more swearing, the music teacher was chastened, the cab driver found it all kind of funny, the journalist thought she could do better.

Tariq leaned forward across the table. He was holding his nose (his latest ruse to cure the hiccups). 'When's K coming on?' he hissed, loud and drunken. 'I didn't bargain for this. I came to see Kwesi. I'm not sure I can take much more . . .' His complaints were interrupted by another hiccup.

Tom looked at his watch. 'I wonder where Karen's got to.'

Freya examined her hands and started to pick at the skin around her cuticles.

'I'm sure she's with your friend Murray,' Ami said comfortingly. That didn't make Tom feel any better.

Paul the poet concluded what he'd prefaced as his penultimate poem and there was rowdy applause. The hippies couldn't get enough; the rest looked forward to seeing the back of him. He gulped from his drink and swilled it around his teeth. His face creased and he made a strange, wet sound of satisfaction.

'My last piece,' he announced. 'Is called "Liberals Smoking Roll-Ups".' And he chuckled to himself. Tariq hid his tobacco under the newspaper.

Tories' teatime sandwiches
Communist coffee cups . . .

The swing-door to the café opened and its hinges creaked noisily. Murray breezed in with Karen, looking a little embarrassed, behind. On stage, the words stuck in Paul's throat. His eyes were wide and he seemed almost dismayed by this interruption. The whole crowd turned to look at Murray but he didn't seem to notice. He was squinting and scanning the room until he located his friends' table. Then, when he found it, he raised a cheery hand and began to excuse-me his way towards them. Paul was staring at him and he said loudly, 'Jaysus! What's your problem?' But still Murray didn't look. He slumped in a spare chair next to Tom and touched him on the shoulder. Tom whispered, 'You all right?' but Murray glanced at him with an expression he couldn't read (scorn, perhaps? What had he done wrong?) and pointed to where Karen was still hovering by the door. Then Murray smiled at Ami, Tariq and Freya. Freya was nodding towards the stage where Paul the poet was tapping his foot in a caricature of impatience. 'Do you mind?' he said. His Irish accent was getting stronger.

Finally Murray glanced towards the stage. He raised his eyebrows and stood up. 'I'm sorry?'

'Can I continue?'

Murray shrugged. 'Go for your life, china.' He sat down.

Paul was looking daggers. He shook his head. He was about to carry on but there was something else he wanted to say. 'Rude fecker!' he spat.

Murray was on his feet in a flash. 'I'm sorry?'

'You're a rude fecker!'

'Why?'

'You turn up late, interrupt me and now you won't feckin' shut up.'

Paul shuffled to the edge of the stage and peered into the audience. He could just about make out the teeth of Murray's wide grin.

'Sorry I was late, china. Got held up, know what I mean? But I didn't interrupt you, did I? You interrupted yourself.'

The whole audience was silent. Some of them stared at Murray, some of them at Paul, most of them at the floor. The café was vacuum-packed in discomfiture: some were embarrassed for Murray, some for Paul, most for themselves. One of the hippies said, 'Can you just sit down?' At the same time, one of the ethnocentrics grunted, 'Just get on with it.' The Jamaicans had woken up. This was the best entertainment they'd had so far. Paul was beginning to look unnerved. Murray was clearly enjoying himself. He sat down again.

If Paul had continued 'Liberals Smoking Roll-Ups' at that point, chances are that the majority of sympathy would have stayed with him. But he couldn't resist another comment and he smiled in what he hoped was a relaxed fashion and said: 'Sorry about that, ladies and gentlemen. What a cunt.'

He lost the rest of the ethnocentrics there and then and the hippies were wavering too and the café was utterly silenced – not a clink of glass or a clearing throat – as if that expletive were some kind of pause-button. Murray leaned back in his chair and swung on the back legs. He picked up Tariq's tobacco and began to roll himself a cigarette. Most of the room was staring at him but Murray was engrossed by his work, the easy smile twitching his cheeks. His manner was so *right* that every group in the café now suspected he must be one of their own.

'You like having the last word, eh, china?' he said, a definite and infuriating note of amusement in his tone.

'You're a feckin' arse.' Paul's voice was beginning to waver.

'See what I mean?'

'Why don't you just shut up?'

Murray held up an apologetic hand. 'Sure. Sorry.'

'Arsehole.'

'And again. The last word.'

The audience began to titter. Even Murray couldn't hold his giggle.

Paul looked bewildered. He raised his script in front of his eyes and took a deep breath. But he couldn't help himself and the word still slipped out of the side of his mouth: 'Fecker!'

That was it. The whole café cracked up. The social worker's harassed expression twisted in joy and his mistress squeezed his hand, the student squawked, the music teacher guffawed, the cabbie rocked and the journalist laughed unironically for the first time in so long it left her confused. The hippies couldn't help themselves, the Jamaicans roared and the ethno-centrics buckled at their midriffs and held their sides. Tom imploded with giggles, Freya buried her face in her jumper, Ami held her head in her hands and Tariq laughed and hiccupped and laughed some more.

Paul the poet didn't know what to do so he launched head-long into his poem but, though he raised his voice to a near shout, nobody could hear it for laughing. And the noise only died down when Paul, still shouting, hit the final line.

'And feckin' liberals smoking roll-ups!' he rasped and the audience collapsed again; eyes watering, lungs hooting, strain-ing 'Oh shit! Oh shit!' as stomach muscles wrenched.

Now even Paul started to laugh. No doubt he didn't want to. He'd probably have rather cursed the lot of them and launched the half-bottle of vodka that lined his inside pocket into one of the walls in an empty gesture of contempt. But he couldn't help himself and a peculiar, unpractised cackle exploded from the back of his throat and, amplified by the microphone, rattled around the café. The volume of his laugh-ter forced everyone to look up and, through their tears, they saw the rancorous poet contorted in mirth. And they laughed all the harder.

It was Murray who finally halted the hilarity. He got to his feet, lit his cigarette and began to clap and cheer. 'Bravo!' he hollered. 'Top man!' First his table joined in, then the next, then the next, until the whole café was on its feet. One of the hippies shouted 'Encore!' but her neighbour hushed her with a finger and everyone was relieved when Paul stumbled off the stage. He was choking on his laughter and, when he exited out back, he was promptly sick in a fire bucket and the taste of bile made his eyes water.

It was a full five minutes before the CCC café finally quietened down. Every now and then, Wordsworth walked on to the edge of the stage but, upon hearing the raucous chatter, he thought better of it. Most of the crowd couldn't even figure what they'd just found so funny and they shook their heads, bewildered, and rubbed their eyes with their hands. But then they remembered some detail (Paul's swearing or their neighbour's expression, say) and they felt the giggles come again and they ruefully rubbed their guts. Kwesi was visible behind the thin screens that served as wings. He was talking to himself and making peculiar gestures with his hands.

Karen finally joined her friends' table, pulling up a chair between Freya and Ami. Murray stubbed his cigarette. He couldn't stop smiling. He leaned across Tom to pat Tariq on the thigh. 'You all right?' he said. 'Where's the wife?'

'All right, Muz. She's at home with Tommy.'

'Yeah?' Murray said. He held his smile, fixed, for just a second. 'Appreciate it, china. Know what I mean?'

Tariq felt a sudden resurgence of guilt so he offered a round of drinks and headed for the bar.

Murray turned to Freya and Ami. He looked like he was about to say something but then another more pressing thought occurred to him and his eyes twinkled at Ami.

'I saw you on TV!' he announced.

'Really?' She was blinking.

'Yeah. Three o'clock in the morning, I turn on the Weather Channel and there you are. "And now it's over to our reporter Ami . . ." What's your surname?'

'Lester.'

'That's it. "And now it's over to our reporter Ami Lester for the latest update from Penrith." Amazing!'

Ami was blushing: 'It's only the Weather Channel.'

'What do you mean?' Murray exclaimed. 'You're on TV!'

He asked about Freya Franklin Hats and his smile took on a new quality and his eyebrows raised a little, mirroring Freya's expression. He took her hand across the table and squeezed it lightly. It was only the second time they'd met but his manner spoke of a long and valued friendship that Freya was only too happy to accept.

'It's early days, china,' Murray shrugged. 'And hats are a speciality business. You don't expect someone to walk past a new shop and think, "You know what? I always wanted a hat", and walk right in. You need a bit of word-of-mouth publicity.'

Freya looked forlorn. 'How do you get word-of-mouth publicity when no one comes into your shop?'

Murray span on his chair and scanned the room. Then he turned back to Freya and the nature of his smile had changed again. 'I'll show you,' he said. 'You got a card?'

'What are you doing?' Freya was smiling, bemused, but she reached into her purse and fetched out one of the gold-embossed business cards (orange logo on blue) that had cost her a fortune.

'Hold on.'

Murray took the card, stood up and weaved his way through the tables to where an immaculately dressed ethnocentric with a nose like a beak and a grey felt beret was sipping on her herbal tea. He bent over her and whispered in her ear. Freya, Karen and Ami watched, fascinated. Even Tom reluctantly glanced round. The woman looked up at Murray and her eyes warned him off. They could see his lips moving and the muscles around his eyes working overtime. There was a moment of uncertainty and then the woman's expression cracked into a smile. She was shaking her head but Murray was nodding in a way that said 'No! *Seriously!*' His hand was resting lightly on her shoulder.

Now the two of them looked round towards Murray's table and he raised a hand at Freya. She waved shyly in return and the ethnocentric waved too. Murray took the woman's hand and kissed her on the cheek and returned to his seat.

'She says she'll be in on Monday,' Murray said.

Freya was shaking her head and giggling. 'Thanks.'

'No problem.'

Tom was staring at Freya and he felt himself bristle (although he didn't try to identify the reasons); god, she could be such a pain. He turned to Murray and his voice came out snide and bitter. 'Charm her, did you, Muz?' he said. 'You always had a way with women.'

Murray looked at him. For a split second anger flared behind his eyes and for the second time Tom thought he must have done something wrong (more than just the comment). What were these silent dialogues, triangles and squares playing out between him and Murray and Freya and Karen? Or was he just imagining? Because then the anger was gone and Murray was chuckling softly. 'Superhero Tom Dare,' he said. 'What the fuck would you know?'

Tom wanted to reply – he wanted to ask Murray what was up – but at that moment Tariq returned with the drinks and a few bags of crisps. He offered a packet to Murray.

'What flavour?' Murray asked.

Tariq pulled an apologetic face. 'Sorry, Muz. They didn't have them.'

'Never mind.'

Back stage, Wordsworth decided it was finally time to get things going again and the music was lowered and the audience chatter subsided to a murmur. He turned to Kwesi: 'You all right?' Kwesi nodded. He was practising his stage face; trying to look tough.

The house lights were dimmed as Wordsworth sauntered to the mic. He shook his head and then licked his palm and carefully pasted back his locks.

'People,' he announced huskily. Then he paused. 'The second half of our show features a poet who some of you may know because he's been dropping lyrical consciousness since time.' Again Wordsworth paused and licked his lips. He'd adopted a curious Caribbean twang to his accent. 'So put your hands together and give enough respect to our very own righteous brother, K!'

Kwesi swaggered on to the stage and the audience clapped enthusiastically. Freya and Karen even stood up and cheered. With the audience still high on the hilarity of Paul, Kwesi would never have a better chance to make a good impression. But Murray leaned across the table to Ami. 'Why's he standing like that?' he asked. There was something weird about Kwesi's bearing. He had his chin raised a little too high in a way that managed to look confrontational and absurd all at once.

Ami shrugged. 'Perhaps he's nervous,' she said.

There was a moment or two of silence and then the music faded up; a sparse and jazzy hip-hop beat. Kwesi began to tap the palm of his hand against one thigh and a couple of people called out 'Bo!' and 'Boo!', sealing their approval. This was going to be cool, wasn't it?

'Yes, my good people!' Kwesi began. 'Back in the days of the Boogie Down Bronx, hip-hop music was the jungle tele-graph for black folk; a poetic communication, the CNN of the street! That's my philosophy of ghetto storytelling and this one goes out to all my bredren and sistren because you know what I'm chatting about! It's called "Babylon on My Tail". Word!'

Kwesi paused and his chest heaved. He closed his eyes for a moment. He was clearly taking this (and himself) very seriously.

> Babylon on my tail. Goodness me!
> Wailing sirens
> Trying to see
> Another brother
> Who never knew his mother . . .

Kwesi kept his eyes shut. Which was a good thing. Because, as soon as he launched into the poem, the audience was silenced in embarrassment like they'd been floored by a punch. The hippies looked at the floor, the Jamaicans tried to suppress their snorts and sneering, and the ethnocentrics shook their heads in astonishment. The social worker sighed, the student reminisced about one off the wrist and the music teacher tried to hear only the drum beats. The cab driver wondered if he'd be home in time for the football and the journalist tutted. Tom, Tariq, Freya, Ami and Karen exchanged glances that said 'It's not *that* bad, is it?' and 'Yes, it is' and they avoided looking at the stage. Only Murray was watching and the smile was fixed on his face as if he'd been caught laughing at the moment of a car crash. 'Fucking hell!' he breathed. 'What's he *doing*?'

It wasn't Kwesi's poem itself that was so gut-twistingly awful but his delivery, manner, accent and vocabulary. He told a fairly standard scarytale of -isms and injustice (all revolutionary catchphrases and unity fantasies); but he repeatedly dropped off beat as if squabbling with the rhythm, he threw out his arms in bizarre, uncoordinated movements that looked like piss-takes of LA gang signs and his accent lurched unconvincingly between New York rapper, ragga MC, sit-com cockney and privately educated son of a Ghanaian diplomat. Slowly the crowd began to fidget and mutter. He described a character in his poem as a 'bitch' and he imbued this insult with such sudden and unexpected misogyny that some of the hippies laughed while others wanted to walk out in protest. 'Booyaka!' he exclaimed and the Jamaicans kissed their teeth and packed up because he sounded like a politician trying to be down with the kids. 'Do we remember Armistad?' he pleaded and the ethnic ethnocentrics looked at one another and said things like 'Well, you certainly don't', while the whites among them thought that, but for an accident of birth, they might have expressed this shit, this pain, this *disappointment*, a whole lot better.

It is a delicate and sensitized kind of skill to represent other people's protests with sincerity. But Kwesi? He was fronting issues about which he knew nothing; ditching his own identity in favour of cardboard cutouts from TV and movies and music. He may as well have boot-polished his African face and sung a Gershwin blues with the Black and White Minstrels. At nineteen, he'd once been stopped by the cops for speeding. Sure. But they'd eventually waved on his diplomatic plates. His only experience of drug culture was an infrequent eighth of weed from the glove compartment of Lucky's Jag and the only thing he ever shot was an occasional amber light. And he visited his mother once a year in a comfortable suburb of Accra.

With his eyes squeezed tight, Kwesi could picture himself as a rebel poet but, up on stage, he came across as half a dozen contradictory black caricatures all at once: an Uncle Tom gangsta, a bush African B-Boy, a crack-dealing Golliwog. He came across as a caricature of himself.

'Babylon on my tail. Goodness me!' he bellowed.

> Police officer officer
> Oversee
> Me?

At last Kwesi opened his eyes as 'Babylon on My Tail' built to its intended climax. But now, seeing the faces of the crowd twisted in various combinations of suppressed amusement, awkwardness and irritation, he found that the words were caught somewhere in the piping between his mind and his gob. His gaze lifted above the audience's heads and his mouth dropped open and he began to blink very fast. It was a sudden, gaping moment of self-realization that couldn't have been more painful if every person present had offered their critique in turn. He was briefly the Jesus of all their disappointments and the instant seemed to stretch as his shoulders slumped and his chin fell and the embarrassment in the café was so tangible it could have been packaged and given out to adolescents shopping with their mothers in fashionable Kensington boutiques.

Murray stood up. He was chuckling noiselessly and he began to applaud very slowly. Nobody joined in.

Tom looked up at him, bewildered. 'What are you doing?' he hissed.

'Rescue mission, china.'

He strode confidently towards the stage and his clapping gradually synched to the rhythm from the sound system. Kwesi's eyes were wide and agonized and starting to blur when he picked out Murray climbing on to the stage and an expression halfway between terror and a smile began to play on his face. The audience was transfixed and silent. Their stomachs still churned with vicarious humiliation but they recognized Murray as the man who'd confronted Paul the previous poet, and they wondered what game he was playing now. And was K in on it?

Murray stopped clapping, slipped his hands in his pockets and stood with his back to the room. Somehow, without his accompaniment, the drum beats seemed to gather pace (or was it just the growing tension?). And when he spoke, he spoke quietly; his tone simmering with soft, controlled contempt. But his voice reverberated around the café without the benefit of a mic.

'What kind of a black person do you call yourself?' Murray said. And the hippies, the Jamaicans and the ethnocentrics all glowed at the sight of somebody who might just be one of their own asking the question.

'What are you saying?' Kwesi sounded bemused, sheepish, broken.

'What I mean to say . . .' Murray's voice came quick.

> What I mean to say
> What does the officer oversee?
> What are you going to be today?
> What kind of black are you going to be?

Murray's improvised scansion was far from perfect and his sentiments far from deep. But the way he spoke, it was as if the recorded bass and snares dropped in with his every word and, to the audience, his every word was exactly the way they'd have put it themselves and they were suddenly on the edge of their seats. Tariq's elbow was frozen, the beer midway to his mouth. Ami's hand was fixed to the side of her head where she'd been tucking her hair behind her ear. Freya and Karen held nervous hands on the tabletop and their thumbs were pink and their knuckles were white.

Tom noticed their interlocking fingers and it surely would have bothered him but he too was hostage to the action on the stage.

Kwesi's brain slowly ground into action and he answered with a dull, almost sleepy inflection. But at least the voice was his own. 'The only black I know how.'

'And what kind of black is that?' Murray asked, dragging K with him like a chip wrapper that snags your foot on the Camden Road.

'It's the black I am now,' K said and he too was beginning to find the metre.

Slowly Murray began to build new poetry out of the rubble of Kwesi's own, firing fundamental questions of race and identity that his would-be accomplice answered with growing wit, confidence and an uncanny capacity for the rhyming couplet. What's more, in the context of K's woeful polemicizing that had gone before, this showdown had a new and political poignancy that was utterly compelling.

'What a set-up!' whispered one hippy under her breath that smelled of clove cigarettes.

'What a devastating conceit!' agreed her boyfriend.

The Jamaicans snapped their fingers in appreciation of Murray's every comment – because didn't it take a Jamaican to express the contradictions of black Britain? – and they glocked their tongues at K's sharp retorts. And the ethnocentrics were dumbfounded at such a brazen confrontation of the issues of diaspora, colonialism and multiculturalism and they wondered whether these two might consider performing at their celebration of Diwali next year (between the Ivorian drummers and the Peruvian panpipes, perhaps).

As the dialogue unfolded, so it heated and sparked as Murray snapped K and K tried to snap him right back (and the cab driver thought, So this is what happens when two clever black geezers get together). Initially Murray had the best of it and the audience started to wince aloud and chuckle with each biting phrase. But as Murray gathered momentum, so K seemed to find assurance, as if biding his time for a killer blow, and he deflected each jibe with skill and irony. The snaps flew and were parried; they were returned with interest and swatted away. And when Kwesi's backing tape ran silent and the speed of the exchange built further into a rolling wave of theses, antitheses and syntheses, some of the crowd didn't notice and the rest figured it was all part of the show. Finally Murray appeared to lose his temper and he strode up to K and shouted at the top of his voice: 'What kind of black are you going to be?'

'Why? What kind of black will you sell me?' Kwesi sneered.

'When you look in the mirror what do you see?'

Kwesi lifted his head a little and spat out the last word: 'That I don't need some white guy to tell me!'

With perfect timing, Murray finally turned to face the audience and there was an audible gasp from every corner of the café as if they were seeing him for the first time. Because Murray, who moments before had been an ethnocentric Jamaican hippy (and a few things else besides), was suddenly, indisputably and unforgivably white.

A single heartbeat was followed by a spontaneous roar of applause. Murray immediately stepped off the front of the stage and the crowds parted to let him through. They barely acknowledged him as they were too busy acclaiming K, who milked their esteem like he'd had five years' practice for just such a moment. White and black and everything in between, they cheered; because Kwesi had won and so redeemed their every disappointment and come to represent them all.

At his table, Murray flopped into a chair and the expression on his face was unreadable. Wordsworth took the stage and asked the crowd to show their appreciation for the performers once more and, at the mention of 'the incomparable K-ster', they again erupted into unselfconscious cheers. Freya and Ami stared at Murray, awestruck. Even they now suspected that the whole show had been some secret plan between Murray and K. But Tariq, Karen and Tom, who remembered their times with Murray at LMT? They knew what he was capable of all too well. Tariq nodded at him shyly and Karen leaned across the table and smiled. 'That was a good thing, Muz,' she said. 'A good thing.' In her head, she compared the whole episode to a movie. Kevin Bacon at the end of *Footloose*, she thought.

Tom ducked his head into Murray's shoulder and whispered, 'Nice one.' And the smile vanished from Murray's face and the muscles of his jaw seemed to tighten a little. For the third time that evening, Tom sensed that Murray was vexed with him but he still didn't know why and he didn't like it. So he leaned forward again and held him by the elbow. 'What's up with you?' he asked.

Murray turned slowly towards him and the stone of his eyes chilled Tom to the gut. He spoke slow and precise and too soft for anyone else to hear. 'You told me about you and Karen,' he said. 'You told me about her new job; about how she was ambitious, how you got left behind.'

Tom nodded. He didn't like the direction this was going.

'You didn't tell me you played her.'

Tom licked his lips. 'So?'

'So much for the superhero. You're a fool, china; a fucking fool.'

Murray shook his head and looked away. Tom felt sick. Kwesi was approaching the table wearing a smile that spanned the city.

7
The art of conversation is dead

When a person's drunk, they talk sense or they talk none; and you can listen to them or not. It's the same as when they're sober.

After Per-Verse, they all went back to Tariq and Emma's house, off Lavender Hill. It was pushing midnight by the time they left the CCC café and it wasn't a good idea but Tariq kept saying 'It's just around the corner' and 'It'll be fine' and 'I'm telling you, it'll be fine'. He was topsy-turvy plastered so his feelings were upside-down. He knew there was fault in there somewhere but, in his drunkenness, he'd managed to transfer it to his wife for making him feel guilty in the first place. Kwesi was on a high and he wanted to keep on drinking so he said, 'Yeah. Let's go to Tariq's. What do you reckon, Ames?' Ami didn't know Emma too well and she didn't want to get involved so she just shrugged a whatever. Tom was buried in his own thoughts; sneaking occasional glances at Murray, wondering what Karen had told him and in no mood to take a decision. Murray was quiet. He looked half-asleep. Karen and Freya did both ask, 'What about Emma?' but Tariq shook his head irritably. 'It's not late,' he said. 'I'm telling you, it'll be fine.'

It wasn't fine.

The others stood shyly on the pavement while Tariq struggled with the latch key to the small maisonette. It was an ex-council terrace of railway workers' cottages but now one of Clapham's more fashionable addresses. Audis and Mercs lined the narrow street and there were Neighbourhood Watch stickers on every window that looked in on uniform Venetian blinds concealing lacquered wooden floors in open-plan kitchens with Agas and breakfast bars.

Tariq rested one hand on the doorframe and bent over the lock, fiddling uncoordinatedly and muttering, 'I never usually have . . . What the fuck? Fucking thing.'

Tom said, 'Do you want me to try?'

But Tariq growled, 'I can open my own fucking front . . .'

When Emma flung open the door from inside, she was already in midstream of a garbled and incoherent invective (half rekindling their earlier argument and half complaining about the hour). But she hadn't expected Tariq to have company – surely not even he was *that* insensitive – and she was brought up short by the sight of her friends, fidgeting and embarrassed, on her doorstep. She was wearing only knickers and a T-shirt that barely brushed her thighs and she pulled the thin cotton down self-consciously and tried a welcoming smile. She stood back to wave them inside but Tom said, 'Sorry, Em. We should just go home.'

'No, it's OK,' she muttered unconvincingly. And then she stiffened it with, 'Really. I'm awake now anyway.'

They shuffled past her, single file, Tariq leading the way into the small living-room. Emma dug him in the ribs as he passed and screwed up her face when she smelled the beer and fags on his clothes and the cheese-and-onion crisps on his breath. Hovering at the back, Freya and Karen glanced at one another. Of course they knew Emma had been suffering from this mystery illness ever since little Tom was born and in the past they'd noted how she was looking drawn and had lost weight. But now, seeing her bare-legged in a T-shirt, they realized the full extent. It didn't look possible that Emma could have had a baby – what? – not much more than six months ago. She was all ribs and elbows and hips and knees; her body was like four coat-hangers in a bin bag. Her complexion was translucent and her hair was lank and thin.

Emma caught their expressions and pulled a wry face. 'Heroin chic's making a comeback, didn't you know? At least I've stopped breastfeeding. Poor Tommy. It was like he was trying to suck on a condom.'

'Shit, Emma,' Karen murmured. 'You look terrible.'

Emma sniffed. 'Yeah? When your friends stop lying to you, you know you're in trouble.'

In the living-room, Kwesi was Carnaby Street; all stilted banter and facial expressions and posing. He was still vibing off his night's success and he chattered to no one in particular while Tariq poured the drinks: 'That was, like, an important lesson for me, know what I mean? Like, Murray, man, you've really, like, taught me something, you get me? It was a reality check. Serious. A reality check; that's what it was.'

Karen pulled the door behind her as she came into the room and she said, 'Do you want to keep your voice down a bit, K?' But it was too late and the baby monitor crackled into life as Tommy's gurgles turned to snivels and then tears and then screams.

Emma looked daggers at Tariq. He shrugged and handed Kwesi an oversized Scotch. 'No problem,' he said. 'I'll go.'

'You're drunk.'

'I'm fine,' Tariq protested and lumbered out of the door.

His footsteps were heavy on the stairs and everyone was listening and embarrassed and Emma threw out 'You see what I have to put up with' expressions that the other women picked up. At one point they heard a stumble and a loud curse: 'Fuck!'

Tariq reappeared with his son nestling against his chest and a roll-up hanging from his bottom lip. Emma flipped.

'What the . . .' she exclaimed. 'What the hell do you think you're doing?'

'What?'

'Give him to me!' She lunged towards him but Tariq span away. The baby began to cry again.

'What's the matter with you?' he drawled.

'Look at you!' Emma's voice was beginning to waver, strung out and twanging like a high wire. 'Blowing smoke in our son's face, Riq? Jesus!'

Tariq went cross-eyed trying to see the cigarette that protruded from his mouth and, when he spotted it, his face opened up in an expression of comic surprise (as if to say, 'How did *that* get there?') and then, equally suddenly, dropped in remorse.

'Sorry. I didn't . . .' he began. But Emma wouldn't meet his eye and she stormed out of the room. Freya looked at Karen and Karen looked at Freya. But it was Murray who went after her.

Tariq's drunken arrogance – always a fragile state – had collapsed into drunken mortification and he looked like he might burst into tears. Tom put his Scotch down above the fireplace and reached out for his namesake.

'Can I say hello to my godson?' Tom asked and Tariq willingly gave up the baby. 'Come to Uncle Tom.'

The baby's face was scrunched up like scrap paper but Tom soon calmed him down. He had a way with kids and he talked to the baby in a kind of tiptoeing adult voice that sounded light-hearted and happy and reassuring.

'God you're a handsome devil!' Tom whispered. 'No wonder your parents gave you such a cool name. Who knows? One day you might be even more beautiful than me.' He began to tickle the child's stomach and he squirmed appreciatively. 'How did your daddy produce a creature like you? Was Mummy with the milkman, was she? Yes she was! Yes she was!' He looked up at Tariq. 'Your milkman a Stani?'

Tariq smiled. 'I think he is as it goes.' He downed a huge mouthful of whisky. He was beginning to cheer up like it was his own belly being tickled. 'Careful, mate. You never know what babies understand. You'll have him growing up with a complex.'

Watching Tom with the baby, Karen found a thin smile frozen on her face. For the first time in ages, she felt a profound (if unsurprising) tide of melancholy and loss lapping against her heart; the kind of sensation that typically accompanies a snapshot of what might have been. She felt briefly confused and hurt, as if Tom was playing a game with her (because that would be nothing new), and her emotions were so acute that she couldn't figure out their substance. He looked at her and smiled and she thought, What do you think you're smiling at? She realized that this snapshot made her hate him more and love him more all at once and it had to be a mistake to imagine those two emotions were black and white and mutually exclusive. She still needed to be careful.

Freya was watching too. Tom looked cute with the baby; easy-natured and content like a Richmond dad. So why had he been snapping at her all night? She bit her lip and looked around the others. Tariq, Ami, Kwesi . . . even Karen . . . they were all watching Tom and Tommy as if hypnotized, their faces gawping in gormless appreciation. There was, she considered, something compulsory about baby-watching and it was a fix of artifice that annoyed her; a second-hand appreciation of virtue when you've abandoned any faith in your own. Well. She had, anyway, for all the good it had done her. Freya found herself squeezing her thumbs tightly in her fists and she self-consciously opened her palms and stretched out her fingers. She didn't want to get so cynical but she knew that was the way she was heading; inevitably, in spite of herself.

She shook her head. No one was talking – they were all still lost in baby rapture – but this silence made her feel like she might burst. She turned to Kwesi (because he still desperately wanted to talk about himself and was the likeliest candidate for conversation) and tried to think of something to say. Eventually she asked, 'So what's next for you, K?' because it was an open-ended and suggestively obsequious question and therefore sure to provoke an answer.

Murray returned from the kitchen no more than ten minutes later. But, by then, a drunken but nonetheless difficult row had erupted with Tom and Karen spitting venom at each other from either side of the room. Between them, the baby was asleep in his pushchair; oblivious and innocent at the eye of the storm.

'It's easy for you,' Tom growled, 'because you don't have to worry about it.'

'Don't have to worry about it?' Karen laughed in a way that said it wasn't funny. 'You of all people should know that's bullshit when I've spent my life worrying about nothing else.'

Murray was munching on something in his fingers. No one took any notice of him and he looked around the other faces. Ami was bemused, Kwesi was leaning forward and poised to speak but he couldn't get a word in, and Freya was wringing her hands and furrowing her brow as if this were somehow all her fault. Tariq was sitting on the sofa. He'd rolled a cigarette and kept putting it in his mouth and then thinking better of it. Murray flopped down next to him.

'What's that?' Tariq asked as Murray popped the last morsel in his mouth.

'Chicken stick. Beautiful.'

'Where's Em?'

'She's coming. Just went to put something else on.'

'She all right?'

'Fine.' Murray patted Tariq on the thigh. 'What's this about?'

'You know, Muz; just the usual.'

'Yeah?' Murray said. 'I haven't seen them for ten years. What's the usual?'

Tariq shrugged and deliberately raised his voice a notch: 'They still get their kicks from fighting with each other. Just, these days, they have to pretend it's actually about something.'

Tom and Karen snapped round to look at him simultaneously and said, 'Fuck you, Riq!' in stereo.

Tariq laughed. 'At last,' he said. 'Unity.'

In fact the conversation had unfolded something like this: Freya asked Kwesi, 'So what's next for you, K?' And Kwesi adopted a serious, intellectual and somewhat agonized expression and said he'd keep 'writing, writing' because it wasn't long before he hit thirty. Ami, who knew nothing of Kwesi's pact with himself, looked puzzled and asked what happened at thirty. 'I stop writing poetry,' he said solemnly but when Ami, wide-eyed and ingenuous, asked why, he didn't know what to say. Tom laughed: 'What then, K-ster? You finally going to get a proper job?' Kwesi looked scared at the thought and Freya, undoubtedly thinking about her ailing shop, said, 'He doesn't have to get a proper job if he doesn't want to.' To which Tom replied nastily, 'You reckon?' and Tariq commented, 'We're living in the real world here, Frey.'

'What about you? What are *you* going to do?'

This was Karen addressing Tom. Of course the question didn't really make sense because it wasn't like Tom didn't have a job. But sometimes meanings are irrelevant compared to tone and Karen's, on the feeble grounds of defending Kwesi, was vicious.

Tom tried to sneer it away. He said he didn't know but he was definitely going to do something. He said he was fed up with being disappointed in people and permanently frustrated and he was definitely going to have to do something about *that*. He fixed on Karen as he spoke and his words were blunt and embarrassed everyone to silence. Except Ami. 'But you're a teacher,' she said, and the moment was gone. 'It can't be frustrating being a teacher. Isn't that the most fulfilling job in the world?'

'You've obviously never been a teacher, Ames,' Tom muttered, helping himself to more Scotch. He'd decided to get pissed. 'Actually, I'm thinking of jacking it in. I mean, I don't know why I'm doing it any more. I thought I wanted to inspire people; at least give them a bit of perspective. But – you know what? – these days I don't think I've got any perspective myself so how can I teach anybody else? You know those teachers you had at school who couldn't get enthusiastic about anything and were always a half-step from cynicism? I've become one of them. These days, you become what you do. It's inevitable. So I've become disappointed and frustrated.'

Tariq indulged in some philosophizing, laced with the melancholia of alcohol. Disappointment and frustration, he announced bombastically, were the twin pillars of modern adulthood.

'That's why I write poetry,' Kwesi interjected, nodding. He only said this because he wanted to say something (preferably about himself) and he didn't consider what it meant, let alone its accuracy.

'What I mean . . .' Tariq continued, oblivious, the pitch of his voice dropping as if weighted down by the wisdom. 'What I mean is that if we looked at ourselves now from a point ten years ago, we'd be depressed and frankly fucked off by what we saw. Disappointment and frustration are the essence of the human condition.' He signalled to Tom to pass the Scotch.

Freya sighed. She was dismayed by the temper of the conversation and she wished she'd left them worshipping at the altar of innocence. 'Perhaps it's good for the soul,' she tried. Tariq raised his glass to her. 'I believe it is good for the spirits.' He slugged heartily.

Tom shook his head. He had his own angle on all this and he didn't want it to fade out with a one-liner. 'No,' he said. 'No.'

According to Tom, it all came down to one thing. Yes, he was frustrated. And yes, he was disappointed. But these days? It was all about money. And he was a teacher, wasn't he? So he didn't have enough of it.

'To think; all these years and I never picked you for such a materialist. What does *that* say?' This was Karen, of course.

Tom smiled without teeth. 'Renting for one gets expensive,' he said.

'Whatever.'

'It's easy for you,' Tom growled. 'Because you don't have to worry about it.'

'Don't have to worry about it?' Karen laughed in a way that said it wasn't funny. 'You of all people should know that's bullshit when I've spent my life worrying about nothing else.'

Tom laughed in a way that said it was. 'Sure. But how much do you earn, Kazza? No. Really. How much do you earn? Why are *you* disappointed? You and Jared get frustrated about the *feng shui* in your Pimlico pad, do you? "No, dear. I told you. The armchair should face the patio." Tough, is it?'

Freya cleared her throat. She knew this was, at more than one level, her fault and she wanted to interrupt. Karen wouldn't let her. 'At least Jared never fucked . . .' Karen began but she was successfully cut short by Tariq who announced as if to the room: 'They still get their kicks from fighting with each other. Just, these days, they have to pretend it's actually about something.'

Tom and Karen snapped round to look at him simultaneously and said, 'Fuck you, Riq!' in stereo.

Tariq laughed. 'At last,' he said. 'Unity.'

The concentration of poison was diluted a little when Emma walked in. She'd put on a pair of baggy tracksuit bottoms and one of Tariq's sweatshirts that hung off her like a poncho. At the front, the cut of the sweatshirt was distorted where Tariq's belly had strained the material. She bent over the pushchair and cooed at her son before wheeling him to the side of the room. She was so skinny that she had to keep adjusting the neck of the top so that both her shoulders didn't slip right through. Whatever tension there was, Emma hadn't noticed it.

Murray stood up from the sofa to make room for Emma and he shifted to the fireplace where he squatted with his back to the wall; beneath the pine mirror and between the mahogany candlesticks Tom and Karen had brought back from a holiday in South Africa a couple of years ago. Emma sat down next to Tariq and, to his surprise, snuggled into his chest. He wrapped an arm around her and squeezed her possessively.

'There a drink for me?' she asked. At Tariq's signal, Murray leaned over to the corner cabinet, retrieved another bottle and poured her a large measure. She took her first sip with a wince.

Ami, who'd been thinking and clearly hadn't noticed the unconsciously agreed ceasefire, spoke up. 'I agree with Karen,' she began slowly. 'I don't think it is all about money. I mean, Kwesi, he doesn't write poetry to make money, does he? And Freya. Why do you make hats?'

'Flower parents who christen me Freya?' she said dryly. 'What else was I going to do?'

'So you're following in their footsteps?'

'No way! That pair of hippies?'

Ami sighed. 'But what I'm getting at is that it's not just for the money, right?'

'I should be so lucky.'

'Right. So I reckon it's really all about personal fulfilment.'

Tariq chuckled. 'You practising for the BAFTAs, Ames?' he said and Emma poked him.

Tom drained his glass. His stomach was getting a little swimmy but he thought his head was still clear. 'You're right,' he began. 'But that's not really what I'm saying. I mean, money's not everything but it is the only abstract signifier of success. Like Kwesi might write poetry for all kinds of reasons – creativity, politics, a chip on his shoulder. I don't fucking know – but do you think he'd be so pent up if he was getting paid?'

Karen and Freya cringed at the dissing but Kwesi was too pissed to notice and he gave Tom some skin, 'Word, my brother.'

'And Freya might make hats out of some missionary zeal for the aesthetic merits of great millinery but, if nobody buys them, what the fuck does it matter? And what about you, Ames? Do you complain about the awfulness of digital TV because of respect for high production values? Of course not. You want to get paid the big bucks; just like the rest of us.'

Everybody stared at Tom. The truth of what he was saying was as undeniable as it was irritating and incomplete. Emma downed her whisky in one and it went straight to her head. Since she'd got sick and lost so much weight, she'd become a real lightweight. She held out her glass to Murray for a refill. 'What on earth are you lot talking about?' she asked.

Tom, Karen, Freya, Ami, Kwesi, Tariq . . . they all looked at each other. It was a difficult question and the answer depended on where you were sitting.

Eventually Tom said, 'Money. So what about you? What do you think?'

'About what?'

Tom shrugged: 'About money. Whatever. I don't know. Like, say, Tariq's business is about to go tits up and you've been, like, fading away for about six months . . .'

Tariq interrupted: 'Easy, Tom . . .'

Emma assumed her husband was being protective of her (and perhaps he was) so she held up her hand. 'It's fine,' she said. 'Carry on.'

'So imagine you had a choice and you could change one of them. Which one do you change?'

'The business,' Emma said immediately.

There was an awkward moment's hush then Freya said, 'Really?' And Tariq peered at his wife in surprise. Karen cleared her throat. 'Come on, Em . . .'

'Come on, Em *what*?' Emma exclaimed. She swilled her Scotch like she was born to it and pulled away from Tariq to look at him. 'I'm sorry, Riq, but there's no point denying it. If you go bankrupt, we lose the house and the fact is I'd rather be sick and solvent than bringing up Tommy on the ruddy street.'

Tariq wouldn't meet her eye. She paused for a moment and Kwesi tried to whisper to Ami, 'This is some serious drama!' But he was too drunk for secrecy and everyone heard and it made Emma smile. She looked at Tom.

'It's not about money as a signifier of success, Tom. Tariq still thinks like that and it's fine because it's what gets him out of bed and on to the tube and into the office and sometimes that's more important than the truth. But that idea is a luxury.

We're just too bloated to see it. But the truth is when you're standing on the precipice, you don't give a stuff about the right clothes or car or postcode. You know what? I'd sell my body for spare parts at the moment; I'd rob a ruddy bank. Because money isn't some kind of abstract symbol to me any more but a real thing. So don't tell me you haven't got enough of it because you don't have the first clue what that means.'

Everyone was staring at Emma. Except Murray, who was staring at Tom. Then everyone shifted their attention to Tom. Except Murray, who now stared at Emma. Tom knew he was being chastised and that, in his defensive and self-pitying state, felt unfair. 'So how much is enough?' he asked snidely.

Emma frowned. 'Have you been listening to me?' She shook her head like this was all just too tiring and lay back down on the soft pillow of Tariq's chest. 'God, I'm drunk.'

Tariq stroked her hair and looked at the ceiling. He didn't want to meet anyone else's eye but, in fact, the rest of them were all examining their hands or staring at the flecks in the carpet anyway. They felt uncomfortable, even embarrassed: uncomfortable that their own problems now sounded too small to air and embarrassed that they still sounded so big in their own heads. Only Murray, who hadn't said a word, was relaxed and he caught Emma's eye over the swell of Tariq's sigh.

'What do *you* think?' Emma asked quietly. Her voice was muffled by a mouthful of Tariq's sweater.

'Me?'

'Yes. You haven't said much, Mr Murray, and I don't know you from a bar of soap. So how about a bit of outside perspective?'

Murray shrugged and smiled. He was so calm that everyone else looked up at him like his state was some kind of wind-chime in a summer breeze, like you couldn't be tense if you looked at him, like he was the gamely blossoming flowerbed in the middle of Hammersmith Broadway.

'I think it's time for some Murray-fun,' he said laconically and Karen, who'd coined the phrase, looked quickly between Tariq and Tom but they were both hammered and didn't look back.

'What does *that* mean?' Emma asked.

'It means there's only one thing for it. I'm going to have to help you rob that bank, aren't I, Em?'

Emma laughed and, with her initiation, Tariq and Kwesi and Ami joined in. It wasn't like what Murray had said was funny but they were relieved at the break in the tension. Freya smiled too. Because she hated confrontation. Karen tutted, 'Murray!' But it was good-humoured disapproval.

Tom was nodding drunkenly. 'No, no, no!' He spoke quickly and overemphasized every syllable. 'Don't laugh. That's a fan-fucking-tastic idea. We should rob a bank. Definitely. All of us. We'll have a . . . you know . . . *gang*. Because *we* . . .' He paused and belched into his hand. 'Are the perfect fucking bank robbers.'

Tariq was still laughing. 'Yeah? How do you figure that?'

Tom straightened his back and cracked his neck and counted off his ideas on five fingers. He was so toped that he looked a little simple. 'In the first place, we've worked together before. As a team. Well, me, Murray and Karen have anyway. Tariq too. At university. Remember Strangers on a Train? The Antiques Trade?' Tariq and Karen were nodding. The rest looked bemused. 'And, in the second place, none of us have got criminal records, do we? So it's not like the cops are going to know where to look. In the third place . . . Well . . . I don't know any bank robbers but I reckon we must be a whole lot smarter than most of them. In the fourth place, it's a one-off job. We do it and go to ground. No one will have a clue. And fifthly . . .' He paused and stared at his little finger like it might provide the answers. 'Fifthly . . .' His brain hadn't got as far as five.

'Fifthly,' Freya joined in, 'we'll be doing it for a good cause so we'll have karma on our side.'

'Exactly,' Tom said.

There was a heartbeat of silence before Tariq put on an American talkshow voice. 'And you guys would do that for me? I'm feeling a lotta love. I'm feeling a whole lotta love. You guys kill me, man. You kill me.'

They all started chattering then. Every one of them had ideas and it felt safe to lose themselves in this harmless little fantasy. They decided Kwesi should do the talking. He could put on that Yardie accent that would throw any investigation off the scent. Ami said she'd be 'on the inside' and Emma liked the sound of that so she said she'd be 'on the inside' too. Neither of them quite knew what this meant but it sounded appropriate. 'What shall I do?' Freya asked dolefully. But Tom said, 'You can make the masks. Designer shit. We've got to look the business.' And there was no spite in his voice and everybody laughed.

Tariq said, 'What about shooters? We need some hardware if we're going to turn over a bank.'

'"Shooters"? "Hardware"?' Emma giggled. '"Turn over a bank"? I'm married to the Pakistani Ronnie Biggs.'

But Murray said, 'Kazza will sort the guns.' It was his only contribution.

'I'm *sorry*?' Karen exclaimed. But then – somehow – she caught on to his train of thought and said, 'Yeah, all right. I'll sort the guns.'

'And how the hell are you going to do that?' Tariq asked. He was loving this.

'You know my ex from way back?' She wished she had a

cigarette so she could exhale coolly, like Stockard Channing in *Grease*. 'You remember Kush? He can get guns.'

Tariq raised his eyebrows and pinched the bridge of his wonky nose. But Tom looked up sharply, 'Kush? You didn't tell me you'd seen Kush.'

Karen shrugged. 'I just ran into him,' she said. 'In the street.'

They talked until three o'clock in the morning. They discussed potential targets, suitable transport and plausible cover stories. They imagined how it would feel to point guns at cashiers and to scream instructions from beneath their stockinged heads ('Masks,' Freya corrected them. 'You'll be wearing masks.'). Even the adrenalin of these mental pictures was almost too much to bear. They touched on the moral implications and dismissed them saying things like 'The insurance company will pay up' and 'It's a victimless crime'. It didn't matter anyway because they were only having a bit of fun, after all. They talked and they drank and they only stopped when the baby woke up and began to snivel and gurgle. It seemed like a cut-off point that brought them back to reality and Tariq and Karen suddenly remembered their nine o'clock meetings and Freya thought about Freya Franklin Hats and Tom remembered a stack of unmarked books. Ami was the first to stand up. 'I should go,' she said. And the others followed suit.

Tariq showed them out while Emma rocked the baby. Karen thought she looked a little happier and healthier than for a long time; glowing even. Maybe it was just the whisky.

As they all said their goodbyes and Murray kissed her cheek, Emma said, 'What about you? What's your role in this caper? It *was* your idea, Mr Murray.'

He straightened up. 'I thought it was your idea, china,' he said but the others picked up on it and Tom said, 'Yeah, Murray. What about you?' and Karen said, 'Yeah.'

Murray smiled and there was a twinkle in his eye and his lips quivered. 'I'm just going to make sure you go through with it,' he said, and the others laughed.

8 Murray tells a lot of stories, including the one about Der Vollbartclub Von Aachen

Murray tells stories about where he's been and what he's been doing; Murray-stories about Murray-fun littered with Murray-isms. He couldn't keep saying, 'You know. Around' and 'This and that' for ever because people would keep asking questions until they got an answer they believed or liked or could live with, at least.

Where have you been, Murray?

'You know. Around.'

Yeah. But what have you been doing for the last ten years?

He shrugs. 'This and that, china,' he says. 'This, that and some of the other.'

No. But . . . seriously, Muz . . . What have you been up to?

He pinches a cigarette and lights it with slow care, his expression creased in concentration. He shakes the match and his knuckles crack and his wrist is so loose it looks like his hand could fly right off. Though he rarely smokes, he inhales deeply like a pack-a-day man and he answers through an out-breath that clouds in front of his face. 'I went to law school,' he says.

Yeah? Which one?

'The one off Russell Square.'

You mean Store Street?

'That's the one. Store Street.'

So you must have known so-and-so. He was there. You know, the guy with the crooked smile and putty features. Or what about such-and-such? Remember her? She went out with wotsisname.

Murray shakes his head. For an instant he looks . . . What? Disconcerted? No. More like confused. But then it's gone. 'Small world,' he says. 'But I was only there about a month, china, then I jacked it in. I couldn't get articles and I wasn't being sponsored so I couldn't afford it.' He thinks for a moment. 'Anyway, Store Street's a big college. Small world but a big college.'

So what did you do next?

Murray flicks the half-smoked cigarette into the gutter and he smiles. Which smile is it? An experienced Murray-watcher might recognize it as number eleven or fourteen or perhaps his eighth smile which is often mistaken for his seventeenth (or is it the other way round?). Whatever. He's getting into his stride, that's for sure.

He travelled, he says. To India. He lived on an ashram in Pune with a sadhu called Sankar who had a beard to his navel, hair to his waist, a thimble penis and a nice line in aphorisms. How long was he there? He shrugs. He can't really remember. Nine months, maybe. A year, tops. The funny thing was that after three months or so, the itinerant Westerners who dropped into the ashram began to assume he was a sadhu himself and sat at his feet when they weren't hanging on his words.

'Perhaps it was my own little sayings,' he says. 'Or perhaps it was . . .' He strokes a finger across his cheek. It is a peculiar, almost sexual gesture. 'You know.'

Your sayings? What were *your* sayings?

He licks his lips. All kinds of things. About materialism mostly. 'Western materialism', they called it. Because wasn't that what the tourists were running away from with return tickets in their bum-bags?

'"They say that money does not grow on trees. Why? Is it not paper?" Or "Selfishness must be distinguished from true faith." Or "It's called capitalism because it's the final state of man. It does indeed *cap it all*." ' That kind of crap.

But what did you actually *do*?

Murray pulls out smile number one; although the nature of his reply depends on his audience. Sometimes he says, 'Not a lot. Just chilled out, smoked hash and got fucked.' Sometimes he says that he meditated for six hours a day and lived off honey and lassi. Sometimes he says that he helped out the sadhu with those buttockless blondes with a taste for the exotic. 'Besides his thimble penis, he didn't have much – what do you call it? – *self-control*, for a holy man. So it was up to me to finish them off.'

Whoever his audience and whatever pay-off he tells them, they say things like 'Nice one' and 'Cool' and 'I know what you mean' and, when they discuss Murray's time in India with each other (which they do), they leave out these details because to speak them aloud would be a betrayal of the intimacy that he surely shared with them alone.

After leaving India, Murray did all kinds of stuff; all kinds of jobs in all kinds of places, like the toy shop in St Albans, for example, and a lot of layabouting besides.

He lived in Jo'burg for a while and took a stall selling fabric in the open-air market in Melville. Was it material he'd bought in India? Yeah. That's right.

'Melville?' This is Tom. He and Karen once spent a month in South Africa during the long summer holiday just after she'd left her job as a lobbyist and they'd stayed a night at the Melville Guest House.

'It really is a small world,' Murray comments.

Tom turns to his ex. 'What was the name of that bar?'

'Ebony,' she says.

'That's it. Run by a Swede called Torben and his black girlfriend. What was her name?'

'Wanisayi,' says Murray.

Karen shakes her head. 'No it wasn't. It was an old-fashioned name. Gladys or Sylvia or something like that.'

'That was her English name,' he says decisively. 'Her real name was Wanisayi. A pretty little thing with those big bright eyes.'

'She was hardly little,' Tom protests. 'Arse like a dump truck.'

'No. I meant little as in young. How old do you think she was?'

'I don't know. About nineteen?'

'Yeah. About nineteen. Twenty, maybe.' Murray cocks his head. 'Wanisayi . . .' he says pensively, as though he will be transported back to the source of the memory simply by speaking her name. His manner suggests something unsaid.

Murray moved on to Bangkok.

How long were you there?

'Any of you ever been to Bangkok?' Murray asks. And when the others all shake their heads he continues: 'Because *that* was a place I could call home, know what I mean? In fact I wouldn't mind going back there some time.'

Yeah? Were you working?

'Just for bed and board. I had a gig at one of the titty bars on the Patpong Road. You know, persuading the sailors and perverts to come in. A lot of London businessmen actually; a fuck of a lot.'

Freya says, 'That must've been disgusting.'

'Sure. But kind of fun too. All those American squaddies looking for lady-boys to remind them of their girlfriends and their able seamen buddies all at the same time. Know what I mean?'

So why did you leave?

'Friend of mine got busted trying to smuggle a couple of

nine-bars in his money-belt. When he got sent down it all got a bit crazy so I figured it was time to move on.'

'It sounds like that movie,' Karen says. And then her thoughts take an extra step: 'In fact it sounds *exactly* like that movie.'

Murray smiles: 'Of course it does. The movie was based on my mate. Andy Donaldson. It was in all the papers.'

The others look at each other uncertainly but Ami says, 'Andy Donaldson? Yeah. That name rings a bell.'

'There you go.'

Murray worked as a potato peeler in a Baton Rouge restaurant (What kind of restaurant? Southern-fried chicken, of course), he was an apprentice tree doctor in Fort Lauderdale and painted telephone poles all the way from Atlanta to Wilmington (experience in a harness was all that was required). He returned to Europe bringing a kilo of charlie (stolen from the Mexicans' Miami cartel) into Charles de Gaulle up his arse. He then sold gram wraps alongside ten-franc models of Nelson's Column beneath the Eiffel Tower (because tourism's a global business). When he ran short of cash he spent six months on the BeNeLux festival circuit playing with a rave didge four-piece called the Doosandonts. Of course he did.

Tom says, 'You never used to be into, like, crime.'

Murray shrugs. 'Like I told you, china. I've changed.'

When he tells Murray-stories, the others – Tom, Karen, Tariq, Emma, Freya, Kwesi and Ami – look at him incredulously. But does that mean they think he's lying? After all, they know that somebody paints poles, somebody deals drugs from their derrière and somebody even plays the didgeridoo over Teutonic techno. So why can't it be Murray?

These days, perceptions of authenticity are at a premium even as authenticity itself becomes ever more meaningless.

These days in London, politics, race and class are less state-
ments of identity than descriptions of the way you choose to
accessorize. Personal validity lies not in fact but in the simple
question, Can you pull it off? At college, Murray's trappings
were minimal so his indisputable authenticity (though endlessly various) was derived from intangible ticks of, say, personality and manner. Perhaps, therefore, his friends' present
(if momentary) doubts come from the way Murray's now
got anecdotes to burn that outstrip all others for thrills and
absurdity. But Tom, Tariq and Karen still remember the
Murray-fun at LMT and the rest have heard many of the
stories so they figure that, if anybody could have lived a decade
like that, it has to be somebody like Muz. Murray was never
Anybody and always Somebody and they *want* to trust him
for the vicarious excitement he gives them: the smell of danger,
the sherbet dib-dab of chaos, the peepshow of potential.
Besides, between belief and incredulity lies the no man's land
of uncertainty; a contested strip of scrub where Murray's
cunning snipers lie in wait to shoot down any sceptic with the
Dutch courage to make a run for the other side. Like when
Tariq doesn't believe Murray's story about Der Vollbartclub
Von Aachen.

Tariq is telling an anecdote to Kwesi. Murray and Tom are
there but he's talking *to* Kwesi. He's drunk and miserable
(again) so he wants to make somebody else – no, not somebody; *anybody* – anybody else feel bad and, on this occasion,
that anybody is Tom. Tariq is already laughing at the prospect.

'When we were at LMT, right, it was around that time
when, like, every student was growing a goatee. You remember that? Like every single student. This was the early nineties,
right? You'd hardly be allowed into further education unless
you had a stupid goatee beard stuck on the end of your
bloody chin.'

Tariq seems to think this is the most humorous and intelligent observation ever because he can hardly get the words out. Kwesi looks bemused. Murray and Tom know what's coming so Murray's not listening and Tom smiles weakly because he's well aware that he's the stooge in this gag.

'So Murray was, like, "We should all grow beards." And I was all, "What the fuck are you talking about?" wasn't I, Muz? And he was, like, "Do you want to fit in around here or not?" Something like that. I don't remember. So we all agree to grow beards.' Kwesi yawns into his palm and Tariq picks up the pace. 'Anyway, the point is we don't see each other for, like, a week or something and then we all hook up in the bar. There's me with some hardcore Paki stubble on my cheeks, there's Murray . . . and he's only got the most beautiful and fulsome beard you've ever seen. And then Tom walks in.' Tariq can't take the hilarity of it any more and he begins to snort with laughter. 'Sorry.' He wipes his nose on his sleeve. 'Tom walks in and he's just got this little fuzz beneath his nose. Just a little fucking moustache like some German exchange student or something.' Tariq packs up again. Apparently this is the punchline but, just in case it's gone unnoticed, he adds, 'It was *so* fucking funny!'

By now Kwesi looks completely bewildered. He tries to laugh but he has no idea what he's supposed to be laughing at.

Tom's smile has dissolved into his face. But he wants to lend his college mate moral support so he says, 'It *was* kind of funny. But I guess you had to be there.'

Tariq doesn't care: 'You should have seen him. You remember, Muz? You remember? That bum-fluff moustache.'

'Yeah,' Murray says. 'I remember.'

'Your beard was the best, though, Muz. Wicked. You should have kept it. Really. You should have done. You should

114

have . . .' Tariq tails off into his pint. There is a heartbeat or two of silence as Kwesi fiddles with a beer mat and Tom rubs a hand over his chin.

'You know what, china?' Murray says. 'Let me tell you something . . .' He sips on his water. It's the first time he's shown any interest in the conversation and the other three lean forward eagerly. 'You know I told you about playing the didge around Belgium, yeah? Well, one time we went over the border into Germany to play a festival in this little town called Aachen. I hadn't shaved for about six weeks – we'd been on the road, hadn't we? – so I had quite a beard coming along.'

Tariq cracks up and sprays a mouthful of his beer across Tom who wipes his face uncomplainingly on his jacket. 'Just that moustache!' he splutters. 'Can't get it out of my head.' He wipes his eyes and looks up at Murray. 'Sorry, Muz.'

'It's cool.' His eyes are smiling. 'All I was going to say . . . Well . . . it was just strange really. I turn up in this little town and they, like, couldn't believe my beard, know what I mean? We were only there a couple of days but, at the end of it, I was like some kind of celebrity. Turns out that beard-growing's the locals' main pastime. It's almost like a sport or something.'

Kwesi says: 'You serious?'

'Serious, china. When the rest of the band headed back for Maastricht, I ended up staying on for a month as a guest of the president of the Beard Club. It was a good laugh. Had my beard coiffured and trimmed and twisted and waxed. Even won some regional competition. In the end I only shaved because I was getting hassle off the cops. This was just after those African bombings and they were really jumpy. Thought I was Al-Aqsa.'

Tariq is staring at Murray. His expression is crumpled in drunken curiosity. Eventually he shakes his head. 'Bullshit.'

Tom and Kwesi turn to him. They'd been thinking the same thing but they weren't drunk enough to say so.

'What?'

'That's bullshit, Muz.' Tariq's drunken hilarity has given way to drunken irritation as Murray's every other story unravels in his mind. 'Jesus! Mr-fucking-Bin-Laden-Bangkok-trannies-coke-up-the-jaxy-bullshit! I tell you something, mate. Trust me on this. When you run your own business, you learn to smell bullshit. And my business is predictive technology. My business is bullshit so I've got a more sensitive nose than most. I don't know about gak up your arse but that's certainly where you're talking from.'

Tom and Kwesi have now turned their attention to Murray. In this instant they realize that none of them have ever really contradicted him before (not so bluntly, anyway) so how's he going to react? Murray smiles and it's a new expression (that Tom, who's recently taking to counting them again, logs as number thirty-eight). 'You think so?' he says.

They hook up again that evening in a Putney pub. It's one of those Irish *manqué* joints with horse brasses, black-and-white prints and seafaring flotsam on the walls. It serves faux-pub-grub from menus faux-written on faux-blackboards for consumption around the faux-coal fire. It was Murray's choice of venue but he's a little late. This time 'the girls' (as Tariq tends to call them) are there too. Well, Emma and Freya anyway. Ami's on her last OB for the Weather Channel and Karen's stuck in some PPP meeting. They choose a table by the plate-glass window. None of them feels very comfortable. This isn't their kind of place; mostly young men – sales reps in suits and lager lads in Ben Sherman – and the odd high-maintenance slapper sipping on an alcopop. Generally they'd either prefer somewhere that sold rioja at ten quid a bottle and the modern pub standards of salmon fishcakes and rocket salads or even what Tariq calls a 'real boozer' with ladies' darts nights and beer bellies propped on the bar. So Tom asks nobody in particular: 'Why did Murray want to come here?'

When Murray appears, he's carrying a small plastic bag. He buys a round before sitting down and it's Tariq, now nagged by an evening hangover, who points to the package. 'So what's that then, Muz?'

Murray hands over the bag and Tariq pulls out a tarnished pewter tankard. There's an inscription on the front and Tariq reads it aloud: '"Der Vollbartclub Von Aachen". What does that mean?'

'The Aachen Beard-Growers' Club,' Murray says.

Tariq sniggers. 'You're joking.'

'No,' Murray says. 'No, china. I'm serious.'

Tariq is staring at him but Murray's face is inscrutable. Emma picks up the tankard and examines it carelessly. 'What's this all about?'

Murray looks at her and starts to laugh. Then he glances at Tariq. 'Long story,' he says. 'Long and boring.'

Tom decides to interrupt because Murray sounds a little tetchy and he doesn't want things to turn nasty. 'What made you want to come to this shithole?'

Murray nods out of the window, through the frosted swirls of shamrocks and harps, and the others follow his eyes. 'The view,' he says.

Freya, who is closest to the glass, is peering outside. 'What view?'

'Over there. The bank. Suburban, middle class, low profile, unexpected. Perfect.'

For a moment there is silence. Murray's tone is both solemn and offhand all at once and they don't know what to make of it. Then Kwesi says, 'You don't really think we can rob a bank, do you, Muz?'

Tariq swills his whisky through gritted teeth. His head is beginning to pound. 'If anyone can, it's Murray.'

Emma tuts. 'It's not about whether we *can* do it, it's about whether we're *going* to.' She pauses. If she leaves it there, it will sound like she's dismissing the idea. But she doesn't leave it there. 'Isn't that right, Murray?'

'Yeah,' he says. 'Exactly.'

At three a.m. Murray is sitting alone in a flat. *His* flat. It's in Hounslow, maybe. Or Harlesden. Or Roehampton. One of those London places that's barely a place at all; more the blink of an out-of-town eye on its way into the city. He is sitting alone in a tatty armchair in front of a huge television at full volume. He scratches a threadbare armrest with the fingernails of one hand, unpicking the material like a playful kitten. His other hand is wrapped around the pewter tankard. It's half full of water and he takes occasional swigs.

The room is furnished but bare and the voices from the TV echo. Apart from the armchair and the television (which, judging by the cellophane on the back, must be brand new), there is a coffeetable, one upright chair and a couple of stools that are tucked under the counter of the open-plan kitchen. There are three doors off this room. Two of them are closed (one, closest to the kitchenette, latched) but the third is ajar and a cold strip-light illuminates white tiles and a pristine basin with none of the debris – toothbrushes, flannels, soap and the like – of day-to-day life. There is nothing in this flat to suggest occupancy: no pictures on the walls, no rugs on the floor, no washing-up liquid on the draining board and no crockery in the sink. There are half a dozen books on the mantelpiece (a bizarre selection including, for example, *Suicide* by Durkheim, *A Short Introduction to Hegel*, *A Hero of Our Time* by Lermontov and a Euripides primer) but even these have a library's coloured labels stuck to their spines and they only add to the picture of impermanence. If anybody were to look around this place, they might think it soulless and a little spooky. But Murray doesn't look around and he doesn't think anything.

The thing about Murray – the one thing that nobody has identified; the thing that might elucidate and bewilder in equal measure – is that he doesn't think anything. Not really. Not any more. Not for ten years. Once, Murray was the personification of consciousness. Whatever you made of him and however he chose to use them, you couldn't deny that he pulsed with ideas and empathy. Sure, he lived in the present with no publicized personal history nor apparent awareness of consequence, but wasn't that simply the perfect persona for London life? But now, while his behaviour – his actions and reactions – suggests a complexity and abstraction worthy of humanity at its most potent, it is really no more than instinct and impulse and as superficial (or perhaps deep) as that. Murray is a ghost of his former self. Ask him what he's thinking: you might as well ask a monkey to explain Hegel – 'I turn the world on its head' – or Big-In-Property to see himself through another's eyes or a super-computer to weep over a movie. If Murray considered this, he'd surely be wondering 'What has happened to me?' and his mind would take one certain stride back a decade. But he doesn't consider anything and his recollections bear as much resemblance to memory as a stranger's photograph album; inadequate and snatched representations that lack the soul to tell their part of a story.

On the TV, Ami concludes her report with staccato sentences – 'This is Ami Lester. For the Weather Channel. On Dartmoor' – and the action cuts back to the studio presenter with the smarmy expression and rainbow tie. He looks out of the box and raises a smug eyebrow. 'And that's all from *Weatherwise* for this week and, indeed, for a while as this is the last in the present series.' He smiles without teeth. 'Thank you for watching. Until next time. I'm Andy Donaldson. Goodnight.'

As the credits roll, Murray zaps the TV with the remote in his lap and, before the colours implode to a single dot of light, he hears the banging at the door. It is urgent and must have been going on for a while, drowned out by Ami's stories of the ponies caught in Devon thunderstorms. Murray gets up slowly, ambles over and turns the latch. It is the landlord, who lives in the flat below and runs the minimarket on the ground floor. He is wearing an apologetic, timid expression and clutching a packet of Murray's favourite chicken roll.

'I'm sorry, Mr Murray,' he begins. He always calls Murray that and it provokes an automatic smile. 'But it is terribly late and we can't sleep with your TV at such volume. I do not like to disturb you of course but Meena is at the market tomorrow and she must be there by five o'clock sharp.'

'Shit! Sorry, china. How thoughtless of me.' Murray grimaces and gestures towards the television. 'I've switched it off now anyway. I'm really sorry, Sankar. You should have come up sooner.'

Sankar giggles nervously. 'No. It is quite fine. I am sorry to bother you myself but you know how Meena is.' He hands Murray the packet of chicken. 'Here, Mr Murray. I brought you this by way of apology.'

Murray takes it and says, 'Thanks, china', but the man is already halfway down the stairs and waves away Murray's gratitude with one hand.

'It is nothing, Mr Murray,' he says. 'It is quite fine. Goodnight.'

'Goodnight.'

Murray shuts the door behind him and flops down in the armchair once again. He is staring out of the window as he rips open the packet and begins to nibble the chicken roll absent-mindedly. A puzzled look spreads across Murray's face and he glances at the meat in his hand for a second. As usual, it tastes unpleasant, soapy, but he hasn't learned his lesson. It's chicken, after all.

Outside, Murray can see the tall oak tree with its fresh wounds. It looks disabled, like an amputee, and the workmen have left some tools in the crook of one stubby branch. Murray peers down into the street and he can see the contractors' fencing in place around the trunk and the sign on the pavement. In the dark, from up here, he can't read it but he knows what it says: 'By council appointment. Melville & Sons. St Albans.' They have been working up the street for a fortnight, ruthlessly hacking back the trees until there's nothing left but the central nervous system to feel the pain. As a rule, they've managed one oak a day but the gnarled old fellow outside Murray's window whose leaves used to tap the glass is taking a little longer and Murray knows because he's been watching.

It's the pigeons that have slowed them down. The pigeons haven't actually attacked the workers but a host of them have been making nuisances of themselves, flying in and out of the branches, knocking off hard hats and shitting in sandwich boxes. 'They're taking the fucking piss!' That's what Murray heard the foreman exclaim and none of his boys wanted to take chances; what with the facts and stories and rumours and gossip that have been circulating around London for . . . For what? A few weeks. According to the foreman, 'The pigeons have gone fucking mad. Headless fucking chickens. Or pigeons, rather.'

Pigeons. Murray is suddenly arrested by images so powerful that he no longer sees anything else. Pigeons. He is transported back in time through a slide-show of the senses that he doesn't understand. Pigeons. He is looking up at the sky and there are dark, heavy clouds; bank upon bank of them. Pigeons. A single bird is on the wall in front of his eyes but Murray realizes he cannot even tell if it is above or below him. Pigeons. Now there are three of them. Now four. Now five. And they're clucking around him as if he were a chick that had fallen from the nest. Pigeons. Murray tries to smile but the muscles of his face are deadened and unresponsive. Pigeons. One is on his leg. Murray can't seem to move his head but he can feel the bird's feet pinching his flesh. The sensation is heavy and light all at once. It's somehow reassuring. Pigeons. Murray realizes his left hand is submerged in water. It's cold but he likes that sensation too. It's as if he were feeling it at a distance. He feels a spit spot of rain on his cheek. Pigeons. Out of the corner of his eye he looks across the chopping water of the Thames to a skimming boat whose oarsman, a blond Adonis, is staring straight at him; he's sure of it. Pigeons. Now he feels a sharp pain in his right palm. He wants to lift it up, to check it out. But he can't. Pigeons. His attention is taken by another bird standing on his forehead. On his forehead! Murray almost bursts out laughing – and he could if he chose to, couldn't he? – but he doesn't want to scare it away. Pigeons. Murray can see the bird's breast rising and falling above his eyes. It has something hanging from the side of its mouth. A worm that struggles pathetically no more than a centimetre from his nose. And what's that? It looks like a globule of red blood on the very tip of its beak. The bird jerks his head and the drop of blood falls. Pigeons. Murray is lying on his back. He decides it's time to stand up. Pigeons. His brain, his body and his will are no longer one.

Murray twitches slightly in his seat and his fingers release the packet that lands face down on the tatty carpet. Now he is still again. His eyes are wide, unblinking and blind. If anyone were to see him they might think he was dead. But there is nobody to see him except the pigeon on the window ledge outside who coos, soft and pitying.

The remnant of content

When a peepnik cocks his head a ninety to the sky, he'll find something reassuring about a flock of pigeons and the patterns they make against the clouds, because their movements seem as natural as the tides or the sway of a willow in the wind. But for a pigeon geez looking down? That's a different story and no mistake. There are patterns among the peepniks, all right, but they are random, changeable, confrontational.

Look at it this way: us pigeons circle and swoop and criss-cross like the most efficient spaghetti junction, while the niks below sidestep and clash shoulders and sound their verbal horns. When we look down we see organized confusion. So is it any wonder that we fly from a heavy footfall or a raised voice?

Of course, all this changed in the aftermath of Trafalgar and weren't the niks as bemused as squibs fallen from the nest? Looking up like the bottom had fallen out of their world (and isn't that some sick joke?). And I'm not beaking about the prelude to the wars, when us birds were divided into two great armies – yes, armies became the right word – and there was some pastiche of pattern reimposed on our flight paths. Oh no. I'm talking about before that; the early days when there was no sense of leadership and us pigeons began to dart every which way with all the composure of fleas and flies and the other miniscularities of flight.

It's no surprise that the niks noticed us birds at that time because you'd better believe I've heard all sorts of stories: numerous accounts of pestering the peepniks and other kinds of confusion besides. There was the tale of the two geezs from the Concrete who collided headlong over Hoxton Square and crashed to terra firma in the salad bowl of a nik picnic. And the one about the old bird in Notting Hill who severed a penthouse pinxen's beak and was battered to death for his confusion. And the tragedy of the coochie-momma who shovelled her own eggs from her own nest and watched them smash on the pavement below because she was just so scared of who-knows-what. And there was me, of course: me and my embarrassing misdemeanour with the four pink feathers pecked from the vani-tarious sweet's headgear while the streetnik desperadoes stood and stared.

The way I scope it, it was memory that did for us. Before Trafalgar, a pigeon would fly towards food and away from danger with all the instincts of evolution. But you tackled that same bird a tick or tock later and they'd have been bemused by any suggestion of hunger or threat. You don't accord? Sure you do. Because every nik's chased a chubster geez from the crumbs of their sandwich lunch in Soho Square, sent him squawking away, only to see him settle a spit distant and begin clucking as contented as a squib with a squirm. So it was memory that did for us. Because memory is about fear first and foremost and any attendant comforts are no more than sugar coatings for the pill. And fear? Well. I've come to believe that the hollowest, most gizzard-twistingest fear of all is about loss. You may not scope it for yourself but the thing that scares you most is what's gone.

What scared me most? You know that old Ravenscourt isn't lying when he says it was the unilluminable nik he likes to call Mishap (for fear of the syllables of his proper name). Yes, sir. And you can consider that information at your leisure.

Now I've told you about the day I saw him at Trafalgar and the night when, I say, the London Pigeon Wars began (with the murder of Brixton23 and that strapping cue-ball pinxen), but I haven't told you about another sighting between the two. Does that make me a lying fuckster? I don't think so because, like I said already, a story unravels at its own pace that has nut all to do with the regular speedometer of time ('He was born. He lived. He died.' What?

You call *that* a story?). Besides, this third sighting can hardly be described as a skyscraper of drama like the other two.

I was perched on a window ledge who-knows-where and I was looking inside (because, as I told you, these days us pigeons like nothing better than to watch the peepniks, transfixed like babchicks in front of a motion flixture). The unilluminable nik was sitting in an armchair with his head lolled back and kinked to one side and his wide eyes staring right past me. Did he see me? I don't think so. His gaze was glazed like a mirror and it left me uneasy because I scoped I knew that look so well; it reflected me and a million other pigeons before the happenings of Trafalgar and the sudden consciousness. But – like that wasn't discomfort enough – there was even more to it than that. Because I knew that I'd seen this inanimate expression on this particular phyzog somewhere before; somewhere a long time ago when I was a squib fresh from the egg.

I can say no more. This is no narrative device but a veritable admission on my part. I can say no more because my memories of so long ago are as wriggly as squirms, elusive and struggling to avoid my pointed beak. How I would love to illuminate what was, I must assume, my first brush with the unilluminable Mishap! And, trust me, I will as soon as I may; as soon as the rain of recollection soaks my feathers and I can no longer fly carefree, as long as my consciousness remains intact (because I fear for it now like a coochie-momma fears for an exposed nest).

Let me put it this way: consciousness is a river that tides and tugs and swirls and eddies stronger than the Thames times ten. The consciousness thereof is an exhilaration like the first gasp of ozone above the estuary and as daunting as night flight into a gale. If you've never known otherwise, you might take it for granted. But here's the thing. The way I scope it, it's a fragile phenomenon and a social disease and it could evaporate like a puddle if enough pigeons reminisce about the missing bliss of ignorance (whether called 'Content' or otherwise) with all the fears of what's been lost therein.

I figure that it must have been around then that Gunnersbury resurfaced. You may have scoped that I'm none too clever with time but I recollect that, after Trafalgar, I didn't see that peachy coochie for a spell, not when the moonacy of memory was at its height. Verity is, pigeons had already begun to coalesce into small groups like oil on the river (finally united by the fear that had divided them or garrulous pigeon nature or divisions between Concrete and Surban, who knows?). But when Gunnersbury reappeared on that oak at Tooting Common? I'm sure that might be called the founding day of us Surbs; when we became more than the sum of our parts and, in some ways, less too.

It was a brisk dusk and the light was nuclear clear and ethereal and magical like only London knows how. There were more birds over the Common than usual, for sure. But don't think we'd come to scope Gunnersbury. No way. Better call it fate or chance or magic or simply fine judgement on that scheming coochie's part.

Nobirdy saw her approach. She was cloud-skimming up high and plunged into our midst like a hawk with the piece of the hulkingest pigeon you ever saw (that she'd pulled from the unilluminable stuff in the rubbish bin in Trafalgar Square) held tight in her beak. There was quite some commotion as she landed on the thick branch of the oak with the hole in its trunk – pigeons winging for a look, coochie-mommas dropping their squirms and the like – because you can bet that every bird knew the story of Gunnersbury and Regent at Trafalgar whether they'd been there or not. Besides, she had that peacock manner (a cock not a hen, mind) and a swagger to her wings that made you scope she must be top bird. And when the peepniks below – bow-wow-walkers, hermetic sexers, all that type – scoped the kerfuffle of feathers? You can bet they headed homewards because you know they'd heard about or read about or seen about the 'crazy pigeons' who'd even attack a nik that hadn't kept an eye on the sky. And isn't that a sugar-coated memory that makes me squawk with delight?

All the clucks and coos ceased as soon as Gunnersbury opened her beak. I can't illuminate why. I'm hazarding that for some geezs it was simply the sight of such a peachy coochie while for others it was their first glimpse of the Remnant of Content. But, for most of us, it was simply an inexpressible (and, let's face it, incomprehensible) assumption that here was a pigeon who might have the answers to the questions we'd only just started asking but already confused the flying fuck out of us. Whatever. There's no doubting she had a captive audience (and – yeah, yeah – I'm fully aware of the ironies of such a comment about a flock of birds with all the freedom of the sky and then some).

'Everybirdy,' Gunnersbury began. 'You'd best come close if you want to hear because a call that dies on the breeze is a waste of breath that might have otherwise lifted your wings a little like the most relaxing thermal. You peep this Remnant of Content? You peep it but do you scope it? It is not a symbol of verity but a piece of the verity itself that has been illuminated to me in a way that even the most loquacious peepnik could never expound. Often verity has as many heads as a squirm shared eight ways in a nest. But this verity? It is a single illumination; not a lamppost but the sun.'

We were all listening and even the toughest oldgeezs were skipping their way forwards for a better look. Did we understand what she was beaking on about? Do me a favour. But, fact was (if my fearful memory serves me straight), this was just about the longest speech we'd ever heard; what with language being so new. And she'd only just started.

'Look at this oak. I perch on this branch, you on that. I perch on that branch, you on this. But the peepniks can chop off this branch or that branch and you know that the tree survives. So where is its oaky core that makes it the oakiest of oaks? The trunk, of course. The trunk is the verity of the oak and that's why I place this Remnant of Content in this hole in this trunk because verity sits in verity as safely as eggs in a sensibly appointed nest.'

Some of the pigeons were beginning to cluck and coo. They were impressed with her verbage but nonetheless bemused by its lack of sense because even us birds know about style over substance (for why else is a magpie never satisfied with a single glistering item?). But then Gunnersbury began to tell her story and she soon shut them up again. How do you scope that? I'll tell you my illumination. A story can always silence the chirpiest geez because it doesn't have to work pinpointedly. Stories are like stormy winds: you cannot see them, only witness their effects and thus praise their power.

'I must tell you a tale,' Gunnersbury began and the warble in her voice was as seductive as a mating coo. 'All of you know that we were not ever thus and thus must have been different before that is to say therefore.' This was hardly the most concise of openings – a simple 'Once upon a time' would have sufficed for me – but nobirdy else seemed much flustered. They were all transfixed.

'Can any of you clearly recall the time before time or the language before language? Of course not. The time before time is a foreign language and the language before language is all words at once. So your memories are no more than snatched phrases and snapshot flicks that illuminate nothing but a pang in your pigeon breast. But for me, Gunnersbury? I have held the full Remnant of Content all too briefly and accepted the full acceleration of verity therein. And thus that is to say, therefore, I must tell you a tale.

'The Remnant of Content? There is no mystery in the moniker. It is a relic of the time before time and the language before language when all pigeons were, indeed, Content in both the fulfilled and full-filled senses of the word. In the time before time, you would not have called me "Gunnersbury" any more than I would have called you "Tooting12" . . .' There was a brief disruption as the mentioned coochie began to coochie-coo in spotlight delight. 'No. In the language before language we would have simply called one another "Content" (as if the language before language had any need for such a word). "Content," I would call. "Content?" And you would call back to me, "Content. Content?" "Content," I'd say.

'In the time before time, we were the flock before flocks existed. We were as one pigeon and moved as one body flapping great wings that could knock a peepnik off their feet with the downrush. So is it any wonder that the Remnant of Content should represent itself to us as the limb of a great bird? No. And just imagine what size Content must have been before that! Its call stopped traffic, the beat of its wing shooed clouds, its span cast shadows across whole London boroughs.

'In the time before time, we lived in the place before place which, in the second language, we now call "sky". Do you really think we were ever defined by the geography of our roosts? Of course not. What sense is there in such descriptions? Tell me. Why do you pigeons depict yourselves through the smallest labels of terra firma when the vast expanse of up above (with all the compass points – including up and down – therein) was once your domain? For the sake of the heavens! Are we pigeons or peepniks?'

A few of the older geezs began to cluck discontentedly at such a comparison but Gunnersbury's head bobbed as if she was one jump ahead of their opinions.

'I know,' she cooed sweetly. 'Believe me I know. I know that these definitions are formed in opposition (for aren't definitions ever so?). I have heard the reports and seen with my own eyes those pigeons from the Concrete who mass behind the magpie-looking geez to chase veritable birds like yourselves from the rich pickings of the city. But that is precisely why *we* – In-Outers, suburbans and the like – must stay united. We are, what I term in the second language, Surbs: unified in this first instance by a misplaced label of place (that was first given to me by the geez with the magpie phyzog) but ultimately by the illumination of Content.'

Gunnersbury paused and all the watching pigeons – how many of us were there that evening? Two hundred? – were silent. Then she peeped directly at me. I remember her bead and the warm breeze that rustled my feathers; warm like the currents above a power station.

'Ravenscourt,' she began. 'You were there at my side. Tell us the adopted nomenclature of that magpie-looking geez.'

'I'm sorry?'

'His name, Ravenscourt. His name.'

'Regent,' I said.

'Yes. And was a name ever so pinpointedly exact? We cannot blame those Concrete pigeons for following that great pretender who promises them no more than they already have. He is an every-geez-for-himself-type fuckster. So how do you illuminate that as a philosophy to follow? I'll tell you how. Because he holds a Remnant of Content of his own that he brandishes like a club, that he hides away to withhold unity, to withhold Content itself!

'Who has heard his rhetoric? What about you, Ravenscourt? Or you, Croydon7? No? I have. He promises those Concrete geezs as many squirms from our Surb commons as they can eat. And isn't that a pretty promise when pigeons like us cannot cross the river to the Strand or Covent Garden or Leicester Square or the City (god forbid!) without being chased like sparrows from a profligate wastebin? How can he tempt them with best bits that were theirs by right when we were all Content? And what does he expect the likes of us Surbs to do but, by the extension of his own philosophy, defend our own Remnant of Content which is all his divisiveness has left us?

'We . . .' Gunnersbury slowed her words and lowered the pitch of her call. 'I say "we" and that word should make your hearts beat faster with pride. We, the Surbs, must work together, collectively, for the illumination of Content. We do not hate the Concrete pigeons nor even the foolish Regent; we pity their misplaced consciousness and will fly strong together until every geez, coochie and squib in London is illuminated. It is our duty and our honour and I promise each and every one of you now, from my perch on this trusty oak on Tooting Common, we shall be Content again.'

Gunnersbury took to the wing, then, a forty-five to no more than tree-top height, and she began to circle the assembly as if the beat of her wings was a rope to knot us together. And the pigeons scoped skywards and, to a bird, cooed in delight. Do you think they all comprehended every morsel of her verbage? Of course not. But you imagine what it is like to be challenged in your new nature by questions that cast doubt on who you are. Especially when you have no answers of your own. Especially when you never even knew such questions existed only a matter of weeks (or months) before. Trust me, when you're haunted by memories of what's been lost, any story will do; none more so than the one told by the charismatic pigeon who has that warble in her call like it all makes sense. Even if the answer she offers is, I soon came to understand, no more than the acceptance of defeat (and not in Regent's beak but in the gizzards of our own natures).

Scope it like this: it wasn't so long (days? Weeks?) before I realized that Gunnersbury knew no better than the rest of us. Do you remember what I told you about the night the London Pigeon Wars began? We were perched on this same oak when Gunnersbury asked me that strange question.

'When you peckchop a squirm,' she began, 'clean down the middle, what are you left with? Are they two squirms that wriggle away or two halves of the same one?'

I said I didn't know and when I looked at her I scoped that she didn't either. So when she squawked, 'This is war', her call strained and excitable, that was a good enough answer for me. But that evening when Gunnersbury rallied us Surbs with the first speech any of us ever heard, we weren't at war then and didn't even scope such a thing on the horizon. We weren't an army but half a flock of pigeons elated by the sweet scent of illumination. And, as Gunnersbury soared and swooped above us, you should have heard the birdsong with which her new-found supporters serenaded their new-found leader. And me? I fluttered up to the hole in the oak where she'd stashed the Remnant of Content because I wanted to clock it for myself. And sure enough, there it was, our great idol, our symbol of who we were, what we'd been and what we'd lost, and it was no more than a scrap of the unilluminable stuff that was dropped into the Trafalgar Square trash by the unilluminable nik whose syllables spell out 'MU-RRAY' – there; I've said it – which is questions and answers right there.

Mishap, I tell you. Mishap. Imagine.

Of faith 10

Tom had always needed something to believe in. Not anything specific, mind; just something with a vivid colour or an attractive smell or a morality that could sound plausible from his mouth. By its definition, faith should be as singular and focused as the London Eye, shouldn't it? But, for Tom, the act of believing was always more important than its subject. Though he never articulated it like that himself.

Tom described Murray as a chancer and Murray described Karen as a chameleon. In fact, Tom was just as much of a chancer or chameleon as either of them; piggy-backing aboard any person or philosophy that might carry him over one of life's puddles. Sometimes the ride was uncomfortable but at least he rarely got his feet wet.

Like most ethical polyglots, Tom's various faiths were both as unbreakable and as fragile as an egg. Squeeze Tom in your fist and you might be surprised by his resilience but catch him an accidental blow and you'd better grab a dishcloth to clear up the mess on the floor. Take football. When he was a kid, the walls of Tom's bedroom in Hampton Wick were plastered with posters of the great Liverpool teams and, in the playground, he was proud to wear Kevin Keegan's number-seven shirt. So, in '91, when he heard about Kenny Dalglish's resignation as manager, he was distraught. He and Murray were coming out of the King's Cross tube when they saw the *Standard*'s banner headlines. Tom paled and rubbed a hand across his scalp in that nervous way of his.

'I feel . . . I don't know . . . *eviscerated*,' he stammered.

'Gutted,' Murray said.

These days, Tom is an ardent Manchester United fan. Look in his cubicle in the staff room of a Harrow sixth-form college and the sole decoration to mark seven years' occupancy is a small Red Devils pendant. And if any one of his pupils mentions the name of Cantona, they're guaranteed a digression. His eyes mist with nostalgia as if he and Eric had learned their trade together playing keepy-uppy on the beaches outside Marseille. Marseille? Is that where Cantona comes from? Tom can't remember.

Tom flirted with religion; Catholicism especially. Perhaps it was the emphasis on style over content that appealed to him. More likely, though, he was attracted by the sense of history – the oblique rituals seemed so irrelevant that they surely couldn't have changed since year dot. For Tom, faith (in whatever or whoever) was a source of identity, and a perception of permanence built an unarguable mass to lend weight to his character (however transitory and coy his beliefs turned out to be). For Tom, Catholicism was like fast food; there was a church on every corner to provide him with a ready-made if ultimately unsatisfying quick fix of self that he inhaled with the frankincense that made him sneeze.

Of course, when Tom met Murray at the Catholic chaplaincy at LMT (to the dubious strains of 'God Bless Our Pope'), it marked his last visit to church for some years. This was partly because he intuited at once – without ever voicing it – that Murray represented an all-consuming form of worship. It was partly, too, because he met Karen the very next day. If Tom's belief in Murray was absolute then his faith in Karen was at least longer-lived. And in this instance the distinction between belief and faith is an important one.

Tom and Murray were sitting in the college canteen. It was lunchtime and there was barely a spare seat as the students lounged and chattered and drank machine coffee and smoked earnest cigarettes. The canteen was an unappetizing place at the best of times with its floors tacky from spillages, its Formica tables patterned with fag burns, and its walls layered with lurid posters advertising the next student drama or gay and lesbian club night. But today Tom was feeling especially unhungry and he pushed his limp chips and greying burger morosely around his plate. It didn't help that Murray was attacking an enormous heap of breaded chicken nuggets with an obscene and slavering relish. There was something grippingly porno-graphic about the way Murray ate: the sounds of his enjoy-ment, the precise manner with which he unwrapped each morsel of meat from its breadcrumb casing, the way he re-peatedly picked his teeth with the sharp fingernail of his right index finger. Tom was transfixed. Occasionally, when he caught himself staring, he would feel a little embarrassed and try to start a conversation.

'So, have you been to the chaplaincy before?' he asked.

'What's that, china?' Murray was admiring a string of flesh that hung from his finger.

'The chaplaincy . . . I was just saying . . . I haven't seen you . . .'

Murray disrobed another nugget, popped it in his mouth and his eyes rolled in pleasure as he spoke between chews: 'Jesus, these are good! These are the bomb, china. These are the good shit. You want one?'

Tom began to examine the backs of his hands. 'No. No thanks.'

He sensed someone standing next to him and looked up. It was a girl. He'd seen her before, knocking around campus. He didn't know her name but she was more recognizable than most. When he'd first spotted her, he'd found himself gawping and wondered if he fancied her. But it wasn't that. She just didn't look like the other girls at LMT. Where most of the students could be immediately identified with one or other social stereotype – the trendies, the crusties, the proto ravers, the Sloanes, the rich Arabs, the academics – she couldn't. She wore her hair in a soft-tinted perm and, as she walked, it bounced above a thick-stitched wool jumper hanging over sky-blue leggings that ended an inch or two above a pair of suede pixie-boots. Her complexion was somewhat filmy and her lipstick pastel pink. Basically, there was something very eighties about her and that was a style too recent to be intentionally retro. In fact, Tom thought, she didn't really look like a student at all; more of a beautician from Anerley or a barmaid from Ongar, perhaps.

She nodded at the free seat next to Tom and almost spilled the Diet Coke that was squeezed on to the very front of her tray. 'Can I sit here?'

It was Murray who answered. 'Course you can. Help yourself.' He sat back, rubbed his stomach happily and inspected the contents of her plate. 'The nuggets? Good choice. Beautiful. Absolutely beautiful.'

She smiled and pointed at the remains of Murray's meal. 'But you're not big on batter, eh?'

'You know how it goes.' Murray shook his head and sulkily began to pick through the breaded casings for any last morsels of meat. They looked like discarded chrysalises, like they'd just given birth to little chicken-breast babies straight into Murray's mouth. 'I don't like to be fussy and I'll eat them if I have to, but why would you wrap up something so beautiful in crap like that? I mean, you know how they breed these chickens? Five hundred to a cage, featherless, with shrunken skulls and brains and bulging breasts. And then they cover them in batter? Whose idea was that? It just doesn't make sense. It's practically disrespectful.'

Murray sounded so bewildered, so personally wounded, that the girl burst out laughing. Tom joined in. She stuck out her hand across the table and Murray took it.

'I'm Karen,' she said. 'Karen Miller.'

'Murray.'

'Murray?'

'Yeah. Just Murray.'

'Oh. You're Murray.'

'Exactly.'

'No. I mean you're *that* Murray. The one who only eats chicken.'

Murray shrugged. 'What a claim to fame.'

'Murray with only one name. Just Murray.'

'That's me.'

Tom was watching chat tennis. But each turn of his neck lingered a little longer upon Karen. She was laughing. There was something about her that appealed to him. She seemed intense and playful all at once. What's more, when *he*'d met Murray for the first time (yesterday), he'd felt immediately daunted by the manic confidence he radiated. But Karen was actually mocking him and, even if Murray didn't rise to her baiting, it still struck Tom as kind of cool.

'But how come?' Karen pressed.

'How come what?'

'How come you're just Murray?'

'I just am.'

'What, you don't have a surname or you don't want to use it?'

Murray looked at her steadily and the tone of his voice was flat. 'Why would I accept the name of the oppressors who raped my ancestors?'

'Right.' She was nodding. She couldn't tell if he was serious. 'Where are you from?'

Murray smiled. 'The Highlands,' he said. 'Culloden was a fucker.'

'Are you always this facile?'

'Yeah, china. Always.'

'I only wanted to know why you didn't have a surname. Guess it's an affectation.'

Murray stared at her for a second (was it Tom's imagination or did his eyes glisten a little?), then he looked away. 'You want to know? You really want to know?'

Karen shrugged. 'Sure I want to know.'

'I come from an abusive home,' he said. 'My dad used to knock me about with anything he could lay his hands on; electric flex, broom handles, saucepans, whatever. Once he beat me senseless with a frozen chicken. Since then I've refused to take his name and I only eat chicken. It helps me remember what I've come from.'

Karen watched him carefully. 'You're joking.'

Murray smiled. 'Yes.'

'That's not funny.'

'You're right.'

'I mean, you shouldn't joke about that sort of thing.'

'Which? The beatings or the frozen chicken?'

Karen tutted. 'Don't be funny. The beatings.'

'Don't be funny. Right.' Murray was nodding. He took a breath like he was about to say something else. Then he held it for a second. 'What about the frozen chicken?'

'What?'

'Can I be funny about the frozen chicken?'

Karen giggled. 'Sure.'

'Thanks,' Murray nodded. He was staring at Karen and his eyes were now a little sleepy. 'That's good to know, china. I'll get back to you.'

'So?'

'So what.'

'Your name?'

'Is Murray. I tell you what, though. You want a good two-part name? What about Tom Dare? That's a real super-hero name right there.'

'Tom Dare?'

Murray cocked his thumb and forefinger into a pistol and pointed across the table. It was a gesture straight from John Hughes, Karen thought. Tom felt like he should cough into his hand or something but he just said, 'Pleased to meet you.'

'Hi.' Karen turned towards him then for the first time. But she didn't actually look at him at all. She was only interested in Murray and Tom was a touch embarrassed. He knew he was no more than an optional extra, a condiment; as if Murray had said, 'You want a good two-part seasoning? What about salt and pepper? That's a real superhero seasoning right there.' Tom stood up and picked up his tray. He wanted to get away. He felt humiliated to be ignored and silly to feel that way. 'I'll see you later,' he mumbled.

'Right,' Murray said. But he didn't look up. Instead he shrugged at Karen. 'Probably got to save the world. Hard life for a superhero. Too many demands on your time, know what I mean?'

Over the next month, Tom began to see a lot of Murray and Murray began to see a lot of Karen. But they never actually met as a three. Occasionally Tom would spot the other two around the college buildings or in the street but they always seemed to be disappearing into a lift or stepping on to a bus. Consequently, all of Tom's earliest info about Karen came via Murray and it always concluded with Murray saying, 'I should introduce you two properly, china. I think you'd get on.'

Karen was from Peckham, Murray said. She didn't know her dad and her mum died when she was thirteen so she'd been brought up by her older sister. She was the first in her family to stay on at school past sixteen and the first to go to college. 'She's a tough nut, china,' Murray said. 'Know what I mean?'

This was a girl who'd pretty much raised herself. She'd got to LMT without any help from anyone and she was determined to make the best of it. Karen had no time for the smug suburbanites nor the rich idlers nor the wide-eyed northerners who seemed to dominate the student population. Oh no. According to Murray, Karen dismissed the college social life, drama, newspaper, sport and the rest. According to Murray, she said 'they're all just games for people with the luxury to play at real life'. He thought this was one of the funniest things he'd ever heard. 'Like anybody ever does anything else,' he said.

Karen was only there to get her qualification and move up and that was that. So she'd head back to South London every weekend. Because, while most of the first years were still bed-hopping between fuck-buddies. Karen had a boy-friend she'd already been seeing for two years; some bloke called Kush.

'Kush?' Tom asked.

'Yeah,' Murray shrugged. 'Rhymes with bush. I should introduce you to her properly, china. I think you'd get on.'

'Why?' Tom asked. It didn't sound likely to him.

'Don't know. Just a feeling.'

A week before the end of the summer term, Tom came across Murray in the inter-departmental library. Murray hadn't been to more than a handful of lectures and tutorials the whole year and he'd walked out of most of his exams before half-time so Tom was surprised he even knew where it was. Maybe he'd been scared into some action.

'Hey, china.' Murray didn't look up. He was bent over a

desk with a pair of scissors, a roll of sticky tape and a stack of what looked like birthday cards in front of him. He was carefully cutting out the middle section of one until he was left with a mini, folded card about two inches square. Pinching the card tightly between thumb and forefinger, he bit off a small piece of tape and sealed it closed. Next to his elbow on the desk stood a finished pile of about twenty similar cards.

'What are you doing?' Tom hissed.

Murray looked around furtively. 'Bored,' he said. 'Just having some fun.' He swept the debris of his enterprise into a bin and carefully dropped the mini cards into the breast pocket of his denim jacket. He stood up, turned away from the desk and ducked down one of the aisles of floor-to-ceiling bookcases. Tom followed.

'You coming on Friday?' Murray asked. He was standing on top of some wheelie-steps and flicking through the pages of a dusty hardback from the top shelf.

'Friday?'

'Mate of mine's running a night at the Union; an end-of-year kind of gig. Should be a laugh.'

'Seriously?' Tom thought that he was taking the piss. Because, as far as he knew, Murray *never* went to student nights.

'Why not?' Murray had taken one of the mini cards out of his pocket and removed the sticky tape with his teeth. Then, slowly, he slid the card into the middle of the book he was holding. He glanced at the cover. '*Suicide* by Emile Durkheim. You think anybody ever reads this?' he asked.

'I doubt it.'

'Me too.'

Murray wedged the book firmly back into its former position and descended the steps. What was he up to? Tom was about to ask but Murray raised an eyebrow and put a finger to his lips. Then he turned down the next aisle. Tom followed but he briefly lost him in the ordered maze of the library. When he found him again, he was already slipping another book back into its place; this time on the bottom shelf.

'*A Hero of Our Time*,' he said. 'Ever heard of it?'

Tom shook his head.

Again Murray headed deeper into the recesses of the library, talking quietly over his shoulder as he went.

'Karen's coming. I've persuaded her to stay around because it's the last night of term. Anyway, I think she's having trouble with her boyfriend. I think he's been getting a bit . . .' Murray paused. '*Les Mains Sales* by Jean-Paul Sartre. Who's he?'

'French existentialist.'

'Yeah?' He replaced the book and chose another. '*The Theatre of the Absurd* by Martin Esslin. Who the fuck's going to read that?'

'Nobody.'

'Exactly,' he said, reaching into his pocket.

Tom was silent as Murray slipped another of his cardboard inventions between the pages. Then he said, 'Her boyfriend's getting a bit what?'

'A bit . . . y'know . . . physical.'

'Physical? What does that mean?'

But Murray was already on the move again, zig-zagging from French Language and Literature through Media Anthropology to Religion and Cults. And this was the way the stilted conversation continued: Tom scurrying in his friend's purposeful wake until Murray's next seemingly random stop, the gossiping about Karen interrupted by questions about books.

Murray reckoned Karen's boyfriend hit her. Tom was shocked. Really? Murray shrugged because Karen hadn't actually told him anything so he couldn't be sure, could he? He said it was just a feeling he got; something not quite right. *The Spiritual Self* by the Very Reverend Desmond Payne? No?

Tom wondered aloud if maybe Murray was mistaken: 'I mean . . . hit her . . . It just doesn't happen.' He didn't quite catch the sardonic reply but it was 'Maybe not in your world' or something like that. Tom was shaking his head. When he thought about Karen being beaten up by the mysterious Kush, it somehow made her even more appealing to him; the sense that she was struggling to outstrip her background, to be more than she was. And then this fucker wanted to knock her back down? For Tom, the *realness* of it all seemed impossibly romantic.

'Anyway, china,' Murray was saying. 'The point is, are you coming on Friday? Kazza doesn't know many people and it would be cool if you could make it. I want to introduce you two properly anyway. I think you'll get on.'

'Sure,' Tom said. 'Of course.'

They were right back where they'd started; standing by the same desk in the library's central work space. Murray said, 'Shall we get out of here?'

But Tom still wanted to know what he'd been up to and he caught him by the arm. 'Those little cards. What was that all about?'

Murray smiled. It was a new and cheeky variation on the expression and Tom realized that Murray seemed to have more different smiles than anyone he'd ever met. One day he'd try to figure out exactly how many, he thought.

'Musical greetings, china. They're sensitive things. The slightest disturbance sets them off.'

'What are you talking about?'

'Just bored,' Murray said through a yawn. 'Just having some fun.'

With that, he turned and headed out of the library. Then,

by the door, he suddenly stopped and Tom almost trod on his heels. Murray reached out a hand and gave the last bookcase a gentle shove.

'What are you doing?' Tom asked impatiently but Murray held up a silencing finger.

'Listen.'

At first Tom couldn't hear anything and he was just about to say so but then, somewhere in the distance, he heard a vague but familiar tune. 'Auld Lang Syne'. It was high-pitched and metallic-sounding and as impossible to locate as a whining mosquito.

Murray was singing along, softly, under his breath: '. . . Should old acquaintance be forgot. For the sake of Auld Lang Syne.'

Tom looked down the library and every working student had raised their head. Some were smiling, some shrugged at each other, some pinched their noses in irritation. Tom didn't think it was funny but he found himself laughing anyway. 'Shit that's childish.'

'Just playing at real life,' Murray said.

11

When Murray got down, Tariq got smacked and Tom got the girl

On the Friday, Tom found Murray inside the party. It was held in the Students' Union bar and the place was already rammed by the time he arrived at half-eight. The venue was almost pitch-black but, at one end, Tom could make out a makeshift dancefloor where a bunch of sweaty ravers were gyrating to fearsomely loud, bleeping techno. They were illuminated in the freeze frames of a single strobe and every now and then they paused in their stuttered movements to throw each other OK signs and thumbs-ups and to mouth stuff like 'You up on one?' and 'Sorted'. The walls were covered in half-hearted balloons and amateurish banners proclaiming 'SCHOOLZ OUT FOR THE SUMMER' in capital letters. The concrete floor was already sweating and slippery underfoot.

Murray was at the bar talking to a skinny Asian guy whose clothes were wannabe trendy and desperately unflattering. Pristine Adidas shelltops poked out beneath improbably baggy combats that were all pockets and zips. On top, he wore one of those Camden-market T-shirts with a cartoon raggamuffin on the front smoking an enormous spliff. The T-shirt was too tight and showed off the suggestive beginnings of a paunch that was incongruous beneath the definite outlines of his scrawny ribcage. He had a nice face, though, Tom thought. He looked like he was both trying to be cool and fully aware that he didn't know how.

'Tom, this is Tariq,' Murray said. 'He's the guy running this. A real entrepreneur, aren't you, china?'

Tariq smiled at Tom and raised his beer bottle cheerily. 'Nah,' he said. 'Just another excuse to get drunk, isn't it?'

The music at the other end of the room faded out to be replaced by some seventies funk and the jittering strobe gave way to some traffic-light spots and a blue wash. Nearby a bunch of dull-looking girls whooped in excitement and made for the dancefloor, passing sweaty, bemused ravers heading the other way. Murray spotted Karen at the door and waved her over. Tom hadn't seen her up close for a while and he barely recognized her. Her perm was gone and her hair was now naturally straight, dirty blonde and scraped back in a ponytail. She was wearing flat-fronted black trousers and a crop-top that cut above her pierced belly-button. Tom was staring at the ring. He'd never met anyone who wore one before and he found it immediately and undeniably sexy. It seemed suggestive, like a naughty signpost down to the waistband of her trousers. Suddenly, Tom realized that Karen was regarding him quizzically as he gazed at her midriff so he pretended his shoelaces were undone and dropped to one knee and kept staring anyway.

Tariq greeted Karen and then made his excuses. He went to have a word with the DJ, who was now playing back-to-back Abba. The dancefloor was packed but that was hardly the point, was it?

As Tom straightened up he said, 'Hi. You look different.'

Karen took his hand cautiously. 'Who are you?'

'Karen,' Murray intervened. 'This is my good friend Tom. Tom, this is Karen. You've met before. In the canteen.'

'Oh,' Karen said. She raised an eyebrow. 'The superhero.'

'Yeah,' Tom said. 'That's me.' He felt lame.

Now the music changed again and the syncopated beats of some generic New Jack swing kicked in. Murray glanced over to the dancefloor and then back to the pair of them. 'Do you want to go dance?' For a moment, Tom thought he was going to be left on his own but then he realized it was a group suggestion and, besides, Karen was already saying no.

'You dance?' he asked Murray. For some reason the idea astonished him.

'Why not?' Murray said. 'Laters.'

He began to barge his way through the crowds to the other end of the room and the swell of people pushed Tom and Karen together until they found themselves face to face. Tom was suddenly and acutely embarrassed. He felt like, if he had ever spoken to a woman before, he certainly couldn't remember how it was done. 'So . . .' he began.

'Murray told me I should meet you,' Karen said noncommittally. 'He reckoned we'd get along.'

'Yeah? He told me the same thing.'

'I don't know why he thought that.'

Tom looked at her carefully. Was she laughing at him? He couldn't really tell. She sounded like she was genuinely puzzled so he just said, 'No.'

There was a moment or two of awkwardness. They didn't know what else to say to each other so they both pretended to contemplate the posters on the wall or the students nearby. Tom found himself nodding, as if she'd said something fascinating which he needed time to mull over. Karen started to twitch half-heartedly to the music. Fortunately Tariq bundled over to interrupt their discomfort.

'Shit!' he exclaimed. 'Check out Murray!'

Tom craned his neck and Karen stood on tiptoes as they tried to see Murray at the far end of the room. He wasn't hard to spot. 'Jesus Christ,' Tom muttered.

On the dancefloor, a zone had cleared around him as Murray got busy. He was an undeniably brilliant mover – rhythmical, loose-limbed and bursting with funk – but there was something disruptive, bizarre and hysterically inappropriate about his style (for a college disco, anyway) as he threw himself whole-heartedly into each new step. And the expression on his face was solemn and oblivious all at once. And his extravagant manoeuvres negated any possibility of dancing as a social activity. And some people watched with their hands over their mouths and others shook their heads laughing and others tutted irritably as his flailing limbs mapped out the majority of the space and threatened to decapitate any trespasser. He was kick-dancing, breaking, locking, winding, stepping and sliding. He did the worm, the cabbage patch, the running man, the robot, the boogaloo and, as the track built to its wailing climax, he flipped from propeller to windmills to a final headspin.

At one side of the dancefloor there was a group of guys who sneered as they watched. They weren't actually from LMT but were students from Imperial who'd heard about the night and decided to gatecrash and they were incongruously dressed in blazers and slacks and pinstripe shirts with designer monograms on the breast. They all had the same haircut, floppy and long and parted in the middle, and the same round-shouldered manner. When they weren't watching Murray, they addressed each other by their surnames and muttered about the 'local birds' and tried to impress the passing talent with their uninterested expressions. Two of them – the two with the youngest faces – were smoking thick cigars and trying to look sophisticated. One of these nudged his neighbour and pointed his Cuban at Murray: 'What's this plum up to?'

'No idea, Jackson. Not a fucking clue.'

'Tell you what, Easton, watch this.'

The fresh-faced Jackson necked the rest of his beer and rolled the bottle towards Murray. His aim and timing were perfect so that, though Murray saw the bottle coming, he was already disengaging the headspin and his movements were momentarily unbalanced. As he tried to take most of his weight on his hands, his right foot, driven by a combination of gravity and the slowing rotation, hit the floor, landed square on the bottle and slid painfully away from the rest of his body. For an instant, it looked like he'd surely lost control and the ring around the dancefloor winced expectantly. But, somehow, he managed to adjust the position of his hips and thrust out his left leg and, as the song's final beat kicked, he landed in a perfect splits.

Murray sprang to his feet as the DJ changed style again, fading up more jittering acid, and the dancefloor soon filled around him. A lot of the girls were staring at him admiringly and a couple of blokes came up and clapped him on the shoulder and pushed their faces into his, their eyes wide and dilated. 'Wicked, man! That was wicked!' But Murray headed straight for the Imperial guys who lined up behind Jackson who puffed out his chest and nervously on his cigar.

Murray was heavy breathing and sweating profusely as he stood toe to toe with the joker. He lifted his T-shirt to wipe his face on the front and his lean belly rose and fell with each gasp of air.

'What's your problem, china?' Murray said. His voice was calm, coloured with nothing more than a hint of confusion.

'No problem.' He checked his boys had his back. 'And if you think Jackson's got a problem, you've got another thing coming; know what I mean?'

Murray furrowed his brow. 'Not really.' He leaned forward until their foreheads almost touched; close enough for a head-butt, close enough to kiss.

Easton caught Jackson by the shoulder – 'Come on. Let's blow this shithole' – and Jackson allowed himself to be pulled away, feigning reluctance. He blew smoke in Murray's face and stubbed his cigar aggressively. As the Imperial posse walked away, he turned back and jabbed a finger, unable to resist a parting shot: 'I'll see you. I'll fucking see you.'

Approaching the exit, Easton nudged his mate and snarled, 'Should have fucking had him', and then immediately dropped his eyes when he bumped into an enormous, rough-looking character coming in. This was the kind of geezer for whom the phrase 'brick shithouse' was coined (albeit, presumably, behind his back) and his florid complexion and squashed features gave him a look of irreconcilable anger. The Guess shirt buttoned to his neck made his head look like an angry spot, ready to burst. He could have eaten the two posh kids for breakfast (and still had room for a full English) but his mind was elsewhere and he barely noticed them. Besides, they were already hurrying away, one of them grumbling angrily – 'Jackson will see him again. You'd better fucking believe it.'

In fact, Easton and Jackson (if not the rest of them) did see Murray again, more than a decade later, although they didn't recognize him and the incident on the dancefloor was long forgotten. By then, Easton's name had morphed in various friends' mouths through nicknames like 'Easter' and 'Egg' and 'Bald-As-An-Egg' and 'Baldy' and, finally, to 'Buzzard'. By then, Jackson's moniker had changed too, though, in his case, it was less a nickname than a title. Because he was, after all, 'Big-In-Property'.

By the bar, Tom, Tariq and Karen had established a tentative camaraderie watching Murray's performance. They were drinking steadily and swapping stories about what would later become known as 'Murray-fun' (the singing cards in the library, for instance) when Karen suddenly froze. 'Oh fuck!' she said when she saw who'd just walked in.

'What's that?' Tom asked, still laughing.

'Kush.'

As Kush sauntered towards them, the crowds seemed to part and Tom, looking up, took a first glance dislike to him. This was partly because of Murray's suspicions and partly because, in Tom's mind, he represented rivalry (though Karen would have been surprised to hear it). Mostly, though, it was because everything about Kush – his size and strut, his cocky charisma – suggested an overt masculinity that could have been bottled for sale (in licensed Soho establishments, say) and Tom knew he could never compete with that. Tariq, who'd heard nothing of Karen and Kush's relationship (not even the rumours), was trying to attract the barmaid's attention. Karen was looking at the floor and whispering, 'Shit, shit, shit.'

Kush was all smiles (untrustworthy ones, Tom was sure of it). 'Wassup, Kaz? When you didn't come down tonight, I was, like, confused, you know? Figured I should get up here and check this university thing for myself, you get me? Figured I could give my girl a ride home.'

'I told you,' Karen began, her eyes fixed on her feet. 'I told you I just wanted to stay here tonight. It's the last day of term. I told you I'd be back tomorrow.'

'Yeah? You know what? I think I remember something about that. But you don't want to just hang round a bunch of students the whole time, know what I mean? Might start getting ideas above yourself.'

Tom was hovering ineffectually. He felt like he had to say something, to make his presence felt, but he didn't know what or how and in the end he just blurted, 'Tom. I'm Tom. Tom.'

Kush looked at him, his smile fixed in place. 'So?' he said. And he turned back to Karen. 'Let's go.'

Tariq rejoined the group holding a fresh pint. 'Who's this?' he asked breezily.

'Kush,' Tom said.

'Karen's boyfriend? All right, mate.'

But Kush was now staring intently at Karen and didn't acknowledge him.

Karen was pleading: 'I'm not leaving. Not tonight. Please.'

'You're not going, are you?' Tariq said. 'The party's just kicking off.'

Kush was holding Karen's hand. It could have been a gesture of affection but, when Tom looked closely, he could see how he was pushing his thumb firmly into her knuckles and the discomfort on her face that flickered beneath the fear.

'Please!' Karen's voice was whispering urgency. 'I'll be back tomorrow. You can stay too if you like but I want to be here. Just this once.'

'We're out,' Kush said and he made to pull her away but Karen tore her hand free.

'I'm not leaving.'

'Yeah,' Kush said. 'You are.'

For a moment, they confronted each other. Karen was biting on her top lip and her face looked drained. Kush's expression was unchanged; mild surprise mingling with arrogance and malicious, one-eyebrow amusement. Tom knew it was time for him to say something but his heart was racing and he couldn't even seem to move, fossilized in a bizarre, hunched posture with his hands clutching the denim of his jeans.

'If Karen wants to stay, she can stay,' Tariq said and Tom looked at him sharply. Even though he knew he wouldn't have got the words out himself, he still felt gazumped.

'What's that?' Kush turned lazily and straightened himself

up, one shoulder then the other. To his credit, Tariq didn't flinch.

'If Karen wants to stay, she can,' Tariq said again. 'It's got nothing to do with you.'

'You telling me how to handle my business?'

'No, mate. You can do what you want. And Karen can do what she wants.'

'And that's what you figure? You figure you're a hard man, do you?'

'Tariq!' Karen snapped. 'Just leave it.'

'No,' Tariq squared up to Kush. 'He should leave it. In fact, he should just leave. All right, mate?'

'Think you're a hard man?' Kush started to laugh. 'You fucking with me?'

His shoulders started to shake and he covered his mouth with a hand. Then his laughter seemed to get the better of him and he bent double and rested his hands on his knees. Slowly he straightened up and scratched his head thoughtfully. Then, suddenly, Tariq was sitting on his backside with blood streaming from the misshapen dough-ball where his nose had just been and Kush was shaking out the punch from his knuckles and pulling Karen away with his free hand tight around her wrist.

Tom watched bewildered as Kush shoved his way through the crowd leading Karen behind and Tariq began to whimper. He shook his head. 'You can't do that,' he said quietly. Then louder, 'You can't do that.'

When Murray arrived on the scene a couple of minutes later to investigate the ruckus, he was initially incredulous and then livid with Tom. Until he heard Murray's anger, Tom was feeling sheepish and inadequate but, given some verbals to react to, he began to get increasingly belligerent.

Murray had his hands under Tariq's armpits and was trying

to help him to his feet. 'What? You just let him drag her away, china? What kind of man are you?'

'What did you expect me to do?' Tom said.

'What do you reckon? Stop him! There are two of you, Tariq gets smacked and you're, like, "Laters". What's that about?'

'It wasn't like that,' Tom said. He couldn't believe what he was hearing. This was deeply unfair. 'I mean, where were you?'

Murray was shaking his head as he manoeuvred Tariq's arm over his shoulder and supported him towards the exit. 'No, no, no, china. Don't try to lay this on me. I didn't see Kush come in, did I? I didn't even know he was here.'

'Where are you going?'

'I'm taking him to casualty aren't I? Get his nose set.'

'I'll come too.'

'What for?'

'I'll go after them, then.'

'Karen and Kush?' Murray was talking over his shoulder. 'What? You think you're going to play the superhero now, china? Bit late for that.'

Tom watched Murray and his patient head out of the door. The other students at the bar had left a respectful space around him, marked out like the silhouette of a body at a crime scene, and, despite the music, the chatter had subsided to a murmur. But now that the victim had left the building, the party-goers began to encroach again and soon they barely noticed Tom standing in their midst; motionless in the ebb and flow of people.

Tom's mind was nineteen to the dozen, a whirlpool of emotions that rose and sank: guilt, regret, anger, impotence, hatred, the unfairness of it all; these and other sensations span in his head before being sucked back under. His breathing was short and urgent and his heart was pounding. He didn't know what he was going to do but he knew he had to do something and he began to stumble towards the exit.

It took him less than five minutes to get to Karen's hall of residence but it was time enough for the sudden churn of feelings to have subsided a little and they now bubbled gently beneath the chilly breeze of fear. But he wasn't going to turn back. He knew Karen lived on the second floor and he double-timed the steps. He doubted there was any real hurry – whatever had happened would have happened by now, wouldn't it? – but he knew that he was more likely to bottle out with every passing second.

He turned into the corridor and checked the board of names on the wall. Karen Miller: 208. That made her third from the end on the left. For a moment, Tom just stood there and listened. He knew that a lot of the students had already left for the summer and he heard no sounds of life. He couldn't hear anything.

His footsteps were loud on the linoleum; lingering sticky sounds that spooked him. As he passed 206, he could see that Karen's door was ajar and his breath caught in his throat like a jacket on a nail. His pace slowed a little but he kept moving. He didn't know whether to make noise, to announce his arrival, or try to sneak up. His ears were pinned back but he still couldn't distinguish anything beyond the 'shlick, shlick' of his trainers. He decided to call out – 'Hello. Karen? Anybody there?' – and he tapped his knuckles gently on the door.

He found Karen sitting on her bed. She glanced up at him. Her expression wasn't what he expected. There was no sign of tears and no scars of a beating. If anything, her manner was cold, detached, almost bored. Only when she lifted her legs on to the bed did her face betray her as it contorted in a wince and her hand gingerly rubbed her belly.

He looked around the room. It was wrecked. In one corner, the chipboard wardrobe (belonging to the college) had been reduced to little more than firewood and Karen's clothes were strewn everywhere; some ripped, others blackened, apparently half-burned. The floor was littered with shards of glass from pictures and photographs and a mirror whose frame now stared blindly upwards from the floor. Tom didn't know what to say so he said, 'What happened?'

Karen tried to laugh. There was that wince again. 'I chucked Kush. He chucked everything else.'

'Right,' Tom said. He sat on the end of the bed. 'It'll be all right.'

'Yeah? You don't know Kush.' Her voice was suddenly faltering. Tom knew she wanted to say more but the words wouldn't come. She settled for, 'I've got to go home, you see.'

'Right,' Tom said and then, impulsively, 'Come and stay with me.'

Karen smiled and he felt a little stupid. 'What for?'

'I don't know. Just to get away. I mean, if you want to. Just until things settle down a bit. For as long as you want. I can, you know, look after you.'

'Yeah?' She nodded. The smile was gone. 'Tom Dare.' She sounded like she was trying out the words for the first time, trying them on for size. 'Maybe you are a superhero after all.' Now, at last, a single tear welled in the corner of her right eye and began to trickle slowly down her cheek. She didn't wipe it away but Tom wished she would because it made him feel uncomfortable. She sniffed. 'Would you . . .' she began. 'You can hold me if you like.'

'Sure.'

He shuffled down the bed and hugged her awkwardly, her face buried in his chest. They sat like that for a while. At one point, Tom thought she'd started to sob (though he couldn't be sure) and he squeezed her a little. She drew a sharp breath. 'Not too tight,' she said.

12
Infidelity as love

Emma has splashed her face from the basin and she's looking in the mirror. Her expression seems caught in momentary surprise. She feels like she barely recognizes the person staring back at her. Perhaps it's because she looks healthier than she has for, what, nine months? Since Tommy was born anyway. There is a flush to her complexion and is it her imagination or can she really detect a fullness in her cheeks? She presses a thumb to her face and when she takes it away it leaves a pale mark, like sunburn does. She cups her breasts gently in her hands and points them at the mirror. She's sure there's more substance to them. They still sag, of course, and her nipples are at twenty past eight, pointing at her feet, but what's a mum to expect? She knew her breasts would swell when she stopped feeding but that was more than a month ago. So now? It seems a bit weird. She lifts them and presses them together. With the right bra I'd have a decent cleavage, she thinks.

Her gaze traces the shadow of her ribs to the jagged outline of her hips. A little healthier or not, she still thinks her pelvic girdle looks like the backend of a bony cow from a news report on some or other drought. Her pubic hair is coarse, thick on her inner thighs and dense in a line to her belly-button. She used to wax and trim it but she hasn't bothered in ages. She remembers that someone's just seen this unappealing undergrowth and she suddenly feels a mixture of embarrassment and bizarre elation and she starts to giggle. She covers her mouth with her hand. She tastes a familiar moisture on the tip of her index finger and she glances down at her chest.

Christ. A tear of milk wells and dribbles from her right nipple. She remembers him taking her breasts in his mouth when she straddled him. Did he taste it? Now she's laughing. What's with this sudden burst of fecundity? Jesus Christ.

The doctors hadn't been able to explain the way she dropped weight. She'd seen all kinds of specialists and the best they came up with was, 'Your body's not absorbing nutrition properly. Everything you eat's just passing right through you.'

'Why?'

None of them had an answer to that and she'd discovered that the higher rungs of the NHS food chain only heightened the verbosity of the replies. Her GP offered an honest 'I don't know' but the knighted consultant blustered, 'To be frank, Mrs Khan, we are as yet unable to ascertain the exact causes of the vicissitudes of your case.'

Emma can't stop smiling. She raises her eyebrows and her forehead barely wrinkles at all. She flattens a palm to it and the skin feels soft and giving. Perhaps it's the sex that has made her look and feel so well. After all it was the first time in more than a year. Sex as nutrition? What would the doctors have to say about that? And it hadn't even been much good. Imagine how chubby she'd look if she'd had a proper seeing to, the kind that Tariq used to give her before they were married.

She feels the muscles of her abdomen contract with a stifled laugh and the spasm expels a dollop of semen down her thighs. She reaches for the loo roll and mops it efficiently. The smell of the stuff is familiar but she's surprised by its strength. Has it been such a long time that she's forgotten or is this a particularly potent batch? She winces at her use of the word 'potent'. Better not be, she thinks.

She drops the pad of tissue paper into the toilet and flushes it away but the stench lingers around her. It's a combination of things: fish fingers and marzipan and a hint of old coins.

But most of all it smells fetid, like an ignored fridge. She finds it somehow sobering that the ingredients of humanity should smell as rotten as the dustbins outside the fried-chicken place on Latchmere Road. Tommy came from stuff like this, she thinks. Stuff *like* this.

She looks up at the mirror again and finds her expression locked in a parody of prudish distaste, the kind of face she pulls when unblocking the sink. She deliberately cracks it into a smile and she thinks how white her teeth look, how her lips are moist and her eyes sparkling.

As the hiss of the cistern subsides, she is called from the other room: 'Em? I think he might be awake.' Her ears immediately prick up to hear the sounds from the baby monitor positioned by the bed. She wonders what the time is. Surely his afternoon nap should last for another hour yet. She can hear her son's gurgling and a plaintive cry and then another. She holds her breath for a moment. Then nothing. Then a contented chewing noise and some sniffles. Just a bad dream but not enough to wake him.

For the first time she begins to feel ashamed and the sensation courses through her like high tide at the Thames Barrier. She sees her expression collapse into familiar knackered patterns. But she gets a grip on herself and somehow transforms the feeling into one of intoxication. I will not be ashamed, she thinks. I'm past shame, I'm too old for shame, I know too much for shame.

She takes Tariq's bathrobe off the back of the door and wraps herself up in it. She ties it at the waist and looks at herself in the mirror again. It hangs off her like ill-fitting fancy dress. Very sexy. She undoes the knot, takes off the robe and drops it in a crumpled heap on the floor. Although she doesn't care about being sexy, she does want to be naked. The mid-afternoon hasn't seen her fanny since Tommy was born and that day she'd had a midwife gazing up her and Tariq squeezing her hand and trying not to look like he was trying not to look. She shrugs for her own benefit. Fuck it, she thinks and the thought catches her. She hardly ever uses that word, not even in her head. 'Fuck it,' she murmurs aloud.

She goes back into the bedroom. Murray is sitting on the edge of the bed but he isn't looking at her. He's craning his neck all the way round over his left shoulder. He looks like he's trying to see his own bum. Side on, his expression looks like one of pained concentration.

She stares at him dispassionately and absorbs all the details she'd had no time for during their frenzied sex. He is lean and his muscles are well-defined in a young-man sort of way. Young man. Yes, that's it. Looking at his bare chest and the smooth contours of his stomach, you'd never put him around thirty. More like a decade younger; twenty-one or twenty-two. He's definitely buff, if you like that sort of thing. But Emma never has. She's always been into something a bit more solid (physically anyway) with manly imperfections and unlikely tufts of hair and an imposing bulk.

She is studying Murray's complexion. She realizes that, apart from Tariq, this is the first naked man she's seen for years and years. There is something strange about Murray's colouring. She knows that he's probably some confused racial mixture but, in this light, he looks more grey than anything else; so different from Tariq's burnished copper. Stranger still is the remarkable consistency of his skin tone. Every inch of him looks exactly the same grey as every other with no blotches, blemishes, scars or shadows. He looks like he's been lovingly painted with an undercoat and never quite finished off.

Her gaze moves to his penis, which is limp between his legs. For a moment she remembers her orgasm and she shivers like a sapling in the breeze, like a recently cured virgin. But she is not a virgin but a married woman with a kid. And besides, it had been fun but nothing special and she'd never been the type of woman who had to struggle to climax. Not with Tariq anyway. Not when they'd been having sex anyway.

She considers for a moment. Certainly she's never felt so detached from her body during sex as she did today. It was a 'push the right button, tweak the right knob' kind of fuck. Fuck. There's that word again. Fuck it.

She is smiling. She is staring at Murray's penis and smiling and she tries not to but she can't help herself. She decides there should be a rule for women; that they should not be allowed to look at a dick unless 1.) They're horny; 2.) It's hard.

There's something ridiculous about a flaccid dick, she thinks. It looks cumbersome, awkward and slightly dishevelled. Like an old man. Isn't that what some blokes call it? Their old man? She has never thought so before but right now she can't entertain a better description. Her imagination is running wild. She pictures Murray's father or grandfather, say, passing on his penis in a bizarre initiation ritual: 'Here you are, my son. This dick has served me well and I expect you to treat it with the respect it deserves. Wash it daily, stick it nowhere you wouldn't stick your tongue and indulge no more than once a week off the wrist.'

She remembers Tariq telling her that nobody even knew if Murray had a family and she finds herself wondering where his dick came from then. Christ. Her imagination really is running wild. Fuck. It must be this bizarre elation she's feeling, this liberation that seems to have everything and nothing to do with what she's just done with one of her husband's oldest friends. Again she giggles and, finally, Murray turns to look up at her.

His expression isn't far from a wince but it doesn't seem to have anything to do with her amusement. 'What's so funny?'

'Your penis.'

'Right,' Murray nods. 'Thanks.'

'Was it your father's or your grandfather's?'

He takes this in his stride. 'Neither. This is one I picked up on the ashram. Swapped it for a pair of trainers.'

Emma is laughing now and she feels slightly stoned, like she used to get when she smoked weed with Tariq when they first met, six years ago. Six years ago? It feels like another lifetime. She'd love some weed now. Fuck yeah.

She stops laughing when she sees that shadow of pain return to Murray's face. He cocks his neck first one way and then the other and he rolls his shoulders a couple of times.

'What's the matter?'

'It's my back,' he says. 'Think you scratched me, china. Hurts like shit.'

'Really? Let me have a look.'

Emma approaches him and he turns round and flops on to the bed on his front. She looks at his back. 'Jesus Christ!'

'What?'

'How did that happen?'

There is a single laceration on Murray's back, about three inches long, just below the left shoulderblade. But it looks nothing like a passion scar, more like he's been impaled upon something. It is deep and wide, raised a little on each side, with fresh blood bubbling in the canyon. Worst of all, it looks septic. The flesh around it is an angry red and there are traces of grey pus at the top end.

'I can't have done that.'

'Done what?'

'This. It's huge. Deep, too.'

She sits astride Murray's buttocks and examines it gingerly but he recoils from her touch. In spite of herself, she's disgusted. She can't understand why. She's never been squeamish. Then she realizes that it's not the wound that's disgusting her at all but the position she's in with the insides of her calves pressing against Murray's thighs and her crotch, still damp, pressing into the small of his back. Forget infidelity, there's an intimacy to this that is utterly inappropriate and makes her feel uncomfortable. Sex can just be sex (not always, but it can be). But this kind of easy nakedness? It feels intrusive, disrespectful to Tariq (and that, she tells herself, was never the intention).

She gets off Murray and stands back. She pushes her hair off her face and she's sure it feels thicker. Yes. Thicker and softer.

'What's the diagnosis, Dr Emma?' Murray has his face turned to one side and his eyes are closed.

'You stay there,' she says. 'I'm just going to find some antiseptic and cotton wool.'

She leaves the bedroom door open to allow the air to circulate and heads down to the kitchen, where the medical supplies are kept. She takes out the Tupperware box from the cupboard to the left of the hob and, as she begins to rummage through it, sitting at the table, she suddenly finds herself enveloped by a soft blanket of nostalgia. She can remember putting this first-aid kit together a couple of weeks before Tommy was born. She can remember how she'd felt at the time: bored and frustrated and overripe like a plum that's about to split. So she'd decided to do useful things and this was one of them and she'd gone to Boots to buy swabs and bandages and plasters and safety pins and antiseptic and witch-hazel and things like that. She'd drawn a red cross on the lid in thick marker pen. Because a proper family should have a proper first-aid kit, she'd thought.

She smiles to herself. She can't remember touching this box since the day she assembled it. So the Khan family's first-aid kit is making its debut treating Mummy's first infidelity. She holds the smile. She refuses to feel ashamed because that's a single step from feeling disappointed in herself which is itself neighbourly to disappointment with her lot. And she knows she's had quite enough of that.

As she picks out the sticky bandage, the cotton-wool pads, the cream and the scissors, she pictures Murray lying on her bed and she feels briefly resentful. Her resentment only doubles when she notices the half-eaten packet of chicken goujons lying discarded on the side. She hates it when some-one messes up her kitchen. She finds her top lip curling in distaste and questions beginning 'What kind of man . . . ?' and 'How could he . . . ?' start whispering at her inner ear. But she checks them right there. Because she knows that whatever blame she attributes to Murray, she has to accept at least half as much again. This was what she'd wanted and she won't regret it.

When your marriage is stretched to breaking point by forces beyond its participants, you have to take extreme measures. This is what she tells herself. And since her marriage had been stripped of sex and passion and value and valuing, she'd needed to find those things elsewhere. She admits that, before sleeping with Murray, she'd had no idea how she would feel afterwards. But now that she's done it, she is unsurprised by her reaction. She sees now that she wasn't looking for love or affection or anything so nebulous. She sees now that she can still get all that from her husband. She sees now that this was just an itch that needed to be scratched. It was, she thinks, like a bungee jump; one of those things that a sane person will do once but only the reckless repeat. She sees now with astonish-ing clarity how Tariq has been emasculated by the twin burdens of fatherhood and the collapse of his business and she sees the subsequent vicious circles of drink and bills and her own frustrations. She sees now how she's been defeminized in the past year.

Until now, any intuition of these things has been drowned out by recriminations and hidden behind accusing fingers. But the visceral nature of the sex she's just had seems to have objectified the facts beyond the selfish reach of her or Tariq's opinion. How could she restore her husband's manhood when she felt like less than a woman? She couldn't. So she has been unfaithful with one of his oldest friends but she did it for Tariq. Her smile is wide and knowing. She'll never be able to tell him, of course, but she has no regrets.

She is idly peeling price stickers off the bandages and cotton wool. She sticks them to the tips of her fingers until she has five sticky talons on her left hand. She splays her fingers and examines them like a woman in a beauty salon.

If she were to regret anything (which she won't), it would be the amount she confided in Murray before the act. She's not sure why she did this. It's not like he pushed her so she assumes she must have felt some kind of compulsion to justify herself.

She told him how she met Tariq, working at Phillips some six years before; how she was a personal assistant in business development and he was the bright spark among the graduate trainees. She recalled proudly how the top brass had talked about him, how she'd overheard the grey suits pointing him out to each other across the canteen and saying things like, 'See that young chap? Typical Asian: ambitious and capable. He's the future. Have your job before you know it.' Things like that.

She told Murray how they'd got together after works drinks on a Friday in a wine bar off Tottenham Court Road.

She told him how the other PAs had got drunk on lime-topped pints, flirted with the middle-aged middle management and danced to seventies disco before skidding into sticky heaps of laddered tights, lager spills and lechery. But she'd had eyes only for Tariq, blown away by his confidence and drive. She said he'd been one of those guys who'd make it, no two ways about it, and it wasn't just her who thought so.

Tariq had been making plans even then, looking around for opportunities and investigating the ins and outs of financing. The future of new technologies? He'd seen it right from the start. It wasn't like he'd been interested in the developments themselves, just the business potential they offered. 'It's like the Wild West,' he used to say. 'It's like the gold rush and the fastest off the blocks is going to get very rich.'

She told this to Murray and he smiled so she protested, 'But he was right, you know? He knew what he was talking about.'

It had been four years before Tariq found a project that suited. A nineteen-year-old wunderkind at Redhill Research approached him with a clunky prototype application that predicted the movement of crowds outside a football stadium. Tariq had seen the possibilities at once and it was less than three months before he'd struck the necessary deal to quit Phillips and set up TEK Systems from offices on Charlotte Street, the up-and-coming area north of Soho where the bright sparks of IT wore ironic T-shirts and baggy jeans and lunched on hummus and tabbuleh in cheap Moroccan cafés.

Tariq had borrowed heavily against the house and Emma had queried that. But he just laughed and shook his head and said, 'The less outside investment, the more money we'll make. As simple as that. TEK Systems. Tariq and Emma Khan. Think about it.' He was so sure of himself.

When Emma told Murray this, he hardly seemed to listen and she became quite strident. 'You don't understand. We had all the major players knocking on our door to buy in to our product. Even up to, like, a year ago. It was so exciting. We were going to be rich. I mean, it's not like it matters. But that's the truth of it. Definitely.'

'And then?'

'And then tech stocks went into freefall.'

Murray shrugged. 'Guess that's life, china,' he said.

What kind of an attitude was that? Hadn't he understood?

She began to harangue him and it was then that she let slip all the little intimacies that now made her blush at the memory. It probably wasn't stuff he hadn't known or couldn't have guessed but that was hardly the point. She told him how Tariq had been so overworked and having a baby hadn't helped, had it? She told him about the drinking. She told him about the lack of sex. She told him how Tariq's fatalism was now as immutable as his confidence had once been. 'It's not about *money*,' she said. 'It's about who he is, how he thinks about himself. With a bit of cash, we could buy our way out of the personal debts at least and he could find another job, start again. But we can't even afford that so he has to keep going. We could lose the house but even that's not the point. Think about what it would do to him. He's broken, Murray. Broken.'

'So what are you going to do?'

'We . . .' she began and she smiled at Murray coyly; sexily, perhaps. 'We're going to rob a bank, aren't we?'

'Yeah?'

'That's what you said. The one in Putney. It was your idea.'

'No.' Murray shook his head and his eyes were narrow; calculating, she thought. 'No. It was *your* idea.'

They moved to the bedroom soon after that.

Emma stands up. She's no longer smiling. She picks up the sticky bandage, cotton wool and antiseptic and heads for the door. At the bottom of the stairs, she pauses and heaves a deep breath. So I'd fuck another man for Tariq, she thinks. I'd even rob a fucking bank for him. *Rob a fucking bank for him.* The words sound ridiculous, even in her head, and the muscles in her cheeks begin to quiver and there are goosebumps on her neck. She'll need to repeat them again and again to make them sound plausible. *For him.* She's strong enough to be honest with herself and she knows that might not be the truth of it. She shakes her head. She's not sure. But does the truth actually matter as long as the story works?

In the bedroom, she finds Murray still lying on his front and his eyes are still closed. But she smiles anyway. She doesn't understand why. Maybe she can't help herself or maybe she just feels like she should.

He says, 'I wondered where you'd got to, china.'

But she just chuckles, bends over him and begins to softly rub the antiseptic cream around the fringes of the wound. She still doesn't know how on earth she could have cut him like this. Without the price stickers, her nails are short and neat. Murray must have skin like tissue.

As she works, the muscles of his back tense beneath her touch. 'Be a brave boy,' she says. She cuts a length of cotton wool and then fastens it across the wound with four strips of sticky bandage. 'There you go.'

Murray turns to face her and she immediately looks away. She doesn't want to see his nakedness any more but she can't help glancing back at him. His expression is blank. Or unreadable at least. 'Again, china?' he says.

'What?'

'Do you want to go again?'

'I don't understand.'

'Sex.'

'No,' she says sharply. And then, 'I mean, do you?'

Murray has started laughing. She's not sure what he's laughing at – it could be her or it could be himself – but she joins in anyway. He reaches for his boxers and jeans. When he pulls on his sweatshirt, his expression twists as the material tugs at her makeshift bandage.

'You all right?' she asks.

'Fine. Yeah. Fine.'

The baby monitor crackles into life again. This time Tommy's definitely woken up and Emma instinctively gets to her feet. She realizes she's still naked. She likes that.

'I guess I'd better go,' he says.

'Right.'

He kisses her on the forehead and, just for a moment, she wishes he would stay and she finds herself asking him, 'Have you ever done this before?' Just to keep him close.

'Done what?'

'You know . . . with one of your friends' . . .'

Murray steps back and examines her, his expression a mixture of hurt and curiosity. 'What kind of man do you think I am?' he asks.

'I don't know.' She shakes her head. 'Sorry.'

Tommy is crying insistently now and Emma finds herself looking towards the door. But she knows she has to ask him one more question, to make sure they understand each other. It's sticking in her throat. 'We *are* going to . . .'

'Going to what?'

'Do the bank, aren't we? I mean, we've got to.'

'Why are you asking me?'

Emma's stumbling over her words. 'Because . . . you know . . . Tariq says . . . you can make it happen, Murray. You're the one who can make it happen.'

'And Tariq wants to, does he?'

'Yeah. I mean, he *will*.'

'What about the others? What about Tom and Karen? What about Kwesi, Freya and Ami?'

'They'll do it.' She's nodding with a certainty she doesn't feel. 'I mean, you know, with a little persuasion.'

He shrugs. 'So we'll do it, then.'

They are standing opposite each other, no more than a foot apart. Tommy is wailing in the background; fearful for where his mum might have got to. Murray rotates his left shoulder a couple of times and raises his eyebrows at Emma. She feels suddenly uneasy, like she knows what's coming next but she can't quite believe it.

Murray says, 'Same time tomorrow, then?' and Emma's stomach twists and she thinks she might throw up.

'I'm sorry?'

He shakes his head and smiles. 'Only joking, china. Know what I mean?'

13
Murray-fun

From the mid-sixties to the late seventies, the UK saw a brief rush of liberal, quasi-Christian publishing (described in the industry variously as the 'Bach effect' or the 'Narnia lag'). Deep in this forgotten forest of good intentions lies a slim volume called *The Spiritual Self* by the Very Reverend Desmond Payne. It was published in 1974 by the now-defunct Church-Temple Press with an initial and, as it transpired, sole print run of 250.

Outside the copyright libraries, there are only four copies still existent. The author's sits in a bookcase in a bedroom in the residential wing of the Highgate Buddhist Centre. This room is rented to the sixty-three-year-old who is now known (personally and professionally) as Tejananda and runs a lucrative psychotherapy practice out of the West End. But, despite the success of both his business and the last five years' meditative contemplation, Tejananda cannot look at the title without feeling a profound if imprecise melancholy.

Of the other three, one props up the till in a Forest Hill junk shop, its spine long since torn off and its contents unknown, and another lies on a table in a café in Playa Del Carmen on Mexico's Caribbean coast where tourists can swap reading material over *frijoles* and guacamole. The third, however, is unique for three reasons: it is the only copy to have changed location in the last five years (having been pilfered from the LMT library by an ex-student less than two months ago), the only one that is ever opened (including, in fact, those in the copyright libraries and the author's own) and the only one that periodically sings 'The Red Flag' (by virtue of a small piece of a greetings card that once prophesied a 1987 Labour election victory).

This piece of card is lodged firmly between pages twenty-two and twenty-three at the end of the former Reverend Payne's introduction (pompously titled 'Self and Other'). If you were to pick up this copy from its place on the mantelpiece in the living-room of the flat above the Indian minimarket in the homogeneous London neighbourhood, you might think that someone had purposefully marked out this section for your attention (especially, perhaps, when you triggered the card's mechanism and heard the opening bars). You would be wrong. This is not to say, however, that you wouldn't find something useful therein that could offer tip-of-the-tongue explanations of issues that have been puzzling you.

The former Reverend Payne concludes his introduction as follows:

There is little doubt that modern Western society regards faith and its implied leap beyond logic with arrogant scepticism. It seems that faith, in its traditional understanding, is as deeply unfashionable as it is contemporaneously ubiquitous. Because it is my contention that we all still believe in something; whether it be the miracle of the atonement, the rights of the trade unions or that a new motorcar will ensure our happiness. Indeed, some reputable commentators with whom I largely concur have suggested that it is faith itself that is significant, rather than its object (the 'Faith as Identity' model).

It is the current trend, however, to dismiss faith with whatever blunt philosophical instrument comes easiest to hand and the most common accusation is that faith is in some way 'selfish'. There is little doubt that such an accusation raises the ire of Christians everywhere but it is my belief that any new spirituality must take account of such criticism. In this humble work (mostly derived from my own essays, sermons and workshops and personal study of Eastern religious traditions), I propose a new understanding which may be summarized in the following ten-point thesis:

1. Faith, especially in its infancy, may indeed be 'selfish' but this adjective rarely offers a complete description.

2. 'Selfish faith' often expresses one or more 'Core Personality Flaw' (for example, arrogance or fear; ambition or self-absorption; conflicted identity or a tendency towards self-destruction).

3. Selfishness must be distinguished from 'true faith' which we may better term 'devotion'.

4. Selfish faith is inherently immature and, in time, usually leads to devotion.

5. Generally, however, faith is cyclical. As selfishness usually extends to devotion, so devotion usually returns to selfishness.

6. These changes in the nature of faith are often (but not always) triggered by a specific event (positive or negative) in a person's life ('Moments of Truth', as I term them, from the subject's perspective).

7. Unfortunately, selfishness may appear devotional and devotion, selfish.

8. The duration of these cycles expands like ripples across a pond before one or other (i.e., 'selfishness' or 'devotion') eventually becomes, in the subject's subconscious, immutable ('The Die is Cast' theory).

9. This immutability is, of course, illusory. Change is always possible.

10. Unfortunately, the subjective nature of faith itself ensures that the faithful rarely attain the perspective to recognize their own nature (or, indeed, exactly what it is they believe in).

Judging by the impact *The Spiritual Self* made on the contemporary religious debate (none) and the author's later conversion to Buddhism, it would be tempting to write off the book as adding nothing to understandings of the human experience. It was intended, as is expressed on page one, paragraph one, as a 'treatise for contemporary Christianity'. But one person who might have found more personal resonance in the Reverend Payne's hypothesis – not least because it correlated with patterns he'd been discussing with his therapist, Tejananda – was Tom. Unfortunately Tom had never read *The Spiritual Self* (although he had once heard it sing, while he was cramming in the LMT library five minutes before the first of his finals). What's more, though he explicitly concurred with most of Tejananda's behavioural modelling, his faith in the therapist was still in its selfish stage and, therefore, he didn't really listen.

An objective reflection upon Tom's relationship with Karen, however, might usefully point to these cycles of selfishness and devotion, identify several Moments of Truth and note the expanding ripples of the cycles through time. If, for example, you attempted to piece together the first fifth of their decade-spanning relationship – the time at LMT – from the information in his therapist's notebook, your story might go something like this . . .

After the incident with Kush, Karen spent most of the following summer holiday living with Tom and his parents at the house in Hampton Wick and it didn't take long for their nascent friendship to blossom into something more. This was partly for the prosaic reason of proximity and partly due to other, less obvious stimuli. In the first place, Tom's parents took to Karen immediately. They asked no questions about why she might need to stay with them, welcomed her hospitably and actively encouraged the relationship (particularly Tom's dad, who saw a girlfriend as altogether preferable to his son's occasional and, to him, bizarre bouts of Catholicism). For her part, Karen had never lived among a nuclear family and she found it enormously appealing. She liked Tom's parents by return but, more than that, she enjoyed their easy manner with each other, their unspoken affections, their cosy routines. Every evening, Mrs Dare would produce a meal (with fresh meat and vegetables as opposed to the cellophane packaging and microwave instructions Karen was used to) and, when he sat down, Mr Dare would sigh in satisfaction and say something like, 'Look at *this*! You're fantastic, my love. You're a fantastic woman.'

Karen felt there was something magically idyllic about such a situation. She felt like Michael J. Fox walking back into the McFly household at the end of *Back To The Future* and she basked in vicarious suburban comfort.

As for Tom, he thrived in his perceived role as Karen's protector. Initially this meant listening to a lot of stories about her ex.

Kush was a small-time dealer, Karen said, had been for as long as she'd known him. It had never bothered her but, in the last year or so, he'd changed. He'd become short-tempered, aggressive and occasionally and increasingly violent. She suspected he was getting high on his own supply. She reminisced about their plans together – her and Kush – how she was going to get a degree and a good job and he'd jack in the dealing and they'd settle down. She talked about this matter-of-factly and Tom listened in silence, nodding his head and prompting with the occasional question. He pretended to be unsurprised and he said 'Right' and 'Of course' and he rather liked his involvement in this other world he knew nothing about, one step removed. And isn't this the very essence of the modern city? When empathy is often less life skill than second-hand (and mostly egotistical?) recreation.

Gradually, these conversations progressed from late night around the kitchen table to small hours between the sheets and gradually Tom started to offer opinions and gradually Karen began to listen to them until they weighed more than any others.

Sometimes Tom drove Karen in his dad's Mazda to the council flat in Peckham; to pick up an item of clothing or a book or for a cup of tea with her sister, Danielle. Then Tom would sit on the threadbare velveteen sofa while Danielle eyed him (suspiciously, he thought) and said things like, '*He*'s been round again, Kaz', and Karen shook her head and muttered, 'So? What do you want me to do?'

With every reference to Kush, Tom half-expected him to come banging on the door at that very moment and he'd square his shoulders and convince himself he was prepared for confrontation. But Kush never did come round; not while they were there.

Aside from Kush, Karen and Tom's other conversations focused mostly upon Murray. At the end of term, he'd taken their numbers and promised to call and somehow, what with his apparent enthusiasm to see them, they hadn't thought to ask for his. In fact, throughout their time at college, they never saw Murray during the holidays and they eventually got used to it and stopped asking why. This is not as surprising as it may sound; universities are frequently hermetic places where many relationships don't stray beyond the last day of term. But that first summer, it struck them as strange and they tried to imagine the reasons and they had ever more fantastical conversations about his possible family background, where he might come from and what he might be up to.

Later, when Tom reflected on how he and Karen got together, he concluded that Murray's absence was probably instrumental. In fact, considering his friend's obvious care for the two of them, he even suspected it was a deliberate ploy on Murray's part since it both provided a connection and left a space which they had to fill together. Certainly when they returned to LMT for their second year, Murray didn't seem surprised to see them hand in hand and Tom felt comfortable in his role as Karen's protector and the protection that this, conversely, afforded him.

For the next two years, Tom's sense of the relationship – the *comfort* – was largely, in his own mind, unchanged. He was devoted to Karen and, indeed, devoted to Murray, too (at the top of an early page in Tejananda's patient notes the word 'BILATERAL' is written in screaming red capitals).

In fact, though Tom has chosen to forget them, there were spells when he lapsed into indisputable selfishness. Two in particular stand out.

When Kush was finally banged up for pushing rocks, Karen insisted upon visiting him and Tom couldn't understand why. Karen shrugged and said, 'We went out for years, Tom. I've got to go and see him.'

'After everything he did?'

'I've just got to.'

'I'll come with you.'

'No,' Karen said. 'No, Tom. I'll go on my own.'

Tom was so angry that, afterwards, he didn't ask how the visit had gone. He thought she was being selfish (a common assumption of selfishness) and so she could cope on her own. And when she burst into tears and told him about Kush's anger and threats (threats against her and, indeed, against himself, too), he hugged her half-heartedly and couldn't resist saying, 'What did you expect?'

Or what about the time, not long after, when Tom was walking past the Curzon on Panton Street? He was stopped in his tracks by the sight of Murray and Karen emerging from the cinema amid the crowds. They were nudging each other and laughing and swigging Coke from the same bottle. It wasn't, of course, seeing them together that caught him off guard but the oblivious and, to Tom's eye, undeniable intimacy of their interaction. What's more, when Karen spotted him, she looked embarrassed. Definitely. And Tom was speechless with jealousy.

'It's *The Breakfast Club*,' Karen said by way of explanation. 'We were passing and you know how I've always wanted to see it on the big screen again.'

Tom wanted to be cool but he couldn't help himself and he turned on his heels and stormed off into Soho. It was a few days before he ran into Murray in the canteen but he was still so angry that he could barely articulate anything.

'You and Karen, you know . . .' he began. 'What . . . I mean . . . you know . . . What . . . it's just . . .'

Murray didn't look up. He was irritably trying to squeeze all the garlic butter out of a chicken Kiev. 'Don't worry, china,' Murray muttered. 'It was just sex. I wanted to fuck your girlfriend and she was, like, "OK, then. Just so long as I've got something to take my mind off it." So I took her to her favourite movie.' He glanced at Tom. 'You do know I'm joking, right?'

'Right,' Tom said. 'Right.'

Of course, these two Moments of Truth that triggered him to selfishness can, in Tejananda's model, be counter-pointed by two others with the reverse effect. It wasn't more than a month after Karen visited Kush in prison that Tom took ecstasy for the first time. The tensions between the couple had already thawed a little by then but it was sharing an E that finally reverted Tom to devotional clarity. Karen said that she'd never taken drugs with Kush, never even smoked a little puff, because it had always seemed so sordid. And Tom, basking on his ecstasy cloud, felt confident in this intimacy which seemed like purity itself compared to alley deals with Peckham crackheads.

As for Tom's brief spell of jealousy, that was turned on its head by an external stimulus. He was superficially reassured by Murray's denials – he never even confronted Karen – but it was the outbreak of the Gulf War that actually triggered the change. He'd been drinking with Tariq and, on their way home, they stopped in a kebab shop on the Edgware Road. Next to the illuminated menu, a small black-and-white TV broadcast the first fireworks of Desert Storm in real time – American pilots throwing victory signs on a Gulf airstrip; flash, darkness, flash, darkness; a mob torching the stars-and-stripes; flash, darkness – and, around the counter, a group of men with Saddam Hussein moustaches shook their heads and muttered in what sounded like Arabic to Tom. Despite Tariq's reassurance that they were probably Turks, Tom didn't want to hang around.

That night he dreamed beerily of chemical warfare and a ravaged London (that looked little different but for the lack of people) and he woke up with a screaming hangover and a poignant sense of lonely mortality. He resolved to find Karen immediately and eventually tracked her down to the Students' Union where she was painting placards for a planned demonstration outside the American embassy. He accompanied her on the march and held the other side of her banner that, on that first day, bore an obtuse slogan – 'It's oil or nothing for Bush!!!' – given weight only by the three exclamation marks. But Tom, in his fragile state, believed that Karen knew what she was doing and his world was safe in her hands. Maybe even vice versa.

Tom himself felt this was a story of significance so he told it to Tejananda in minute and excruciating detail and, between yawns, the therapist wrote, 'DECREASING CIRCLES OF SELF? Soya milk PROTECTOR VS PROTECTED? onions, cracked wheat EFFECTING – pilates six p.m. Don't forget breathing exercises! – VS AFFECTING.'

Despite these occasional hiccups, a speed-reading of the therapist's notebook makes it difficult to disagree with Tom's assertion that the two years of the relationship at LMT were the most . . . the most *what*? Tom inserts the word 'comfortable' at this point but an objective observer might find a simpler word like 'successful' more useful. And, if you believe the weight of evidence from the case notes, the main reason for this was Murray.

Murray was Tom and Karen's spice, the piquancy, the zest, the consciousness, the added value. All successful couples have it; a shared passion of philosophy, activity or sex (even all three, if some show-offs are to be believed). Tom and Karen had Murray. That is not to say that they didn't share the other things too but, in the aftermath of their split, almost a decade down the line, Karen couldn't help but notice how those passions had faded in Murray's absence.

Such transference may sound implausible but, for his part, Tom must have agreed because look how your story of the relationship (third-hand via Tejananda's scribbles from Tom's reminiscences) concentrates on anecdotes about Murray.

Murray was entertainment and, for their last two years at LMT, Tom and Karen indulged in Murray-fun – individually, as a couple and with Tariq too. Murray-fun? It came in all sorts of different forms; planned and spontaneous, momentary and drawn out, safe and dangerous, pointless and pointed, kind and vicious and utterly delicious.

Tom told Tejananda about the confidence tricks. Like games of Find the Lady on Holborn street corners where Murray would deal the cards and he or Tariq played the stooge. Murray's fingers were deft and his timing immaculate and he took cocky American exchange students for up to a ton. But sometimes he liked a mark's style, especially if they were a made-to-measure sucker, and he'd deliberately lose all his winnings and more besides and he seemed to get off on the expression of bemused pleasure on the mark's face as he or she tucked away a fat roll of tenners.

Or what about the Antiques Trade? This was a convoluted scam which began with Murray buying a knackered carriage clock or dusty painting or some other nick-nack from a junk shop for a fiver. Then he'd put on a dark suit and black tie and wander into a quiet, mid-morning pub. He'd order himself a Scotch, lay down the clock, say, on the bar and engage the landlord in conversation. Generally the exchange went something like this.

'Can I get a bit more ice, china?'

'Sure.'

'Ta.' Pause. Nod. Shake head. Swallow. Sigh. 'Don't suppose I could ask you a favour, could I?'

'You can ask, mate.'

'Well. Thing is, I'm on my way to a funeral. My granny. St Mark's/Joseph's/John the Divine down the road . . .'

'Sorry to hear that.'

'Thanks, china. But it's not like we were close or anything. She was a typical old Jamaican/Italian/Irishwoman, all patois and plantain/memories and moaning/pope and potatoes, and she never forgave my old man for shacking up with a white woman/my mum for marrying a Libyan/me for lapsing, know what I mean? So I hadn't seen her for years. Anyway, point is she left me this tatty old clock. To be honest, I'd like to just bin the stupid thing . . .'

'You can't do that, my son. She must have wanted you to have it. You'd never forgive yourself . . .'

'No? No, china. Guess you're right. But I don't really want to take it to the funeral with me, do I? I know it's small but the fucking thing weighs a ton. So what I was going to ask is, any chance I could leave it here for an hour or two? I mean, not for long. I'll just go to the funeral and sandwiches after and I'll be back to pick it up this afternoon.'

'No problem, mate. I'll just stick it behind the bar.'

'You sure? I don't want to put you out.'

'No trouble at all.'

'Thanks, china, I owe you one.'

During the lunchtime rush, a couple of hours later, one of the others went into the pub, smartly dressed and carrying a briefcase. It was usually Karen because the combination of her newly dreadlocked hair and the sombre attire achieved exactly the right mixture of bohemia and business. She sat at one end of the bar and ordered a sandwich and a mineral water. Then, after ten minutes or so, she noticed the clock and called over to the barmaid. She just wondered where it came from, she said.

The barmaid shrugged. She'd never seen it before. She called out back. 'Barry? Young lady here wants to know about this clock.'

Karen then examined it under the landlord's curious eye. She hummed and hahed and asked if he'd consider selling it. He shrugged nonchalantly. 'Why? You think it's worth much?'

'I'm not absolutely certain,' Karen said. 'I'll have to get my boss to have a look at it but I'm pretty sure it's a Westphalen.'

'A what?'

'Westphalen. Swiss, 1920s, hand-made. They only made a couple of dozen.'

'But it looks like junk.'

'I know. Pity that this one's not in great nick. But you must have felt how much it weighs.'

'Yeah, I have as it happens. I know it's small but the fucking thing weighs a ton.'

'Exactly!' Karen nodded and smiled. 'You can always tell a good clock by its weight, its . . . umm . . . mechanical density.'

'Right.' The landlord scratched his head, mulling it over. 'So it's worth a lot?'

'Tell you what. You let me nip out to the cash point and I'll give you 400 quid for it right now.'

'Four hundred?' He chewed his thumb, lips and gums. 'I thought you said they only made a couple of dozen?'

'They did. But, as you said yourself, it looks like junk.'

'Right.' The landlord thought for a minute and then came to a decision. 'Sorry, love, but I don't think I want to sell it. Been in the family for years, know what I mean?'

'Fair enough.' Karen sighed, took a scrap of paper from her pocket and jotted down the digits. 'Tell you what, though. If you change your mind, call this number.'

'Yeah? All right, love, I'll have a think about it. You never know, I might just give you a bell.'

Murray came back into the pub around twenty minutes later. The landlord greeted him with a smile and asked him how the funeral went.

'Depressing,' Murray said and held his jaw in one hand as if the recollection still troubled him. 'And now I'm going to stare at that bloody clock for the next five years feeling too guilty to chuck it out.'

'I'll take it off your hands.'

'What's that, china?'

'I said I'll hold on to it. I mean, if you really don't want it.'

Murray pondered for a moment before shaking his head. 'Nah. I can't do that. It's like you said, I'd never forgive myself. I mean, the old girl must have wanted me to have it. Like you said.'

'So let me buy it off you.'

'Buy it?'

'Yeah. I mean, I quite like the look of it. I buy it off you and then you can buy something nice to remember the old lady by. She'd like that. I'll give you a hundred quid for it.'

'A hundred?' Murray laughed. 'It's not worth more than a fiver.'

'But I like the look of it and with a hundred notes you can buy something really nice, know what I mean? I don't want to rip you off, now do I?'

Murray shrugged. 'OK.'

Presumably, later that day, the landlord called the number on the scrap of paper and got straight through to Sotheby's. Presumably, for a heady second or two, he really thought his luck was in. Karen always gave Sotheby's number. For some reason it tickled her. If Tariq was playing the expert, he gave the number for Scotland Yard. With Tom it was always Westminster Council's refuse department. Although none of them ever actually heard the phone call being made, there was definitely something pleasing about personalizing Murray's gag a little.

At first they worked this scheme in two or three pubs near the LMT campus around Farringdon. But in their third year Tariq moved to student digs in Archway and Karen chose a college room in Southwark Hall on the South Bank; so they spread their net wider, north and south.

On one occasion when Tom posed as the expert buying, in this instance, an amateurish watercolour of Lymington harbour, he swaggered into the pub to find a community policeman discussing alarm systems with the landlord. He turned straight round. Murray, who was waiting outside, was livid and insisted he go through with the plan. According to Murray, the presence of the law only improved the whole situation. 'It'll make it seem more legit,' he said. 'You think some copper's going to know shit about paintings?' Eventually Tom agreed to go back in and he pulled off, though he said so himself (and to everybody else), the performance of his life.

Later, while Tariq was counting the money, Tom said, 'Of course, I would never have done it if it hadn't been for Muz.'

Murray raised one eyebrow. 'It's a game. You don't just stop playing when you don't like it. Games have to be finished. That's the point of them. They're self-contained.'

'I was just saying . . .' Tom began but Murray was shaking his head.

'You are what you do, china. So if you don't do it? You're . . . Well . . . I don't know what you are.'

In fact the Antiques Trade was a rare manifestation of Murray-fun that might be described as explicitly criminal. But, the way Tom told the story to his therapist, when Murray first set out its mechanics for his friends, this actually seemed to bother him more than the rest of them. Usually nerveless and single-minded, he was clearly uneasy and it was the others who talked him round.

For her part, Karen was apparently unbothered. 'It's a scam,' she said. 'It works on the greed and dishonesty of the landlord and if they're greedy and dishonest enough to give us a hundred quid then that's their problem.'

Murray smiled. 'I never had you fingered for such a crook, Kazza,' he said.

Tom logged Murray's expression as number fifteen and commented, unthinking, 'She went out with Kush for years. She's used to breaking the law.' Then, without even needing to look at her, he dropped his head and said 'Sorry' because he knew that she hated any mention of her ex. Especially from him. Karen tutted and shook her head irritably. In a way, of course, Tom was right. Because her morals were of the overreaching variety, big issues that needed demonstrations and placards rather than the trivia of interactions that, in her experience, always required pragmatism and a little manipulation.

Tom was the complete opposite. He made no outward complaint about the plan but, at some hidden level, the prospect of such a brazen con filled him with doubts to match the thrills. So he justified it aloud, to himself as much as the others. 'We're not telling any lies,' he said. 'We only say the junk *might* be worth a lot of cash. We never say it *is*.'

As for Tariq, his enthusiasm for the Antiques Trade was altogether simpler. As far as he could tell, Murray's scams were his only source of income and, if this stopped him scabbing a tenner every Friday night, then that was good enough for him.

Some hours after one session with Tom, Tejananda the therapist flicked idly through his case notes. In the margin of an early page he found he'd scrawled the following: 'moral compass with behaviour as magnetic north rather than vice versa? another example of *fin de siècle* (or, perhaps, *naissance?*) malaise. possible magazine article.'

Despite the cryptic nature of this scribble, Tejananda knew precisely what he'd meant and he suddenly felt quite deeply moved; so much so that he felt compelled to take a break from his work to drink a cup of green tea and write a postcard to the orphan he sponsored in Tanzania.

Generally, Murray-fun was naughty at worst. Walking along the street with Tariq, he saw two beat coppers coming the other way and he caught Tariq by the arm, pointed at the policemen and shouted 'Run for it!' at the top of his voice before scarpering in the opposite direction. Tariq, utterly bemused, ran after him because . . . Well . . . because he did.

Murray kept to the main road until he was sure the cops were following and then he ducked down a sidestreet and immediately stopped.

When the police caught up, Murray seemed surprised by their attention. 'We're just playing It,' he said. 'I saw my kid brother and I thought he'd spotted us.'

'Are you having a laugh, sunshine?'

'Yeah, china,' Murray said. 'You?'

He was only arrested once, by a heavy-handed scumbag who figured he might be able to do him for some or other misdemeanour. And didn't Murray love that? Especially when a uniformed inspector forced the PC to apologize through gritted teeth. 'I am sincerely sorry for my mistake.'

'What mistake was that?' Murray asked.

'For assuming you were fleeing a crime scene.'

'When, in fact, as I explained to you, china . . .'

'When, in fact, you were playing a game of tag.'

'It,' Murray said. 'It was It. No problem.'

He loved that.

Once Murray headed to the Wandsworth Arndale Centre armed with a dog lead and a pair of dark glasses. Within minutes, he had twenty people searching vainly for his guide dog and shouting 'Behemoth! Here boy!' at the tops of their voices. He persuaded the mall's manager to make an announcement over the tannoy: 'If Behemoth is anywhere in the precinct could he please meet his master at the information point.'

Even Tejananda, spiritually centred as he was, graciously admitted the comedy in the set-up.

Once, Murray challenged Karen as she was coming out of the Our Price on the Charing Cross Road and he asked for her autograph so ostentatiously that a small crowd soon gathered. Laughing, she signed for him and, as Murray backed away, he was accosted by a chubby couple with Brummie accents and turquoise shellsuits. 'Who's that?' they asked.

'Karen Miller.' Murray brandished his autograph proudly.

'Who?'

'Karen Miller!' he enthused. '*The* Karen Miller.'

'Karen Miller?' the man said. 'Right.'

'She looks smaller in real life,' Murray said. 'Doesn't she?'

The woman agreed, nodding her head. 'Not as pretty, either.'

But Murray's favourite games were rarely one-offs and some – the Antiques Trade, Cop It, The Race Card and Knock Down Ginger (a bizarre bar piece involving vituperative rants against a supposed illuminati of redheads, left-handers, albinos and the like) – were tweaked, repackaged and re-enacted on numerous occasions. One, Strangers on a Train (Murray's undoubted favourite) must have gone through at least fifty versions.

Strangers on a Train was, in Tom's opinion, the very archetype of Murray-fun, conjuring amusement from a simple premise (in this case, the captive audience of a tube carriage). It worked like this: Murray and whichever henchmen he chose would get on different carriages of the same train. Then, a couple of stations later, they would meet up as strangers and, with Murray as ringmaster, play out a scenario (sometimes rehearsed, sometimes improvised, sometimes a one-liner and sometimes a devilishly complicated vignette). In one situation where Tom, with Murray as the nudging friend, chatted up Karen, you could almost feel the carriage's collective heartbeat swell with the innocent charm. Three stops later, Tariq joined the carriage carrying a bunch of flowers that Tom apparently bought off him for fifty quid and, offering them to Karen, he seemingly broke her shy and flattered resistance.

Tom and Karen got off at the next station, hand in hand.

But Murray liked to stay on the train to watch the middle-aged women fold their arms, unconsciously holding themselves, and the businessmen who looked suddenly distracted and the couples who leaned intimately against one another.

Other scenarios included the one where Murray posed as an itinerant preacher-cum-healer. This worked particularly well during his beard-growing phase. He restored Tom (wearing the Arndale Centre shades) his sight in front of a public that, depending on how Tariq and Karen geed them up, could be astonished, incredulous or spiteful.

Then there was the deaf argument, in which Murray and Tariq silently confronted each other across the carriage in ever more ostentatious and aggressive sign language that the other passengers couldn't ignore. Tom got on a couple of stops later and, after a minute or two's thought, he started signing in an apparent attempt to mediate the disagreement. At first Murray and Tariq would watch him, mollified. But then, just as the train entered a station, he threw some outrageous gesture and they turned their anger on to him and began pushing and then slapping him around. By the time the doors opened a three-way brawl had erupted and they bundled out on to the platform, kicking and punching and wrestling until the train pulled away and they could lie on their backs, out of breath and bursting with laughter.

They loved the way this little narrative was played out in complete silence, the way any background chatter was quickly suppressed by the volume of their movements, the expressions of the other passengers who could only communicate their confusion in sign language of their own – raised eyebrows and shrugs and darting glances.

Murray's enthusiasm for Strangers on a Train seemed limitless and he could surely have conjured endless scenarios if the others had shared his verve. But the game required such exhausting showmanship that, by the second term of their final year, it had petered out. Besides, by now, they had other things on their minds.

Tariq was running the student ents pretty much full-time; booking bands, organizing club nights and setting up all kinds of bar promotions. It wasn't that he was particularly *into* it but it allowed him, he said, to develop his 'entrepreneurial skills' with a view to the future. He had tried, unsuccessfully, to get an MBA place for the following autumn so he had signed up instead for a graduate training scheme with Phillips ('Just for a couple of years, to learn the ins and outs of business'). His ents work also allowed him to drink pretty much full-time and he was beginning to develop what Tom later christened 'the twirtysomething London body'; round shoulders, concave chest and a ballooning paunch.

Karen was kept busy both by her conscientious attitude to her studies and her growing involvement in all kinds of student pressure groups. After the previous year's marches during the Gulf War, she now chaired APT (Anti-Poll Tax) Action, SAL (Students Against Loans) and DRA (Date Rape Awareness) and she orchestrated the protests against visiting lecturers. Initially, this last exercise was intended only to scupper the planned visit of Norman Tebbit but she soon found that the majority of invited speakers could be regarded as politically unsuitable for one reason or another. This was democratic liberalism at its least democratic and least liberal.

Generally Tom accompanied her to these demonstrations and meetings. He wasn't all that bothered by these 'issues' himself but he liked to be at her side and watch her passion and, especially, to see the awe with which she was regarded by her fellow students. Karen was very much the leader, the firebrand, and he couldn't help but take vicarious pleasure in her status.

Tejananda's notebook is mostly filled with précises of Tom's stories but there is the occasional direct quote. One is from their last session; from the same day, in fact, that Tom ran into Murray in Trafalgar Square. 'When I met her, she had, like, a boyfriend who beat her up and . . . a fucking perm and pixie-boots, know what I mean? But by the time we left college she was, like, on this committee and that committee. And she had, like, dreadlocks and a nosering. And that was down to me. It was. It was down to me.' Beneath this outburst, the therapist has written, 'TEARS. RECRIMINATIONS AND GUILT? FAITH AS DEBT? NB replace tissue box.'

Of course, when he wasn't so angry, Tom did acknowledge Karen's converse influence over him. After all, if it hadn't been for her and her colourful umbrella of a social conscience, would he really have applied for a PGCE? At the time this had seemed like something to be grateful for. In retrospect, when he bent over the coffeetable in the flat he couldn't afford, filling in all the new paperwork he couldn't fathom, it sounded more like an accusation.

Approaching their finals, it was only Tom who found time to see Murray regularly (partly because he knew that teacher training didn't require a top-notch degree). They saw a fair bit of Tariq, too, but that was more by virtue of the latest version of Murray-fun: peddling pills at student nights.

The con was simple. These student events were relatively well-policed with the college contracting a local firm for external security. But, with Tariq working behind the scenes, he was always at the venue early and he could carry in Murray's supply. When Murray arrived, he picked up the drugs and pushed them at ten quid a pop, handing on a pound's commission to Tariq for every sale.

The first time Tom saw Murray dealing, he was shocked.

Because there was a difference between, say, scamming some greedy landlord and pushing drugs, wasn't there?

Murray had just come off the dancefloor and they were standing in a corner of the Union bar when two nervous first years approached, identically dressed in smiley T-shirts and stars-and-stripes bandannas. Tom watched astonished as Murray produced a couple of small cellophane bags from his pocket. 'You want to buy a vowel, china?'

'Two Es,' one of the students said and handed over a twenty.

When the deal was done, Tom exploded: 'Jesus, Muz! What the fuck are you doing? Dealing drugs? Shit!'

Murray peered at him quizzically. In the darkness of the bar, Tom could hardly see his face but, as the spots flashed, he caught a glimpse of his laughing eyes. 'What's this, Mr Superhero?' Murray hissed. 'An attack of ethics?'

'You're no different from that fucker Kush!'

'Yeah?' Murray laughed. 'Let's go talk to Tariq.' He caught Tom by the arm and almost frog-marched him to the office where the promoter was lounging behind a desk, his eyes sleepy, already hammered.

'Hey,' Tariq slurred. 'How's business?'

'You knew about this shit?' Tom exclaimed. 'Shit!'

Murray handed Tariq a fistful of crumpled fivers. 'Tom Dare's on the moral highground,' he explained. 'Got a touch of vertigo.' He sat on the corner of the desk and turned back to Tom. 'Look, china. Just shut up a second and listen. All right?'

The students turned up at college and they were getting into raving, weren't they? Buying everything from the ethnic pants to the mix CDs to the fluorescent bloody T-shirts. But this lot at LMT? They were just typical Home County Sloanes or Arabs or middle-classes from the burbs or wannabe travellers; so what did they know? Basically they just wanted to get pissed but, since they'd started hearing about, listening to, *getting into* acid house, they thought they should probably start dropping a few sweeties: Doves, Rhubarbs & Custards, Pink Calis, Strawberry Trips, Disco Biscuits and Snowballs.

'Peer pressure,' Tariq said. 'So Muz provides a service.'

'By flogging them class As?' Tom protested.

'It's just aspirin,' Murray said. His smile was broad and confident; smile number one. He opened the door of the office, beckoned Tom over and pointed to the dancefloor that was a mass of thrashing limbs. 'Look at them, china. They think they're high. High on life more like. High on *life*. It's a beautiful thing.'

'And lager, of course,' Tariq said and burped into his hand.

'Yeah. So I provide a service. Give them the illusion of excitement, keep them off the hard shit and maybe even help their hangovers into the bargain.'

Tom still wasn't convinced. Not until Murray said, 'I don't even tell a single lie. I say, "Do you want to buy a vowel?" And if they say "A", they get an aspirin or Anadin or anti-histamine and if they say "E", they get an E-Lax.'

'E-Lax?'

'A laxative.'

Tom stared out at the teeming bodies that lurched into each other, apparently wired. He started to laugh. 'Cool,' he said and he took half Murray's supply there and then and began to deal himself. He gave Murray all the profits because he didn't really need the money and, besides, that made him feel a little better. Because he was only doing it for the spice, because it was funny.

A month or so later, the pair of them were sitting opposite each other in the canteen. Behind Murray a bunch of oyster-voiced Sloanes were joined by a baggy character with a Madchester haircut and a parka.

'Hey, Frankie, man. What happened to you on Friday night? We all went back to Henry's for coffee and a smoke.'

'Don't talk to me about Friday, know what I mean? I was sorted. Completely fucking sorted. You wouldn't believe it, like. Had, like, four Es and went back to my room, like. So I'm sitting there, high as a kite with Joy Division on the headphones and, you know what? Next thing I know, it's four hours later, like, and I've only gone and fucking shat myself.'

'Are you serious?'

'Serious? Course I'm fucking serious. They were some blinding pills, man. Blinding.'

Tom and Murray looked at each other. Murray raised an eyebrow. 'Blinding,' he said and they both cracked up and laughed so long and hard that Murray couldn't finish his drumsticks for his aching guts.

Of course, the drugs scam couldn't have worked indefinitely. They dealt with the (admittedly rare) complaints by refunding the money and blaming a 'dodgy batch' but the students, even the Sloanes, were getting more suss and someone would have twigged in the end. It didn't matter. By now, it was a couple of days before the end of the year and, as Murray said, 'So you'll go and be a teacher, Tariq, some kind of business bigwig and Karen will find someone to pay her to organize storms in teacups.'

'What about you, Muz?'

'What about me, what?'

'What are you going to do?'

'Me?' he shrugged. 'Somebody's got to look out for you lot, haven't they? When you need someone to knock you into shape; know what I mean?'

Tom let this go. It was typical Murray. 'Hopefully it won't be a full-time job,' he said.

'You never know, china,' Murray smiled. Number five. The most winning of them all. 'You never know.'

So the story you're telling of the first two years of Tom and Karen's relationship (which includes Murray – 'BILATERAL' says the red ink – and Tariq too) reaches its conclusion on their last day at LMT. This was an important day for numerous reasons. It marks, of course, the end of Tejananda's case notes – although this day took up four sessions and thirteen pages of his notebook – concluded by the words 'SELFISH FAITH', which labels, unknowingly, the following year of the relationship (coinciding with Tom's PGCE). But it also marks what Tom and Karen denoted as their second anniversary, the day that Kush was released from prison and the last time any of them saw Murray for a decade.

It was a Thursday. Tom had packed up his room the previous night and spent the whole morning running around, choosing presents. He picked up a bottle of Moët and a bunch of daffodils. He also bought *St Elmo's Fire* on video because he knew she didn't have it. He'd always wanted to get her some underwear but he'd never quite dared. So today he bought her a pair of edible knickers. Just for a joke.

He was supposed to meet her for lunch in the canteen but she didn't show up. After about twenty minutes he started to ask around. Cecily from the SAL Committee hadn't seen her. 'But there was some bloke looking for her,' she said.

'Some bloke?'

'Yeah. This massive guy with a shaved head. Didn't look like the kind of person Karen would know at all. I told him to try Southwark Hall.'

'Shit,' Tom said. 'Kush.'

Karen had told him a month before that Kush was up for early release. But today?

Tom sprinted to the station. He could feel the champagne

bouncing in his rucksack. The flowers made it hard to run so he dumped them in a bin. He caught the Northern Line to Waterloo. On the train, a middle-aged woman with a walking stick stared at him. At first he thought it was because he was so jumpy. Then he realized he vaguely recognized her. It had been one of the games of Strangers on a Train about six months earlier when Murray had apparently restored his sight. He remembered her because she'd got quite worked up and begged Murray to cure her arthritis. But today he didn't appreciate her attention because he was so sick with nerves and unformed fears and, when he got up at Waterloo, he felt like he had to justify himself. 'I saw you staring,' he said. 'I was blind and he made me see.' He didn't know what he was saying and the woman looked upset.

He two-timed the steps out of the station and ducked away from the crowds down to the South Bank. He glanced up at the sky and weighty clouds were banking over the skyscrapers and the rising breeze made him blink. The atmosphere was, he thought, perilously prescient. Was he going to make it there before Kush? Whatever. This time, if there was a beating to be taken, he swore he was ready for it.

Southwark Hall was a gated compound right on the river. In the evenings, it was often busy with *cognoscenti* theatre-goers shortcutting to the National but, at this hour of the day, there was no one around. There weren't even any students. Tom figured a lot of them must have already left for the summer.

As he crossed the flagstone courtyard, he realized he had no idea what he was up to. If Kush was there, what was he going to do about it? And what would Kush want? Tom pictured a stir-crazy thug dragging his ex out by the hair and beating her senseless. Was that realistic? Kush probably wouldn't show up at all.

The door to Southwark Hall was opened by a keycode. Tom knew it by heart but the door was latched open. His stomach dropped and his imagination immediately rewound exactly two years to another hall of residence on the other side of London. This time Karen's room was on the ground floor – a third-year privilege – the first on the right. The door was shut. He knocked.

It was a couple of minutes before Murray answered. He seemed surprised. Not half as surprised as Tom. Nor as relieved. He was smoking a cigarette. That was unusual but not unheard of. He was wearing a T-shirt and jeans, no jumper, and his feet were bare. He looked a little dishevelled but Murray always looked a little dishevelled.

'Muz!' Tom exclaimed. 'What are you doing here?'

'Kush got out today.' Murray took a drag on his cigarette. The smoke lingered between them, picked out by the shaft of light from the open front door. 'I heard he was round the university, looking for Karen. Thought I'd better get down here, china, know what I mean?'

'Thanks,' Tom said. 'Right.' He looked at Murray curiously. There was something in his manner. An edginess. 'You all right?'

Murray smiled without teeth. 'Cool. I thought you were Kush, didn't I? Thought things were going to get hectic.'

'Right,' Tom said. 'Where's Karen?'

He walked past Murray and they clashed shoulders for a second because Murray didn't get out of the way. There was a short, shadowed corridor (the tiny en suite loo and basin on the left) which opened up into Karen's room. Tom looked around. The double bed was unmade and crumpled. The desk under the window had been cleared for the end of term. One of Karen's bras hung from the back of the upright chair. That wasn't like her. Tom felt like he was seeing the room for the first time. It seemed somehow unfamiliar. There was a smell in the air; a mustiness. It was probably just the smoke. Although she had an occasional cigarette herself, Karen hated people smoking in her room. Tom had a nagging sensation in his middle. He knew what it was but he tried to ignore it. He was being stupid.

Murray followed him into the bedroom. 'She's in the shower,' he said. 'She was crying. Worried, I think. She wanted to take a shower. To calm down.'

Tom nodded. The communal shower-room was at the end of the ground-floor corridor. 'Why was the door shut?'

'What's that, china?'

'Why was her bedroom door shut? If she's taking a shower . . .'

'In case Kush showed up.' Murray went over to the window. It was one of those modern ones with double glazing and several ways of opening. Murray tilted it a little. 'The smoke. You know how she hates the smell of smoke.'

'I know,' Tom said and sat on the edge of the bed. His hand stretched over the undersheet. It was warm. He began to feel a little sick.

There was a knock at the door and Murray hurried to answer it. His movements were curiously uncoordinated; lurching and clumsy. What had happened to his usual poise? Tom could see Karen silhouetted in the doorway. She was barely covered by a small towel that was wrapped around her breasts. Another was turbaned around her head. Instinctively he looked at the full-length mirror with the hooks beside it. Sure enough, there was her dressing-gown; a huge, soft-towelling cream bathrobe with a hood like a boxer's. He'd bought it for her last birthday. It had been a thoughtful present; to keep her warm to and from the showers.

Karen shuffled into the room, one arm clasped across her

cleavage. Her face was pink and her expression taut but she flashed him a smile. 'Hiya!' she said. It sounded like such an impersonal greeting; vacuous, with open-ended jollity. Tom couldn't speak. She grabbed the dressing-gown and disappeared to the en suite to dry herself and put it on.

Murray was leaning against the wall. He produced another cigarette and lit it. Where the hell did these cigarettes come from? He'd never owned a pack in his life.

Tom shivered. He felt physically cold and detached, like he was watching himself on a security camera. And when he spoke, it was as if he were hearing his own voice on the radio or an answering machine. 'What's going on?'

'Sorry, china?'

'What have you been doing, Murray? What the fuck have you been doing?'

Karen emerged. She had a towel in one hand and the other ran through her locks, untangling them. Her face was its usual porcelain again but there was still a flush around her neck and jaw. She stood next to Murray. 'What are you talking about?'

'You, Karen.' Tom turned his attention to her. 'What game are you playing? You think I'm stupid?'

'Now wait a second, china.' Murray was holding up a hand. 'I came down to keep an eye on Kazza. You've really got the wrong end of the . . .'

'Oh, fuck off, Murray. Just get out. Go on. Fuck off. I don't even want to look at you. Get out.' Tom could hear his voice shaking. He was amazed it had any control at all. Murray glanced at Karen. 'Don't even fucking look at her, Murray. Just get out.'

'No,' Karen protested. 'What's the matter with you, Tom? You're being an arsehole. *You* get out.'

Tom felt a sudden pain behind his eyes. Tears. He didn't want to cry but there was something about the removal in

Karen's tone. He'd heard it once before. When Kush had trashed her room. Two years ago to the day.

Murray said, 'It's fine. I'm going.' Karen touched his arm – a gesture that twisted Tom's guts – but Murray added, 'No. It's cool. I'm going.'

Tom found himself starting towards him. 'Yeah. Get the fuck out, Murray. I don't want to see your face again, Murray. Don't come near her. You hear what I'm saying? I never want to fucking see you again. Never.'

When Murray was gone, Tom and Karen had the fight to end all fights. Tom kicked it off with all the macho vigour and incoherent ranting of the typical cuckold. Karen kept shouting at him to leave, to just leave. But he said he wasn't going anywhere until she gave him some kind of explanation. Karen seemed to calm down a bit and there was the shadow of a smile on her lips.

'Are you laughing at me?'

'Explanation of *what*?'

'You and Murray.'

'There is no "me and Murray".'

Tom couldn't believe she denied it and he talked about the dressing-gown, the smoking, the way she'd greeted him, the bed that was still warm with their bodies. Karen was shaking her head. What? So those minutiae of behaviour had nothing to do with the fact that her ex might come round any moment and knock seven bells out of her. Oh no. They meant she was fucking Murray. Of course they did.

Tom was getting desperate. 'What about that day at the Curzon?'

Karen stared at him. Her expression was bewildered; blank like Clapham Junction billboards. 'What the fuck are you talking about?'

It was about half an hour before Tom started saying sorry.

And he kept on saying sorry for a little more than a year. Sometimes he meant it and sometimes he didn't. Sometimes he wondered how his evidence could have seemed so certain and sometimes how it had been so easily refuted.

It was only in therapy that Tom finally figured it out. At their last session, Tejananda suggested, 'Perhaps they did have an affair. How would that make you feel?' He chose his words carefully. 'After all, you yourself . . . strayed . . . in the end.'

Tom thought about this for a moment and a guilty nausea welled in his belly. 'No.' He shook his head. 'No. I don't think so.'

'Do you think Murray was the kind of person who'd have an affair with his friend's girlfriend?'

'Yeah,' Tom said quickly. 'Yeah I do. But . . . it's funny but that only makes me more certain that he didn't. Because the way we were, the three of us, she'd have told me in the end. Definitely.' And he realized this was the first time he'd believed that unequivocally.

Of course, the real point about all this – and the reason you're telling this story (courtesy of Tom via his therapist) is that, after Murray left Karen's room on their final day at LMT, they didn't see him again for ten years. Initially Karen blamed Tom. But when he said, 'What? You really think anything I said would have had that much effect on Murray?' she had to concede he had a point.

'I guess that's the thing about Murray,' she admitted. 'He was always such a chancer.'

And what about Kush? After all, it was his release from prison that triggered this Moment of Truth (from the subject's perspective). Well. He never showed up, did he.

14
What goes up must come down

Do you object if I take a ninety from the narrative thrust and detach myself like a sulky coochie from the flock (who's just dropped the squirmiest squirm into the reservoirs at Barnes, say, or lost the handsomest geez to some harlot rival with no charms but a coy coochie coo)? After all, I never set myself up as a war historian, chronicler of chaos or top-storey storyteller so this process is as novel to me as it is no such thing to most niks. And that is imprecisely my point.

In the aftermath of consciousness, it is no surprise that the more cerebral geezs – if you can use such an adjective of a vanitarious species with acorns for brains – looked to nik knowledge for explanations of the here and now (which had, of course, before Trafalgar, been indistinguishable from the there and then and the where and when too). I have already said that 'consciousness is a blessing in disguise' but, the way I scope it, the niks know that better than anybirdy – or at least did so once upon a time – and that's the verity.

Consciousness is as raw as the Thames at Tilbury in a November nighttime so no wonder they dress it up in all kinds of winter woollies. Let me illuminate it like this (and nuts to the niks because I can be a feisty fuckster given the right thermal to think upon): do you peep more about a peepnik from his thoughts or his threads (and I'm not just beaking about his logos but his *logoi* too: the stories that he tells about himself, that are told about him, that unravel in his every gesture and affectation)? It's his threads, right? So cash savouries conceal themselves behind high walls in Hampstead as surely as streetnik desperadoes conceal themselves like genies in Bethnal Green bottles and poor blaxens slide past questions with more questions (like, 'You think I give a shit?') while city slicksters slide past answers by sliding CDs into multichanger car stereos that provide other answers (like, 'All you need is love, doobedoobedoo').

If memory is about fear and fear is about loss then most niks have figured out or had figured out for them by a collective unconscious (and isn't that a phrase that illuminates pinpointedly?) that the easiest solution to the hazards of now, then and even when is to forget and the very first thing to forget is how to think. And that is to say, therefore (as the loquacious coochie Gunnersbury might have it), that, in this city, the prognosis for peepniks is procrastination; to forget exactly what it was that made them niks in the first place. So what am I saying? I'm saying don't look down on me from your comfy cumulus when I tell you that us pigeons proved ourselves to be just the same. After all, we've got threads of our own. We're a feathered species so it's no wonder we're feather-brained.

The verity is that it's the consciousness of consciousness that matters rather than consciousness itself. Look at it like this: four fat oldgeezs with breasts that brush the Tarmac of a park playground peck up peepnik crumbs and the like and beak on about god-knows-what. A febrile feline with a frenzy to feed is circling but these arrogant chubsters are saying things like, 'Who does this puss-puss think he's going to catch? There's no cover in the concrete and we'll fly in a flash.' So they let that Tom narrow their angles, pick a pigeon and poise to pounce. And when he does pounce and he catches his prey in his Tomcat chops, you can be sure (because this is what a bird-brained oldgeez is like) that the pigeon will squawk, 'But I can fly! I can fly!' And if the Tom has anything more about him than bloodlust, sun worship and a love for his own anus (which, let's face it, he doesn't), he'll reply through a mouthful of cartilage, joint and feather, 'Not now you can't, geez. Not now you can't.' And he'll have a point, too. If you're not going to fly when it matters, you may as well be flightless. Without consciousness of consciousness, you're barely conscious at all.

I've already explained that my understanding of time is about as efficient as a squib's first mindmap of their locality. Nonetheless I remember the day, hour, minute . . . No! *Instant* when I was fully (and I mean consciously) conscious for the first and, so it seems, only time with pinpointed exactitude.

I was soaring high above my home roost, middle of the day, scoping the bow-wows below with their sweet mistresses and keeping a beady eye out for any RPF renegades who might be straying my way. It was London beautiful with a cut-glass sky and breezes that tickled your feathers as you surfed them but nothing more exceptional than that.

Suddenly, like an air shooter's crack (and haven't I heard a few of those in my time?), it happened. What *it* was I can't say but I can tell you how it felt. It felt like time accelerated and slowed, space expanded and shrank and sound was cacophonous and particular all at once. I could see everybirdy – and I mean everybirdy (peepnik and pigeon) – rushing past me, above me, below me, through me without a sideways, upwards, downwards or inside glance. The noise was like thunder; not a clap but a round of applause, a standing ovation, an 'Encore! Encore!' But even as they zipped by like so many fleas and flies so they moved in slowtion too and I could hear their every question: the whys and wheres, hows and whos and, most numerous of all, the 'What the fucks'.

Then (or, rather, when; or, rather, at exactly the same time) I caught my breath and before (or, rather, when; or, rather, as) I knew it, I'd sucked everywhere into my meagre pigeon breast and I felt like I was sure to choke. The dome of St Paul's, the Thames Flood Barrier, the British Museum, the London Eye, Battersea Power Station – all my favourite perches, all the places the peepniks seem so proud of – were pressing against my lungs so I blew them out just as fast as I could. But as I blew so they accelerated away from me beyond the horizon until I was left squawking, 'Come back, come back', no better than a squib to his coochie-momma. Even as I heard my own call I scoped I was short of breath and I felt like I was drowning in the middle of the vast ocean of everywhere and I ducked my phyzog under my wing just to hear the reassuring pip-pip-pip of my pigeon heart.

And then? And then it was over and I looked down and saw the same bow-wow below still chasing the same stick and the same sweet still fiddling with the straps on her babchick's perambulator.

I was fuddled and flummoxed, believe you me, but there were a few things that I knew to have verity and they weren't facts so much as forebodings. First, I figured that choking on a squirm in your home roost is no different to drowning in a Thames tide. Make of that what you will. Second, I reckoned that being everywhere was no different to being nowhere and I was surprised to surmise that this probably applies to all the other 'every's and 'no's too. Third, I heard from a little bird who tweet-tweeted in my ear that the consciousness of consciousness is both power and weakness right there. If consciousness is a blessing in disguise then the consciousness thereof is a wolf in sheep's clothing; only this wolf has been dolled up like Dolly for so long that, these days, he'd rather run with the flock than acknowledge his wolfish nature. And this, whether you scope it as inadequately metaphorical or adequately oratorical, leads me to precisely the spot I intended.

After this brief exhilaration of the consciousness of consciousness, what do you think I did next? Did I hunt it down again like the superlative rubbish bin that you occasionally observe in an obscure London square? Did I humbly contemplate the weakness and power therein or the implications of both thereof? No. I needed the fellowship of the flock so I called out to Acton29, a gossiping geez, who was perched in a nearby willow next to Ealing423, a dull hulkster who flew a whole lot faster than he thought. Let me tell you something: if Trafalgar provoked the consciousness of consciousness, there were still plenty of pigeons who could have learned a thing or two from a sparrow and Ealing423 was one. He had all the brains of a squirmy squirm that's been peckchopped in half so many times that it's basically – however Gunnersbury might try to aphorize – all anus.

Acton29 was beaking all kinds of birdshit about a coochie I may have mentioned called Finchley440. Finchley440 was a harmless little number who gooned over Gunnersbury like a nik youngen with a crush – Gunnersbury coos, 'Fly!', she coos, 'How high?' You know the type. But Acton29 had got his tailfeathers in a tangle and no mistake.

'Who does that mangy coochie think she is?' he was squawking. 'Following Gunnersbury around like a squib on its maiden flight? Track-stopped like an idle pigeon at a peepnik window? Anybirdy would think she was somebirdy the way that one carries on. But she's not. She's a mangy nobirdy, that's what. Finchley440? I mean, that's all you need to know right there. For starters, she's hardly a Surb at all. And apparently, after Finchley16 got squishsquashed by twenty tons of North Circular Nissan, that bird-brained coochie started calling *herself* 16 like nobirdy would notice.'

Ealing423, who was, when you think about it, caught on the loose talon of an insult, squawked precisely zilch. And me? You think I set Acton29 as straight as the crow flies? You think I even flew above it and shut him up with the expression of my exhilarated experience? Then you haven't been following. No. I bathed in that birdshit as happy as a starling in a sandpit.

After Trafalgar, a schism surely divided the London pigeons as a lightning crack divides the sky and two armies (Surb and RPF) slowly squared up to each other like two thugalicious hulksters haggling over who owns the pot to piss in. But just because us Surbs shared a loathing (and, perhaps more pertinently, the definition therein), that doesn't mean we were what you might term united any more than the peepnik haves and have-nots. In fact, it was no time before we splintered into cliques and coteries that bigged up and did down mainly on miniscularities of prestige and reputation that hadn't even existed a matter of weeks (or months) earlier. We were, you might say, spinning threads of our own because while birds of a feather may flock together that surely doesn't mean that they all see eye to eye.

Of course, I'd like to tell you that I took a bird's-eye view of this pigeon pettiness but that wouldn't be the verity. And doesn't that leave me with one ding-dong of a dilemma? Even as I beak on, you see, I feel the words slipping away from me as though I bury each one with its utterance. I'm desperate to get this out but I'm struggling to remember why, let alone hit upon how. I hazard it's partly for all pigeons but partly just to coo, 'I am. And I am me,' before it's too late and the particularities of language have lapsed once again to nothing more meaningful than 'cluck, cluck, cluck' and 'squawk, squawk, squawk'.

The way I illuminate it, the veritable consciousness of consciousness may be an enlightened and benighted state but that's not to say there's no sliding scale which ultimately descends to the dull selfishness of instinct. I see it in us poor pigeons, of course, and I see it in the peepniks too: one moment you're a deity who is both at one with and looking down on London all at once, the next you're no more than a pick 'n' mix of genes that are flapping to fight their way out of your bag of bones. And I'm no deity; not any more. I'm but a spit from a dumb animal; another gormless geez for whom 'better' and 'worse' are just binary finery crammed into my chromosomes.

Once upon a time (weeks or months ago), I'd have put this fate of affairs down to the unilluminable nik I named Mishap; because I'm still sure he's at the root of all this as surely as I don't know why or how. But now I begin to wonder whether the consciousness of consciousness is something like a state of grace which, once achieved, will ineffably degrade and this fact is as defiant and definitive as the failings of our flesh and the rhythm of our heart (personal, peepnik and pigeon) that hears its final drum roll even as the egg cracks or the umbilicus snaps. Is it, therefore, our capacity that defines us or our footling failure to fulfill it? The niks know nut all, trapped as they are on terra firma, and they couldn't envisage the verity even if they so chose. But us birds can fly as high as we want (or near enough) and there's one thing we know with certainty and its implications for us are, as you can imagine if you engage your mindeye, far more pertinent and pernicious than for the peepniks. What we know is this: what goes up must come down. As simple as that.

That very same nighttime I winged it to Tooting Common. To be veritably veritas, I wanted to be close to the Remnant of Content, our idol of what's been lost (and, if you think about it, are idols ever else?). If that illuminates something for you, feel free to fly with it.

I circled a couple of circles with an eye out for RPF renegades (because we didn't want their spotters to spotlight our stash) and then settled on the branch next to the hole that held our fragment of the unilluminable stuff (a hole that some gullible geezs had already christened 'the shrine'). It was a moody night; the kind when shooting stars signify solipsistic portents and every breeze whispers the same. My feathers were ashivering and no mistake.

'Ravenscourt?' Gunnersbury was sitting on the lip of the hole. Her phyzog was all surprise and I hazard mine was the same. She looked like I'd just dragged her out of Nod without a by-your-leave and there was something about her manner, a vulnerability to be veritas, that made her seem, at least to my amber bead, even more perfectly peachy (like that's possible).

'I was just checking out the lies of the land,' I cooed, soft like an oldgeez to his favourite squib. 'I wanted to make sure it was safe. The . . .' For some reason I was struggling to strike the right word. 'The shrine.'

Gunnersbury made a noise that seemed to gurgle right out of her gizzard, somewhere near a laugh, I hazard, and her phyzog flicked towards me infused with some semblance of something. 'You too?' she warbled. And I didn't know what to make of that.

An observation: peepniks are putty-featured creatures whose phyzogs are chock-full of expression. For example, when a savoury says, 'I love you', or some other sentimental schmaltz, scope his eyes because if he doesn't blink you can bet he's a fibbing fraud. Or when a sweet says, 'No, I haven't just fucked your best friend' (or, more likely, words that add up to the same), scope the twitch of her lips to know the verity: none and she's innocent and angry; plenty and she's unsullied and upset. But a little twitch followed by a conscious stiffening? You may as well ride your cock horse all the way to King's Cross for a poke of paid pathos. You didn't know that? Like I said, pigeons watch peepniks for fun and probably know nik nuances better than the niks themselves. Whatever. The point is that the appearance of us birds is capable of no such subtlety so if a pigeon with a penchant for the palimpsest (peachy coochie or not) is suffering the delusions of allusion, you'd best ask for some straight squawking.

So I said to Gunnersbury, 'What's that supposed to mean?' And I figure she felt the frankness of my call because she looked away and ducked her head, coquettish like the heroine of a motion flixture.

Then she started beaking. 'Ravenscourt,' she began. 'You're a faithful geez, aren't you? I mean, when the tick tocks you're not going to flee the flock. A faithful Surb geez through and through, that's you.'

'Faithful to what?' I clucked dubiously. To be veritas, I figured she'd found a god complex, which is easier than you might think for us birds, who can, after all, shit on most things from a great height.

'Exactly. To what? That's the nub of it, the point of the pin, all right. To what?' She extended her wings and flapped them a couple of times. It was an idle movement, like she was vanitariously scoping her own span. 'You were there, Ravenscourt. You scoped the scrimmage, that starling geez Regent and the frenzy in my own feathers. You witnessed me fight over the Remnant of Content and you know this is no shrine but mere symbol at best. You're no moonatic; you figure what's going on even if you can't illuminate it. You figure it was just a pebble in a pool and the splish-splosh turns to ripples and even they iron themselves out in time. You figure all those bird-brained fucksters only put me on the bird-table, in the spotlight, because they don't know what else to do. But scope it like this: somebirdy's got to make sense of this even if there's no sense to be made, you accord?'

'I scope that you've started to credit your own dawn chorus.'

'Yeah? You reckon? So what you doing in this neck of the woods that's a fair old flight from your home roost?'

That got me. 'I don't know and that's the verity,' I cooed, soft and low. 'What's your excuse?'

Gunnersbury beaded me then and her beads were glinting: 'I'm on the nighttime watch. Guarding our Remnant of Content. Guarding our shrine. Because I can't get a geez to do a gig I won't do myself, can I? And tomorrow I'm leading a bin raid right into the heart of the Concrete jungle. The way I scope it, us Surbs deserve all the nik niblets and best bits of the city bins, Ravenscourt, and we'll show Regent and his RPF rabble that they can't scare us off with spotters squawking above the bridges. You accord? Can you gulp that through your gizzard, geez? Because I want you at my right wing.'

'Why?'

'Because you're a faithful Surb geez, my friend.'

'But why are you leading a bin raid?'

'Because I'm a leader and London is ours to win.'

'Right you are,' I murmured. 'Right you are.'

After that we were silent like the city.

To be as blunt as a woodpecker's beak after a month in the Concrete, I don't know how you've got me pigeonholed. Maybe you scope me as a gullible geez or maybe a well-intentioned do-gooder who thinks too much and knows too little. Then again perhaps you just think, 'He's a rat with wings. Why should I give a flying fuck?' Up to you. Because the thinking tricks of a few mixed-up niks are like water off this duck's back. But however you've got me figured, there's one verity I come back to with the regularity of a homing pigeon and you're just going to have to take it on trust.

Everybirdy wants to follow. There; I've said it. Everybirdy wants to follow, whether physically or metaphysically, and when the carcass has been stripped it all comes down to faith. In an ideal world, you'd want to follow somebirdy or something that you knew inside out and upside down and back to front too. In an ideal world, you'd want to know – and, more than that, *understand* – history, personality, cause and suchlike. But this is not an ideal world so, as fly comes to fall, you just want to follow. So now you know.

You can love that or you can leave it but it won't stop it being veritas. And I'm one geez who does give a flying fuck. And prior to passing pedantic judgement you might want to verbalize this verity too: I give a flying fuck and, more to the point, I can.

15

Reality. Television

It might seem surprising how easily TV Ami was convinced.

They met at the Kensington end of Hyde Park. Ami had just been at her agent's office. Since the end of her stint on the Weather Channel, she'd been in there most days, walking the fine line between pushiness and desperation, confidence and panic.

Emma called her on her mobile out of the blue. Ami seemed distracted. She was sitting on one of the leather sofas in reception, pretending to read the *Stage*, and pulling smiles at the hasbeens and wannabes who came in and out – eighties comedians clutching corporate-video scripts in nicotine-stained fingers, brassy former soap stars who were these days all slap and no dash, reality-TV rejects with makeover outfits and wide eyes, and male-model types with puckered lips, particular profiles and T-shirts that revealed the line of hair from navel to crotch. The real stars? They never went to see their agent. Oh no. Their agent went to see them, in fashionable restaurants, private members' clubs or boutique hotels that were themed around Barbarella or Gaudi or Grand Central Station.

'Ami? You there?' Emma asked.

'Yeah. Sure. How are you?'

'OK. Tommy's playing up. I think his milk teeth are sore.'

'Really?' Ami soothed. 'It must be so difficult for you.'

Emma was mildly irritated. What was that supposed to mean? She found that most people talked to new (or newish) mothers exactly how they talked to their babies so that words mattered far less than tone of voice. 'Who's my little man?' became 'How are you coping?' and 'You're my little man' became 'It must be tough'. They might as well just coochie-coo at you. Just because you'd had a kid, it didn't mean you couldn't think straight, did it? Or maybe it did.

'Look. I just wondered if you fancied a coffee some time.'

'A coffee? Sure,' Ami said vaguely. 'That would be nice.'

'Where are you?'

'Now? Kensington. With my agent.'

'Kensington? Really?' Emma checked her watch. 'Actually, I'll be there in about half an hour. I'm picking up some . . . some stuff for Tommy. You want to meet?'

Ami's shrug was almost audible. 'Sure,' she said. 'Why not?'

At the other end of the phone, Emma raised her eyebrows at Murray. He nodded.

The four of them – Ami, Emma, Murray and Tommy in the pushchair – walked up past Kensington Palace, past the gates where a sea of flowers once lapped in memory of Princess Diana. Ami was chattering about her meeting. Her agent had seemed excited, told her he had really good news, got her hopes up. But then it turned out to be nothing more than TVX offering her another series as the 'croupier in a bustier'. 'I mean, soft porn?' Ami exclaimed. 'On cable?' She'd told her agent she'd have to think about it.

Emma was barely listening, just making the right noises. And not just because she could do it too. No. She was thinking about the time she and Tariq had come here a couple of weeks after Diana was killed. It wasn't like they'd cared. It had been Tariq's idea, a thoroughly honest act of morbid curiosity. She liked that about him; his brazenness.

They'd been here at dusk, stood in this very spot and stared at the flowers and the people who kept silent, candlelit vigil: middle-aged men with alcohol-bulbous faces, mothers with teenage kids, elderly couples in scarves and overcoats with brass buttons. The way they'd been talking on the way there, Emma was scared she might laugh which, in retrospect, seemed ridiculous. Because, in fact, she was ambushed by a bubble of sadness that slowly swelled in her stomach until, much to her surprise, she couldn't stop it bursting in a sudden series of choking sobs. She'd wept like a baby though she didn't really understand why. It certainly wasn't for Diana. If anything, she was weeping for herself, for the brief, gaping immediacy of her own mortality. She'd buried her face in Tariq's shoulder and he squeezed her tight and didn't say a word.

Now, Emma remembered the overpowering stench of the flowers; sickly sweet, the olfactory equivalent of a dress in orange and aqua or too many marshmallows. She remembered how it had seemed so appropriate, the scent of beauty putrefying. Now that she was thinking about it, she appeared to be able to conjure that smell as if it had hung in the air around here for the last few years, unaffected by changes in weather or the nearby expulsions of millions of car exhausts. But this smell seemed slightly different. In addition to the sweetness, there was a hint of musky warmth.

Emma found herself unconsciously sniffing. She looked at Ami, who was still chattering on about her career or lack thereof, and wondered if she could smell it too. She recalled Tariq's retort whenever she accused him of farting in bed. 'That's your top lip, Em.' The thought prompted a quick internal smile.

She turned to Murray who was pushing Tommy at her side, and she suddenly, sickeningly, realized the smell was coming from him. It wasn't strong and it wasn't dirty but it was definitely there, a smell somewhere between sex and death that reminded her of the day they'd . . . She felt like she might gag.

Ami was saying, 'So, Murray. What are you doing here in the middle of the day? Shouldn't you be working? I know Em's just a housewife but what about you?'

Murray shrugged, 'You know me.'

'Not really,' she said and she attempted a laugh but it sounded uncomfortable.

They pottered on in silence for a bit after that. Ami glanced up at the sky and saw the sun manfully trying to poke his head out from behind a cloud. Scanning left and right, she noticed how grey everything looked. This was hardly a revelation. Though she'd lived in London all her life, she'd travelled enough to know that this was the most colourless city in the world, in which even the trees and flowers had the faded quality of a black-and-white photograph. This wasn't a metaphorical observation, either; rather a seemingly intrinsic feature of London's washed-out light (though that didn't, of course, negate the possibility of an apposite metaphor). She took a couple of deep breaths. Maybe things weren't so bad. After all, if celebrity was a ladder then her problem was that she'd chosen only to look up and never down. There were, she knew, a whole lot of people who would die to be in her shoes and, when you looked at it like that, it made you feel a little better. It's important to enjoy where you are as much as you'll enjoy where you want to be, Ami thought, and she congratulated herself on her perspective.

She looked around and consciously appreciated the sight of baby Tommy snoozing in his pram, the Swedish couple snapping pictures by a statue, the Lycra buttocks of a fit guy who jogged past grunting like a caveman and, oddly, holding an umbrella like a relay baton. Simple things. She enjoyed the crunch-crunch of the gravel path underfoot, which sounded like chewing muesli. Unfortunately, as soon as she thought that, she began to think about the chimps in pyjamas – 'What

do your little monkeys eat for breakfast?' – and she remembered how she'd been mistaken, more than once, for the
girl in the advert; a girl who was certainly more famous than
her (for being in an advert!), probably younger and already
playing a mother. She began to feel miserable all over again.
Something had to change.

Tommy woke up and started to grizzle so they sat on a
bench to give him a bottle: Ami, Emma and the baby, and
Murray; all in a line.

'I'll take him if you like,' Murray suggested.

But Emma said, 'It's fine.'

'Really.'

'No. Really. It's fine.'

Ami asked if either of them had a spare cigarette. Emma
said, 'I didn't know you smoked.' She didn't, not really; just
fancied one. Emma nodded. She didn't have cigarettes anyway; hadn't smoked since she got pregnant. Murray didn't
have any either.

Then Murray leaned forward and said to Ami: 'So we're
going to rob this bank, then.'

'What?'

'This bank. For Em and Tariq. It's all planned.'

Ami laughed. 'Yeah, right.' She could really use a cigarette.

Murray was staring at her. 'What do you mean, "Yeah,
right"? We all agreed. And the whole thing depends on you.'

'Me?'

'Yeah,' he snapped. 'You. You're going to be "on the inside",
remember? It was your idea.'

Ami was slightly taken aback and her smile became a
stuck-on expression. She tried a scoff, 'I thought Emma was
on the inside too.' But Murray shook his head. 'Not any more.
Plan's changed.'

She didn't really know what Murray was on about, nor

whether to take him seriously. She'd never seen him aggressive and that confused her all the more. I mean, he had to be having a laugh, right? But it certainly didn't look like it.

Murray shook his head in an exasperated way and said, 'Em?' Like he was appealing to her for reason.

Their plan was unfolding exactly as anticipated and it was Emma's cue to take over. But she nonetheless felt uncomfortable as she passed him her son, contentedly suckling on the rubber teat. Murray got up then and walked a little distance away, rocking Tommy in the crook of his arm. He was still shaking his head, apparently irritable, as if to say 'You talk to her'.

Emma moved closer to Ami on the bench. She took her hands briefly and then let them go as if she couldn't presume such an intimacy. Ami watched the way her bony fists clenched and unwrapped, clenched and unwrapped.

She explained it to Ami like this. Look. Things were desperate. They were going to lose their house, weren't they? No. Seriously. Lose their house.

'So you're going to rob a bank?' Ami said. 'You're winding me up, right?' And she tried a disbelieving giggle. But Emma was eyeballing her so intensely that it never made it out loud.

Ami! That was exactly it. That was exactly what they were going to do. That was exactly how desperate things had got. Sorry. Look. She didn't mean to snap but how else was she supposed to react? What would *she* do in this situation? Just sit around and wait for the bailiffs? Watch Tariq drink himself to death? Raise her kid in a *fucking* – Emma rarely swore but Murray had told her it would add conviction – council B & B? Tom had been right. A one-off job? They'd never get caught. Think about it, Ami, think about it. Please. Tom had been right. Never even be suspected.

Ami said: 'I'm sorry, Em, but . . .'

Emma covered her face with her hands for a moment. They were cool against her eyelids. Murray had said this would happen. And he'd said what would happen next.

Emma spoke through her wrists. It was fine. What was she thinking of? Sorry. Ami must think they'd gone completely crazy. She lowered her hands. They'd just had such a good idea, that was all. Trouble was it depended on casting Ami. It wouldn't work without her.

'What is it?'

What?

'The idea.'

No. Forget it. It didn't matter now.

'Really? You may as well say. What is it?'

Emma was smiling feebly. It was simple really. If you wanted to rob a bank, you had to have someone on the inside, someone who worked there, right? So they'd wanted Ami to get a job as a cashier. Something like that.

Ami said, 'Oh.' It didn't sound like much of a starring role. Emma continued.

But how was Ami going to get a job in the specific bank they'd targeted? It wasn't possible. Even if she got accepted, she'd probably have to do all kinds of training and placements and she might not even get posted to the right branch at the end of it. So they'd had this idea. Well. *Murray* had had this idea. Emma shook her head. Ami would probably think it was daft.

Look. She, Ami, was always saying how TVX wanted to break into terrestrial telly and were just looking for the right format. So why didn't she pitch them something? A reality-TV show based around real workplaces, a different one each week or maybe even one each series, depending on how it went. You'd set up hidden cameras around an office, say they were a new security system or whatever, and create a real-life soap opera. You'd see all the office romances, affairs and power games; find out who was nicking Julie's Slimfast from the fridge, that Trevor was downloading porn all day, that Mr Cunningham was cooking the books and fiddling his expenses, that kind of thing.

Emma paused. Ami looked completely nonplussed but she ploughed on regardless.

And Ami? She'd be the stooge, right? She'd be the viewers' point of access, the continuity, the mole, the focus, the *star*. If there was a story they didn't catch on tape? Ami could relate it in a piece to camera. But they weren't talking trash here, no way. This would be high-quality, popular programming. There would be sex, sure. But it would be *real* sex; not like Hollywood but justified and plausible. There would be comedy but you wouldn't be laughing at these people. Because there would be tragedy too and it would be human tragedy, *real* tragedy. Like when Annette's mum has a heart attack or Darren, the office junior, gets knocked off his moped. This would be real life, right? Only on TV.

Emma was watching Ami. She suddenly realized she was pushing the right buttons. Ami said, 'So what if they recognized me?'

Who?

'The people in the office.'

They wouldn't, would they? Emma smiled.

Then Murray stepped in. He was now standing in front of them but concentrating on the baby, persuading the bottle between his lips. Murray said that if she got recognized, she could make a joke of it, couldn't she? How she looked like that girl Ami Lester off the telly.

Ami said, 'Right. I could say, "That stuck-up bitch? No way!" Something like that.'

She looked to Murray for approval but he was still

encouraging Tommy to take a little more formula – You're not full, are you? Come on, china. Just another sip.

Ami turned to Emma. It *was* a good idea – a really good idea – but she still had some reservations; some queries about, you know, the exact format. Emma nodded. Of course she did. But that was hardly the point, was it? The point was to have a pretext to work in the bank. Ami looked perplexed but she still muttered, 'The bank. Yeah. Right.'

Emma reassured her. Because this was the beauty of the idea. All she had to do was convince TVX that the show had potential. She could explain to them that she just needed to do some research with the validity of a credible production company behind her. Like, in the first instance, all she'd want is to use their headed paper to write up a proposal and borrow a DVC. She'd take them to one of the businesses she was thinking of including in the show – a high-street bank, say – and explain to the manager that she just needed to test the water. Like, do a couple of weeks posing as a work ex. Something like that.

'What if he says no?'

But Emma just laughed. A bank manager wasn't going to say no to TV Ami, was he? She would stress the good publicity. She could say, 'It'll be good for me and good for you. Good for both of us.' The guy would think he'd died and gone to heaven.

Emma could see Ami was hooked; wanted to be, anyway. Ami said, 'But I'm never going to actually make this show, am I? Not if you're going to . . .'

No, no, no. Hold on. Because this was where it really got good. Emma glanced quickly at Murray but he appeared not to be listening – You're all right, china, aren't you? Lovely. Yum, yum, yum.

If . . . Emma began. If, for whatever reason, they didn't go through with the robbery, then the idea for the show was still a strong one and Ami would have lots of material to work with, wouldn't she?

'We'd have to pitch for a pilot,' Ami said. 'That's how it works.'

Sure. If, for whatever reason, nobody was interested in the idea, she'd still have blagged her way into the bank. So couldn't she sell the footage to *Channel 4 News* or somebody? As, like, a special report about lax security in our high-street banks. Surely that was just the kind of thing they'd go for on a slow-news day and it would help establish Ami as a serious journalist, wouldn't it? Like on *Tomorrow's World*. Or *Watchdog*. An undercover reporter. That kind of thing.

Ami was nodding. She was swallowing this, all right.

If, on the other hand, they did go through with the . . . you know . . .

'The what?'

The bank job. If they did, it would be all over the media. And look who'd be on the spot? Ami Lester, TV presenter, working undercover on her new project. And guess what? She'd have secretly filmed the whole thing on her DVC. She'd be a hero, an overnight celebrity. Even more of a celebrity, that is.

Emma said, 'I mean. When you think about it, what have you got to lose?'

Murray handed Tommy back to her with an 'I think he's had enough' and she nodded and absentmindedly burped her son over her shoulder. Tommy spewed up a little milk over her T-shirt which she wiped away with a tissue.

Murray was now rummaging in the pocket of his jeans and he pulled out a crumpled packet of ten cigarettes. 'Look what I found!' he announced and offered them to Ami. 'You want one?' Ami gratefully accepted and Murray lit it with a flourish.

He was squatting in front of her, his hands resting on the bench either side of her thighs. She had to turn her head a little to exhale, so she didn't blow smoke right in his face.

'I mean, Tariq and Emma . . .' he muttered. He looked sideways at Emma and nodded respectfully. 'Sorry, Em. But you really need our help.'

'It's fine. It's true,' Emma said quickly. And then to Ami, 'But, look, if you've got problems with this – like, moral problems – just say. I mean, I know it sounds kind of mad. If you just think it's wrong . . .'

'No,' Ami interrupted decisively. 'It's not that. Like you said, you're desperate and what have I got to lose? I mean, it's good for me too. Not that I'm selfish because you know I'm devoted to you and Tariq, Em. I'd do anything for you.'

Murray said, 'Devotion can *appear* selfish.'

'Exactly. So I'll talk to the guys at Tit TV a.s.a.p. After all, if we're going to do this, I ought to get on with it, right?'

'Right.'

'Right.' Ami flicked her half-smoked cigarette on to the grass nearby. She felt good.

They walked back down to Kensington High Street together. Emma remarked, 'We never even had that coffee', but Ami replied that she wanted to get into the production company that very afternoon, to make a start. Murray said he was going to stroll up to Notting Hill and visit Freya's shop. He asked Emma if she wanted to come but she thought Tommy was looking a little tired and they ought to head home.

'Look at that!'

It was Ami who spotted the pigeon beneath an exhausted and unhealthy-looking sapling and they stopped to investigate. The bird, a tatty-looking creature with uneven feathers and what could only be described as a limp, was repeatedly circling the slim trunk. But it wasn't the bird's movements, odd as they were, that caught the attention so much as the bizarre, palsied twitches of its head and the low grumbling sound that seemed to emanate from somewhere deep within its breast. And it continued its narrow circles, again and again, as though this road to nowhere was its only hope.

It really seemed to bother Ami. 'What's it doing?' she exclaimed. 'It looks demented. It looks so weird; so, like, *human*. I mean, what's going on with the pigeons in this city?'

Murray was shaking his head. 'It's lost its mind,' he said quietly.

They watched it for a while, fascinated in spite of themselves. God knows how long it had been beating this path and god knows how long it could stay at it. People jogged, hurried or strolled past. Some threw the three of them a curious sidewise glance but none stopped.

Emma said, 'Have you noticed how many people are carrying umbrellas at the moment? Even though it's OK weather.'

Ami looked around and saw she was right. 'Yeah. I saw that earlier. There was even a jogger holding one. What's that about?'

'I don't know. Tariq reckons they're worried about the pigeons and want to have something to beat them off with. It's like when everyone's freaked by terrorism and all those people buy gas masks. I mean, it makes sense really. The pigeons are being really weird.'

'*Fucking* weird,' Ami said and then she giggled. 'But carrying a brolly? As a weapon? Shit! When did that happen? London's gone crazy.'

'It's amazing what people can get used to,' Murray observed. 'Even think is a good idea.'

They stared at it a little longer; like they expected the pigeon to do something else, add a little quirk to its already quirky performance. But it just continued its deranged patrol around the tree trunk; grumbling to itself like an old tramp or bag lady.

Eventually Murray said, 'Let's go.'

But Ami protested, 'But what are we going to do? I mean, we can't just leave it.'

'Do? What do you want to do?'

'Maybe we should tell someone. Aren't there park keepers or something?'

'Tell them what? "Excuse me, china, one of your pigeons has gone mental." Like he'd give a flying fuck.'

Emma said, 'He's right, Ames. There's nothing we can do. Come on. Let's go.'

'But it's suffering! Look. You can see it. It's suffering.'

Murray made a strange grunting noise. 'Join the club. We're all *suffering*. It's only a pigeon.'

'I just think it should be put down or something.'

Murray took out a cigarette and lit it quickly. Emma was watching him. He suddenly seemed fidgety, shifting from foot to foot. He took a sharp drag on his cigarette and twisted an arm back over his head like he was trying to reach an impossible itch. She wondered what he was thinking.

He walked over to the tree and squatted down by the pigeon. The bird didn't fly away or even appear to notice him; it just carried on circling. Murray said, 'Do you want me to?' the cigarette dangling from his lips.

'Want you to what?'

'Wring its neck. Only take a second.'

Emma made a yuk noise but Ami thought about it and said, 'We ought to do something.'

'Do you want me to or not?'

'I think so,' Ami said and then, 'Yeah. Go on. It's for the best.'

When Murray picked up the bird in his left hand, it suddenly squawked into life and began to thrash against his grip. Ami exclaimed, 'Shit!' and Emma unconsciously stepped forward, in front of Tommy's pram. Murray tried to grab the pigeon's head in his right hand but it was twisting this way and that, pecking and sniping. Eventually he caught it, wrapped his fist around the head and gave it a sharp yank. Its body fell limp.

'Are you all right?' Emma asked.

'Yeah. Just it bit me.' He scrunched his face and his eyes tight shut. 'Poor fucking thing.'

He tried to take his right hand away, to open his palm to show her. But when he did, the pigeon's head came with it, snapped right off the body and hung by its beak from a small wound in his hand. Emma gasped and Ami said, 'Jesus!' Even Murray looked a little disturbed, dropping the body at the foot of the tree. He carefully unpicked the beak from his flesh and Emma gave him a tissue, which he pressed into his hand. He shrouded the head in another tissue and then lobbed it into the nearest bin.

They were quiet as they began to walk away then Ami said, 'Do you think we did the right thing?' And Murray started to laugh. Emma and Ami soon joined in. It was kind of funny when you thought about it.

16

Pyaa-pyaa duppy

Freya Franklin Hats was tucked into the backstreets between Notting Hill Gate and Ladbroke Grove that estate agents had begun to call Westbourne Village. Freya had chosen her location well since the neighbourhood was up and coming and beginning to teem with small businesses bursting ambition. A graphic-design studio with glass-blocked front was cheek by jowl with an exclusive lingerie shop, all clean lines and somewhat clinical décor; an organic delicatessen that appeared to have been entirely furnished in hessian sat snugly next to an ethnic outlet selling cheap exotica from the four corners at phenomenal mark-ups. Freya had been lucky to sign her lease when she did because even her tiny space, broadened with mirrors, would now have easily exceeded her budget. Certainly, many of the area's longer-serving residents – generally immigrants of all creeds, colours and exotic tendencies – were already being squeezed out by the rising prices. Such is the nature of London, where bohemia is chased, even in its celebration, leaving only the most pallid ghosts of multiculture in its wake.

Freya Franklin Hats was busy. Or, at least, just about as busy as a boutique hat shop should get. Probably busier. Because it's not like we're a supermarket, Freya thought.

The 'we' was royal as she was still running the shop on her own and she was almost beginning to miss the empty days when she could take her time over coffee, ensure her book-keeping was just so, practise her latest mantra and fantasize about the glamorous customer who was sure to come in at any moment. Because now there was a steady stream through the door.

Some of them were indeed glamorous, or rich anyway (same difference; like the London borough of Kensington *and* Chelsea) but a lot were just browsing. There were dark-skinned Italian women, elegantly dressed with elegant friends, who pored over the quality of Freya's beadwork and stitching. There were Japanese women who were super-polite and spoke no English and could have been any age between fifteen and fifty. There were Americans with college T-shirts, blonde highlights and hockey players' thighs who asked, 'Can I get your stuff online? I *can't*? That's, like, so retro.' And there were English roses who bloomed in front of the mirror only to wilt as soon as they left the shop to be confronted by Jasper's breath and then Jasper – 'How are you, my dear?' – who, perhaps enjoying the new prosperity, seemed to have taken up permanent residence on the kerb opposite. Freya made a mental note to ask him to move on. Again.

Although the shop was busy, this busyness probably constituted no more than fifty customers a day. But the trouble with hats was that they, and those who tried them on, required individual attention. The way Freya saw it, a hat was the highest species on the evolutionary scale of apparel. A T-shirt was just a T-shirt. A top was a top, not a shirt. A pair of jeans, however fashionably labelled and personally styled, was still only a pair of jeans. Even a suit, bespoke tailored and lovingly individual, was nonetheless a suit. But a hat? Apart from shoes, whose function left little room for manoeuvre, and socks, whose every attempt at flamboyance led nowhere but embarrassment, hat was the only item of clothing that referenced just the part of the body it covered and nothing of its own nature or design.

What's more, for Freya, a hat's success or failure was always discovered in its wearing. Some designers seemed to view hats as works of art – sculptures of velvet and net, reed and plastic – that found their best expression in shop windows, alone. But Freya knew a hat could be measured only in its symbiosis with its owner; something which depended not just on the shape of skull or style of dress but also upon the confidence of bearing, the quality of smile, the tendons of neck in turning, even the bob of shy head. Consequently, before a sale, Freya felt compelled to elicit her customers' true nature right there and then on the shop floor. For how else would she know if her creation really suited? And she surely owed them that; both hats and heads alike.

A self-possessed, bright young thing, for example, could try on an effervescent marvel that bubbled berries and beads and look every inch the It Girl as she preened in front of the mirror. But what use would that be if she flailed in the breezes on the downs or flushed with her second glass of champagne or flopped beneath the gaze of a dozen men? So Freya would gently tease out her customers' insecurities as she teased the hat to its perfect angle. 'Because what's the use of a hat that only looks good in the bedroom?' she said and smiled reassuringly. Another sale.

Anyway. The point was that, after those first struggling weeks of sell-a-hat-pin, buy-a-latté, Freya Franklin Hats had undoubtedly picked up. But Freya was just too hectic to consider exactly how this might have happened, let alone the implications.

Of course, it had helped that the beret-wearing ethnocentric woman Murray charmed at Per-Verse had turned out to be a minor aristocrat in disguise. When not slumming it with slam poets, she was a Home Counties girl with a double-barrelled surname and plastic on Daddy's account and, the following week, she'd come into the shop with a wedding emergency.

Freya had done her proud with a creation of understated elegance with an unusual, irregular brim that granted a certain nobility to the woman's otherwise unfortunate nose. And Ms Home Counties was so thrilled that she recommended the shop to her friends and Freya became the marriage's main milliner, with no less than three hats featured on the pages of *Tatler's* 'Party Scene'. As Kwesi put it: 'Good job you came to my gig. And thank god Murray spotted the toff muff in mufti.'

Lately Kwesi had taken to hanging around the shop a lot and, oddly, that had helped too. His triumph at the CCC seemed to have done wonders for his confidence, though it was hard to tell how brittle this new shell might be or whether, as Freya considered it, it was largely a bedroom hat. But he'd certainly learned that manner was everything and self-possession was nine tenths of that law so he'd taken to leaning on Freya's counter with a street scowl on his face that he counterpointed by throwing warm, complimentary remarks and even the odd couplet of verse in the direction of the exclusively female clientele.

He'd been there when the ethnocentric toff muff came in and her evident delight at meeting Kwesi – the K-ster, K the poet – had encouraged him further; especially when she'd asked him in that champagne-and-oyster voice to 'drop some lyrical bombs'. He was only too happy to oblige and, following the visits of her friends, this became a regular feature of Freya Franklin Hats and countless wealthy women were utterly charmed by this cool black dude who offered them personal poetic praise at those daunting moments of heightened, hat-buying vanity. Truth be told, Kwesi generally trotted out the same lines again and again – stuff about 'porcelain skin and summer wind' and the hat as 'The soul's cap, the soul clap / Pause; applause' – but since the purchase of a hat, even for the recklessly rich, was a biannual activity at most, it didn't much matter.

At first Freya had been dubious about the benefits of Kwesi's soul claptrap but the response had been so unanimously positive that she'd bitten her tongue as customers bought her creations while buying into a perceived urban chic. Kwesi had even begun to talk about delaying his fast-approaching thirtieth-birthday retirement and both *ES Magazine* and *Time Out* had been on the phone suggesting they might feature Freya Franklin Hats in their shopping pages.

Freya remembered what Murray had said to her at Kwesi's gig. He'd been right, all she'd needed was a bit of word-of-mouth publicity to achieve the success that now seemed so rightfully – fatefully, even – hers. Where, very recently, London had been a fortified castle surrounded by a deep moat and guarded by elves and goblins who pissed on your head from the battlements, she now found herself standing on those same ramparts, looking down at all manner of peasants as, behind her, fine ladies in Freya Franklin Hats called her down to eat from the hog on a spit.

So the only trouble with this new position was that she was so damn busy. Her stock was selling as fast as she could make it and the nine-to-six flow of customers (ten to four on Sundays) left her no time to even glance at her business plan, let alone figure out how she might reschedule her loan or find a shop assistant with the necessary mixture of innocent candour and knowing bullshit. What's more, it didn't help that, apart from Kwesi, several other acquaintances had taken to regular visits as if she had time to burn.

There was Jasper, of course, and he proved a tricky tramp to shift, standing outside for hours at a time, quaffing Special Brew and attempting to engage every customer and passer-by in convivial conversation. He would move on with a humble bow any time Freya asked but he would always reappear within ten minutes or so; a cigarette butt between his fingers and that toothless smile curling his face like an autumn leaf.

In fact, Jasper wasn't too much of a problem since his manners were at least as unfailing as his stench. But Jasper's presence on the pavement often attracted Learie, the Jamaican with reputed voodoo skills, who had recently developed a new aggressive streak and begun to harangue all-comers in indecipherable patois.

On one occasion, Learie had got quite out of hand and well out of order with a smart woman of Arab appearance and Kwesi had taken it upon himself to try and sort it out. Unfortunately Kwesi's greeting – 'What's up, my brother? You cool?' – had only provoked Learie further.

'Brudda?' he'd exclaimed and advanced upon Kwesi brandishing a bottle. 'Ku pan bag-o-wire yout' come een like 'im stoosh bakra. Cho! If I still hef the bucky me hefe shot teeth in yuh, son, fe real.' And Kwesi had been forced to beat a hasty and uncomprehending retreat.

Aside from Jasper and Learie, there was also Big-In-Property Jackson. He'd come in a couple of days after the shop had opened. There was a church in the area that he was thinking about converting into studios, he said. He was passing and he decided to, you know, see for himself.

Jackson looked around the shop with what seemed like genuine interest: 'What's this? Felt? And you stitched the sequins?' But Freya couldn't take her eyes off the dressing on the end of his nose that sang absurdity above his button-down collar, double-breasted lapel and lilac silk tie. 'It's not as bad as it looks,' he muttered. 'They said it won't scar but there's always plastic surgery. At the end of the day, Nick Jackson'll do what's right for Nick Jackson.'

He took to dropping in every once in a while and, though she was busy, Freya decided she liked him a lot better since he'd lost a chunk of nose to a pigeon. Disliked him a lot less, anyway.

After one visit, Kwesi said, 'What's that guy want?'

Freya shrugged. 'Apparently he's working round here.'

'You reckon he's trying it on?'

'Trying it on?'

'With you I mean.'

'What? No way.'

'I hope not, Freya. I mean, the guy's scum. He's a no-holds-barred, self-important wanker. Definitely.'

'You don't like him?' Freya laughed. 'He's not that bad, K.'

The next time Jackson came in, he stood in the very middle of the shop and nodded approvingly while Freya was sat behind the counter, snipping a few loose ends off a new design. He said, 'You've got a good set-up here. You should let Nick Jackson introduce you to a few people some time, make a few connections.'

Freya said, 'Sure. Why not?' without looking up but she did wonder if Kwesi was right and maybe Jackson was trying it on after all. She dismissed the idea quickly because she was somewhat off men at the moment and wasn't up for a relationship. And besides, she didn't really have the time. But she couldn't help feeling flattered nonetheless.

Part but by no means all of the reason Freya was 'off men' and part but by no means all of the reason she had little time was that Bast was still pursuing her with thick-skinned vigour. He came by at least once a day, flopped into the one armchair (brown leather, distressed) and lounged like a lord; feet on the coffeetable, legs spread and groin to the fore. Absentmindedly, and occasionally chuckling, he flicked through the back issues of *Vogue* and *Glamour* that sat on the coffeetable. The armchair was meant for bored boyfriends but that's exactly what Bast considered himself to be.

He'd wait for a lull in trade and then leer at Freya over the top of his magazine until she felt compelled to speak first. 'What are you doing here, Bast?'

'Oh. Hey!' he'd exclaim, as if surprised to be interrupted in the midst of a fascinating article about clitoral versus vaginal. 'Just wanted to check you were all right, darling, that's all.'

'I'm fine. You working yet?'

'Me? Working? Just checking out some opportunities, you know how it is. Doing a few bits and bobs for Lucky.'

'You're dealing?'

'Bits and bobs, bits and bobs. Nothing permanent. So. Look. When are we going out again anyway? What's the plan?'

Gradually, Freya's dismissals of Bast's clumsy advances became ever more blunt. It went against her nature to be brutal, that's what Freya thought. But she told herself that she had a lot of stuff on her plate and he had to get the message, didn't he? So in the end, when the time came, she was as unarguable as a car horn. 'Look, Bast,' she spat. 'I don't want to go out with you today and I won't want to go out with you tomorrow and I'll never want to go out with you again. Do you get that?'

Bast shot a glance at Kwesi, who was desperately looking out of the window as if trying to read a receding number plate.

'So why did you hit on me?' Bast said quietly.

'What?'

'It was *you* who hit on *me*, remember?'

'I don't know . . .'

Freya's mind flashed back to the night she'd met him at the twenty-four-hour Esso. It had been the day the shop lease was finalized and she'd rung Tom, hoping to find some company, to celebrate; nothing special, maybe a glass of wine and a bowl of pasta. But Tom had said he was too busy with marking and lesson plans and he was all 'Sorry, Freya, but what can I do?' So she'd got drunk on her own and then stumbled down to the garage for an ice cream; a treat. Bast had been buying Rizla. He had some weed. He was there.

'I don't know,' she blinked coldly. 'I must've been desperate.'

Within ten yards of Freya Franklin Hats, Murray had to deal with two of these timewasters in quick succession. Bast clattered his shoulder as he hurried down the street but he didn't stop or say a word and Murray didn't either. Murray was too busy checking out Learie, tottering towards him with his eyes narrowed and suddenly sharpened like two pencils.

Learie walked right up to him until their faces were no more than licking distance apart. He swayed back to take a mouthful from his bottle of clear spirits and sluiced it around his teeth. Murray didn't retreat an inch but his expression flickered with something – an innocence, perhaps – which would surely have been unrecognizable to anyone who knew him. Learie's breath was hot and sour and his spit flecked Murray's cheeks and lips as he spoke. 'Yuh smell dat renk evil, bwoy, no true? Why else pyaa-pyaa, maga duppy come monks this new Babylon? Nah cut yai, man! I-and-I speak same tongue.'

'Babylon?' Murray whispered.

'New Babylon, star. *New* Babylon.'

'Me? Evil?'

Learie's face cracked into a rotten-toothed smile. 'No, man. *Babylon!* Yuh hear me? Feel no way, duppy! Feel no way!'

Freya was standing in the shop doorway. 'Murray?'

He turned and his face cracked into smile number one; the most trusted and least specific, the catch-all, lighthouse smile. He brushed past Learie and didn't look back. 'Hey!' he said and he peered inside as he gave her a hug. 'Check out all the hats! You could be anyone in a shop like this.'

She squeezed him too and thought nothing of his sharp intake of breath when her hands joined, tight around his back.

Murray stood back and checked her up and down. She was wearing a black suit, tailored and flattering. Her unruly dirty-blonde hair was strictly pulled back in a bunch and the pink of her throat looked like a delicate statement against her pristine white shirt. She appeared somehow older, reined in, professional. 'Look at you!' Murray said.

Kwesi was overexcited, like a kid seeing his favourite uncle come Christmas. His veneer of calm fell away and he gripped Murray's hand, saying, 'Cool, cool, man. You cool? Where you been?'

'Familiarity breeds contempt, china.'

He raised his eyebrows at Kwesi as if asking a question so Kwesi said, 'No, man. No. What you talking about?'

Murray laughed. He looked at Freya, who was now back behind the counter. It was the same look he'd given her when they met at her launch party and it was powerful enough to make her stomach lurch and she noticed her forearms were flushed and her heart fluttered. She didn't know why. There was nothing sexual in his look; but she still felt like she was being sized up, unwrapped for eating.

She peered deliberately out of the window. 'I don't know what's going on with Learie. He seems really screwed up at the moment. What was he saying to you?'

'Who?'

'The tramp. Outside.'

Murray blinked and wiped his right hand across his mouth. He then examined it curiously. Emma's tissue was still stuck to the beak wound. He said, 'I just saw that boyfriend of yours. What's his name? Bast?'

'He's not my boyfriend.'

'No?'

'That loser?'

'A loser?' Murray smiled. 'Right. And you don't want to mix with losers.'

Kwesi said: 'There's a new man in town, isn't that right, Freya? You remember that guy Nick Jackson?'

Murray shook his head. He slowly peeled back the tissue on his palm. The cut was black and wet.

'You remember, man,' Kwesi said. 'The geezer at Freya's party who got bitten by a pigeon.'

Murray shot Freya a glance. Her face was hot and she knew she was now blushing properly. She felt like a schoolgirl.

'Right,' Murray said. 'Right.'

Kwesi went out for a sandwich. Freya said she was OK thanks. Murray asked if K would be passing a proper food shop because he was peckish and fancied some chicken. Like, whatever there was. A corner shop might have wings or breasts vacuum-packed in cellophane. If not, there was always chicken roll.

Kwesi, who'd heard about Murray's peculiar diet but never thought much about it, said, 'Oh yeah. You only eat chicken, right? What's *that* all about, Murray, man?'

Murray looked at him and his eyes were dancing. 'It's about function, china. You know there's no such thing as a wild chicken? Free-range, corn-fed, battery-farmed; they're all raised to be eaten. It's their only purpose, you know?'

'Yeah,' Kwesi said. 'And that's why I'm vegetarian.'

'No, china. You've got to eat chicken. Otherwise what's it for? It's a question of respect.'

'Are you serious?'

'Totally,' Murray smiled. 'Imagine we were all like you. The nation would be drowning in chicken shit within a week.

Function, respect and responsibility in one bite-sized mouthful; it doesn't get any better than that. How many more reasons do you need? Then again, I like chicken.'

'What if I can't find any?'

'You can always find chicken, china. If they don't have any roll, pick me up some stock cubes. Or chicken crisps. I can always lick chicken crisps.'

Kwesi was laughing. 'You're joking, yeah?'

Murray looked momentarily confused. 'No, china,' he said. 'I like chicken. That's what I like. Chicken.'

When Kwesi left, Freya was immediately uncomfortable. The shop suddenly seemed very quiet and she felt like there was a lot of unsaid stuff between Murray and her that was just hanging out in the atmosphere around them; as real and as unseen as the exhaust fumes over Elephant & Castle, Swiss Cottage or any of those other big London junctions. But what 'stuff' that could be, she had no idea. Because she and Murray? They hardly knew each other. Nonetheless, she went out back to the little cloakroom-cum-office and put on a CD – the first that came to hand, a nondescript acid-jazz compilation; anything to drown out the sounds of silence.

Murray was looking over one of her hats, turning it in his hands like a potter. 'This is crazy!' he exclaimed and he'd picked on the very design of which she herself was most proud. It was a black rubber base, almost like a swimming cap, that extended in two licks to cover the wearer's ears (imagine, say, the sculptured shape of a Sassoon bob). The scalp, meanwhile, was covered with light aluminium chains that circled to the crown. It was part twenties society, part mediaeval helmet and part cyber chic. She was yet to sell one and she knew why: it was way too funky for her clientele. But personally, Freya loved it best. She figured it reflected her perfectly even though she knew she could never wear such a hat herself. And, while that appeared to contradict her whole theory (of hats and their owners), it only made her love the design all the more; as though it were in some way aspirational, as though one day she might become the kind of person who could carry it off.

Freya said, 'Thanks.' But her discomfort was growing. Murray's words, his manner, his . . . *being* . . . seemed oddly confrontational, although she knew there was no specific reason to make her think so.

Murray carefully returned the hat to its stand. 'It's good, china. You're doing pretty well, eh?'

'Yeah. Sure.'

Freya turned away. There was something about Murray that made her feel accused, defensive, as though 'doing pretty well' actually meant 'doing the devil's own work'. So she was relieved when the shop bell rang and two girls walked in chatting busily in French. Early twenties and wide-eyed with cheap handbags, she knew their type and she knew they hadn't any money to spend but she was pleased with the distraction nonetheless.

Freya went to help them. They said they were just looking, thanks, and began to try on one hat after another. Generally such behaviour irritated her – especially when she knew they were just messing about, killing time – and she could have politely got rid of them by pointing out prices and hovering over their every move. But right now she was happy to let them play and even encouraged them with appreciative chatter. She glanced at Murray. He'd swung himself up on the counter and he was swinging his legs, crossing and uncrossing them like a clown. He was poring over his hand again and Freya caught a glimpse of the dark circle in the middle of the palm, like stigmata.

The prettier of the two girls – all olive skin, blonde highlights and shocking-pink lipstick – had put on the cheapest hat in the shop. It was Freya's take on an Irish Walker, the traditional houndstooth material set off by an amber band embroidered with gold detail. The girl was posing in front of the mirror, laughing while her friend pulled faces at her. Freya felt suddenly nostalgic. She remembered when she'd had fun just trying things on, just for the sake of it. In fact, now she came to think about it, she couldn't figure when that had stopped being true. It must have been when the shop opened. She caught sight of her own reflection. A tired, thin-lipped, hardened expression was frozen on her face.

'*Superbe.*' This was Murray speaking. '*Choisissez celui-là. A n'en pas douter.*'

The girl looked at him: '*Vous êtes Français?*'

'*Non! J'ai passé du temps à Paris. Aussi en Belgique.*'

She nodded. At first she seemed unsure what to think, like maybe he was mocking her. But she had the confidence of one who knows no better and she inclined her head, coy and coquettish.

'*Vous trouvez vraiment?*'

'*Celui-là vous va à merveille,*' Murray said and then he smiled. This one was a dazzling number; a smile so bright it was like a sunrise that peeps over the horizon for a moment before suddenly washing the landscape in its brilliance. Freya felt another unexpected pang of nostalgia. Or perhaps this time it was jealousy because it was connected to the thought of how young Murray looked. And the girl? What else could she do but return the smile and buy the hat?

On their own again, Freya tried a laugh. She said, 'You're as good as K.'

'At what?'

'Selling hats.'

'I think you're doing all right yourself, china.'

'Getting there.'

'No. You're a success. You're successful. You've made it. Freya Franklin Hats. It's great. You must feel great, eh, china?'

Freya stared at him. She felt her temper rising and the fact that angry tears were beginning to needle the backs of her eyes only made her angrier still; as did Murray's continued contemplation of his right hand, pressing his left thumb into the palm and then squeezing his fist around it. 'Are you laughing at me?'

Murray looked up. Where moments earlier he'd been like an animated teenager, his face was now drawn, blank and exhausted and that just made Freya feel all the more bewildered. 'No. I just said you must feel great, china. And I meant it. You're getting what you want, you're where you want to be, doing what you want to do. You must feel great.'

'There's more to life than hats,' Freya said and she tried a weak and winning smile but it didn't work.

'Like what?'

'What do you mean "like what", Murray?' Freya snapped. 'Like believing in something. Like being a good person. All that stuff. What are you getting at? If you've got something to say just spit it out.'

'Selfishness must be distinguished from "true faith".'

Freya paused, confused. Then, 'What does *that* mean?'

'Like Tom.'

'What's like Tom?'

'Selfishness must be distinguished from "true faith".'

Freya chuckled and it came out just as bitter as she intended. 'What are you talking about, Murray? You sound like a five-pound guru. This what they taught you on the ashram? I'm just saying I need something to believe in. Yeah, Tom too. I don't know about you, though. Really I don't.'

'So that's why you fucked him?'

'What?'

'That's why you fucked Tom.'

'What are you talking about?' Freya was suddenly cold; bitterly cold and her skin was goosebumping and her breathing came in quick gasps.

'I'm just saying, china. That must be why you fucked Tom. I mean, you met him first, right? And then you met Karen. You knew they were going out. In fact, more than that, because they'd been together for years; they were, like, partners. But then something happened, an opportunity, a moment of truth. And you needed it. In that instant you said to yourself, "This is what I need."'

'It wasn't like that.'

'Right,' Murray nodded. 'What was it like?'

Freya was gaping at Murray and her eyes were icy and bright but her mind was lurching elsewhere: to her and Tom in that bar piping Sade; to the way he tugged at his hair, a nervous twitch; to the hand on her leg that said she was a good friend, a good listener; to the speed drinking for excuses and reasons; to her front door to call it a night; to her phone to call a cab; to her bedroom to call a spade a spade and to her bed to call him her boyfriend for just one moment. And Freya thought, It *was* what I needed and it *was* exactly like that. But, sometimes, when need and desire intersect, you call it love because you don't have another word for it nor another experience to set it against.

'Fuck you, Murray,' Freya said. 'Is that what you think? What the fuck's it got to do with you?'

'Nothing.'

'Who are you to judge?'

'I'm not. I'm not . . . judging . . .' His eyes were fixed on her but she couldn't read anything in them. They were glazed, distracted. It was almost as if he were half asleep, half dead, and he pressed his left thumb into his right palm again until he winced. 'I don't think ... any more ... I don't make judgements,' he said. 'I don't know how to. I'm just asking questions.'

'Well, don't!' Freya snapped. And then more softly, 'It's none of your business.'

Murray dropped his head for a moment and then drew a sharp breath that whistled through his teeth.

Freya said, 'What have you done to your hand?' And Murray held it up for her to see. Seeing it spanned like that, she was surprised by how small his hand was. The wound glistened but it was dark; more like a hole than a cut. It looked quite bad but Freya couldn't resist a sly laugh. 'You been playing Jesus again?'

Murray grimaced. 'A pigeon.'

'You and your pigeons!' Freya snorted. 'You had a tetanus shot?'

'No.'

'You'd better. They're dirty things. What were you doing?'

'Wringing its neck.'

'Right.'

'Ami asked me to.'

'You always do what someone asks?'

'Don't know, china,' Murray said. 'You?'

Freya reached behind the counter. She pulled out a white silk scarf that some effeminate City boy had left behind the previous week. She handed it to him. 'Here. Use that.' She'd never seen Murray like this; pitiful. She'd heard from the others, Tom especially, how Murray played to his audience, she'd even seen it herself. But she hadn't expected this. Was this just more – what was it Tom called it? – *Murray-fun*? Freya said, 'I'm not a bad person, you know? Really I'm not.'

And when Murray didn't reply, she asked, 'What are you thinking?'

He shrugged. He was wrapping the scarf around his hand. 'I'm not sure I think anything, china. People are what they do. The motivations can be good and bad and the results can be good and bad. But people are just what they do, as simple as that.'

'I guess . . .' Freya began. 'I just feel like a flower in the shade, you know? Like I poked my head out of the earth and I had to dodge the other buds and shimmy and crane until I could see the sun. But even seeing the sun, I look down at my stem and it's too long and twisted and fragile and it could be snapped just like that.'

She closed her eyes and pressed the heels of her palms into the sockets until she saw swirling patterns in purple and green and shooting stars. She attempted to picture Murray sitting just opposite her but found it impossible. Every time she tried to add features to his face, they turned out to belong to someone else – the lips of that newsreader, the nose of the bus conductor on the 94, the bone structure of some rapper jostled for position – until what she pictured looked like a photofit pasted on a police-station noticeboard.

She heard Murray say, 'At least you feel like a flower.'

'You're weird, Murray. You know that?'

He chuckled and she lowered her hands and now he looked completely different again: revitalized, radiating good health; his eyes sparkling and his lips twitching with good humour. Freya sighed and then, in spite of herself, she smiled. She didn't know why, it was some sense of an unknown and un-specific but nonetheless delicious absurdity. Murray returned her smile with interest.

Kwesi came back in then and Freya pretended to look at her watch and said, 'Where have you been?'

He said, 'Sorry. I was looking for chicken. There was nothing in the corner shop so I had to go all the way down to the supermarket.' He pulled a packet of barbecue thighs out of the plastic bag he was carrying and held it out to Murray.

'Thanks, china,' Murray said. 'I'm touched.'

He took the packet, tore it open and bit deep into a juicy chunk of flesh, sending chicken juice squirting down his T-shirt. He made a noise of appreciation that wasn't far from sexual.

'Do you have to do that in here?' Freya said. And then, 'Just don't touch any of the hats, OK?'

Murray squeezed out 'Lighten up' through the gaps in his bolus and Kwesi laughed, 'Yeah, Freya.' Freya smiled but she found it hard to lighten up when Murray ate like such a pig and his face, hands and clothes were already orange with the luminescent barbecue sauce.

He paused over his second thigh. 'So we're going to rob this bank, then,' he said.

'Yeah?' Kwesi's eyebrows were jumping off his forehead.

'Who's "we"?' Freya asked.

Murray belched into his hand. 'You, me, K, Em and Tariq, Tom and Karen.'

Freya was laughing. 'The magnificent seven,' she said.

There was a pause while Murray took a mouthful and Kwesi sipped – thoughtfully, he hoped – on his coffee.

'Why would we do that?' Kwesi asked.

'I don't know, china. Because Em and Tariq are about to go bankrupt and need our help. That's a good reason. Or how about a sortie into race warfare? I mean, for you, me and Tariq, my brother. Fight the power. That'll do, too. Or perhaps it's an act of artistic expression or a conscious rejection of the social contract or entrepreneurial spirit or post-millennial ennui. Or maybe – *maybe* it will represent an existential moment of definition. Maybe. Then again, perhaps it'll just be a laugh, you know?' Murray shrugged and smiled and he glanced at Freya. His teeth were orange-stained too. 'The important thing is that we're going to do it. As simple as that.'

Of happiness

17

Karen is sitting in a coffeeshop in one of the busy sidestreets between Blackfriars and St Paul's. She's just walked across the Millennium Bridge and her face is untypically pink, whipped by the wind off the river. She paused for a minute or two in the middle of the bridge and contemplated the view of each bank, dominated behind her by the monolithic magnificence of the Tate Modern and ahead by the cathedral's great dome. Although the bridge has only been reopened for a few months, this is already her favourite London spot.

In the summer of 2000, Karen and Tom had been among the throngs that trooped across this bridge on the day of its first opening and, when it started to sway so alarmingly, they clung to one another for support. It was closed for more than a year after that.

This morning Karen read an article about the bridge's design flaws in one of those free magazines that lay around the canteen at work. According to the article, the engineers had expected the bridge to be able to move a little; indeed such flexibility was part of its strength. But what had caused it to swing so much that the people crossing struggled to keep their footing? The answer, it transpired, was simplicity itself. Apparently the engineers had not allowed for the fact that the footsteps of a crowd of pedestrians will always tend to slip into synch: left, right, left, right. Consequently, as the crowd walked across the bridge to one drum, their unanimous stride pattern carried enough force to start it swaying. What's more, as it began to move so, with one mind, the crowd had to adjust their step in order to keep balance and thus accentuated the swing.

This little article was the catalyst to set Karen thinking and now, hunched over a table in this fish-bowl warmth, she can't stop. All kinds of different stuff; that free-range type of thinking when ideas come and go, in gangs, pairs and individually, like the passengers on a mid-afternoon tube to nowheres like Stanmore or West Ruislip.

When she sits down, the first thing she thinks is that she doesn't do this much; this thinking. She doesn't have the time. She wonders if this is an excuse but, on second thoughts, she realizes it's absolutely spot on. She's so busy. She works, she has meetings, she chatters to friends and acquaintances, chatters to Jared, drinks, smokes the odd cigarette, can't bring herself to ring her sister, catches the headlines, fucks occasionally, reads the same five pages of the same book every night for a month and sleeps easily and without guilt. She's so busy reacting; to a memo, to chatter that fuels chatter, to ancient, ill-concealed inadequacies, to war and terrorism, to impatient nudges and ultimately to the day's ineffable rhythm. She's so busy.

She remembers something Jared says, his mantra: 'Nothing *makes* you happy. Happiness is a by-product of what you do.' And she remembers Murray's riposte and the laughter in his voice, 'But you're happy, right?' Now, she doesn't think she believes in happiness. Then again, she doesn't think much.

Looking around, she is suddenly shocked by the décor; the pictures so formulaic you seem to see straight through them to the bare walls, the pine chairs with the check seat covers, the marble-patterned Formica tables. Though she has been into this very coffeeshop a dozen times before, she notices for the first time that it is furnished around a quaint golf theme located somewhere in fifties Americana. She is briefly fascinated by the idea that someone presumably designed all this – this peculiarly specific abstraction – presumably at vast expense. The anonymous quotes on the ceiling: 'The game of golf is a long slow walk punctuated by occasional moments of optimism, but generally characterized by crushing disappointment . . .' The words 'CRUSHING DISAPPOINT-MENT', 'OPTIMISM' and, indeed, 'GAME OF GOLF' are capitalized.

She considers all the suits and shoppers dropping in to this coffeeshop to revive themselves with Styrofoam highs and she is suddenly equally shocked by the hubbub; so many people with so many different things to say! She has a bizarre sensation that maybe she's been struck mute and if someone approached her now she wouldn't be able to form any words at all or, if she could, they'd be somehow cancelled out by the white noise. She knows this is fancy but she nonetheless considers the difference between the dumb and the merely silent. There is no difference, she concludes, until the silent choose to speak.

She wonders about Tom; what it was that made her call him. They've been apart for a long time now but, when challenged, pressurized or upset, she still dials his number without fail. Is this instinct, habit or a mixture of the two? It's not like she does it without understanding the implications but she always goes ahead anyway. She suspects it's not a good thing. It's unfair on him and probably unfair on herself as well. But Karen figures that this is something that defines people, especially people in relationships (however successful, failing or over): the capacity to do stuff that they know is bad – even bad for themselves – and, what's more, to keep on doing it again and again.

Of course, Karen had assumed it would get easier. She had assumed that, in time, the bits of Tom's heart, personality or perhaps just routine that had embedded themselves within her would begin to decompose, maybe even fertilize a new relationship. But that hasn't happened. How could it when she still calls him any time she has a worry? This makes her angry with herself and, more to the point, angry with Tom, too. Again, she knows it's unfair but that's the way it is.

Now that she thinks about it, she realizes she's jealous of Tom and that only makes her all the more angry. Specifically, she's jealous of his certainty.

When they first met, she'd found his eagerness to love her almost bizarre, as threatening as it was welcome. After all, her only previous boyfriend had been Kush so it wasn't surprising that she thought of men as heavy bodies to dodge and parry and relationships as an ongoing series of battles and ceasefires in which she was the lone guerilla, living on her wits, sacrificing everything. Tom's promise to look after her (however unlikely) had, therefore, seemed like it must be a cunning ruse, a plan to make her drop her guard and open herself up for the killer blow. But she was a girl raised on high-school movies in which star-crossed lovers find redemption in the final-frame clinch so she had to go along with it; almost as a matter of principle. And besides, Tom had been so certain.

Tom had always laughed at the way she could watch *Some Kind Of Wonderful*, *The Breakfast Club* and *Pretty In Pink*, of course, again and again. He said, 'What happens next? That's what I want to know. It's typical Hollywood. The movie ends at the point they get together but, in real life, that's when it starts to get difficult.'

Karen was puzzled he could be so disparaging about the archetype while seeming so sure about their future together. He, on the other hand, couldn't understand how she had more belief in a fairytale than she did in her boyfriend. In the end, though, it was her faith that was proved right and she who suffered for it. Where was the justice in that?

If she was honest with herself – and she was – Karen did admit that, for the majority of their time together, Tom's certainty, his unquestioned commitment to them, had been a solid foundation for the relationship. After the initial hiccups of her distrust (not of him particularly; of anyone), that commitment gave them thick roots that allowed their branches, flexible with youth, to knot and entwine with speed and confidence.

Karen admitted too that she had come to take his conviction for granted. She admitted that, as her career progressed and accelerated, she had stopped worrying about the foundations or roots and concentrated instead on what she considered the cosmetic – the décor of the relationship that needed sprucing up and the buds that now occasionally failed to blossom. When, for example, she had begun to work seventeen-hour days for the campaign team, she had figured this was no more than peeling wallpaper, a superficial problem to be dealt with at a later date. And when she'd subsequently gone off sex and found Tom's every touch sent the wrong kind of shivers down her spine, she'd dismissed it as a dry spell which required no cure but the changing season. Because their relationship was certain, wasn't it? That's what he said.

Only it wasn't certain. It wasn't.

She'd come home one night after a tough day of conference calls, copy editing and computer headaches to find Tom sitting up in bed fully clothed. It was past three a.m. and his breath was thick with alcohol and she could read his face like a banner headline. He said, 'We need to talk.' And she said, 'Tomorrow.' Because she knew what was coming and she was simply too tired.

'I've been with someone else.'

He blurted it out just like that. It should have been, in some ways, a Hollywood moment, loaded with tension and drama. But London's not Hollywood and Tom is no Tom Cruise and his eyes were unfocused and his cheeks sagged.

'With who?' she asked and even those two words seemed to exhaust her further.

'It doesn't matter.' Tom was shaking his head. 'The point is we have to talk.'

'I'm going to sleep,' she said quietly. 'I've got an early start. Would you mind sleeping on the sofa or something? I don't want to look at you.'

Tom was bewildered. It wasn't what he was expecting. 'But we need to talk.'

'No,' Karen said. 'No. You've done it. What's there to talk about? You've done it already.'

She'd tried to throw him out the next day but he refused to go. It took her a week to sort out another place and she left. In between, they barely exchanged a word. Tom was bitter and angry (which she certainly didn't understand) and hardly ever in the flat; and when he was he was drunk. Karen was just numb. Her mind and her emotions seemed to click into a cool rationality that brooked no argument and rendered any conversation pointless anyway. She didn't cry at all, which surprised her. The only time she cried was a couple of weeks later.

This was because it was a couple of weeks before Tom started begging her to come back. He took to hanging around outside her building – she'd moved to a bedsit in Kilburn; a *bedsit*, for god's sake – and swearing his undying love. He'd accost her at the door and say, 'We're meant to be together, sweetheart. You know we are. Some things are meant to be.' And, for all the desperation in his face, there was that certainty again.

At first she wouldn't even acknowledge him, let alone let

him in. But in the end she had little choice because he was becoming such a nuisance and her neighbours – above her, below her, to left and right of her – were starting to look at her funny when they crossed on the stairs.

As soon as they were inside and he was perched on her one chair while she slouched on the uncomfortable futon that dug divots into her back, she saw he was hopeful and she knew she had to dispel that pretty quick.

'I love you,' he began. Like he still thought *that* would make it OK. 'We're meant to be together.'

She shook her head and she felt her eyes prickle and burn. 'How can you be so sure?'

'Karen!' he exclaimed. It was like he expected this and he had his answer down pat. Jesus! He almost looked smug. 'I've always been sure.'

'No,' she said quickly. 'No. Because if you're sure you don't fuck around.'

'It was a mistake,' he said. 'A lapse.'

'No way. Because if you're sure, if you're certain, if you're absolutely positive, you don't make mistakes. Because you're sure. That's the point.' She felt a lump the size of a plum in her throat and the first sob almost choked her as she fought with it. 'Jesus, Tom! Jesus!'

He tried to comfort her then but she wasn't having it. He'd become a heavy body and she was the lone guerilla again, fending him off. His touch, his smell, the look of pity on his face – pity? How dare he! – repulsed her.

'Go,' she said. The tears were coming fast now. 'Please. Get out.'

'We have to talk, sweetheart.'

'No. There's nothing to talk about. I was never sure, Tom. I was never sure. But *I* never made a mistake. *I* never lapsed, *I* never fucked someone else. Please. Just go.'

They'd been having variations of the same conversation ever since; some civilized, some raw and angry, but basically the same. And Tom still didn't get it.

The truth was that Karen didn't hate his certainty and she reckoned she understood where it came from perfectly. But that was why she was jealous; because this certainty – however misconstrued, misplaced or plain mistaken – was such an act of faith. And faith came so easily to Tom. It was easy for him with his loving family in a semi-detached in Hampton Wick to believe in anything he wanted and, what's more, to stop believing with few repercussions (she had, after all, witnessed his occasional spurts of devoted Catholicism). It was easy for him to believe that there was someone out there (Karen or whoever) who was meant to be with him, with whom he could live happily ever after and say so with unshakeable devotion. Lucky Tom. But Karen? She'd never believed that and the one person she'd met who might have convinced her otherwise had shown that, for all his faith, he couldn't be faithful. And trust, like many things, is most highly prized by those who've known it least. So no wonder she stuck to her movies, thanks very much. And yet . . .

Karen checks her watch. Tom is late. Tom is never late to meet her; never. And she feels a brief pang of desperation and she suddenly wonders if the moment she's long expected has finally arrived; the moment when he finally admits that they weren't meant to be together after all.

She shakes her head and plays with the froth where her coffee used to be, scooping it up on her teaspoon for mouthfuls of bubbles. Her relationship with Tom is, she thinks, as confusing as an Escher sketch or the Soho one-way system; a complex conundrum of impossibilities and queries whose answers solve nothing. She can't be with Tom because he's so sure that it's right and she can't trust that. But if he lost his certainty, of course, she couldn't be with him anyway. She could forgive him his infidelity if she thought he was truly weak but how could she build a life with someone weak? Maybe if he changed, she could give him another chance. But if he changed then he wouldn't be the Tom that she'd so wanted to believe in. He'd be yet another shape-shifter, no better than Kush, whose many faces (well, two) only confirmed her fears that she couldn't trust anyone. He would no longer be the Tom she fell in love with.

So Murray calls *her* a chameleon? At least her changes reflected the search for viable identity rather than unconsidered inconsistencies of character or brief hiccups of desire.

Of course, Karen knows that her thinking is flawed but she forgives herself easily because she tries not to think about this too much and, besides, it's essentially about how she feels and she may as well question the weather as question that. Nonetheless she is able to admit that she still wants Tom even as she knows they can never be together (and that at least sounds like a balanced equation). What's more, she knows that people do change – her, Tom, the lot of them – whether she chooses to acknowledge it or not. After all, she'd seen Kush again just the other day and hadn't their meeting been evidence enough?

After she ran into him in Brixton, Kush had called her at work. God knows how he got the number but she couldn't be bothered to protest. He said, 'We should catch up, know what I mean?' And when she asked why and he said, 'For old times' sake', she almost laughed. But she arranged to meet him for lunch at the Admiralty, an expensive joint just off Strand. 'My treat,' she said though what she meant was 'my turf' and she hoped he'd feel every bit as uncomfortable as she thought he might.

He turned up reeking of expensive aftershave and wearing an expensive suit that was tight around the shoulders, waist and thigh and lent him all the class of a baked potato. His thick neck and bald head poked out pinkly from his collar like the head of a penis from a gripping fist. Kush? Of course he hadn't changed at all.

She recalled the way he used a knife and fork for his asparagus tips and then complained, loudly, on his way back from the gents that the food had made his piss smell dodgy. She recalled some of the stories he'd told and the conclusions she'd drawn from them; that he'd graduated from junior gangster to minor gangster, cutting deals around South London and battering some other poor cow no doubt.

The change, therefore, was in her. She wasn't surprised that she was no longer scared of him; she'd expected that. In fact, part of her wanted Kush to lamp her right across the table so she could laugh all the way to A & E at the prospect of having him sent down. Nor was she surprised that she still found him in some ways charming. There was that street savvy she'd always admired, of course, and she also recalled how she liked the way his voice softened to barely a whisper when he was trying to be serious – a mark of confidence or insecurity, she'd never been able to tell. What did surprise her, however, was the idea that she'd once tried to plan a life with him and, more to the point, once found this monster in some way physically attractive. He was, she now realized, an oaf. It was nothing to do with his capacity for violence nor the pathetic tics of machismo that found form in his every expression. Instead it was the clumsiness of his movements; the noise he made – a wheezing sigh – when he sat down, the sight of his fat mitt wrapped around a crystal bulb, the way he accidentally kicked her under the table when he crossed his legs. Presumably, at one time, she hadn't noticed this lumbering; perhaps she'd even liked it. But now the idea of being close to him conjured only images of beasts mating.

She remembered too that he'd been oddly interested in Tom. He said, 'So you still with that geezer, then?'

'What geezer?'

'That geezer you met at your college.'

'What? Tom?' she laughed. 'No. Not any more.'

'This Tom bloke. He never said anything to you, then?' Kush's tone quietened with gravity and Karen was curious.

'About what?'

'Nothing.'

'About what, Kush?' she pressed.

'Nothing, nothing.' He looked momentarily uncomfortable. 'I just ran into him one time, that's all.'

Karen stared at him. She'd never seen him look so awkward; almost nervous, almost guilty (and not just the meaningless hangdogging he used to adopt after he hit her, either). 'Really? He never mentioned it.'

'No?'

'Why? What happened?'

'Nothing happened,' Kush said quickly. 'Just wondered, that's all. Trying to catch up with your life, aren't I?'

When they left the restaurant (he insisted on paying, which tickled her), they ran into Jared, hurrying back to the office with his lunch in a neat, New York-style paper bag that contained, no doubt, a roasted-vegetable wrap, an individual pasta salad with black olives and pesto, and a bottle of mineral water. Jared kissed her on both cheeks and shook Kush by the hand and either didn't engage in or, more likely, didn't notice the territorial games Kush played with those minimal twitches of his eyebrows and jaw. She introduced him only as 'someone I work with'.

Karen said goodbye to Kush with a single peck. Momentarily

he held her by the shoulders, his hands exerting a little too much pressure, and he said very quietly, 'Anything you need, Kaz. Anything at all, know what I mean?'

Then he jumped into a pristine Beamer that must have been parked, unpenalized, on a double yellow for almost an hour and a half. Karen smiled. There were those street smarts again, the kind she'd forgotten all about, that told her London was a place of countless different codes and etiquettes and it was nigh impossible to learn them all. These days, she did asparagus while Kush did double yellows and that was that. She laughed as the engine roared and the bass bins began to boom some nondescript UK garage and Kush nosed into the heavy traffic before ducking back into the bus lane and speeding away.

She walked back to work with Jared. He slung a casual arm around her shoulder and asked, 'Who was that?'

'Kush? My ex. A long time ago.'

'Right. He looks . . .'

'He looks what?'

Jared chuckled apologetically. 'Well. I was about to say he looks like a lout.'

'A lout?' Karen said. 'Yeah, he is.'

And, while it was the perfect description, she was nonetheless surprised that she now went out with a guy who not only used the word 'lout' but accompanied it with a slight nose wrinkle of distaste. She'd changed, all right.

Karen checks her watch for the twentieth time in twenty minutes. She's beginning to wonder if Tom's stood her up but she can't believe he would. Of course, she'd call him but he must be the only person in the city who doesn't own a mobile. Even as he thinks this lends a certain Luddite radicalism, it reveals itself as nothing but affectation. That's Tom all over.

She's finished her coffee and she considers getting another. Trouble is, the place is packed and she'll probably lose her seat. Of course, she could leave her phone on the table and most people will recognize this marks her spot. But someone who isn't most people will nick it. Alternatively she could leave her newspaper but she isn't sure if that constitutes a staked claim. In a pub, maybe, but in a coffeeshop? Maybe not. It's all a question of etiquette again and she resolves to stay put and give Tom a little longer.

There are two things, two *worries*, that she wants to talk to Tom about and they both have a name. One is called Jared and the other Murray. In some ways these worries, these *problems*, are connected and in some ways they aren't. Maybe she'll mention what Kush said as well; if she remembers.

Of course, Karen knows it's unwise and probably unfair to talk to her ex-boyfriend (Tom) about the new model (Jared) but, by now, she's been over and over this in her head and she knows she'll do it if she wants to so there's not a whole lot of point in fretting. Besides, who else is she going to talk to? She's already tried Tariq so her only real alternative is Murray and he's a problem in his own right.

Her essential difficulty with Jared is that she's beginning to suspect he's a bit of a dick. God. Tom'll love that.

She's not quite sure how this – this dickness – has happened. After all, she's been seeing the guy for some time, been living with him for three months; and then suddenly, out of nowhere, she's been confronted by the unignorable notion that he's a dick. What's more, it isn't even as if Jared's been hiding something that he's only now begun to reveal. If anything, it's more like she's simply seeing it for the first time, like someone just switched on the light. She hasn't stopped thinking he's basically a good guy – intelligent and motivated and still, even, kind of attractive for a posh boy. But right now, his goodness comes across mostly like piety, his intelligence as pomposity, his motivations are suspiciously ambitious and what once looked louche now seems increasingly like awkwardness.

She spoke to Tariq about it because, besides Tom and Murray, he's her oldest friend. She said: 'I mean, how does that work? Surely you don't just wake up one morning, look over at the next pillow and decide your partner's actually an idiot.'

At the other end of the phone Tariq, who was, she figured, most likely drunk again, burst out laughing. 'Kaz!' he exclaimed. 'That's *exactly* how it works! That's how it's been with every girlfriend I've ever had. You're attracted by a great pair of tits or whatever and then, one day, you take your eyes off their chest for a minute and think, "Blimey! You know what? You're a right arsehole."'

'He's not an *arsehole*.'

Tariq found this so funny he could barely speak. 'Arsehole, prat, whatever. Why do you think you don't stay friends with most of your exes? It's nothing to do with awkwardness or history or any of that bollocks. It's because you don't actually like them much.'

'I've only really got Tom,' Karen protested. 'I don't think like that about him.'

'Well. There you go. The basis for any decent relationship: not thinking your partner's an idiot.'

'You can't think like that, Riq. Does Emma know you think like that?'

'Em's never really had any tits.'

'Be serious.'

'I am being serious.'

'It's not very romantic.'

There was a pause and what sounded like a sigh. Then again, Tariq drank and smoked so much these days that his every breath was heavy like a sigh. 'I don't know, you know?' he said. 'I think it *is* kind of romantic. To wake up next to the same person every single day and not find them irritating; to basically, fundamentally, intrinsically still like them. To be honest, I think that's about as good as it gets. And you can let that lift or depress. Up to you.'

'So,' Karen said slowly. She'd had enough of this conversation. 'How are you two, anyway?'

'We're all right, you know. We're good.' Tariq spoke with certainty, finality. Clearly he'd had enough of this conversation too.

Karen's problem with Jared started, she thinks, when they met up with Murray. Of course, that can't have really been when it started because she reckons it's been there all along. But it was the first time she noticed, anyway. Murray had rung her up – when was this? Last week some time – and they met for a drink after she finished work. Their conversation, incidentally, was the source of the other problem she wanted to talk to Tom about.

She took him to the Oxo Tower and they sat at the wrong side of the bar looking out over the wrong view of London: i.e., not the Thames, Temple and Embankment but the half-hearted, grubby towers of Southwark. But it was a beautiful evening and they spent some time just staring out of the window and even the wrong view looked right enough.

They'd only been there about half an hour when Jared rang and suggested he come to join them. Since they were deep in serious and disconcerting conversation, Karen raised her eyebrows at Murray but he shrugged, so she said, 'Sure.' Because what else was she supposed to do? Nonetheless she was nervous. Although Murray and Jared had met before, the night of Freya's launch, they'd hardly exchanged two words. At the time she thought she was nervous at the prospect of

Jared meeting Murray because you never quite knew which Murray you were going to get. But in retrospect she reckons she was actually intuitively nervous about Murray meeting Jared because at some level she must have known that her boyfriend was a dick.

Jared behaved like a fool from the moment he arrived, ordering himself a Martini and ostentatiously leaving his platinum card behind the bar – *anybody* can have a platinum card these days – before awkwardly folding his long body into a seat like a letter into an envelope and combing his fingers through the thick weight of his blond fringe.

He then turned to Murray and said, 'So *you're* the chap I've been hearing so much about', and smiled this peculiar lopsided smile; the kind of strained expression one might pull when finally brushing your fingertip against a ballpoint dropped under the sofa. For some reason, Jared clearly regarded Murray as a threat and his response to this was to bray loudly about himself, his job and just how important, successful and all-round fucking fabulous he was.

It didn't help that Murray was at his most modestly charming, something that threw Jared's boorishness into, for Karen, ever more embarrassing relief. Murray laughed dutifully at each anecdote, nodded noncommittally at every bumptious assertion and made all the most polite noises of encouragement when called upon. Despite this, Jared seemed determined to be patronizing, dull and generally disagreeable.

At one point, for example, he asked: 'So, Murray, do you know this part of town, this neck of the woods, do you?'

Murray said, 'I do as it goes, china.' He pointed a finger out through the opposite wall. 'Because Kazza had a room just down there when we were at LMT; Southwark Halls.'

Jared turned to her and his expression flickered 'I didn't know that'. Karen felt obliged to say something but before she could get a word out, he'd already looked away and embarked on another story about himself.

'After Oxford, when I moved down here for post-grad,' he announced, 'I used to scull this part of the Thames every day of the week. Of course the boat clubs are west of here; Putney, Hammersmith, Barnes, places like that. But I found there's nothing quite like rowing through the heart of a city. It's the looming buildings and the wash of river traffic combined with the exhilaration of hard exercise. Sometimes a police launch would pull alongside because you're not supposed to row this stretch. But you know what? While I was on the river, I didn't care about anything.'

'I've never really understood rowing,' Murray observed mildly.

'It's very scientific. An almost trance-like state combining intense concentration, mechanics, physiology – because you have to be very fit and strong – and an understanding of . . . No . . . a *oneness with* the ebb and flow of the currents.'

'That's cool, china,' Murray smiled. 'I just always thought it looked like a seriously knackering way of going backwards slowly. I mean, you don't even notice what's going on around you, do you?'

Karen suppressed a giggle but if Murray was taking the piss, Jared certainly hadn't registered. 'Of course you do!' he protested. 'I saw all sorts on the banks: schoolkids having sex, tramps scavenging the sludge, wrecked cars. Once I even saw a body.'

'Seriously?'

'I swear it. Right near here. Some poor fucker laid out on the bank. But I wouldn't expect *you* to understand rowing, Murray. You can't understand something until you've done it.'

'True enough. True enough.'

Later, in another of Jared's prolonged monologues, Karen

noticed Murray staring out of the window again and she interrupted her boyfriend to say, 'What are you thinking, Muz?'

Murray turned to her and she was somehow shocked by
his face. He'd always been racially indistinct, of course, but
now, in this bar gloom, it was as though all colour had drained
out and left him with the complexion of veal. What's more,
his eyes were glistening like dark puddles under a lamppost
and his expression seemed unbearably sad. He gestured
towards the outside world. It was a beautiful dusk and the sky
was a palate of red and orange that washed even the drabbest
nearby buildings a gentle shade of pink. His lips twitched with
the vaguest sort of smile – one Karen didn't recognize; one to
be added to Tom's compendium. It was such a minimal expression and yet she thought, just for an instant, that it con-
veyed the most profound heartbreak. Then it was gone.
'Not a lot,' he said. 'You know me, china. I'm not one for a
lot of thinking.'

Karen tutted at him until he continued.

'I don't know. I suppose I was just wondering about the
light in London. All day every day, whether it's bright and
clear or driving rain, this town looks as grey as a Pathé
newsreel. Then, sometimes, you get a sunset like this one and
it's like a postcard. You've got to ask yourself if somebody's
taking the piss, know what I mean? It's like that line: "The
first requisite to happiness is that a man be born in a famous
city." I'm not so sure about that, you know?'

Karen said nothing. Even Jared had briefly shut up. Murray
suddenly looked very puzzled.

'You remember when we were at college? In the summer,
people would go to exotic parts of the world and when they
came back they'd always talk about the light; how it made
everything look so colourful. I wonder, if I'd gone somewhere
like that, whether it could have made me happy.'

Karen said, 'But you've been to loads of exotic places.'

Murray blinked. 'Sure. But when you describe those places, you ever wonder whether you're actually saying what you think you're supposed to; like you're actually describing something secondhand from TV or the travel pages or whatever?'

Jared jumped in. 'Nothing *makes* you happy,' he declared. 'Happiness is a by-product of what you do.'

Suddenly Murray's face flashed with a familiar animation and his voice hummed with laughter. 'But you're happy, right?'

'You know, Murray, I am. Because I'm happy with what I do.'

Karen and Jared left Murray on the South Bank and caught a cab on Blackfriars Bridge. As they rode home Jared said, 'Murray seems like a decent chap.' It was the first time Karen had ever heard anyone describe Murray as 'decent' but she didn't say anything because her mind was elsewhere.

Karen doesn't believe in happiness. Or, rather, she doesn't believe in happiness for herself. But, if she did, she'd probably have to admit that she subscribed most closely to Jared's view since her every decision, for as long as she can remember, has been taken with an appreciation of exactly this in mind. Simply, she has studied people who seem happy and tried to do as they do. That's the only reason Murray can call her a chameleon.

As a kid, she saw the girls who smoked countless cigarettes and laughed as they jumped into their boyfriends' cars. Ironically, this was how she ended up with Kush. As a sixth former, she was taught by a young graduate with flopping hair, attractive earnestness and a pretty, fashionable girlfriend who sometimes collected him from the gates in a convertible Escort. So she decided that she should get a degree too. When she first went to stay with Tom at the house in Hampton

Wick (while on the run from her own life), she loved to watch his parents' relationship – even their bickering couldn't disguise affection and intimacy – and she resolved to build the same with their son. Back at college, she watched the young women in the cafeteria who endlessly discussed the ills of the world. She envied their certainty (of course) as much as she admired their values and it wasn't long before she joined them.

In her final year, when talk turned to careers, she noticed that the most sorted students were already interviewing for City jobs, graduate-training schemes and the like. So that's what she did, too. By virtue of what had gone before, however, her applications had a political consistency and she landed a job with a small firm of green lobbyists. She was later head-hunted by the party, who convinced her that her passions would be better served assisting one of the junior members of the Shadow Cabinet.

In the interview, it was hard to say who told more lies (prospective employer or prospective employee). At least, at a fundamental level, Karen only wanted a job (to earn more money, pay the bills, get on), while her would-be boss seemed desperate to convince her of a cause where they both knew there was none. Nonetheless Karen was still soon dispirited by the pragmatism and lack of certainty in her new work even as she was aware that it suited her perfectly. She was dispirited by the lack of faith even as she came to understand that was a kind of faith in itself; that politics was now a one-trick pony in which success was the only measure of success (and that wasn't just party politics, either).

Sometimes Karen wondered if she'd simply been born in the wrong time, growing up only against the background of Thatcherism. If she'd been born in a different era, perhaps she'd have found a plausible cause by virtue of class or gender, say. But now? Such an idea was barely imaginable. She didn't despise the party for any specific policy; but their lack of principle, the breadth of their church, gave them a bagginess that could only ever be tightened in tricks of light or language. There was, in fact, nothing to believe in. Sometimes Karen wondered if she'd only been hired for the working-class South London kinks to her accent – something which her job, ironically, ironed out within three months. Such homogeny, she thought, perfectly encapsulated the death of meaningful politics. And, what's more, she didn't care.

When she met Jared, therefore, it took him little time and few lies to persuade her that, in the aftermath of devolution, local politics might prove to be a more interesting arena. Because she didn't really care about that either. Much more to the point was the fact that Jared struck her as a self-possessed individual and she knew that was exactly what she wanted to be. So she's been working for London ever since.

Every decision Karen has made, therefore, has been based on this simple equation but, if she thinks about it (which she tries not to) and if she's honest with herself (which she is), she's rarely been happy. Every step she has taken has been to travel down a road lined with contentment and yet all these steps have more or less disappointed (no different, apparently, from the game of golf). And if she's often failed to notice this, it's only because she'd already set her sights on the next horizon. She considers Tom's analysis of her favourite American movies and maybe he has a point after all. Because getting the boy, getting the job, getting the high-school prom dress . . . they've all proved to be false dawns. If anything, she realizes that the happiness she has experienced has come in brief snatches and in fact was mostly snatched with Tom – their first holiday together, a picnic in Bushey Park, the night he got back from a PGCE training course and she knew she'd missed him so much and loved him so utterly. So why had he gone and let her down? Certainly she knows that happiness is not a by-product of what she does now; not after yesterday.

Yesterday Jared called her into his office and there was something different in his manner; an embarrassment, perhaps. He didn't get up or kiss her cheek but suggested, awkwardly, that she might 'pull up a pew'; almost as if they'd never met.

He asked her what she thought of the 'whole pigeon situation'. She hadn't known how to react to that so she smiled and said, 'I didn't realize it was exactly a *situation*.'

Jared nodded very seriously and told her they'd been getting hundreds of complaints about pigeons flying headlong into blocks of flats, dropping dead out of trees, harassing steeplejacks, crane operators and park keepers, and settling in groups on children's windowsills and squawking at all hours of the night. Karen struggled not to crack up and managed to suggest that this was surely a problem for the London boroughs – local pest control, that sort of thing. But Jared said, 'We need to be seen to do something, to take a position.' And the look on his face and the tone of his voice stunned her to silence at the prospect of what she realized was coming next.

He told her that she was being taken off the transport committee to, in Jared's words, 'head-up pigeons'. He even had the cheek to imply that this was in some way a promotion and Karen didn't know whether to laugh or cry. Although, in fact, she was so angry that she was dry of mouth and eyes anyway. When, however, her boss/boyfriend used the phrase 'Pigeon Czar', that was the final straw and she stood up stiffly and stalked to the door. She turned and said, 'You . . .' She was so exasperated that she couldn't get out the second word but it didn't much matter because saying it was only for her own benefit anyway. And she knew what it was, all right.

Karen gets up. It's been more than half an hour now and

she's had enough of waiting. It looks like Tom's let her down too. And though Tom, of course, once let her down worse than anyone, she's surprised nonetheless. The coffeeshop is still jammed and there are so many conversations going on and she's not part of any of them. She's feeling sorry for herself and suddenly very lonely. She tucks her mobile into the breast pocket of her suit as usual. She thinks of how Jared always says it 'spoils the line'. Dick.

She steps out from behind the table and she's about to leave when she notices that a pigeon has wandered in through the open door. She bursts out laughing.

This pigeon is a healthy-looking bird, fat and slate grey with the swagger of a beat policeman. It saunters around the entrance for a while, its head bobbing left and right as though disapprovingly checking out the clientele. Apart from Karen, nobody seems to have noticed and it ruffles its feathers a couple of times as if put out by the lack of attention. It is, of course, unusual to see a pigeon in a coffeeshop but Karen thinks wryly that, if this is the extent of the 'pigeon situation', she can probably cope.

Disgruntled, the pigeon hops out of the door. As the pigeon leaves, Tom comes in. He sees Karen straight away and raises a hand but there's no apology, no *mea culpa* in his expression. In fact, if anything, he looks kind of cocky. She immediately dispels any thought of discussing Jared let alone Kush. But they must talk about Murray.

18
Getting on with it

Tom was feeling better than he had for a very long time; the best he'd felt since the horrors of breaking up with Karen, anyway. No. Even longer than that. Because Tom was feeling so good that he could even admit to himself that things hadn't been great for a while before they'd actually split. Previously, Tom had found this a difficult idea to acknowledge because, in his desperate certainty, he'd been keen to accept all responsibility for what had happened; to lay all the blame on his mistake, his infidelity. But he was now coming to terms with the proposition that such an explanation was really just an easy way out – and not just for her but for him too. After all, the story of a perfect relationship that he'd screwed up with one error, tragic and fateful, was easier to bear than the idea of a true love that they'd both neglected until it began to wear, unravel and finally (and prosaically) fall apart. So Tom was feeling unburdened and it granted him a lightness of step; as if he were walking on the moon and pushing off too hard might see him sail away into space. In some ways this was frightening but, for the moment, he felt nothing but exhilaration.

He'd just had his final session with Tejananda and this had been his decision rather than the therapist's. In fact, Tejananda had been quite put out (albeit in a very understated, Buddhist kind of way) and this was why he was late.

During the session, Tom related everything Murray had told him in their conversation last night. Not the stuff about the bank job, of course (because he wasn't sure about the

271

niceties of client confidentiality when it came to armed robbery), but the stuff that was relevant to his state of mind; specifically the talk of Karen, specifically of Karen and Murray, specifically of their last day at LMT.

He told Tejananda how upset he'd been and he listed the emotions that had fizzed through him. He'd felt betrayed, of course, but somehow that had proved to be a brief pain. The deeper agony was one of emasculation that left him feeling inadequate and, more to the point, with a bizarre and profound sensation of loss, as if his identity as a man had literally been taken away. It hadn't helped that Murray had been so calm; not exactly unapologetic but surprisingly unfazed (considering this was a secret that had been rigorously protected for a decade).

Tejananda flicked through his notebook. 'And yet Murray was very judgemental about your relationship with Freda?'

'Freya,' Tom corrected him. 'And it wasn't exactly a relationship.' He shook his head as though the mannerism could provoke a sense of irony as opposed to vice versa. 'Murray said that was different. Because I hadn't actually wanted to have sex with Freya anyway.'

Tejananda nodded as if he understood perfectly and commented, 'Desire defines us. Desire destroys us.' Because when he didn't know what to say but felt he had to say something he had a tendency, common among therapists, to get a little gnomic.

Tom then told him how his feelings of emasculation had given way to anger. In fact, he'd never been so angry and Murray's ongoing placidity had only provoked him. In the end, Tom had completely lost his rag and lashed out. It hadn't been a typical scrap between combatants who don't really know how to fight, a chaos of arms and legs that inevitably ends in stalemate and exhaustion. Rather, Tom had thrown one clean jab that caught Murray below his left eye and sent him flying off his chair. He described in proud and lascivious detail the sound of his knuckles against Murray's flesh, the sight of Murray sprawling on the pub carpet and the way his eye had swollen and closed with almost supernatural speed.

Tom said that, now he reflected upon the incident, he realized he'd never felt superior to Murray before and it felt good. Tejananda muttered something about anger as a necessary and functional expression of . . . something or other. He swallowed the end of this aphorism and it drowned somewhere in the back of his throat.

'So!' The therapist sat forward, spinning his ballpoint on an index finger. 'How do you feel about Karen now?'

'About Karen?' Tom looked puzzled. Like that was a question he hadn't considered. 'Like I always felt. I mean, some things are meant to be, aren't they? This is about me. I feel differently about me.'

'And how do you feel about you?'

'I don't know.' Tom frowned and then, slowly, the expression dissolved and relaxed into the broadest of smiles. 'Better.'

Only at the end of his allotted time, when Tejananda took out his Palm Pilot to schedule a further appointment, did Tom admit that he wasn't planning on another visit. 'OK,' Tejananda nodded as if he'd been expecting this. 'If you don't mind my asking, what led you to such a . . . a decision?'

Tom shrugged. 'I guess I'm feeling better. I thought it was time to . . . to just *get on with it*, know what I mean?'

'I do. I do know what you mean. And that's good, isn't it? That's good.'

'Right then.'

Tejananda then tried to explain that, in fact, they still had a lot of work to do, plenty to *address*.

'Do you think so?' Tom sounded surprised.

'I do. I do think so.'

He said he suspected Tom was experiencing the brief euphoria that was so typically a corollary of the revelation of a Moment of Truth. In fact, this conversation with Murray, this new knowledge, had most likely triggered a shift in the nature of Tom's understanding of his relationship with Karen. Perhaps, within the mental framework – 'the brainwork', if you will – in which they'd been talking, it represented the movement from devotion to selfishness.

Tom said, 'Really? If anything I would have thought it was the other way round.'

Tejananda shook his head. Apparently Tom was missing the point. It didn't matter which way round, the point was that this Moment of Truth had sparked change and who knew what the repercussions might be? For example, Tom had frequently talked about his relationship with Karen in terms of Murray, that is to say *bilaterally*. Did he remember that? Did he remember Tejananda's use of the word 'bilateral'? Good. Because how, in the light of this new knowledge, would he now represent the relationship? What stories would he now tell, about himself, about Karen, about Murray? How had those stories changed?

Tom said he didn't know but guessed he'd find out. And he was OK with that. Besides, he claimed he'd never really got this whole bilateral thing anyway. This was, of course, a lie but basically he'd had enough of talking, hadn't he.

Tejananda's veil of composure was starting to slip. There was a tightness at the corners of his mouth and his gaze of beatific calm was beginning to pinch around the eyes. Was this fellow being wilfully obtuse?

What he was trying to explain, he explained, was that Tom's trust had been completely broken. In fact, he'd asked Tom in a previous session whether he trusted Murray and Tom had said he did. Did Tom remember that? Yes? And now that trust, that *faith*, whether selfish, devoted or whatever, had been utterly – the therapist paused here – trampled.

'I know,' Tom said and Tejananda was reassured to see a stricken look crumple his patient's face. It was, however, quickly blinked away. 'But, like I said, I guess I've just got to get on with it. And I feel different, you know? I feel a real certainty. I feel like I've reached that stage you were talking about. What was it called? The Die is Cast theory.'

'Quite. But I'm sure you remember that the Die is Cast was always an explanation of perception rather than truth. It's about perceived immutability when, in fact, change is always possible.'

'Exactly!' Tom exclaimed. 'That's exactly what I'm hoping for. Because how else could Karen change her mind?'

'And that's still what you want?'

'Of course it's what I want. The Die is Cast.'

As far as Tom was concerned, this was the last word. Tejananda, however, had other ideas and insisted on trying out several further arguments as to why they needed future sessions. Frankly, the more the therapist said, the more Tom was convinced he'd made the right decision. The way Tom saw it, if a therapist claimed you should continue seeing them over and above your own judgement, then they either knew you better than you knew yourself (in which case you were probably a whole lot more screwed up than you'd realized) or they were actually something of a charlatan. Tom, who knew he wasn't very screwed up, was beginning to suspect the latter. Or, to put it another way, he was coming to understand that what he'd mistaken for devotion on Tejananda's part was, in fact, selfishness.

By the time Tom finally left the West End practice, therefore (half an hour late), he felt even better than he had when he'd gone in. 'Unburdened' *was* a good way of putting it (since he certainly felt released from guilt and worrying and, now, worrying about worrying). However, with connotations only of the removal of bad stuff, 'unburdened' didn't sound quite positive enough. 'Elated': that was better. After all, in the last couple of days he'd stood toe to toe with Murray (literally) and won, and toe to toe with his therapist (metaphorically) and won that too. He knew that both feelings of superiority were almost certainly temporary (and, in the case of Murray and his disclosure, undoubtedly flawed) but wasn't that all the more reason to enjoy them? In fact, he struggled to distinguish which victory was more satisfying. His dealings with Murray were clearly the more significant but they were nonetheless rooted in dark emotions and problems as yet unsolved. But with Tejananda? It was a cheap success, sure, but there was something delicious about seeing a Buddhist therapist, whose very nature was calm and aloof authority, reduced to ill-concealed, if understated, irritation and bullshit. Whatever. He was certainly looking forward to seeing Karen anyway because he had a thing or two he wanted to say to her. He wasn't entirely sure what one thing or the other thing might be but there was a thing or two, no doubt.

When he walked into the coffeeshop, however, his lightness immediately vanished, if only temporarily. He saw Karen standing by a table and she looked slightly dishevelled. Her power suit appeared somehow too big for her and one knee was kinked, as though about to buckle. Her mouth was frozen, as if in spasm, in a ghoulish smile like a snapshot of someone reluctantly laughing at themselves. Strands of hair, loose from the ponytail that generally gave her the appearance of business-like severity, now inelegantly framed eyes that were sunken and exhausted.

Tom felt his heart pop. She looked completely familiar and completely unrecognizable all at once. He felt like he was seeing someone for the first time in the flesh whom he'd previously met only in his dreams. Or perhaps the other way round. She looked, he thought, vulnerable in a way that only those who don't know how to be vulnerable can.

She said, 'You're late. You're really late.'

'Sorry. I was with my therapist.'

'Your therapist? You're not still doing that, are you?' She was defensive, catty. 'You must be the only school teacher in the country who can afford a therapist. Dad paying, is he?'

'It was the last session,' Tom said and he smiled. 'I'm cured.'

Reluctantly, Karen smiled too. 'Yeah? What was wrong with you?'

'Not sure. But I'm better and that's the main thing. Success.'

'Success,' she nodded. 'Exactly.'

'Exactly.'

Tom went and bought coffee. Karen didn't want another one but she accepted it anyway. The taste of it made not just her mouth but her whole insides feel filthy. She sipped at it resolutely while Tom, who'd regained most of his levity, small-talked with some animation. He asked whether she'd been in to Freya Franklin Hats. She had. Impressive or what? If anybody deserved a bit of success, it must be Freya. He asked whether she'd seen Emma and how she was doing. Karen said Emma was doing good, actually; seemed to be feeling a whole lot better. 'You see?' Tom smiled. 'We're all feeling better. It must be in the stars.' He told her that he'd run in to Tariq the other day and he was a lot more chilled too. He was heading for bankruptcy, of course, but at least he and Emma were getting on OK again, yeah? It must have been tough on both of them when Emma was so sick. Karen shook her head and said vaguely that she hardly thought that was the whole problem. Right, Tom nodded and took a deep mouthful of coffee.

Karen was beginning to relax and when he said, 'What about you? How's life in the corridors of power?' she forced a chuckle and told him all about her new position. She knew she was opening herself up to piss-take but had decided she didn't care.

In fact, though, Tom genuinely seemed to think it was quite an opportunity. 'Come on!' she scoffed. 'The Pigeon Czar? Are you having a laugh?'

But he protested his seriousness. 'I don't know,' he said. 'The pigeons *are* behaving very strangely at the moment. Who knows what's going to kick off?' Tariq claimed that businessmen had begun to carry umbrellas to beat off any attack and he related a story that Ami had told him about a manic-depressive pigeon she'd found in Hyde Park. Murray had wrung its neck.

'Murray did that?'

Tom shrugged. 'Yeah.'

'Actually, there was one in here just before you.'

'One what?'

'A pigeon.'

'In here? What was it doing?'

'No idea. It just kind of swaggered around a bit; like it was casing the joint.' Karen laughed. She still thought her new job was 100 per cent bogus and she still doubted the sincerity of Tom's enthusiasm but she felt a little better nonetheless; so much so that when Tom asked her, 'And how's Jared?' she managed, 'You know. OK', without even thinking about it.

Tom drained his coffee and leaned forward. 'Can I tell you something?'

She studied his face, looking for the tell-tale signs of angst and guilt that usually signalled their conversation's descent into justifications, recriminations and, frankly, boredom. But they weren't there. If anything she detected something like a sparkle in his eyes so she said, 'Sure.'

'It was Freya.'

'What was Freya?'

'That I slept with. It was Freya.'

Karen blinked and looked away and ran her tongue around her teeth. She felt thrown, duped. 'I thought we were past that,' she said quietly.

'Past what?'

'Why are you telling me now? I thought we were past that.'

'We are past that. It was a long time ago. That's why I'm telling you now. I mean, we still have a relationship, don't we? I think it's time to be honest. I need to be honest.'

'Why's this about what you need?'

'I think you need to be honest, too. And don't be angry with Freya. Please. It wasn't about her. It was about me.'

Karen was struggling to retain her composure. Tom hadn't *got to her* like this in ages. What was wrong with her? Last time had been round at Tariq and Emma's and she'd blamed it on the sight of him holding his godson. But now? Was she just feeling fragile or was it the difference, the new confidence, in his manner? Either way, she felt familiar sensations of anger and hurt bubbling to the surface and her voice was taut.

'All right,' she said. 'I'll be honest. Honestly, it's not for you to tell me how to feel about Freya, is it? Honestly, I'm not angry with Freya. I was but now I can't be bothered. Because, honestly, I knew it was Freya. I always knew it was Freya. Of course it was fucking Freya.'

'You knew?' Tom's face was a picture. 'Who . . .'

'Tom! Nobody told me. I'm not an idiot. Believe it or not I loved you like crazy. I spent years watching you, you know? I enjoyed your expressions. I enjoyed the way you looked at me. You don't think I saw the way you looked at Freya and knew exactly what had happened? Jesus, Tom! You say you want to be honest. Why? I don't know what this therapist has been telling you but I really think you need to fire the fucker.'

'I have,' Tom said. And then he burst out laughing. He actually burst out laughing! Karen was confused. She was beginning to think he might be deranged.

'I don't know what you think's so funny,' she said. 'I don't want to talk about this.'

'OK.'

'It's not why I called you. I don't want to talk about it.'

'Fine. You want another coffee?'

Tom pushed his chair back and got to his feet. Karen shook her head. She said, 'Judging by the state you're in, I'm not sure you should have one either. You'll be bouncing off the ceiling.' But Tom just beamed at her.

By the time he returned with another giant beaker accompanied by a chocolate-chip cookie the size of a frying pan, Karen had steeled herself for the main event. 'Look. I wanted to talk to you about Murray.'

Tom slurped through the plastic lid and then winced as the hot liquid scalded his lips and left sandpaper bumps on his tongue. 'That's funny. I wanted to talk to you about exactly the same thing.'

'Really?'

'Yeah. Murray told me what happened.'

'What happened?'

'Between you and him.'

'What did he say?'

Tom blinked and bit his lip. It was his turn to be disconcerted. He couldn't believe they were about to discuss this after so long; nor that Karen was being so straightforward. He began to feel lighter than ever, as though he had now pushed off too hard and was indeed floating away, high above the table, heading for the ceiling. Fuck it. There was nothing else to do but go with it.

'Actually he was really calm,' he said. 'Which made me pretty fucking angry.'

'Exactly!' Karen exclaimed. 'He's actually persuaded everybody to be in on it, that's what gets me. I mean, Tariq's a drunk, Emma's desperate and Kwesi thinks the sun shines out of Murray's arse. But Ami? And Freya? I thought Freya had more sense.' She looked at Tom and her eyes narrowed. 'Then again . . .' she added.

Tom dropped back into his chair with a bump. 'Right,' he said. Although he wasn't sure what was right. Right, he had no idea what she was talking about. Right, he supposed he was going to have to wait to confront her. Right, that was OK since he'd already waited a decade. Right.

Karen was getting quite steamed up. 'You can't just walk into a bank these days and say, "Your money or your life,"' she hissed. 'For god's sake! They must have panic-buttons and bulletproof glass and all that kind of thing.'

'Oh. Right.'

'They're not even going to make it behind the counter.'

'Right,' Tom nodded. Then he said, 'Actually it's a pretty ingenious plan. Ami's already got a job in the bank.'

Karen snorted, 'You're joking!'

'No. Seriously. She persuaded her TV company and the branch manager that she should do undercover research for a show. You know what Ami's like when she turns it on. She did her whole telly-eyes thing and they really went for it. She's working there right now. She told me she's enjoying it.'

Karen gasped, incredulous. 'I don't believe it.'

'Honestly.'

She stared at him curiously. 'You're not part of this mad plan, are you?'

'I don't know,' he shrugged. 'Why not?'

'I thought you said you were angry with Murray?'

'That was . . . something else. Doesn't matter.'

'Why are we even having this conversation?' She shook her head. 'This is crazy.'

'Why? The way I look at it, it's no different from all the Murray-fun we had at LMT. Shit, Karen, you had no problem with the Antiques Trade and that was basically stealing, same as this. I mean, come on; don't tell me you have moral problems with it. It's a one-off and you're doing it for your friends. It'll be a laugh. Murray? He's untouchable. You know he is. It's just another scam. Let's face it, you can trust Murray 100 per cent . . .' He paused. 'When it comes to scams, anyway.'

'You do know we're not at college any more, Tom. We're actually grown-ups these days.'

'Right. So we should pull a grown-up scam.'

'This isn't a scam. Stop calling it a scam. This isn't even stealing. This is a bank robbery. You realize Murray's asking me to get Kush to find us some guns. Guns, Tom. You really think that's a good idea.'

Tom started laughing again. He was revelling in this exchange. The thought that Karen was looking at him as crazy and reckless was new and exhilarating. 'Like you said, it's a bank robbery. What do you think we're going to use? A pair of scissors and a couple of steak knives? Nobody's going to get hurt. It *is* a scam. It's a bluff, isn't it?'

Tom took a big bite of his chocolate-chip cookie and munched happily. He broke a piece off and offered it to Karen. She declined. He realized he was floating once more and, looking down, he liked the self he saw and the way Karen was watching him. He loved the idea he was the kind of guy who calmly ate biscuits while discussing bank robberies. He felt like he was in a movie.

He dropped another bombshell. 'I'm quitting my job.'

'What?'

'Yeah.' He picked a crumb from the corner of his mouth. 'Jacking it in. Teaching, I mean. I'll see out the end of term but that's it.'

'Why?' She looked almost personally hurt.

Tom shrugged. 'I don't know. I think I became a teacher because it fitted with you and me, you know? But I don't have that any more. I just feel like I want to do something for me. Besides, apologies to any political sensibilities and all that, but it's a shit job and it's only getting shitter. I'm permanently knackered and, the money I'm on, I can barely afford my rent.' He glanced up and met her eye, unblinking. 'Don't look at me like that. I'm not having a go at you. This is just about what I want. I need to try something else.'

Karen said, 'So you're going to leave teaching and rob a bank. You're really going to do this?'

He laughed. He felt *peculiar*. He couldn't find the word for it. He felt *perfect*. 'Rob a bank and leave teaching. That order,' he said. 'I think so. I mean, if you don't want to be part of it, that's fair enough. Your life's going well, right? You've got a good job, a nice place to live and a successful boyfriend. You're on the top of the ladder peering down at the rest of us, know what I mean? But me? I'm barely even on the bottom rung. No. Please don't look at me like that. I'm not complaining. Really I'm not. I'm not bitter, I don't think I'm especially unlucky or life's unfair, I'm just telling it like it is. I've known Murray longer than anyone and I know he's really up for it. And me? I want to do something, you know? I want to do something big. I *need* this.'

'What if you don't have guns?'

'Then I guess it's back to the steak knives.' Tom smiled and polished off the cookie. 'I've still got them.'

'Got what?'

'You remember Riq and Em's wedding? You remember we forgot the present? You remember what it was? Conran Shop, set of twelve, hundred quid?'

'We never gave it to them?'

'Uh-uh,' Tom shook his head. 'Been sitting in a box under the basin ever since. I guess you could say we owe them.'

Karen's phone rang. She looked at the display and Jared's name flashed up. She ignored the call. She shut her eyes for a moment and licked her lips. She was feeling very peculiar too; super-sensitized as if she could feel every part of her body at once, distinguish every scent (coffee, of course, but vague traces of exhaust fumes, perfume, sweat and disinfectant as well) and hear every individual voice above the hubbub – 'You should have got it. You'll get it. You're going to get it. 'You'll just have to wait that's all. Bide your time. You'll get it.' 'You coming tomorrow night? Yeah? Should be brilliant.' 'I try and manage twice a week. It gives me so much energy. Even if I only use the treadmill.' 'They'll go for it. Of course they'll go for it. What are they going to do if they don't go for it? They'll go for it.' 'There's, like, one every three blocks. We're becoming, like, *so* Americanized. Listen to me! Every three *blocks!*' 'I don't know. You know what it's like. I just can't seem to get myself out of it.' 'You all right?'

The last voice was Tom's and she opened her eyes. She blinked at him and smiled thinly. 'Just tired, I think.' Looking at him now, at his concerned expression and the way he ran a hand through his hair (his long-standing mannerism of nervousness), she felt suddenly and deeply nostalgic. At first she couldn't figure where it came from but then she was forced to accept she was nostalgic for the certainty she had indeed once known (if never admitted). Without thinking about what it may or may not mean, she reached across the table and took his hand and squeezed it gently. When she spoke again, her voice was barely audible. 'You know you said my life was going well?' she whispered. 'I'm not so sure any more. I'm not so sure.'

19
Inklings of inevitability

I am peck-pecking at the Clapham Common earth just south of Lavender Hill (and isn't that a typical contradiction of nik nomenclature with its reek of railways and exhaust emissions?). I'm half-heartedly squirrelling for squirms but mostly just enjoying the cool consistency of this sumptuous soil beneath my beak.

I'm wondering how you scope my scoop so far: do you divine drama in my divulgences or do my own awful agonizing and my species' skirmishes and scrimmages strike you as no more than a feathered fuss over not a whole lot? Feel free as a bird to be asinine in your assessment as it won't bother me. Because one part I can positively pinpoint is this: however petty us pigeons may appear to the peep-niks, however dull our divisions and paltry our politics, consider the impact they had on a feather-brained flock that had just now known no such thing. Before Trafalgar, before consciousness, before Gunnersbury's grasp of the word 'war', there were squirms for all squibs and best bits for everybirdy and endless bins where birds burrowed without even the blink of a bead to acknowledge London's lavishness. Sorry to beak on about it but that's the way it was. What am I trying to illuminate? I'm saying suspend your superiority because our pigeon pettiness was certainly significant to us. To be veritas, a lot of peepnik problems seem pretty petty to me too. Empathy, therefore, is what I must emphasize to ensure illumination.

Nonetheless I'll sheeply admit that, as I tiptoe across these squirmy casts and dodge the packets and papers that blow across the patchy grass, the current content of my daily drudge is (I hazard; since I haven't the reassurance of recollection) not so different from the time before Trafalgar and the construction of consciousness.

Whether, therefore, with a peepnik penchant for exactitude, you call this war or simply bedlam in a bird-bath, I can veritably verify that life still goes on.

This is not to say that my whole pigeon personality is not sometimes shock-stilled with the chilly-chill of freezing fear and foreboding as I presently potter on this hiatus before the horizon, teeter on this precipice of the present, falter on this fault line of fate. But, fact is, I've still got to find my foodchits, I still gulp honest ozone into my bursting breast and I still scope Gunnersbury as just about the peachiest coochie this side of the City. 'Life goes on,' I squawk; and isn't that nik knowledge right there?

Even as this call carelessly coalesces into something like solid sound so my vibrato diverts a bounding bow-wow who's stalking a stick nearby (as bow-wows do). He's yomping towards yours truly, all drool, trailing tongue and concealed canines, so I take a vertical to the bough of a beech nearby.

This bow-wow's a feisty fuckster and no mistake. Generally these peepnik pets – four-legged fops the lot of them – have all the attention span of a squabblesome squib. But this one? He's pawing at the trunk, high on his hind legs, his breath like death actually atrophying the air around me until it feels like some kind of shrinking prison. I'm hardly bugged by this bothersome beast but you can scope that his ambition amuses me. Does he presume this pigeon will just jump into his yawning jaws?

A full flutter distant, I can scope his morose master mouthing half-hearted hails that the bow-wow inevitably ignores. This savoury is an old knackered in threadbare threads with lank grey hair that licks his lobes and tickles his temples. He's a sullen sort with an unappealing apathy, mitts in the pits of his pockets and a cigarette cherry hanging limp from his lower lip.

Nearby a cash young couple in casual cashmere are steering a stabilized youngen on his babchick's bicycle and they haven't scoped his big brother toddling towards my tree fixed in fascination by the barking bow-wow and the geez that goads him from a branch above. This little fellow is all flushed fresh phyzog and goldilock charm beneath his burgundy beanie but I wish he wouldn't come so close to this salivating sack of savagery with his turbulent temperament. Fly away, youngen! At least flee!

To be veritas, it's none of my business and it's not like no niks ever rushed to rescue a bird being torn wing from wing by a pernicious pussy. Nonetheless, as I scope the bow-wow's attention abstracted by the warm woolly bundle of bones, I shriek and squawk with all the bravado in my breast: 'Up here, you fatuous fuckster! Up here!' After all, what have I got to concede for my concern? Nut all. But the behemoth's brain has already been sidetracked by the sideways sight of the nik youngen and he growls and gallops at him with a ferocious focus that ruffles my feathers, no doubt.

The youngen yelps helplessly even as the bow-wow butts him to the earth and reveals his gnashing gnashers before sinking them deep into the tender flesh of a trousered thigh.

Now the poor poppet's parents have noticed the absence of their elder offspring all right. The sweet is a swell of screams as the cash savoury sprints to his son's side. The bow-wow's owner comes quickly too but his shouts are as ineffectual as September sun. The bow-wow is shaking its head from side to side, tossing its peepnik package this way and that like he was a bag of bird food.

To be veritas, the youngen's oldgeez is fairly frosty. He clutches the creature's collar and his guttural growls match or even trump the beast's own. He thrusts one hand into its mouth and hits its heaving flank with his fist again and again trying to jar the jaws apart.

It's only a moment before the bemused bow-wow drops his peepnik prey and sidles sheeply away, mewing like a miffed and plaintive pussy. The youngen's soon smothered in maternal mollycoddling and, to listen to the lungs on him, nowhere near death's door, not even perched on the porch of passing away. But this isn't going to stop the savoury from attacking the old knackered with a cavalcade of curses and a sharp selection of slurs: you stupid fucking this, you old fucking that, you ignorant fucking the other and so on.

Though I like to peep the peepniks as much as the next bird, I quickly lose interest since such tiffs are two a penny on any suburban street or Concrete concourse (are you looking at me? What did you say? Excuse me but this is a fucking queue, right? All of that). Like I said, the ins and outs of a nik contretemps can seem a trifle trivial to a pensive pigeon. Like I said, empathy is a two-way street.

Besides, there's something about this scenario that starts me in some conscious contemplation. I'm focusing on the youngen whose fresh phyzog was fixed on the barking bow-wow. One moment he was an awestruck audience while the very next he was startled into a starring role (or at least the specious spotlight of the expendable extra). Isn't this a cautionary tale for us all (peepniks and pigeons alike)? Though we tend to take top billing in the motion flixtures on our mindeyes, we still have a contrary capacity to watch ourselves over packets of popcorn on pot bellies until the beastly behemoth bites us back to some semblance of reality and we suddenly see ourselves scuppered on the very same soundstage. I'm thinking on the wing so fly with me. Because I'm sure there's a niblet of knowledge in here somewhere.

Take the two tyrants (or is that tyros?) of our feathered factions: Gunnersbury and Regent. When I consider the current conundrum of our fractured flock, I consistently conjure the context of their Trafalgar tantrum as they squabbled over the unilluminable stuff that was bunged in a bin by the unilluminable nik. But this recollection casts the cantankerous couple in roles of responsibility that might just be missing the point of the pin. After all, does a leader always come up with a cause? Or are they, the leaders, merely expelled by the frenzy of fate, spat into the spotlight by the harbingers of happenstance? What I'm trying to illuminate is this: would our destiny have differed if two other birds (one geez and one coochie) had been first to Trafalgar's trash? And, if so, how much?

If my instinct is now inclining me towards some inkling of inevitability, I confess I find little comfort therein; not least because these ponderous ponderings pester me with a new nugget of vicious verity that now yawns for yours truly as surely as that monster's mouth.

Scope it like this: once again, I'm reeling with the recollection of the night Brixton23 was murdered above the Brixton Tarmac. I recall that honest Surb geez's querulous calls, Regent with his magpie phyzog and Gunnersbury's desperate declaration of war. Most of all, however, I pinpoint the memory of Mishap's shooter shot that laid out the thugalicious pinxen in the car park below. Specifically, I remember peeping the scene in the consequent chaos and the way Mishap glanced up and looked me straight in the bead.

Suddenly, even as I pitter patter in nervous circles as the winsome wind soughs through the boughs of this beech, I recognize I may as well be beating my wings from between that bow-wow's teeth. Am I the most vanitariest pigeon to suddenly wonder whether yours truly, a nobirdy oldgeez from the most random suburban roost, could be the very acorn of it all? Is it my consciousness that clutters my bird brain with these inane imaginings? Or, in fact – let me frame this query correctly – is this sorry situation maybe less a measure of our bird bosses, less about the time before time, less about consciousness, the consciousness thereof and, indeed, contemplation therefore and more about Mishap and me?

Oh words! Oh consciousness! Is this the very essence of abstraction: that consciousness and clarity should call it a day when you're on the very verge of the verity? Stay frosty, geez. Stay frosty, old Ravenscourt. Because this narrative will untangle with or without your concession of complicity.

OK. I'm going to set this straight; or as straight as I can; or as straight as the crow flies (which, though a nik might not know it, is not always so straight). I am starting to suspect that there is a connection between Mishap and me that dates back to the time before time, the language before language and the flock before flocks existed. What is it that assures this assumption? I cannot illuminate. But there is something in his unilluminable phyzog that is as familiar as it is frightening; some manner in his movements; some charisma in his character. Most of all, however, I am coming to the conviction that my brief exhilaration of the consciousness of consciousness might not have been an exceptional experience after all. Perhaps I experienced it in the time before Trafalgar, when I was no more than a squib, when I was eye to eye with Mishap's inscrutable bead: certainly these are the shadowy images in the senile dimension of my mindeye, a motion flixture that casts his semi-comatose corpse into the sludge and slurry of a rising tide. Veritably.

And yet, even as I ascertain as much, I recall that memory is about fear and the hollowest, most gizzard-twistingest fear of all is about loss. And what have I lost? Memory. And there's the hubris and hilarity of circularity right there. As my words wander off, therefore, and my consciousness continues to collapse, I realize with another inkling of inevitability that all will be illuminated as surely as, when it happens, I will no longer have the conscious capacity to comprehend. It's Mishap, I swear.

As I cogitate on all these conundrums, I find I've fluttered down to terra firma once more and I'm scrabbling at the dirt with my pigeon toes and bobbing my beak at this barren soil like the mooniest moonatic. I know that revelation is coming but – aside from the conscious capacity to comprehend it – will I even have the appetite to appreciate it? If consciousness is a blessing in disguise then I'm starting to suspect that illumination may be an illness after all.

20

The drama and the farce of it

As a rule, given the choice, you would want the significant, definitive events of your life to be characterized by broad drama rather than narrow farce. When such an event looms on the horizon, it's primarily for this reason that people fall into tried and trusted archetypes or so-called traditions of behaviour. A church wedding, for example, is generally regarded as the traditional means by which a young couple announce themselves to the community. These days, however, a church wedding can also be thought of as a safe, if unimaginative, dramaturgic bet. After all, the priest has done it before, the guests know what to expect and you're probably guaranteed 'ooh's and 'aah's at the right moments and the prerequisite album of happy memories. In fact, therefore, the wedding is no different from the proposal on bended knee. While society may have once imbued such an action with the tradition of romance, it is now ascribed by the individual in the moment; by the boy who genuflects and takes the girl's hand because, most of all, he's scared of screwing up. In fact, therefore, the proposal on bended knee is no different from the fear of being knocked down by a car in yesterday's underwear. Behaviour is driven by fear of farce. This was what Tom thought anyway.

Karen, on the other hand, regarded Tom's hypothesis as very middle class. She got what he was saying, all right, and she agreed that avoidance of embarrassment could often be regarded as a primal motivation. After all, she understood that nobody wants to die on the toilet and, though from a plebeian background herself, she was English nonetheless. However, she couldn't help but surmise that the emphasis Tom placed on this smacked of privilege.

When they were going out, Karen quickly learned that Tom would always make do rather than make a fuss. He hated to haggle with a cab driver or question a restaurant bill, on the basis that it was 'more trouble than it was worth'. Of course, Karen thought this was easy for him to say because, whether school teacher or TV executive, he'd always get another cab and eat in another restaurant merely by virtue of his upbringing. But her? Her mum died when she was thirteen so she'd spent much of her adolescence dealing with prying social workers or trying to borrow a fiver off a neighbour or in endless, desperate queues for five minutes with a bored housing officer or, later, ignoring the patronizing advice of a middle-aged GP when she clocked the bruises on her shoulder and upper arm. She was used to embarrassment, you see.

In fact, Karen figured that she could reasonably extend this class-based analysis of Tom to other aspects of his personality. She wondered, for example, about his capacity to regard world events as somehow definitive of *him*; to take them so personally. After all, she'd always been the one with the political spirit; the one who'd marched and rallied and, eventually, made a career out of it. But it was him who was most spooked by the '91 war with Iraq, by the came-to-nothing threat of the millennium bug and by 9/11; as if any of these events had the slightest practical impact upon his life. This was, she reckoned, an illustration of the middle-class quality of distant empathy; while the white collars had room for it, the *hoi polloi* were just too busy scraping by. What's more, in Karen's experience, its flipside was often a peculiar apathy to more proximate, prosaic scenarios.

Although Karen insisted this was at least half a compliment, it's perhaps not surprising that Tom took offence and, claiming that she was missing the point, he changed tack. What he'd been trying to say was simply that the desire for appropriate drama, which was both stimulated by and combined with the modern penchant for a hyperbolic story (with nods to everything from Hollywood to soaps via the red tops), had led to ever more numerous learned behaviours appropriate to life's more extreme circumstances. If, he said, he was ever in a room and someone lobbed a grenade through the window, he'd probably dive on top of it; not as an act of bravery but simply from desire to fulfil the script. All these stories you watch, read and hear, he explained gravely, gave new meaning to ideas of fate.

Karen laughed at this and suggested it was a good job his theory would never be tested. She said that, the way she saw it, in extreme circumstances people generally reverted to type.

Again Tom baulked. It wasn't just in questions of heroism, he said. You could apply it to almost anything. Take tennis players. Before the late seventies none of them grunted as they served, whereas now they all did. In fact, you could walk past park courts and find kids who grunted with every shot, even when they were knocking up. What was that about? Either it reflected an intrinsic change in the modern game or, more likely, it was just a learned behaviour from a youth spent watching Jimmy Connors or, these days, the Williams sisters.

So what?

So lately Tom had been wondering if the same could be said of sex. He suspected it used to be a quiet kind of business whereas now sexual grunting was pretty much a required soundtrack. Were the wordless moans, oh yeses, oh gods and oh fucks *really* spontaneous and irrepressible markers of pleasure or simply expressions of a new fucking etiquette?

At this point the breadth of the conversation itself narrowed considerably. When Tom first started talking about church weddings and the like, Karen had carefully steered the conversation elsewhere in case he was building up to the clumsiest and most unwelcome proposal of his own (after all, with Tom's capacity for prevarication and inopportune timing, anything was possible). Now, however, she took Tom's reference to the joys or otherwise of sex as a (thinly) veiled insult with a whole lot of history; not least because he accidentally lent the phrase 'new fucking etiquette' a frustrated and offensive tone rather than the intended meaning of revolution in bedroom convention. She therefore responded with a barrage of (unveiled) comments about, among other things, his sexual prowess which left him at first bewildered, then hangdog and finally irritated enough to retort in kind.

Of course, all this confusion and subsequent bickering would probably have been avoided if Tom had ever properly learned (in therapy, say) to speak his mind. But he hadn't. You see, although Tom began talking about an abstract idea applied to hypothetical situations, he actually had a very specific event in mind. Specifically, he was thinking of the night they went to buy guns from Kush. Specifically, he was trying to address (in the most circuitous and, perhaps, middle-class fashion) his regrets with regard to both the drama and the farce of it.

It was undoubtedly, for Tom, a momentous and definitive occasion just as surely as, for Karen, it seemed to have been easily forgotten or, perhaps, wilfully ignored. It was also an occasion that had mixed dollops of the broad with lashings of the narrow to leave an altogether unsavoury aftertaste.

On the arranged midweek night, they planned to meet at eleven thirty at Emma and Tariq's. And that was pretty much the end of the harmony. They couldn't even agree who was going to attend the rendezvous.

Emma suggested (and assumed the others would concur) that the party should consist of Murray and her (as schemers in chief), Karen (since she'd set up the deal and knew Kush) and Kwesi (because he was 1.) the biggest; 2.) could do that Yardie accent, which might impress a small-time gangster; and 3.) had once claimed in a poem to have had dealings with the mobs hooked in to the West African diamond racket). This was, she proposed, a group of about the right size to lend each other support and demonstrate to Kush some kind of weight of numbers.

Unfortunately, however, it was Freya who'd fronted the 600 quid to buy, as Karen informed them with a smirk, 'three shooters'. ('That sounds like a lot of cash,' Tom commented. Karen shrugged. Like he'd know.) And, since Freya Franklin Hats had begun to grow and blossom, so had something else. Freya described it as 'self-confidence' while others were already beginning to use words like 'self-importance' or even plain 'selfishness'. Whichever way you looked at it, it meant that Freya reacted to Emma's proposition by saying, 'I think I should be there.' And then, 'Seeing as it's my money.'

In the cold light of day (or even the muggy night of a London summer), this was hardly a rational response and the others were quick to say so. What did she think they were going to do? Run away with the wad for a slap-up dinner and a West End show? And besides, a night of gun-buying in a South London car park was hardly the hottest invitation in town. But as Freya's self-confidence (or self-importance) had increased so, as is typical, had the depth of her stubborn streak and she wouldn't be swayed. So Emma looked to Karen and Tom, who both shrugged. It was OK. There was room for five in the Volvo. Karen took the brown envelope full of cash and tucked it into her handbag.

Ami and Kwesi took no part in this debate. Ami was playing

with her DVC; reviewing the day's material and already imagining a final edit. She had some great footage of Dave Purbright, one of the personal bankers, refusing a young couple an overdraft extension. His grave and patronizing demeanour was wonderfully undercut by Ami's surreptitious camera angle, which showed the glossy cover of a wank mag protruding from his desk drawer. This show was a winner. As for Kwesi, he was playing with Tommy, who was in turn playing with the badge that said 'Ami Lester: Trainee'. Considering the hour, the baby was surprisingly good-natured. Infected by Emma's own nerves, he hadn't been able to get to sleep and he calmly turned the badge in his hands and then sucked on a corner while Kwesi, whispering in kiddy tones, tried out a new verse on him. The K-ster was doing all that he could to appear similarly calm, to give the impression that arms deals were second nature (which was, after all, what he'd claimed, in oft-repeated rhyme).

Then Tariq came in from work and the atmosphere really soured. He was drunk. Of course he was; it was after pub closing time. Today, however, he'd far exceeded his usual levels of inebriation. Whether it was an especially bad day at the bankruptcy coalface or the thought of the night's activities had driven him over the edge was impossible to tell, since he was pissed beyond coherence. As hard as he tried to look repentantly sheepish, he couldn't stop his eyes rolling, the constant swaying and occasional belch.

Emma was livid. She'd intended that he'd babysit while she was out buying guns. But she could hardly leave her son in Tariq's care, could she? He tried to give her a hug and repeated, 'It's fine, fine, fine', over and over like a mantra. This only made it worse.

Ami pointed out that she was staying behind anyway and would happily keep an eye on Tommy. Emma said thanks and pulled a strained smile; but she wasn't really comfortable with that. Wasn't *comfortable* with it? This, in turn, put Ami's nose out of joint; all the more so when Emma added, thoughtlessly, that looking after the baby required more than just 'keeping an eye'.

Tom was gently chastising the drunkard, saying things like, 'Come on, Riq! I thought you were making more of an effort', and, 'It's hardly helpful, is it?'

Tariq was nodding dolefully. 'It's fine,' he said. 'Fine, fine.'

Until recently, Emma had surely appreciated any allies on the battleground of her marriage. Now, however, she was suddenly defensive of her husband. In the last couple of weeks she had, in her words, 'tried so hard' and 'made all kinds of sacrifices' and the last thing she needed was some outsider, well-meaning or not, putting his oar in. So she hissed at Tom: 'Leave it out.'

Tom was taken aback. 'I'm sorry?'

'It's fine,' Tariq slurred. 'Really. Fine.'

'This is between Riq and me, OK? None of your business.'

'OK, OK,' Tom muttered. 'Shit.'

Karen was the only one who seemed unaffected by the rising tension; this was partly because she secretly suspected they weren't going to go through with the whole thing anyway. 'Where's Murray?' she asked and they all looked at each other and then to their watches.

'He'll be here,' Tom said.

'And what are we going to do?'

Emma, who was now strung like a top C, said: 'What do you mean, "What are we going to do?"'

'I mean, who's going on this outing, then? What are we down to? Me, Freya, Murray and Kwesi: is that the idea?'

'No way!' Emma snapped. 'I'm definitely going.' They all stared at her. A few minutes earlier she'd been the one who'd tried to explain to Freya that buying guns in a car park was hardly the height of glamour. Now she was being obstinate in exactly the same way. 'I'm going,' she said. 'And that's that.'

'So who's going to look after Tommy?'

'Not me. Apparently,' Ami mumbled.

'I will,' Tom volunteered. He bent down, rubbed the baby's crown and gently disengaged his fingers from Ami's badge. 'He's my godson. I've done it before. *And* we get on like a house on fire, don't we?' He mock-frowned. 'I said, don't we?' Tommy gurgled appreciatively and stretched out an arm to reclaim his new toy.

Emma was shaking her head. 'No. He's coming too.'

They all stared at her again. Tom said, 'Em?' while Karen burst out laughing. 'Are you serious?' Freya growled, 'Oh, for god's sake!' and loaded the exclamation with all her new-found pomposity. Tariq, who'd sobered up enough to pour himself an enormous Scotch and hand another to Kwesi (who gulped it in two), said, 'We'll all go. It'll be an adventure. Why the hell not?' And he embellished his words with an expansive, magnanimous gesture as if he were actually saying, 'The Milky Bars are on me!'

In the end, this was what they agreed. Or, if not agreed, *concluded* at least.

Emma said she'd been thinking about it and her reasoning went like this: the more of them at the meet, the more that were implicated and that would head off any future discord and stop anyone backing out. Tom observed that they were *supposed* to be friends; they were *supposed* to trust one another. Emma reminded him that they hadn't even done anything yet and they were already squabbling. Karen suggested that Kush wouldn't be expecting such a posse and might feel threatened. Emma asked how he was going to feel threatened by a mother and baby. Karen shrugged. She was just saying. Privately she thought the more the merrier since, she figured, it increased the possibility of the loss of collective bottle.

Freya said nothing but adopted an attitude of aloof disdain. She'd been practising and had it nailed. This lot, she thought, couldn't run a piss-up in a brewery (apart from Tariq, who could run a piss-up in Mecca). Tom recognized, with circular logic, that if they were all going then he had to go too since, apart from Mr and Mrs Khan, he was the only one with a car.

Ami grumbled that they could say what they liked but she wasn't going anywhere. She said that she still couldn't see any thrills in the proposed mission and she didn't say that Emma had pissed her off besides. This briefly led to further arguments (which had Freya tutting and sighing) until Emma pointed out that it didn't really matter since Ami was effectively implicated anyway as she'd already started work in the bank. 'Whatever,' Ami said but she wouldn't look up from the mini-display of her DVC.

Tariq, whose lager fuzz had now been largely cleared by the whisky, was becoming absurdly garrulous and enthusiastic. 'It'll be brilliant,' he babbled as he gave Kwesi a refill. 'Buy some guns, rob some banks, brilliant! It's got to be better than predictive bloody technology, anyway. I'll tell you something, I bet my smart-arse computer didn't predict I was going to rob a bloody bank!'

Tariq thought this was the funniest thing he'd ever said (possibly even heard, trumping the depressed pigeons) and doubled up in hysterics. He then farted accidentally, belched violently and winced as though he'd just taken a mouthful of god-knows-what. He quickly poured himself another.

Kwesi immediately held out his glass again. Having abandoned any affectation of poise, he was eagerly playing catch-up. He was certainly well aware that the whole lot of them piling into two cars with a baby on board and driving to a

Brixton car park to buy guns was a bad idea (and it didn't take his imagined experience with Ghanaian gangsters to tell him that). Nonetheless, he'd signed up for this madness and *they*'d all agreed that *he* was going so he felt a good deal happier to be one of six (six and a half, including Tommy) than of four.

It's arguable that if they'd taken the time to, variously, sober up and calm down, they might have come up with a different plan, even abandoned the scheme altogether. But they didn't take the time. Because it was about then that Murray finally turned up and, typically for Murray, he made quite an entrance (albeit a very untypical one).

Karen answered the door but the others all heard her exclamation – 'Jesus Christ!' – and, when Murray stumbled into the living-room, they each dropped similar and some fruitier curses. He looked terrible. In fact, more than that, he looked like someone else (no mean feat for someone who generally looked like anyone).

It's hard to know where to start. He was wearing a grey T-shirt with a blue hoodie knotted at the waist of his dark jeans. Just below his left shoulderblade, the thin marl was clinging to his flesh and a dark, wet patch of what could only be blood covered a large part of the material. His right hand was still knotted with the silk scarf Freya had given him in the shop but it too was now black and soiled. Worst of all, his face looked like a Picasso. His left eye was grotesquely swollen, gummed shut with yellow pus and seemingly balanced on the bulbous purple ledge where his cheekbone was supposed to be. It gave his whole aspect a bizarre, cartoonist lopsidedness that was both repellent and oddly sympathetic. Or was that worst of all?

Later, when Tom recalled Murray's appearance, what he remembered most was the colour of his skin. Or rather its lack. In certain lights at certain times Tom knew Murray could look black, white, Asian or any cocktail of any races you'd care to name. But now – was it just in this light, at this time? – he looked like . . . like he'd been drained. Tom couldn't express it any better than that. His skin tone was somehow dull and transparent all at once. This is not to say that you could see his veins or the definition of his musculature; rather the opposite. It was as though he were actually no more than a particularly dense fog; real and present but if you tried to touch him you'd be scared he'd dissolve in your fingers. Tom thought that was the worst.

Later, when Emma recalled his appearance, what she remembered most was the smell that seemed to flood the room when he entered. It was a smell she recognized at the same time as it was utterly unfamiliar, as if the overwhelming strength of it had transformed it into something of a completely different nature. The stench was so visceral it almost seemed to take shape and Emma imagined great hulking brutes that represented tag teams of armpits and arseholes, drains and dishwater, abattoirs and ashtrays, cocks and cunts slugging it out invisibly in the wrestling ring of the living-room. Emma thought that was the worst.

Perhaps because he didn't know the origins of any of Murray's individual wounds or perhaps because he was so bladdered, it was Tariq who was first to frame his expletives into something like a question: 'Fucking fuck! What the fuck happened to you?'

Murray attempted a smile but, with the state of his face, it was a freakish expression that matched nothing in Tom's database. And was it Tom's imagination or did he really spot black gaps in Murray's mouth where teeth used to be? Surely his single punch couldn't have caused damage like that. 'This and that, china,' Murray said. 'You know how it goes.'

'But what happened to your face?' Tariq asked and he

half-expected him to launch into some cock-and-bull story about bare-knuckle boxing in a Dartford dive, a bar fight with fifteen Frenchmen or a kicking from Combat 18. Consequently he was half disappointed when Murray said simply, 'I slipped.'

'You *slipped!*'

'Yeah.'

'What about your back?' This was Ami.

Awkwardly Murray turned to her and his one good eye looked puzzled. 'My back?'

'What on earth happened? You look like you've been cut.'

He tried to shrug but the movement sent a shiver of pain through him. 'Like I said, china. I slipped.'

'And your hand?'

'That?' Murray's face curled into the same ghoulish smile. '*That* was a pigeon.'

'For god's sake . . .' Tariq began. But he was interrupted by his wife, who exclaimed a little louder than was necessary, 'No. It *was*, Riq. Me and Ami were there, weren't we?'

There was a heartbeat's hush. Then another. 'Whatever, Muz,' Karen said softly. 'We're going to have to take you to casualty.'

'What?'

'You need to see a doctor. You look awful.'

Murray shook his head. 'For a few cuts and bruises, Kazza? You're joking. I'm fine and, besides, we've got work to do, haven't we? We should be going soon so who's coming?'

Freya said, 'We all are.'

'Except me,' Ami added.

'Right then,' Murray nodded and suddenly seemed to regain some of his usual assurance. 'Just give me something to eat and clean me up a bit and I'll be right as rain.'

Kwesi started to laugh but managed to cork it. 'Yeah, man. I hate to say this Murray, man, but you really hum.'

Emma took control then. She led Murray upstairs by the hand, found him a fresh towel and left him to shower. She shouted down to her husband, 'Riq! Can you find me the first-aid box.'

'What first-aid box?'

'It's in the cupboard to the left of the hob.'

Tariq rummaged, drunk and half-hearted, but couldn't find it so Emma had to look for herself. She took out the antiseptic, bandages and sticky plaster. Then she opened the fridge. She had in fact stocked up on all kinds of snacks for this evening, to give her friends something to chow on before they left. But she'd forgotten all about them what with all the fussing. She'd bought some boneless chicken breasts especially for Murray and she fetched them out and tipped them on to a plate. She realized that the shock of Murray's appearance and her consequent busyness had calmed her down no end.

Tariq was watching her blurrily. 'You're such a housewife!' It was a comment that, once upon a time, would have infuriated her but now she could take it on the chin. In fact, she almost agreed.

Next door, the others were sitting in near silence. Kwesi was helping himself to more booze while Ami had returned to her camera. Tom was rocking his godson on his lap. Freya watched him curiously and Karen watched Freya and then said, 'K. Can you pour a little one for me?' At some point, Kwesi tried, 'Is it just me or is this really weird? I mean, cool, cool, you know? But weird.' The rest made vague noises of agreement but had their own reasons to find that they didn't feel like talking.

When she heard the shower pump click off, Emma headed back upstairs with her makeshift medical supplies and the plate of chicken. The bathroom door was open, billowing steam, and she realized Murray must be in their – her and Tariq's –

bedroom. Her stomach tumbled as she knocked on the door.

Murray was sitting on the edge of the bed with a towel around his waist. He looked forlorn, pathetic, and Emma didn't reject the feelings of intimacy that rose in her because they were compassionate rather than sexual. She was sure that nobody else had ever seen Murray like this; a fleeting hopelessness and naivety in his eyes. Until recently, of course, she would have been right but Freya had already seen momentary flashes of the same as he sat on her counter; Karen, too, high above London in the Oxo Tower.

Murray said, 'I figured I could borrow one of Riq's T-shirts.'

'Sure,' Emma said. 'Of course.'

Then neither of them spoke at all as she tenderly swabbed and dressed his back and hand. She cleaned his palm and covered it with gauze and a pad of cotton wool before wrapping it tightly. But, even as she did so, a new stain began to spread across the material. This close to him, she began to notice the same stench again; only now it sickeningly mingled with the artificial, sweet perfume of soap.

When she turned to his shoulder, she discovered her original bandage, wet from the shower, hanging limp and filthy. She gingerly pulled it away and the wound she revealed somersaulted her already fragile guts. Though she wasn't squeamish, she'd never seen something like this before. It looked somehow fresh and fetid at once. The lips still held a vague pinkish tinge but they were attached to strips of grey, dead skin that, steeling herself, she snipped away with scissors. Murray couldn't feel it and he didn't flinch. The heart of the cut was still wet and bloody – which was odd because its colour was dark, the colour of clotting. She mopped and patched it as best she could.

She knelt in front of him and he was as docile as a trusting child as she rubbed a little antiseptic into the welt on his cheek and carefully around the eye socket. She said, 'I can't really do much about this. Unless I give you an eye patch.' She tried to inject a lightness to her voice but, in spite of herself, it crackled with doubt. 'This one will heal on its own,' she tried.

'Sure, china,' he said. 'That's fine.'

Emma sat back on her haunches and contemplated Murray's battered face. The pitiful expression had vanished and left no shadows. 'Are you all right?'

'Apart from the pain? Yeah. Good.'

'No. But, I mean, the . . . on your shoulder. It hasn't healed at all. Are you sick?'

'Me?' Murray did his lopsided smile. 'I'm ticketyboo. I thought you were the one who was sick. How are *you* doing?'

'I'm better.'

'And how's Tariq?'

She shrugged. 'Drunk.'

'And you and Tariq?'

She stared at him for a moment, trying to read his expression. Then she frowned and shook her head. 'I brought you something to eat,' she said. 'I'll leave you to get dressed.'

When she was gone, Murray discarded the towel and examined his reflection in the wardrobe's full-length mirror. He shut his good eye and stood like that for a moment. Then he tilted his head contemplatively. He wasn't thinking but at some instinctive level there was some overwhelming realization growing inside him; something so basic and so inevitable that it required no more processing than, say, hunger. He blinked at himself and his eyes pricked with a feeling that wasn't pain.

He found a can of Tariq's deodorant. It was lying on the floor, fallen from the chest of drawers. He picked it up and sprayed himself all over, holding the nozzle down for a full minute until he began to wheeze, shrouded in a mist called Cool Blue, and his whole body was covered in a fine white powder. He dressed as quickly as he could. The clean T-shirt took the longest since his left arm was almost immobile. He slipped on the hoodie and zipped it right to the neck.

He sat on the edge of the bed, rested the plate on his lap and began to tuck in to the white meat with mechanical haste, each of the four breasts requiring no more than two giant mouthfuls. He couldn't remember the last time he ate. It must have been a packet of Sankar the sadhu's chicken roll. He sat for a moment with his right hand resting on his stomach and his eyes darted towards the door. He hadn't time to reach the main bathroom so he made for the en suite instead. He knelt over the pan, shut his eyes and regurgitated the food in four mighty retches. He flushed the toilet and stood up. He felt a little better. He pressed the heel of his gored, bandaged palm into the bruise of his left eye. He opened his eyes and checked his reflection again, this time in the mirror over the basin. He looked a little better, too; a little less grotesque. He strode out of the bedroom and slammed the door behind him.

Tom was standing at the bottom of the stairs, looking up. 'You all right, Muz?'

Murray sat down on the top step and rested his elbows on his knees. He peered down at Tom, narrowed his good eye as though staring from a great distance and stretched a strange smile. This one had no number; with the freakery of Murray's face, classification was impossible.

'I'm losing faith, china,' Murray said. 'You know what that's like, right?'

'Losing faith in what?'

'I don't know. In my friends. I mean . . . you know what that's like.'

'Yeah,' Tom said and momentarily his tone hissed with acid. 'Yeah. I do.'

'You're not going to let me down are you, china?'

'Murray!' Tom exclaimed. 'In the robbery? I never let you down. Not when it comes to Murray-fun.'

'I'm not talking about that. I just mean in . . . I don't know . . . in *life*. Because I only wanted to look out for you, you know? Like I said I would. Ten years ago. That's what I said. But I feel like I've come to a realization. I feel like this is my moment of truth.'

'Moment of truth?' Tom almost choked to hear Tejananda's psychobabble thrown back at him. 'What's your Moment of Truth?'

Murray suddenly appeared puzzled and his voice came out at a whisper that Tom couldn't decipher. 'It's something I read,' he muttered. 'I think I'm dead, you know?' And then he tried it louder. 'Dead.'

'What are you talking about?'

'I said I think I'm dead.'

Tom gazed up at him and tutted; then tried an expression of mild concern. 'What are you talking about? You all right, Muz?'

Murray snorted, an odd spasmodic sound somewhere between a gurgle and a laugh. 'Yeah, china. I'm good. I guess it's about time we got going.'

Sainsbury's car park

They went in convoy, Tom leading the way in the old Mazda his dad had given him and the Volvo following behind. Karen automatically made for the Mazda's passenger seat and Murray slid in the back and lifted the hood of his top and pulled the drawstrings tight so that he looked like a boxer after a hard fight. With these two for passengers, Tom thought it might be an opportunity to address a ten-year-old secret. The timing could have been a lot better, of course, but he had a vague sensation of urgency; like he might not get another chance. But then Emma, who had her drunken husband next to her and Kwesi amusing the baby in the back, suggested Tom took Freya too. Tom said 'no problem' but obviously the extra passenger (especially considering who it was) ruled out that particular plan.

Ami waved them off from the door.

It was only a ten-minute drive and the roads were quiet, which was reassuring; alongside Clapham Common, into the High Street with its shuttered pubs, and a shimmy right and left to Acre Lane with its ghost-town atmosphere of boarded takeaways and litter blowing like tumbleweeds. Nobody spoke. Tom wondered if the others were nervous. He wasn't. He was thinking about the webs of secrecy. He knew that she knew about them while she didn't know that she knew and she didn't know that he knew. As for him? He knew everything. That kind of thing.

He pulled into the supermarket car park and it was, thank god, deserted apart from Kush's BMW parked right in the middle of the space. The man himself was leaning on the bonnet. He was wearing a black leather coat, smoking a cigarette between his forefinger and thumb, looking every inch the gangster.

'He's on his own,' Karen said. 'That's good.' She suddenly realized they were actually going to go through with it and there was no backing out now.

Tom parked facing the Beamer's nose and Emma pulled in alongside. Karen got out first with Tom next to her and Freya just behind. Kwesi and Tariq were side by side, the former now every bit as drunk as the latter. Emma had planned to leave Tommy in the car but he was grizzling. She took a moment to slip him into his harness and he quietened a little with his head next to her heartbeat. Murray was skulking at the back.

At the sight of this motley group, Kush started laughing. 'Oh dear, oh dear,' he said and flicked his butt. 'What are you doing to me, Kaz? Who the fuck are this bunch of motherfuckers?'

Karen said, 'Let's get on with it. Have you got them?'

'Got them? Got what exactly?'

'Come on, Kush. The guns.'

'The *guns*?' He widened his eyes in ham amazement. 'I've no idea what you're talking about, love.' He looked directly at Kwesi, who seemed to shrink beneath the weight of it. 'You know what she's talking about? No? What about you?' He turned his attention to Tariq and his expression suddenly fixed with recognition. 'Well! Look who it is! If it's not the Paki hard man. How's the nose? Fucking hell, Kaz. All these years and you're still hanging out with the same lot of losers? I have to say I'm disappointed.'

'Look . . .' This was Freya and she sounded pompous. 'It's a simple deal. You've got the guns and we've got the money. If you don't like it, we'll take our business elsewhere.'

Kush smiled broadly. 'Yeah? Motherfucker! Check you out. What's your name, darling? I'm Kush.'

He held out his hand towards her. She looked disconcerted and backed off a step. 'Freya,' she said.

'You don't want to shake my hand, Freya? That's a shame. I like a woman who talks tough, know what I mean?' He looked at Karen. 'Eh, Kaz?'

Tommy began to whimper and then cry and then it took just seconds to explode into a full-blown tantrum. Emma tried to shush him as she rocked him back and forth but his screams seemed to tear the night like it was a thin satin sheet. The sound wound the tension tighter and then tighter again.

'Do you mind shutting your baby up?' Kush said. 'Fuck, Kaz! What are you trying to do to me?'

'Let's just make the exchange. I know you've brought them and I've got the money right here. Last time I saw you, you said you'd help me out. You remember? "Anything I can do." That's what you said. So did you mean it or not?'

'All right! All right! You trying to make me feel guilty? You know I'm a man of my word.'

Karen knew her ex-boyfriend was enjoying every second of this; revelling in the control. His cue-ball head wrinkled and flattened as he played out every little game he wanted. She glanced at Tom. His hands were deep in his pockets and he was staring at the ground, nudging a pebble with his foot. Emma had walked a little distance away and was urgently cooing to her baby. Karen caught sight of her face and it was haggard, desperate. Freya looked, frankly, terrified. To their credit, both Kwesi and Tariq were trying to maintain some kind of front; albeit with a lot of Dutch courage and not much conviction. And Murray? He was still hovering at the back, his face completely shadowed by the hood. What was he playing at? She could have used a bit of support.

Kush opened the rear door of his car on the driver's side and pulled out a black sports bag. He laid the bag on the bonnet and unzipped it. 'Sigs and a Delta,' he said. 'Quality hardware.'

Tom shuffled forward and peered inside. There were three guns, all right. Two of them were dark, dull and threatening but the third was a shiny silver, the kind of thing James Bond might carry. Tom felt like he should say something but he didn't know what. In the end it just slipped out: 'Nice.'

Kush glanced at him with unconcealed disdain. 'You ever shot a gun?'

Karen, relieved and eager to get this over with, took the envelope of money out of her handbag and handed it to Kush. He took it without looking at her. His gaze was still trained on Tom, who was doing his utmost to meet it. 'What's this?'

'Six hundred.'

'Six hundred? What for?'

Now he turned to her and her heart plummeted. She saw a familiar flicker in his eyes – an aggression, a macho thrill – and she suddenly knew it was all about to go wrong. 'Like we agreed,' she prompted.

Kush nodded, opened the envelope, checked its contents and slipped it into his coat pocket. 'Right you are, Kaz,' he said. 'Trouble is, things just got a lot more pricey.'

For a moment nobody said anything; silence, punctuated only by Tommy's occasional whimper. Then Karen managed, 'What?'

'Look at it from my point of view.' Kush looked up at the sky and rolled his fat neck. 'I didn't know you were going to bring the world and his wife – let alone his kids – now, did I? I mean, think about it: you turn up on your own and there's not much risk for me, you get me? "My girl Kaz isn't going to grass me up." That's what I thought. Though, judging by your expression, I might've had that wrong too. And then you turn up with all these motherfuckers? Well. You can see my concern. I don't know what you're going to do with these shooters but, judging by the state of you lot, it's fifty-fifty to go pear-shaped. And that's a whole lot of motherfuckers who recognize my boat, you get me? You're asking for what you might call a considerable leap of faith and that costs a considerable amount of money and, let's be frank, I reckon you lot can afford it.'

'Look . . .' Karen began. Then, 'Sorry . . . But . . .'

'In fact, to be honest with you, I'm quite tempted to walk away from this shit right now. Six hundred notes? Not a bad night's work. You can call it my consultation fee and put it down to experience, know what I mean?'

Karen desperately looked around her friends – Emma, Freya, Kwesi and Tariq. Surely one of them would say something? But they all looked as bewildered and defeated as she felt. She didn't look at Murray because, by now, he was standing so far back that he was right at the fringes of her vision. She didn't look at Tom because she knew he was shit in situations like this; or, rather, she knew he was shit in situations that, compared to this, were a walk in the park (and not a car park at that). After all, for all his stated desire and attempts (both successful and failed) to look after her, he was, essentially, a coward.

And yet it was Tom who spoke; Tom, who'd failed to stand up to Kush once before, who'd just come out of therapy, who saw this, however absurdly, as yet another Moment of Truth (they were coming thick and fast). 'We've paid you the money so just give us the fucking shooters . . .' he said. 'Guns.'

Kush's mouth slowly peeled into a wide grin. 'Mother*fucker*!' He annunciated the word precisely, loaded with admiration and irony. 'Aren't *you* the surprise package? So why should I do that?'

In spite of himself, Tom found that he was slowly moving forward. He felt a bizarre detachment, the same kind of lightness he'd experienced a few days previously after his last session with Tejananda, as if he were floating. In this moment of abstraction, he considered it somewhat ironic that, at this potentially most definitive of moments, he should feel so overtaken by events. 'Because that was the deal,' he said.

'So?'

'Because you're not going to take our money.'

'No?' The grin had thickened into a scar on Kush's face. 'And why's that, then?'

'Because I'll take that bag off you myself.'

Karen said, 'Tom! Don't be stupid. Forget it.' And Freya, who'd lost any semblance of composure, stretched a squeal into a word that sounded something like 'Please!'

'Yeah? You going to be a hero?'

Kush opened the flap of his coat and placed his right hand on the butt of the gun that stuck out from the top of his jeans. It was a perfectly executed movie moment and Karen knew that Kush loved it. But she knew too that he wasn't to be messed with; he was way too unstable to be trusted to behave rationally when he had a weapon in his pants. She hissed, 'Tom!' but he was still, slowly, approaching the gangster. Tom glanced at her sideways and she saw a flash of panic on his face. It was as though he couldn't stop himself, as though his feet were on coasters. He felt – or was this just informed by location? – like a runaway shopping trolley heading for a smash.

For an instant, Kush looked uncertain, like he didn't know what to do next. But he did have the gun, after all, so he pulled it out and trained it on Tom's forehead. That stopped Tom, all right. And Freya let loose a curious strained scream like a holed balloon and Kwesi exclaimed, 'Goodness me!' like the privately educated son of a diplomat that he was (because, as Karen observed some months later, in extreme circumstances people generally revert to type).

Freya's whines set the baby off again, too, and now Kush, for all his confidence, was beginning to feel more than a little rattled. He turned to Karen, though his gun was still ready to pop a hole in Tom's head. 'What you want them for?'

Karen saw no reason to beat around the bush. 'It's a bank job,' she said.

'A bank job?' Kush exclaimed and he started to laugh again. He couldn't believe what he was hearing. 'What are you doing to me, Kaz?' he spluttered.

The gun still raised, he made a move towards the bag. It was time to get out of here. Easy money but now it was time to go. But then he saw the geezer strolling towards him from the back of the group. Of course he'd sussed him earlier but he hadn't given him too much thought since he hadn't said anything and was just hovering in the shadows. Now, however, this geezer was approaching and he dropped his hood and Kush said, 'Fuck!' and automatically shifted the gun's aim and backed away a step or two.

'You all right, china?' Murray said.

Karen looked between them. She didn't know what was going on. She knew that, with the state of his face, Murray's appearance was somewhat gruesome. But it wasn't like Kush had never seen cuts and bruises before and, besides, in this half-light Murray didn't look nearly so bad. Nonetheless she admitted that there was something in Murray's manner that made 'fuck' seem like a reasonable response. It was as though Murray had flicked a switch and turned on the full force of his personality and it was as dazzling as the bathroom light at three a.m. There was an almost tangible calmness about him;

his movements seemed to have a swaggering rhythm of their own, his gaze was like glue and it can't have just been her imagination that granted his whole being some kind of aura of perfect otherness, as if he were a touched-up photograph. In fact, she realized that she hadn't seen this full extent of Murray's charisma for years; certainly not in this time he'd been among them. She realized that all the flashes he'd shown – at Freya's party or Kwesi's gig, say – had been no more than that, flashes; like tracer fire preceding the main assault. Because this? This was different.

Kush said, 'Long time.'

'True, true,' Murray smiled. 'How long's it been?'

'Must be ten years. Looks like you took another beating.'

'What goes around comes around, china.'

'What's that supposed to mean?'

Murray shrugged. He was now closer to the sports bag than Kush himself and he was looking inside. Again Kush had his eyes pointing one way and the gun another. Again he was staring at Karen and he looked strangely disconcerted. 'You said you weren't seeing this motherfucker!' he said. 'That day we met. I thought you were with that posh cunt.' He spat the words like pellets.

Karen was completely bemused. 'What?'

'That day we met,' Kush said again and then his eyes darted back to Murray. His voice took on an odd mollifying quality. 'It's Tom, right?'

'No, china. Murray,' Murray said. 'And these are replicas.'

'What? What you talking about?'

'I said these are replicas. I used to work in a toyshop, china. You think I don't know toys when I see them?'

'They're reconditioned. They shoot bullets. What more do you want?' Then to Karen. 'After all these years, Kaz. You still seeing *him*?'

'Seeing who?' She didn't know what was going on.

'You sure it won't blow my hand off when I fire it?' Murray was reaching into the bag. Now Kush fully turned his attention to Murray and jabbed his gun repeatedly at him, like it was an extension of his index finger. 'You keep your hands to yourself!'

Murray was smiling. Smile number two: the power smile that lets you know exactly who's in charge. 'I've got to check the merchandise, china.'

'I said keep your hands up!' Kush was just a couple of yards away from him and his expression was stretched with a panic Karen hadn't seen before. His hand was flexing, tight around the grip of his gun. The others were frozen. Freya's face was a cartoon of terror. Tariq and Kwesi were dumbstruck like kids in front of B-movie horror. Even Tommy was silent, clutched tight to Emma's chest. Tom murmured, 'Murray', and just for a second Murray glanced at him and the brow above his good eye jumped up and down as if to say, 'Are you ready for this?'

Murray's right arm hadn't moved an inch. It still hovered over the sports bag. 'Why are you so surprised to see me?' he asked.

'What?' Kush's gun hand was quivering. 'Are you fucking crazy? Just back off.'

'I thought we were doing a deal. I just wondered if you knew.'

'Knew what?'

'Knew what you did. Ten years ago. I mean, I can see it in your face, china. You've been trying to forget. But you know, all right.' Murray leaned forward and dipped into the bag.

'No! Just back off. Back the fuck off.' Kush's voice cracked and leaped an octave.

In that frozen second, Karen thought he sounded like a

pleading child in the grip of a playground bully. In that frozen second she felt the collision of forgotten terror at his hands and visceral overwhelming hatred. In that frozen second, the only thing that moved was a dark object that dropped through her line of sight so slowly it seemed to flicker like cine film.

It was impossible to tell which pressed the fast-forward button – the impact of the dead pigeon crashing on to the BMW's windscreen or the gunshot that rang out an indistinguishable instant later. Time suddenly accelerated into a chaos of images that later, in private, they each reassembled into their own personal collage. There was Freya, screaming and hysterical and being shushed by Tariq. There was Emma, sitting on the Tarmac, rocking the baby as she rocked herself, her face washed out and pallid. There was Murray, stock still with the gun hanging against his thigh. There were Tom and Karen checking Kush's corpse. When they turned the body and saw the gory mess of the face, Karen gasped and Tom covered his mouth. God knows what this reconditioned replica fired but it certainly wasn't a clean bullet. There was Kwesi running to the edge of the car park before dropping to his knees and spewing acrid whisky puke all over the place. Then, remembering some newspaper story he'd once read about a criminal conviction based on DNA in vomit, he took off his jacket and began to desperately mop at the puddle.

Each of their individual collages contains some of these snapshots and not others but one image unites them all. Because they all looked up when they heard the cacophony above their heads and saw the living blanket of pigeons tear itself apart and fly off alone, in pairs and groups to north, south, east and west and up and down.

Some months afterwards, when Tom propounded his theory of farce, he probably had his own collage of these moments after the shooting unrolled in his mind's eye: Freya's unruly hair wet with snot and tears, the stomach-turning, bloody offal where Kush's right eye used to be, Kwesi's jacket dripping pungent puke and the ubiquitous pigeons. But he didn't admit it to Karen, of course.

If he had, he might have been surprised to hear her come up with an admission of her own. Because her explanation of Tom in terms of his white-collar background (though it certainly had roots in her experiences of college and, in fact, every day thereafter) was distilled that very same night.

Specifically, Karen discovered that for all her friends' uselessness in the face of real danger and for all their tendency to fret about the rights and wrongs later (even if only in terms of abstract questions), their thick-skinned capacity to cope in the immediate aftermath was breathtaking. Sure, there was a couple of minutes of tears and tiffs, retching and rebuke, but thereafter the level of no-nonsense practicality and quickfire justification was impressive and spoke, she thought, eloquently of the twentysomething, middle-class trick of locating yourself at the very centre of your moral universe.

At the height of her hysteria, Freya shouted at Murray, 'You shot him! Oh god! You shot him!' and they all turned accusing eyes in his direction.

But then Murray said, 'He pulled the trigger first. His gun jammed. What was I supposed to do? Wait for him to have another go?' And they all accepted that explanation without further question.

Tom said, 'Right. That's right', and none of the rest knew whether this was a confirmation of Murray's version. And none of them asked.

Tariq said, 'So what do we do now?'

There was barely a pause before Emma replied, 'Do? We don't do anything. We get out of here. No one's seen us. No one knows we're here. It's just another dead drug dealer.'

Tom did briefly try and protest: 'Hold on. Somebody's died.' But he was drowned out by Freya: 'Emma's right. Let's go.' He looked to Karen but she just shook her head. She couldn't pretend to feel something she didn't.

Kwesi had found a Sainsbury's carrier bag and dropped his sick-sodden jacket inside. He said, 'What about evidence? What if we've left evidence? Tyre tracks. That kind of thing.'

Emma, who was probably the coolest of the lot of them, managed a chuckle. 'A Mazda and a Volvo parked outside Sainsbury's? Big deal.'

Tariq went to the car and took a pair of driving gloves from the dashboard shelf. Slipping them on, he strode purposefully across to the corpse and, crouching over it, rummaged through the coat pocket until he found the envelope of money. Straightening up, he handed it to Freya in a businesslike manner. 'Right,' he said. 'Now we can go.'

In fact, the only clue that they'd had an evening in any way out of the ordinary came in their refusal to meet Murray's eyes. This wasn't about whether they blamed him or not, merely that he was the main connection (aside from the body, of course) with what had happened. So they couldn't look at Murray any more than they could look at Kush's bloody wound.

Only when they were getting into the cars did they even take notice of what Murray was doing and, with their chatter, but for the merest hint of solemnity, you might have thought they were leaving a pub. Emma was taking Kwesi and Freya. She was fretting about finally getting Tommy into bed. He'd be a nightmare tomorrow. Kwesi had asked to sleep on the sofa. Freya wanted to call a cab from their house. 'I'm a businesswoman these days,' she said.

Leaning on the passenger door, Tariq saw Murray holding Kush's black sports bag. He shook his head. 'You're bloody joking, aren't you?' Then they were gone.

Tom had already started his engine. Karen called to Murray, 'Come on, Muz. We should go.' Her tone was gentle. He had his head tilted back, contemplating the black and empty sky.

'I'll make my own way, china,' he said. Did she really hear his voice break? Did she really see his Adam's apple bob in his throat?

'Come on, Muz,' she said again.

'Don't worry about me, Kazza. I'll make my own way.'

Tom drove her home. Or back to Jared's house, anyway. They barely spoke, which suited Karen just fine. She wanted to establish how she felt to have seen her hated ex-boyfriend killed. There were certainly impulses telling her she should care; broad impulses of the 'human life is sacred' variety. But in the narrowness of herself she knew that she didn't care. Not at all. She tried thoughts like, 'The world's probably a better place without him', to see how they sounded in her head, to give the event the wider significance that a death surely merits. While these abstractions functioned well enough, she knew they didn't really fit. Because she just didn't care.

At one point Tom said, 'We shouldn't have left him.'

But, as she didn't reply, the words just hung in the air between them for a moment or two before slowly evaporating. Karen didn't even know if Tom was talking about Murray or Kush.

Studying Tom's profile, she found she was gradually overwhelmed by an understanding of the connection they shared and, in its simplicity, she found it extraordinary that she'd never put it together like this before. Tom, by virtue of his ongoing need for faith (in God, in therapy, in Murray, in her), was aspiring beyond the mundane security of his background while she, by virtue of an upbringing that ever tried to drag her back, aspired to precisely that mundanity. A botched gun deal in a Brixton car park, therefore, surely brought them closer together. So they met once again in the no man's land of ambition; a safehouse of unspoken but mutual secrets.

Tom parked the car outside Jared's flat in Pimlico. Rather than leave the engine running he switched off the ignition, which seemed like a statement of intent. The lights were on in the living-room and the curtains were open and they could see what must have been Jared's sinewy torso and legs up-turned against the bright, white wall.

'What's he doing?' Tom asked quietly.

'Yoga, I guess. It's good for his back.'

'At four in the morning?'

'He must be waiting up for me. He's probably worried.'

'Where did you say you were going?'

'I didn't. We're not really talking at the moment.'

She opened the door and leaned across to kiss him. Of course, she'd kissed him a thousand times since they split up, but, as her lips met his cheek, she immediately knew that this one was different and she held herself there for a moment and shut her eyes and heard his intake of breath. When she finally pulled back, he said, 'You can stay at mine if you like.' And when she didn't answer, he blustered. 'I'm not trying . . . Really . . . I just meant . . .'

'No. Thanks. No,' she said. And then added, 'Not tonight', and even as she said those last two words, she realized they promised a future and, what's more, that was precisely what she'd meant.

'You OK?' Tom asked.

'Considering.'

He nodded, 'Considering.'

She got out of the car and slammed the door. Looking up at the window, she saw that Jared was still locked in his headstand, upside down. Even as Tom pulled away, she stood there for a moment and thought about the men in her life –

Kush, Tom, Jared and, she guessed, Murray too. Briefly, achingly, she wondered if all relationships were based on no more than coincidence of aspiration.

22 The London Pigeon Wars

As the tongue-tying's multiplying, so I know I've no time for bush-beating and I'd best be blunt as a woodpecker's beak after a month in the Concrete. For all her indubitable qualities of leadership and loquacity, and her indisputable skill for scoping the nuts and niblets that stayed stuck in the gizzard of a geez, Gunnersbury was no general and that's the verity. This is neither diss nor disloyalty. Such tactical acumen is by no means natural for a pigeon who was raised (as we all were) with no great grasp of the fabulous fortune of this London larder; so only god knows how Regent, the geez with a magpie phyzog, should have proved himself such a born soldier. But it's a tract of fact nonetheless and one we were soon to regret.

After the murder of Brixton23 above the Brixton Tarmac, Gunnersbury was very vocal about vengeance and, to be veritas, we had her tail feathers to a bird. We were all, like, 'What to do? What to do?' cooing on cue like squibs for a squirm, but Gunnersbury incubated her ponderings for no more than an hour after the Declaration of War before hatching her plan.

It was an idea that she ill-advisedly devised as 'the invasion' but, in its aftermath, became known to us Surbs simply as 'Paddington' (as in 'battle of'). And, even though I missed the horror's heart of it (and that's surely why I'm still here to beak on to you), that's a word that ruffles my feathers and curls my pigeon toes and no mistake.

Let me briefly illuminate the geography of the situation so that you might manifest a mindmap. Put simply, the division between RPF and Surb was a division between In and Out with Regent's hordes locked on a Concrete strip that stretched north from Westminster to the West End and Marylebone and then east along the river to the City, Stepney and Bow. In principle, therefore, us Surbs ruled the rest of the roosts in a wide circle around this RPF turf. That makes us sound like the powerful posse, right? Right. But in practice it was a whole lot more complicated than that.

In the first place, the majority of Surb strongholds were to the south and west; ticking clockwise from Deptford to Camberwell to Brixton to Streatham to Wandsworth to Hammersmith to Shepherd's Bush to Kensal Green and outwards from there. And the other suburbs? Theoretically, for example, Neasden, Golders Green, Hampstead and Highgate were Surb territories and the peaceable pigeons from such roosts surely claimed camaraderie with Gunnersbury and our gang; but they weren't much involved when the feathers started to fly, not after Paddington anyway.

Similarly, Regent, mostly through the guile of the gregarious Garrick, had secured support in Hackney, Stoke Newington and Leyton but these alliances didn't bother us too much because we knew there were pockets of Surb resistance in places like West Ham, Wanstead and Walthamstow that would at least make them doublethink before concluding to come to our commons and find squirms for their squibs.

In the second place, our strength was also our weakness. While we might have reigned over the rump of the roosts, that was a whole lot of compass to control (especially when you deliberate the down and up as well as the other four points). And as that frosty geez Regent made a virtue of the concentration of his isolation, so we were stretched as thin as the wind. I'm not making excuses but that's the acorn of the matter.

Gunnersbury's plan? That peachy pigeon's plot was simplicity itself and was rolled out just two days later (though, as I've already illuminated, two days can seem like a lifetime on the accelerated mindclock of cock and coochie). After the abomination of Acre Lane, you can bet that both sides in this soon to be war had reinforced their lines of spotters flying high over our bird boundaries (generally the young hotheads who could stay airbound for hours on no more than the conviction of their conscience). So I was to lead a raiding party of just twenty-five heartland hulksters to try and break the RPF line above Southwark bridge.

The way Gunnersbury illuminated it, it didn't matter whether we succeeded or failed just so long as we squawked for London and beaked with enough braggadocio to bring Regent's forces flocking from the Concrete. Then we could hightail it back to Surb safety where a tough young coochie called Lewisham6 would be waiting at the head of a 100-strong squadron. They weren't there for a set-to, skirmish or scrimmage but merely to provide a body of beaks to track-stop the intruders (if they reached that far) and hold on for support. Our deployment was, you follow, only diversionary.

After our Southwark assault had turned the enemy phyzog, Gunnersbury herself would lead a full attack at the head of 500 beaks to the west. They would, she assured us, easily overwhelm the spotters at Notting Hill before swooping behind the bulk of Regent's followers to surprise them at, say, Westminster – or Lambeth at the latest. All being well, the enemy would be driven into Surb territory and then scattered before our fury and, meanwhile, Gunnersbury and her closest consorts would be free in the Concrete to seek out Regent's own Remnant of Content. Gunnersbury was confident and confidence is catching.

Now, as I've illuminated myself for you, you may ponder what yours truly, a pensive pigeon with an appetite for analysis, made of this scheme that looks (with the benefit of hindsight anyway) blatantly bird-brained; a scheme that patronizingly predicts no worst-case scenarios and relies less on its own brilliance than on the opponents' disarray. After all, I'd experienced the brief exhilaration of the consciousness of consciousness so didn't that lend any objectivity (or bird's eye, if you will) to my view? Well. If you still cogitate upon this conflict like that, my friend, then you clearly haven't scoped the full scoop and you may as well fly back to cloud-cuckoo-land. The verity is that for all my consciousness, consciousness thereof and, indeed, contemplation therefore, I was still as confused as the next geez. And, like I've illuminated already (if you've been following), everybirdy wants to follow. So now you know.

I can't pinpoint the precise second when I realized it was going wrong.

My raiding party engaged the RPF spotters above Southwark Bridge right enough but there was barely a peckchop in anger. Certainly, we were some fearsome flock with thugalicious geezs like Sutton9 and Furzedown on my either wing and the enemy were squawking in terror when Tooting16 (who went by the nikname St George) sent some poor youngen whose breast had barely greyed plummeting to a Thames tomb (the second victim at a pigeon's beak, I hazard). Nonetheless, I was trebly surprised when they turned tail. I was surprised because we were well-matched for a scrimmage, because they surely expected reinforcements and, most of all, because there was Garrick himself at the forefront of their flight. What was that geez doing on the frontline? Generally he was never more than a wingspan from Regent's side.

I was doubtful of what to do. Did my raiding party chase them back into the Concrete jungle where we'd surely run into rough resistance before too long? And, if the bulk of their beaks weren't heading here then, for the sake of the heavens, where were they?

In the end, I'm shamed to admit, it was St George who took the decision. He called to me, respectful like: 'What now, chief?' But I prevaricated and procrastinated until he squawked, 'Let's get after them!' and set off in pursuit: 'For Content! For Content! For Content!'

So I followed my followers and justified it to myself with the thought that we would surely meet Gunnersbury's invading army if we could stay out of trouble and back-double west over Embankment and Piccadilly.

Garrick of course had other ideas and was soon leading us into the heart of the City and away from our Surb fellows. The atmosphere was a strange one because the skies were as silent as surely as the streets below were the usual hub of nik hubbub. As the RPF spotters headed further north and further east, I was developing disquiet. What if they were playing us at our own game and there was a posse poised to pounce in Spitalfields or Shoreditch?

'Hold up, geezs!' I called to my fellows. 'My bird's eye sees some starling shiftiness. We'll have this hunt another day. Now's the time to find our invasion.'

Despite some discontented contempt (from Sutton9 most of all who was near smoking with bloodlust) they swallowed my orders like a squirm – good geezs all – and we took a right-angle, dropped a forty-five and headed for the Notting Hill line, flying low for cover, almost brushing the buildings with our breasts. Nobirdy can predict might-have-beens, of course, but I reckon I made the right call; especially considering what we found in West London.

It was over Hyde Park that we first scoped them; scores of pigeons heading in to the Concrete. I didn't recognize a single one but, like I've already illuminated it, the features of a phyzog are difficult to differentiate for us birds, and initially I assumed they must be the vanguard of our Surb army. But then the cacophony of their calls conspired into a chorus that, to be veritas, made my feathers shimmer and almost snap in terror:

> The coochies and the geezs
> No squibs or pussy teasers.
> When Regent will instruct us
> We peckchop those Surb fucksters!

OK, OK . . . it was a ridiculous, ribald rhyme, only worthy of the playground babchicks. But it chilly-chilled my blood nonetheless. Some of them looked hurt or haggard, all right, but most of them were joining in this triumphal song at the very tops of their calls.

The peepniks crane their necks
Begin to look perplexed
When the RPF come calling
You know the Surbs are falling!

Luckily, or intuitively, perhaps, I'd dropped us lower still and we were skimming the Serpentine and Long Water, unseen as this bad bunch flew overhead. But you can bet we were full of foreboding as we cleared the park at Lancaster Gate and different kinds of noises – honks and shouts and sirens wailing – gave us our first clue of what we might find.

The nik traffic was track-stopped throughout the area and even the pedestrian peepniks were shock-stilled by what lay ahead. We caught niblets of their panic as we passed – 'What the . . .' 'Why the . . .' 'How the . . .' – typical niks who know nut all and are ever questions and no answers.

As we flew up Craven Road, I realized there were now no other birds in the sky (neither Surb nor RPF) so I took a steep seventy to get a better look at what was going on. My god . . .

As my consciousness degrades so too my grasp of language surely slips away like a squirmy squirm from the beak. But in this instance I'm limited not by my diminishing descriptive powers but by horrors that would have flummoxed the most talented tongue-twister. As I looked down like god himself, I scoped that a rough rectangle, bordered by Eastbourne Terrace, Bishops Bridge Road, Praed Street and the Westway and including both station and basin, was now no more than a mass grave for our Surb fellows. Hundreds of pigeon corpses littered the Tarmac and pavements and lay in pigeon-shaped dents in car bonnets and roofs. Shop windows had been shattered by dying birds who must have been desperately trying to pull out of their final free-falls. The Westway was chockablock after a speeding Transit had – I'm hazarding here – met a fleeing geez head-on and jackknifed across the carriageway and rolled upturned to a stop before four, five or six cars piled into its wreckage. I scoped several ambulances, pairs of policemen in sun-yellow jackets, bab-chicks who wailed at the carnage of it, sweets sweetly weeping and savouries who shook their heads and said, 'What the . . .' 'Why the . . .' 'How the . . .'

I peered down at my fallen fellows, seemingly all Surbs to a bird, and I felt like my poor pigeon heart, no bigger than a berry, might burst with sorrow. Sutton9 was at my right wing. His phyzog was all pity but at least his brain was still ticking over. 'We should go, chief,' he squawked.

We found the drabs and dribs of our mighty invasion had flown to Barnes Common, just south of the river. If I'm going to straight-talk and crow-fly, then I must concede that it took some time to establish the exact events since every single one of those pigeons was all shock and staring beads. They clucked around and cleaned each other's wounds but none was adequately *compos mentis* to paint a proper picture. In the end, I had to piece it together myself with the same tender care and heavy hopelessness that you'll see in a coochie-momma as she tries to piece together the shell of a dropped egg.

It turned out that a huge RPF force, around 1,500 beaks strong, had been right there at Paddington when the invasion hit their territory. When their spotters fled from Notting Hill, so Regent was waiting just a mile up the road, hiding in the eaves and awnings, unseen by Surb scouts. As the triumphal invasion flew cooing over-head, so the RPF emerged from hiding and sent fear and frenzy flooding through the flock and carcasses cascading to the Concrete. Indeed, Gunnersbury herself, who was at the back of the bunch, was set upon by three fucksters and would surely have perished but for the furious intervention of Finchley440, who beat them off one by one.

That poor coochie had made it back to Barnes but she'd taken a terrible gouging and goring and was fading fast by the time I found her, all alone in the arms of an oak. Even as I fluttered down next to her, I could see the light dimming in her amber beads. 'For Content,' she cooed, soft and mournful. And I replied likewise, if only to give her death dignity. Because, to be veritas, I already knew it was all birdshit.

When I located Gunnersbury, that peachy coochie was a firework of fury. She too was surely shocked but, the way I scoped it, her indignance was ignoble and veritably vanitarious. Maybe it was the god complex of which I'd already seen signs, but the way she was beaking on you'd have figured she were protesting the cheek that her plans should have been so disrupted rather than the deaths of a dozen dozens of her own.

I tried to ask her, 'How did Regent know where we'd attack?' But she wasn't even interested in this most quintessential of questions.

Instead she preferred to rant and rave with a tremulous timbre to her call; as if this defeat were in some way a personal slight. Perhaps if I'd pushed my point a whole lot of pigeons would have been spared. But I didn't push my point so you can scope, without illumination, I think, that sometimes the slipping of my consciousness feels like a blessing (with no disguise) or a sheep in wolf's clothing.

'Regent figures they can hold out?' This was the kind of stuff Gunnersbury cooed. 'But who has the numbers? We do, Ravenscourt. We do. And we'll overwhelm and overrun them with our battalions of beaks until they beg for the unification of Content.'

I did query her, veritably I did. 'Gunnersbury! What are you squawking about? Look who you're squawking to! You don't have to sell me a line. I'm not some naïve nik who can be diverted by a pleasing phrase or glistering goods. It's me. Your right-wing!'

But Gunnersbury just scoped me and kinked her peachy phyzog: 'You're a faithful geez, aren't you? A faithful Surb geez, through and through.'

I don't blame her. Perhaps, for the sake of the heavens, her consciousness was already coming apart and as a consequence her consecution was already faltering and flawed. But that is not to say that she was not responsible for the subsequent suffering.

Subsequently, Gunnersbury ordered two more massive assaults on the Concrete – one across the river at the South Bank and one at Wapping – and they were each as disastrous as the other. Sure, we slaughtered many of Regent's followers (who were, of course, no different to us but for the geography of their roosts) but we always came off worse.

To get to the acorn of it, you need to scope that Gunnersbury had no serious strategy beyond our greater weight of numbers. So she figured that if she got enough pigeons in one place at one time and passion-peppered them with her awesome oratory then that was job done. And when she sent these vast armies off – generally rag-tag crews who'd no more spark than a sparrow but had gone gaga for Gunnersbury's grandiloquence and agog for her phyzog – they were ready only to be butchered by the well-drilled RPF army.

At Embankment, for example, Regent did no more than execute the self-same plan that served him so well at Paddington. His forces hid under Hungerford Bridge before ambushing our fallible flock as we crossed the river. Our losses were again heavy and I can picture the whole scenario in my mindeye, no doubt. But I have no desire to illuminate it further and, besides, perhaps you have memories your own selves from the nik newsprint – the camera-clicking pinxen who was bumped from the bridge by three grappling geezs to a Thames-quick quietus; or the shattered space pods and snapping cables on the great Babel wheel that had sweets and savouries shrieking; or the greatest and gruesomest dogfight I ever saw that locked Regent and Garrick with Sutton9 for a full minute before that suburban heartlander (who was indeed the very heart of us Surbs) spiralled to oblivion.

Instead, therefore, I wish to pinpoint only two points about this particular catastrophe. One: our losses would surely have been even heavier but for the anarchy of our army, who mostly fled at the first peep of the Pigeon Front. Two: our losses would surely have been heavier but for the appearance of Mishap, staring into the murky river where it flows beneath Jubilee Gardens. You thought I'd forgotten about him? I hadn't. And here's why.

God knows who first spotted him and god must assume that they knew nut all about him. For starters, I figure he was my own personal philosophy and I never squawked about my thinkings and, for seconds, I barely recognized the savoury. He was unilluminable, of course, but now you could have hazarded him as a knackered nik without being dissed for your description. And though he was no pinxen, brownsen, blaxen, yellowsen or greysen, his phyzog was a splash of plum purple and no mistake. Nonetheless his presence sent all the pigeons into a fleeing frenzy. So how do you explain that?

He didn't do anything; just peered into the Thames like he figured it might hold some answers. But it was as if his very being bewildered the lot of us (RPF and Surb alike) and the chorus of our catcalls and curses coagulated into wordless screeches and squawks that were reminiscent, to use Gunnersbury's verbage, of the time before time and the language before language. So you can bet that we turned tail one and all, each guided by no more than gut instinct.

I tell you this partly because it saved a lot of lives but mostly because it illuminates the fact, in case you'd forgotten, that this old bird was constantly and consistently cognizant that the unilluminable nik was at the acorn of it all. But I digress . . .

As for the other great assault at Wapping, it was, if anything, a fiasco even more fatally feather-brained in its formulation.

Scope it like this: after the South Bank, you can bet that us Surbs were already struggling to convince our constituents of our cause, even those naturally inclined to support it (pigeons with religious relish for the Remnant of Content, pigeons who took a shine to Gunnersbury's wholesome white breast, pigeons who liked the war talk of best bins as birthrights and territory as turf). So we were forced to sweep the suburbs simply to round up enough reinforcements to fashion a flock.

Now, Gunnersbury's plan was that our great gang would gather in Southwark Park before setting off over Lower Pool, Shadwell and Whitechapel for the city's eastern backdoor (this was the very limit of her tactical nous and even this soupçon of surprise was something I'd pressed upon her). Unfortunately, of course, our raggedy recruitment was hardly rigorous in its regimen so the vast sea of pigeons that congregated on that Common was full of phyzogs that might as well have been a thousand eggs for all I could tell them apart.

Even as Gunnersbury took a high perch to deliver her heartening homily, therefore ('A great prize requires great sacrifice'; 'The illumination of Content is justification right there'; and all the usual fuzzy stuff), I was already full of foreboding. Like, I called to some geez who was busy with a best bit in his beak: 'Who are you? I don't recognize you.'

And he called back, frosty as you like, 'I'm Bermondsey71. You?'

'Ravenscourt,' I said. 'And who brought you here?'

'Nunhead8,' he replied. 'And that peachy coochie Nunhead24.'

Bermondsey71? Nunheads 8 and 24? I'd never heard of any of them. But what was I going to do? We needed the numbers. Nonetheless, my doubts doubled and then some.

When Gunnersbury had finished speechifying, we all took to the wing and for a moment I thought what a fine and powerful sight we must have made, some 3,000 pigeons blocking out the sun over Jamaica Road. Indeed, to tell the verity, I even had the brief sensation that maybe our coochie leader had been spot on all along, that everything was going to be all right. But, trust me, that feeling changed quicker than you can say, 'Oh shit!' from your slick nik lips.

Before we even reached the river we were confronted by a posse of maybe 100 RPF pigeons with Regent to the fore. Can you picture the joy on Gunnersbury's phyzog? She was fronting a force of 3,000 so surely that magpie-looking geez's comeuppance was up-coming. Unfortunately her expectations were not long lasting.

Regent was hovering on a breeze and he looked as cocky as a geez displaying for the peachiest coochie in the certainty that his luck's in. He called loud and proud: 'For the conquering of Commons! For squirms for all squibs! For the defence of our dustbins! For the power of the Pigeon Front!' In that instant I got an insight into that geez's mindset, all right. Not for him the highfalutin rabble-rousing of the rights and wrongs of religion, the moral masticating and the power politics of personality; all he cared about was success and it was an unprincipled principle whose simplicity surely served him well.

His words, though, were a signal and suddenly all was chaos and terror as our army tore itself apart from the inside. How many were there? Maybe 500, maybe more of Regent's faithful followers had distributed themselves throughout our throng. I scoped that they'd joined us on Southwark Common and, as anonymous as the Tower Hamlets towerblocks, been welcomed with wide wings.

Now, at their leader's command, they attacked the geezs with whom, moments earlier, they'd shared a squirm and noshed on a niblet. It was a most devious deception that threw us Surbs into confused commotion and even our bravest birds were soon high-tailing it hither and thither. For how are you supposed to fight the unidentified enemy within?

'Thames! West!'

I heard Gunnersbury's strained squawk over the horrific shrieks of both killers and killed and I and perhaps forty other faithful who still clung to that coochie (though now we didn't know why or what for) followed her flight. For all my criticisms of our leader, you should scope that both her courage when facing the phyzog of fear and her ingenuity in the eye of the storm were indisputable.

Of course, Regent and his posse pursued but it's veritable to say that, if Gunnersbury were no grand tactician, she knew the intricate ins and outs of a close-quarters skirmish, no doubt. We led those poisonous pigeons quite a choreography around Tower Bridge; swooping under, back-doubling, splitting up and reuniting, teasing and testing them with our intricate manoeuvres. It was here, I'm shamed to admit, that I claimed my first and only victim. I spotted a fat Concrete coochie scoping this way and that just a tree height above me so I took a vicious vertical and caught her full in the breast with my beak. Even now, though my consciousness collapses and recollections recede, I can still remember the crunch of her bones, taste her blood and feather, hear the pip-pip and final pip of her beating pigeon heart. Indeed, it was difficult to detach my head from her innards before she dropped to the bridge below, landing no more than a stride from a peepnik perambulator and making a shocked sweet scream like lorry brakes at an accident. I'm shamed to admit it both because of the chilled thrill it gave me to have popped a fellow pigeon and because I can claim no more than one victim of the thousands that died. That is, when you ponder it, another conundrum only civil wars can explain.

One other recollection of Wapping: in the end, Gunnersbury secured our flight by leading us, tight to the turf and goose formation, right past the Tower of London. Wasn't there some joy in dodging the Beefeaters and, especially, looking back to scope Regent himself, trackstopped by a couple of crows who then chased him away with instinct's disregard for his dignity? The exhilaration I felt as I fled in Gunnersbury's slipstream – my old-bird wings beating at a full 120 bpm – still ruffles my feathers at the thought of it.

It was only after this third disastrous defeat and the extermination of excessive numbers of our number that Gunnersbury finally agreed to a change of tactics. Even then it was probably force of circumstance that swayed her more than any recognition of wrongdoing.

Scope it like this: Regent's real skill lay in his know-how of our every formulation. Paddington? Embankment? Wapping? He knew our every plan. The consequent conclusion, therefore – ironic considering the feather-brained nature of this conflict (though is war ever any other way?) – was that the RPF victories were primarily the result of infiltrated intelligence. Of course, this came as no surprise to yours truly. After all, haven't I already illuminated the peculiarities of pigeon nature? Before Trafalgar, before the consciousness of consciousness, we knew ourselves only as birds of a feather so more delineated definitions never came naturally. What's more, the territories of Surb and RPF were ever misty in their mapping and the values of each flock full of fluctuations. Most of all, however, for all the typical Surb accents and Concrete conceit, it wasn't as if you could tell a coochie's conscience or a geez's allegiance just by scoping them. It wasn't like we had nik uniforms – whether formal or fashionable – to label us, so we were arguably only what we claimed to be in a given instant.

Do you scope what I'm trying to illuminate? You should do, I think. Because these days I'm not sure the peepniks (uniforms or not) are much different. For all my fascination with the unilluminable Mishap and conviction that niks like to hide behind their logos and *logoi*, I can't avoid certain observations. Take complexion: aren't London peepniks ever more mixed palates (if not entirely unilluminable)? Take logos: aren't cash suits often filled by niks speaking faltering foreign tongues? Take *logoi*: aren't City slicksters as likely to slip into street slang as any streetnik desperado? These days, this city is populated by a conundrum of representations so no wonder the niks are confused and stay close to the coteries they know best. So, at this crucial point in the Wars, us pigeons were exactly the same.

Put simply, you peep a geez and you call, 'RPF or Surb?' and he calls, 'Surb', what are you going to do? Peckchop the fuckster just because you don't like the dart of his bead? Intelligence was, therefore, everything.

Gunnersbury may not have accepted this analysis but we were so downright decimated that she had little choice but to savour my solution. And so we abandoned any grand scheme of a great army and rearranged our remaining loyal birds into raiding parties; that is to say insular cells, ten to fifteen strong, where every bird knew every other.

The conception was clear enough: the RPF surely couldn't penetrate these posses that would report their activities only to Gunnersbury, Lewisham6 (who was becoming increasingly influential) or myself. We gave these raiding parties no specific plans but merely the freedom of the sky to wreak havoc where they could: to propagate our propaganda (whatever that might be) to any RPF who might waver in our direction, to attack enemies keen on combat and even assassinate any of our own Surbs suspected of spying. Essentially, then, we gave the cue for chaos.

Let me quiz you: how do you measure the merits of a method? Certainly the war now turned against the rampant RPF but to whose benefit is an altogether equivocal equation. Sure, we caused carnage in Concrete and Commons alike, but to what end? Do you really think, for example, that a few words from Gunnersbury, Lewisham6 or me could conserve the conception of our cause? No way. Our raiding parties were soon as random in their processes as they were ready in their prosecutions. We were soon no more than terrorists with principles prostituted to the continuation of conflict. What was it all for? Though, at least initially, Gunnersbury still beaked a believable battle plan, the verity is that none of us now knew. So both the RPF and Surb flocks fractured into gruesome gaggles that served only their own ends and had no more to unite them than the certainty of their selfishness.

Now here's another query for you to get your beak (or nik nose) into; a real 'Which came first, the coochie or the egg'-type dilemma. As us pigeons splintered into ever smaller denominations (and even some raiding parties divided and subdivided again), so the diminution of our consciousness accelerated. We were dumbing down by the day. But which was the trigger? What I'm planning to pinpoint is this: was our ignorance a product of our failing faith or vice versa? It's a problem that ties this old geez's bird brain in knots and no mistake.

Does it bother you? I scope it does not if you're a peepnik with the composure of complacency so try this on for size instead. In her various verbage (oratorical and otherwise), Gunnersbury repeatedly returned to the time before time, the place before place, the language before language and the flock before flocks existed and she described this as a state of Content, an idyllic and harmonious London Eden (for what creatures have ever succeeded in this city so well as us pigeons?). What's more, I believe that coochie was honest in her approbation of Content as appropriate aspiration. And yet, as I feel my consciousness collapse, I can't help but question whether Content is where I'm heading and, assuming that's the verity, is my consciousness, consciousness thereof and, indeed, contemplation therefore a worthy price to pay? Scope it like this (and whether peepnik or pigeon it's a concept to consider): is Content really the height of my dreams and will I ever, even, dream again?

As the London Pigeon Wars unwound into petty and prosaic parody of what had gone before, I spent increasing time at Gunnersbury's right-wing. Although (or maybe because) she retained her reason far longer than most, the depredation of her own dreams hit hard and I felt she needed a friendly phyzog at her side.

Even for us, words came less easy now, so we took to taking timeless, silent flights high over London. The lines of spotters were long gone so there was no great danger beyond the raiding parties (of either side) that had retained their integrity if not their intelligence and still made like moonatics for the opportunity to tear a pigeon wing from wing. But those pigeon posses? They now had nuts for brains and couldn't keep up with our city sense.

Sometimes we scoped one of our formerly faithful geezs banqueting at a bin, following a foodchit or baiting a bow-wow. Once we scoped Furzedown, once Acton29, and we called to each of them. Acton29 took a forty-five and didn't look back, like we were contesting his claim. Furzedown, though, glanced up at us and there was not a niblet of recognition on his phyzog; his beads were as opaque as the buttons on a slick babchick's cash overcoat. Gunnersbury took such things tougher than me. I figure this was partly because of her god complex and vanitarious nature and partly because I'd already considered this conclusion way back when I first made connections with the unilluminable savoury I call 'Mishap' (for fear of the syllables of his proper name).

With the Wars winding down, however, at least we had the freedom of the London sky and so explored Common and Concrete as we saw fit. We pecked squirms in Soho Square and ravaged rubbish bins of their best bits without caring who beaded us. Indeed, even the peepniks who would have once shoo-shooed now hurried away or shock-stilled and stared as we tore a crust between our two beaks. They'd surely never taken such notice before!

Eventually we even toured Trafalgar. I hazard that it was in some way inevitable that we'd end up there before too long; that fate should feel that the end of the end should reflect the beginning's beginning.

We came in from the north and, since this was the very heart of RPF turf, we kept a steady high altitude, at least until we'd scoped the lay of the land. It was peculiar because we barely peeped a pigeon as, with growing confidence, we dropped little by little until we decided to catch our breath on Nelson. It was the first time I'd sat on that perch since you-know-when.

Suddenly, Gunnersbury's feathers ruffled and I saw a glimmer in her phyzog. 'What?' I cooed. 'What you scoped?'

That coochie didn't reply but took off on a dipping seventy and I automatically swooped behind. She slowed no more than a tree top from the ground and, for a moment, hovered on a thermal before, with its passing, winging a tight circle.

Now I scoped what she was beading and my call caught like gristle in the gizzard. I heard words on her breath – 'Garrick! Regent!

Lewisham6!' – the first she'd uttered in a day. There, below us, on the transparent, upturned nothingness where a lion should stand, those three pigeons were struggling in a starling-tempered skirmish on the slippery surface. Lewisham6 was proving herself a feisty fuckster as she held her own among the pecks and jabs and tearing toes, and in her beak clung to something I couldn't scope.

Then, for an instant, the mêlée of feathers parted and my bead fixed and, in spite of myself, I squawked a wordless sound. Next to me Gunnersbury cooed, 'Content', all soft and gentle, and she directly dived to join the fray and suddenly there were four pigeons hammer and tonging it for god-knows-what.

You know something? Despite my pinpointed positiveness of the pointlessness of it all, I would have lent my beak to the cause – veritably I would – but for a couple of considerations. First, I scoped with incontrovertible conviction that this was no Remnant of Content but a scrap of the unilluminable stuff that was dropped into the rubbish bin by the unilluminable nik named Mishap. In itself, this wouldn't have been enough to stop me but I found myself floating on a sensation of hopelessness and, contrarily, hilarity that swelled in my breast like a bubble. Has war ever been so worthless? Second, before I could collect my consciousness, I peeped the thugalicious peepniks, holding sticks and bats, and surrounding the transparent upturned nothingness with a thick nik net that they cast over the two geezs and two coochies who still scrimmaged even as they were dragged from the slippery surface.

In my mindear, I can hear their calls as they thrashed about with no hope of escape. 'Fuck off!' they squawked. 'Fuck off! Fuck off!' And I figure that if these are the first words of any tongue, they're most likely the last too.

Half-lifes

In the days after Murray shot Kush dead in the Sainsbury's car park, the others reacted in various different ways though with one common consequence.

Tariq and Emma, for example, threw themselves into their marriage with almost autistic enthusiasm. Emma began to cook for her husband every night, a wide variety of recipes made only from the organic supermarket's freshest ingredients, while Tariq rushed home without even stopping for a swift sharpener let alone anything to chase it. Over these dinners, they talked rapidly – about their financial situation, Tommy's latest gurgle, the pigeons, the state of their relationship (which, they agreed, had been through a rocky patch but was now stronger than ever). And when the words petered out, Tariq stubbed his roll-up and led his wife to bed where they had uncomplicated and mostly satisfying sex. Afterwards, if either of them were awake long enough to find uncomfortable thoughts come knocking, they'd shake the other and insist on round two until Emma's thighs ached and Tariq's back began to spasm.

Freya, on the other hand, dismissed the events surrounding her first and last attempt at criminality with what looked, in her mind's eye, like a vindicated shrug. Although in what way she was vindicated is anybody's guess. Freya didn't much care. She had a business to run. Anything Kwesi thought or felt was expressed through poetry which, though abstract, evolved a new and uncompromising viscerality which reassured him in something he'd been thinking for a while: thirty was both too young to retire and too old to change your ambitions. As for Tom and Karen? They deliberately avoided the subject. But that was easy enough. It wasn't as if they were unused to carefully negotiating paths around uncomfortable and unexpressed mutual knowledge.

The one common consequence, therefore, was that they hardly talked about what had happened, let alone about Murray, the guy at the centre of it all. And so their plans to rob the bank were dismissed by silence. In fact, the only person who really wanted to discuss any of it was Identikit Ami. When Tariq, Emma, Freya and Kwesi got back to the Lavender Hill house that night, Ami had elicited only the briefest explanation of events and subsequently had the vague and shameful but nonetheless undeniable feeling that she'd somehow missed out. And so with the very thinnest material of vicarious experience, she conjured in her imagination a televisual narrative somewhere between cop drama and a live feed from the CNN chopper. Indeed the others' refusal to talk about it only seemed to sharpen both images and plot.

One strange attribute of all stories (and most memories too) is that their truth lives only in their telling. After all, both are social constructions and, if they remain unexpressed, soon begin to decompose. This is not to say that they die or disappear altogether and elements may be recalled with the trigger of a specific smell or flashing image. But, untold, they have a half-life and quickly degrade. There remains every clue to what they once were but they are now arcane and require a considerable commitment of time and effort for their reconstruction. While, therefore, it might seem extraordinary that this group of twirtysomethings could step over memories of Kush's bloody corpse without breaking stride, it was in fact anything but.

In humanity's brochure there's always been a paragraph or

two of marketing puff about the power of memory; the capacity of individuals and groups to learn from experience. Only in recent editions, however, has this been marked with a footnote addressing the contrary potency. And even now, the ability of people to forget what's best forgotten (and the strength that can be found therein) is granted far from equal footing.

That said, of course it is easy to imagine scenarios in which this bunch would have been unable to ignore what had happened. If, for example, any one of them had chosen to break the unspoken vow of silence, it would surely have forced all of them to confront it. Therefore, in fear of precisely this, they now spoke rarely with any of their friends they considered likely to crack. Tom and Karen felt safe with each other; Emma and Tariq the same; Freya and Kwesi too. None of them were particularly sure about Ami but that was OK because she was working nine-to-fives in the bank and spending most evenings in an editing suite with the guys from TVX who professed themselves 'pumped' by the potential of her reality show.

Similarly, if they'd seen Murray then of course the memories would have come flooding back. But they didn't see him or hear from him and they told themselves, relieved, that this was just typical of Muz. Except Tom. Because Murray rang Tom once, a couple of days after the shooting.

'All right, china?' There was something weird about his voice; a stiltedness like he was slightly out of breath.

'Murray? You OK?'

'Fine.' Tom heard what sounded like a gulp.

'What have you been doing?'

'This and that,' Murray said. 'This and that.'

'You sure you're all right?'

'Fine.' He was suddenly impatient. 'Are we going to do this, then?'

Tom heard the question but didn't know what to say. 'Do what?'

'The bank, china. The bank.'

Tom sighed: 'Muz . . .'

But Murray immediately cut him off. 'Right. Right. And the others? Emma? Riq?' There was a pause and Tom said nothing. 'Right.'

'Come on, Muz. It went wrong, didn't it? It wasn't, like, Murray-fun any more. I just want to forget all about it.'

'It's a game,' Murray said. 'You don't just stop playing when you don't like it. Games have to be finished. That's the point of them. Self-contained. You don't stop playing football when it starts raining. Because then you forfeit, china, know what I mean?'

Murray sounded urgent, almost pleading, and Tom felt peculiarly exasperated. 'I don't care, Murray,' he snapped. 'It's time to grow up, you know?'

'Exactly. You are what you do.'

'And what you don't do. Look . . .'

'Tom.' Murray was suddenly very distant and very desperate. 'This is for me, china. I just want to finish it.'

'I'm sorry, Muz, but . . .'

The phone clicked and there was the dial tone; though Tom kept it to his ear for a moment as if expecting something more. He felt empty and briefly very sad. Murray had never asked him for something in that way before; never sounded so imploring. Then again, it was probably just a tactic. Because nobody knew how to get what they wanted quite like Muz. Was he letting him down? Maybe. But it was no betrayal compared to Murray's with Karen a decade ago. He shook his head and smiled as though someone were watching. He didn't tell anybody about the conversation – who would he tell? – and he made a conscious, if unadmitted, decision not to think about it. It was difficult at first but then there were the pigeons and Karen came to stay with him that evening and he had other things on his mind.

Of course, another situation that could have compelled the former would-be bank-robbers to talk about what they had and hadn't done might have been a degree of media coverage. If Kush's murder had taken place in a slow news week and prompted the leader-writers to proffer opinions about gangland, say, or the growth of gun crime, it's a fair bet that Tom would have been poring over the papers, Kwesi garrotted by guilt and even Tariq and Emma's lovemaking unable to forestall the inevitable conversation for long. It was fortunate, therefore, that the news was instead chock-full of another story that held London in its appalling thrall and enveloped every one of them to varying degrees.

While Karen's new role as 'Pigeon Czar' had sounded to her (and indeed to her boss and boyfriend, Jared) like a career cul-de-sac masquerading as a poor gag, it soon placed her at the eye of the most extraordinary and unexpected storm.

At first the reporting from West London was sketchy, even joked about by the DJs on local radio. But, within an hour, amateur footage began to make it on to the TV channels along with live broadcasts from the scene and suddenly the whole city was paralysed in shock.

Some of the material was certainly disconcerting. Though it had claimed no lives, the pile-up on the A40 gave up distressing pictures of twisted metal and bewildered talking heads bandaged above bloody T-shirts. There was also a van that had spun across the hard shoulder and broken the crash barrier to hang by its front wheels from the very edge of the flyover; a nod to just how much worse it might have been. Similarly, the shattered windows, the shop floors strewn with glass and bird blood and the numerous washed-out faces of schoolkids, bus drivers and the first policemen to the scene, these all made for extraordinary television.

Nonetheless, it wasn't the visible horror that stunned the city nearly so much as its cause. After all, broken shop windows and car crashes far worse than this were hardly unusual. But pigeon battles raging in the skies and pigeon corpses raining from them were an altogether different matter. The fear, therefore, was in the loss for an explanation. It was as if the city were pitched into a bad dream with all the crazed internal rationality such fantasies are built upon. The atmosphere was as though London were being punished for some awful but unknown crime. It felt like its very fabric was pulling itself apart at the seams which you could now see had been frayed for a long time. Was this another quirk of nightmare logic or a byproduct of the inevitably knowing press coverage?

The population began to panic, albeit in a restrained and rather orderly way. They didn't take to the streets, let alone cut loose in spats of rioting and looting. Rather, the vast majority retired to their living-rooms and drew the curtains and watched the television reports.

In one newspaper, a columnist suggested this reaction was symptomatic of the post-historical view of Western society; that it (society) was no longer regarded as something to be shaped, changed or even overturned but rather as little more than an elaborate myth whose exposure was simply too scary to contemplate. The journalist wrote: 'We retreat into our single cells, the very nuclei of our comfort zone, for fear that any action might further undermine our elaborate deceit. We batten down the hatches, stock up on baked beans and pray that when we finally open our front doors the myth will have somehow survived.'

Despite the abstruse argument and mixed (indeed, contrary)

metaphors, this article led the journalist to be invited on panel discussions on both television and radio. On one of these she sat side by side with the former clergyman turned Buddhist therapist Tejananda, who supported her hypothesis with his own. 'Without faith we have nothing to believe in,' he said. This line was unkindly picked up by several Sunday supplements in their sneering weekly round-up of notable quotables.

In the evening of the first great battle of the London Pigeon Wars (as they were soon dubbed by some smart hack), Karen accompanied the mayor to the scene of the chaos and was introduced to the media in her new role. Everyone agreed that, considering her lack of experience, she handled herself with some distinction.

She ran down the list of casualties and stressed that, while this bizarre occurrence was not to be taken lightly, shock and superficial destruction actually far outweighed serious injury. The driver of the Transit who'd lost control on the Westway was in a critical but stable condition and among the other motorists there were several broken limbs and numerous cuts and bruises. But it wasn't, thank god, nearly as bad as it looked. Otherwise, a few pedestrians and shop workers had required minor stitching for injuries sustained from flying glass. Nothing more. She praised the emergency services for their impeccable conduct.

By far the most serious incident, therefore, had seen an elderly man – Karen checked her notes: Learie Benson – who'd suffered terrible head trauma when hit by a falling corpse as he slept on the pavement. He had passed away soon afterwards in St Mary's A & E, though the attending consultant pointed out that the level of alcohol in his blood stream had hindered treatment and undoubtedly contributed to his demise. This story briefly sparked press attention; especially when they discovered that Benson's best friend was telling anybody who'd listen that the deceased had been haunted by premonitions for some weeks (in particular, this friend with a Knightsbridge drawl said, of a 'PR PR duppy'). But then they found out that both men were notorious local winos and their interest quickly evaporated.

Karen fielded questions with aplomb. No, of course the mayor's office hadn't been prepared for something like this but an investigation was already under way. Yes, they had been fully aware of the strange behaviour of the city's pigeons before now and that was precisely why she was in place as Pigeon Czar. Yes. That's right: 'Pigeon Czar'. No, they had no explanations as yet. Yes, people should remain calm and continue to go about their daily business as they had no reason to suspect this was other than an isolated occurrence.

Despite the genuinely distressing scenes of carnage – a square mile of London that looked like a bomb had hit it; shattered windows everywhere; and policemen in fluorescent jackets and rubber gloves collecting the limp avian corpses in dustbin bags – Karen enjoyed herself. She knew she'd done a good job and later, in a taxi, she rearranged some ideas that had been troubling her. She realized that, finally, she wasn't doing something she'd chosen in the futile pursuit of happiness but rather something she'd fallen into, however reluctantly. She recalled Jared's epithet – 'happiness is a by-product of what you do' – and she figured that she was now certain he had it right and that gave her two reasons to be grateful to him.

Since Karen's appointment to her new role and her furious reaction to it, the couple had been treating each other with arm's-length civility. This hadn't been difficult with Jared always working late and plenty of space between them in his kingsize bed. Indeed, Karen had begun to wonder if this was how relationships now ended; not with any deliberate decision but with a gradual waning instead.

Tonight, however, as her cab crawled through the streets of South Kensington and Chelsea towards the Pimlico flat, she felt a rush of warmth for him. It wasn't that she thought their situation reparable; nothing so specific. Rather, with the events of the day, she had the vague notion that he was somehow good for her. This lasted about half an hour from the time she walked through the door.

Jared was eating a stir-fry and drinking red wine. He hadn't made her any food and the wine bottle stood empty on the side. When he said that he hadn't known what time she'd be home, she nodded.

He'd watched her on the news and thought she handled the whole situation very well. 'Top job,' he said. 'Good girl.'

She made herself some toast. They were out of butter. She looked in the bin and there was a butter carton. She saw he'd thrown it away unscraped. She hated that kind of waste.

Jared joined her at the kitchen counter and dropped the substantial remains of his dinner into the rubbish bin, which, as far as Karen was concerned, added insult to injury. He then stood in the doorway and, reaching up his hands, hung from the frame; stretching his back. He said he'd been thinking. He said he hadn't expected the whole pigeon situation to be quite so serious. Nobody had. He'd been thinking that it might need a more senior hand on the tiller. 'Just thought I'd throw that out there,' he said. His back made a clicking sound.

Karen chewed her dry toast and swallowed. She shook her head. This wasn't going to happen. She pushed past him and, when he caught up with her, she was putting her toothbrush and a clean pair of knickers in her handbag. He said: 'What on earth's the matter with you?'

'Dick,' she muttered. 'Fucking dick.'

Karen headed for Tom's. She considered Riq and Emma's but no, Tom's was better. She didn't call him, just turned up on his doorstep. He didn't seem surprised to see her.

The first thing he said was, 'So you're quite the media star now?' he smiled. 'Ami will be jealous.'

'You said I could come and stay.'

'Sure.'

She briefly worried that he'd get the wrong idea. But, beyond the boundaries of right now, she wasn't sure what 'the wrong idea' was. Besides, she should surely have known Tom better than that. Because he was never better than when looking in on someone else's crisis.

He asked her if she was hungry and ordered pizza. She ate and watched herself on the late night news while he busied himself in the bedroom and then dumped a duvet and pillow on the sofa.

'I should get some sleep,' she said.

'I made up the bed for you.'

'The bed? I'll take the sofa. No problem.'

'Don't worry.' He shook his head. 'I'll take the sofa. I often sleep here anyway. These days.'

'Thanks. And sorry.'

'What for?'

'I don't know.' She shrugged. 'Just sorry to put you out, that's all.'

'You're not putting me out. I said you could come and stay, didn't I? Stay as long as you like. If you need anything, there's still a few bits of yours in the wardrobe.'

'Really?'

'Yeah. A few things.'

When she went into the bedroom she immediately remembered the last time she'd been there; the day she left almost a year ago. The recollection confused her and sat her down on the bed . . . his bed that was once their bed and, tonight, was her bed. That confused her too. Tom didn't seem to have changed anything. There was the same linen, the same books piled on the floor (books that, in fact, belonged to both of them) and the same happy photos on the cork board. She wondered if this lack of change said anything about Tom's desire to hang on. Probably not. It probably said more about his lack of care for his environment. She noticed the pair of boxer shorts scrunched up and discarded in a corner. They'd probably been there a year too.

She looked in the wardrobe for something to sleep in and found one of her own old T-shirts. She hadn't missed it. She changed and slung her suit over the back of a chair. Even the chill in the air was familiar as she slid herself under the covers. She had the strangest sensation; as if she'd just blinked and a year had passed and nothing was different. This irritated her. It felt like a comfort trap and she wondered if it would irritate her enough to fight it.

Tom poked his head round the door. He just wanted to say goodnight.

She pulled the sheet up around her chin. 'Goodnight.'

Tom lingered for a moment and ran a hand through his hair. 'It's like the first time you stayed at my parents'. You remember? After . . .' A combination of the next name in this memory and the look she gave him stopped him right there. 'Anyway,' he said. 'Goodnight.'

Karen's popularity with both press and public alike was quite sufficient to ensure that the mayor himself rejected Jared's suggestion that he should take over the management of what had now moved, officially, from 'situation' to 'crisis'. Karen was shocked by Jared's vitriol in defeat but at least it confirmed, as if confirmation were needed, that their relation-ship was over. She was utterly sanguine about this. She'd seen it coming of course and her only worry (about where she might go) was eased by the fact that Tom was a model of selfless and unoppressive support (as he'd always been, she conceded, in situations like this). Besides, she was simply too busy to think much about it; first with the excitement of her new position and profile and then trying to cope with each new pigeon blood bath and, more pertinently, the city's response.

For various reasons, the reaction to the second great battle of the London Pigeon Wars was almost hysterical. It didn't help that the news networks were ready for it this time and all led with graphic footage of the slaughter over Embankment which they balanced with expert opinion from zoologists, animal behaviourists, and biological anthropologists who took turns to say exactly the same thing in the different languages of their professions. They were mystified.

What's more, while in the first outbreak the public had been able to take cover in shops and offices, there were fewer places to hide on the South Bank and certainly not for the pedestrians who found themselves caught in the middle of the chaos as they crossed Westminster, Waterloo or Hungerford bridges. Consequently, the number of human injuries directly caused by pigeons was far higher.

Nine people suffered serious concussions after being hit by falling or low-flying birds and one child lost an ear to a crazed attack, another a significant chunk of her top lip. Worst of all, an American who tried to take photographs of the battle was hit square-on by three fighters and the angle of their impact and the force of the blow lifted him clean off his feet and bowled him over the railings and unconscious to his death in the Thames below. This prompted concerned transatlantic phone calls at governmental level and the *New York Times* headline 'London pigeons call time on tourism' above pictures retrieved from the victim's camera.

The collateral damage of this second battle was worse, too; certainly more costly. Both Charing Cross and Waterloo stations were forced to shut down for a full day in order to clear their concourses, platforms and tracks of hundreds of the dead and repair numerous minor faults caused by severed wires and the like. At the London Aquarium, a couple of dozen birds somehow found their way inside and, driven to ever greater frenzy by the confined space, killed many fish and then flew, kamikaze-style, into the thick tanks, cracking most and even puncturing a couple. Some of the aquarium's most valuable and exotic residents, presumably used to an altogether more peaceful life in warm waters around Pacific archipelagoes, were put down on veterinary advice, their nerves shot to pieces.

Unsurprisingly, the National Theatre and Royal Festival Hall had several hundred windows broken. Their dull grey buildings were also, however, redecorated with buckets of blood, shit and feathers and they appealed for volunteers to help clean up the mess. 'Our cultural pride and joy on the South Bank now looks like a Croydon car park after a particularly torrid Saturday night,' wrote one acerbic diarist. 'No change there, then.'

As for the London Eye, the glass in every capsule was smashed and one pigeon hit a supporting cable with such preternatural momentum that it snapped and whipped loose across the promenade where it connected with an unfortunate arse, breast and head, causing nasty fractures of Japanese coccyx, German sternum and Scandinavian skull. The wheel itself was stopped in its tracks and it took the London fire brigade more than six hours to rescue every passenger. One, a member of a touring Australian netball team who was also a structural engineer, was threatening to sue.

By far the worst impact, however, was on the psyche of the

city that quickly lost all semblance of confidence. Those who could, of course, stayed indoors. But those who couldn't moved like shades through the streets. There was no Dunkirk spirit, just a plague of surreal fear (and it is the surreal, after all, with its confrontational difference that often makes us most aware of reality).

It was as if the whole of London had visited the same deranged chiropractor. Where previously the city's eyes had concentrated on the patch of pavement six feet in front of them, they were now permanently fixed on the skies above giving everyone the appearance of rapturous born-agains. There were countless pedestrian collisions.

Buses were empty and tubes (regarded as safe from the pigeons) jammed to a standstill. Internet chat-rooms were loaded both with sick jokes about American tourists and new, ornithic interpretations of Nostradamus. Enterprising umbrella salesmen (generally East African) made a killing flogging brollies that, they claimed, incorporated a reinforced aluminium structure (i.e., the spokes); while enterprising street hawkers (generally Eastern European) sold T-shirts with a picture of a plume and the slogan 'My —— went to London and all I got was this lousy feather'. Schoolkids were learning new, pigeon-referencing hopscotch rhymes that they practised in breaks now spent in gymnasiums, classrooms and corridors.

By the time of the third great battle of the London Pigeon Wars, Karen found herself increasingly strained. Nobody held her personally to account but there were ever more generalized questions about the mayor's ability to deal with the situation.

The human death toll had risen to six. Aside from Learie Benson and the American tourist, there was now the Transit driver from the Westway (whose condition had suddenly deteriorated). Then, a teenage girl was set upon by two birds as she walked on the Mile End Road and suffered numerous cuts to her face and hands. Though she in fact died of secondary infections (after refusing to go to hospital), she was the only confirmed victim of wilful pigeon attack. Finally a young couple driving home from a South London pub swerved to avoid an oncoming flock (that 'looked like they were playing chicken', according to one passerby) and both were killed instantly in the collision with a tree. Ironically, it was the same Gypsy Lane tree which had accounted for Marc Bolan twenty-five years earlier and aged T-Rex fans held candlelit vigil nearby; some drawn by the fateful coincidence and others distressed by the destruction of the small memorial stone.

The advice at Karen's official briefings now changed. Londoners, she said, should probably stay indoors and avoid all non-essential journeys until the crisis was brought under control. In retrospect, this change of tack was a mistake since it only fuelled the sense of vulnerability and surreality.

Of course, it didn't help that the third great battle took place over Wapping; something that fuelled press paranoia no end. There were calls for more policemen on the streets and, on the letters pages, for the deployment of the army or a mass poisoning programme. Karen pointed out that you couldn't really have soldiers taking pot shots at every passing pigeon while laying poison all over the city was hardly a responsible reaction. She pleaded with London to stay calm and leave the problem with the proper authorities. But this didn't stop several vigilante groups taking to the streets armed with nets, capturing any birds they could and beating them to death with cricket bats and squash rackets and a strong if somewhat ill-defined sense of moral outrage.

Then there were rumours – at first ridiculed but soon taken more seriously – that this was some kind of terrorist attack. Exasperated, Karen pointed out there was no evidence to suggest as much but the rumours persisted and the newspapers that dismissed them still reported the gossip. After all, if you could train pigeons to home, was there any reason you couldn't train them to fight? There was talk of cloning, genetic tampering and, even, robotics.

It was within a fortnight, therefore, that the pigeons were the only business at hand and London was at a standstill. Many people took Karen's advice about non-essential journeys to include their commute to work and business suffered. The stock market lost confidence, fell, and then plummeted with the perception of lost confidence. Foreign airlines were threatening to suspend service to Heathrow, Gatwick and City for fear of pigeons flying into the engines at take off or landing, though there had been no suggestion of such incidents thus far.

Every section of every newspaper covered nothing else: news, editorial, travel, science, financial . . . and all others too. The sports pages, for example, were full of the cancellation of major fixtures across the capital while senior health writers offered worrying predictions of the pestilence that could follow if thousands of undiscovered pigeon remains on London's parks and commons were left rotting for the vermin. Even the style sections reported, variously, that the latest accessory for clubland was a catapult hanging from your back pocket, that extreme fashionistas had taken to wearing polyurethane masks, that dinner parties were the new restaurants.

It was at the height of this hype that two papers and a magazine decided to profile Freya Franklin Hats. Looking for an appropriate angle for the zeitgeist, they were quite taken with two hooks in particular. First, by Kwesi, whose poetry now brimmed with references to the pigeons. And second, by Freya's favourite design that, up to now, no one had bought: the chainmail-encased rubber cap that covered the wearer's ears with two licks. Perfect pigeon wear, the journalists thought.

All three publications, therefore, came up with near identical illustrations for their features: a picture of a ranting Kwesi addressing Freya in the chainmail hat. In one, this image overlaid a montage of pigeon photographs. In another, Kwesi was asked to wear a bright yellow beak on a piece of elastic. In the last, the studio was designed to look like the set of Hitchcock's *The Birds* and Freya was styled after Tippi Hedren (excepting the hat of course). But the straplines were always printed in Freya Franklin's colours (orange on blue) and the principle was always the same.

The day after the first of these features hit the streets, Freya's stock of her favourite hat sold out in ten minutes (she'd only made five) and she rushed the pattern back to her Indonesian manufacturers for a substantial reorder. In fact, though, the very exclusivity of the design only heightened her contemporary cultural cachet and secured her place among the elite of London's milliners. Big-In-Property Jackson dropped by to congratulate her on her success. His nose was almost healed but the slight scarring combined with his inevitable appreciation of the Pigeon Wars seemed to have granted him, in Freya's eyes anyway, a charming and almost otherworldly humility. He hung around until closing and then accompanied her back to her studio flat where she just about managed to rustle up a pot of spaghetti Bolognese on the two-ring hob. She told him she was hoping to move soon. He said he might be able to help.

One of the feature writers of the Freya Franklin story suggested there was irony in Kwesi reciting his freeform poetry to the wearer of this particular hat since the rubber licks over the ears ensured they wouldn't hear a single word. The K-ster read this comment with interest but decided, in his state of ever-burgeoning confidence, that this was really more feature than flaw. He posted this cutting to his mother back in Ghana.

With Freya's support (and, importantly, her new-found 'name'), he began to plan a show around the pigeons, the hats and this very idea; a show he launched a couple of months later in a subterranean Soho gallery. Pitched as the 'bridge between installation art and spoken word', 'The London Pigeon Wars' was an interactive experience which allowed the audience to wear various Freya Franklin creations (all of which had this particular auditory design quirk) while Kwesi performed several poems from a bird's eye perspective. 'I think many people believe the pigeons were trying to tell us something,' he explained to a late night BBC magazine show. 'This is my attempt to address what that might be.' The piece won several prizes and secured Kwesi a sizable grant from the Arts Council that came through the day before his birthday.

Anecdotal evidence

24

With the media frenzy heightening as public confidence fell, Karen was under growing pressure from within the mayor's office to come up with an answer, though nobody had a useful suggestion as to what that might be. They'd employed numerous experts from numerous different fields but, to a man, they'd been as baffled as their TV counterparts. Now the mayor himself, with Jared's prompting, was threatening to take personal control of the crisis.

But at exactly the same time as Freya was splashed all over the papers, Karen remembered what Jared had said when appointing her to this job: 'We need to be seen to do something.' And she made a connection, had an idea and called Tariq.

Tariq understood her proposition immediately and was in her office at eight the next morning. She told him it didn't matter exactly what he produced just so long as it had a story they could sell to press and public alike. 'Do you know what I mean, Riq?' she said. 'It's no disaster if you can't come up with a solution; we can blag our way around that. But what I have to show is a new way of talking about the problem.'

'Of course, of course,' Tariq said. 'Of course.'

She hadn't seen Tariq this enthusiastic for years; not since his days running student ents at LMT. In fact, she'd forgotten he had it in him.

She assigned him an office on her corridor and he got to work straight away. He brought in his chief computer monkey and requested every scrap of information they had on the pigeons' behaviour and movements: photographs, maps, eye-witness accounts, reports from all the relevant experts and so on. The next day, when she knocked on his door, he looked up beaming and clearly chuffed with himself.

'I haven't finished,' he said. 'But you'll be pleased to know that so far I'm pretty sure it's ending.'

'What is?'

'The London Pigeon Wars.'

Karen burst out laughing. 'Really?'

'The algorithms never lie, Kazza.'

'So why?'

'Why what?'

'So why's it ending?'

'No idea,' Tariq shook his head. 'My programme only tells you what's happened, what's happening and what will happen. It doesn't give reasons.'

As soon as Tariq had finished his calculations and was certain of his findings, Karen called a press conference for the next day. They planned what they would say precisely, weighing every word and its potential impact, so that she was guaranteed to take the credit and he to gain maximum commercial exposure.

'Good morning, ladies and gentlemen,' Karen began. 'I'd like to introduce you to Tariq Khan, managing director of TEK Systems, a computer software company at the very cutting edge of predictive technology. We have been working side by side throughout this crisis and have now made a significant breakthrough. I'll allow Tariq to run through TEK's findings and then we'll take some questions.'

Tariq's performance was exemplary. He gave the assembled journalists just enough technical explanation to ensure they felt smart and, importantly, important before cutting directly to what, he and Karen had agreed, was the heart of the story.

Whichever journalist, Tariq began with a smile, had coined

the phrase 'London Pigeon Wars' was unwittingly very accurate. Because what appeared, from ground level, to be little more than random violence was in fact highly structured combat between two well-organized armies (or, if you like, air forces).

With a map of London projected on a screen behind him and a pointer in his hand, he carefully explained and illustrated the way the conflict had unfolded; the major battles, minor skirmishes, incursions, retreats and what he supposed to be the two main areas of control. By the time he finished and Karen joined him on the platform, the press room was a cartoon of bewildered silence.

The first question was, 'Are you serious?'

Absolutely. The journalists could find all the data in their press packs. Because of the nature of the discoveries, the mayor's office had decided upon a policy of full disclosure. So they were free to check the findings with any experts they chose. Although, as Tariq pointed out, he and his team were the leaders in this particular field.

'What exactly is this technology *for*?'

Good question. It was a predictive technology that enabled pattern modelling of apparent chaos. It was designed primarily as a business tool with obvious potential in the areas of market research and analysis but it could be used to establish a system for any seemingly random series of events.

'If you're right, Mr Khan, how come these systems weren't spotted by the authorities in animal behaviour?'

Tariq laughed. He couldn't answer that since he wasn't one himself. He guessed, however, that those guys had probably (and reasonably) only looked for patterns previously recognized in birds or, perhaps, the wider animal kingdom. He couldn't say for sure, of course, but he assumed this particular situation – this London situation – was unprecedented.

'This is all very well and interesting but we don't really care about what's going on nearly so much as getting it sorted. So the real question is: what are you going to do about it?'

Karen answered this one. They had already established several procedures that they expected to have a significant impact on the situation within the next few days and resolution within a fortnight. She couldn't go into exactly what they were since they involved the use of several instruments that were protected by the Official Secrets Act.

She successfully suppressed her laughter. This had been Tariq's idea. 'Remember, Kazza,' he'd remarked. 'You're a politician these days.' The Official Secrets Act was a kind of unverifiable catch-all since she knew from experience that central government and the City of London never knew what the other was doing, let alone what MI5 were up to.

'I'll take one more question,' Karen said.

'Karen, do we have any idea why the pigeons are fighting this . . . this war?'

This time Karen allowed herself a smile. It was a journalist she knew and a query she liked. 'Of course we only use words like "war" and "armies" to explain what's been happening, Henry. We will investigate the birds' behaviour but the first thing is to bring this crisis to the swiftest possible conclusion.' She paused and raised her eyebrows in a wry expression. 'It's important not to get carried away with the anthropomorphisms. They're only pigeons, after all.'

As Tariq had predicted, the London Pigeon Wars now began to peter out; both in fact and in the city's consciousness. And if their brief dominance of London life was surprising, the speed of their passing into rarely spoken folklore was arguably even more so. There was still the odd incident – an attack on a pensioner, twenty-five pigeon corpses found on Peckham Rye – but press and public had lost interest.

As news hits the news section first before, depending on its import and momentum, working its way through the rest of the paper, so the reverse is true. While the pigeons were off the front pages in a matter of days, they did linger a little longer in features and comment. Some notable writers offered their explanations – occasionally fantastical, generally unremittingly turgid – of what had happened. But they slowly (as is typical of the self-appointed intelligentsia) cottoned on to the fact that public enthusiasm for the subject didn't match their own. As for Karen's promised investigation, it never materialized. And nobody noticed.

With the pigeon story swiftly evaporating, therefore, news editors (both print and broadcast) were like junkies who, after a fortnight of pure hits, would now settle for any kind of ropey fix. So they latched on to a minor high street bank robbery with a vigour that smacked of desperation. On closer investigation, however, it actually threw up several good hooks.

For starters, there was the fact that the bank's security system sounded for a full fifteen minutes before the police turned up. It transpired this was because the Met had become so used to the endless false alarms caused by rampant pigeons, that they'd assumed this was just another. Consequently the perpetrator had simply walked out into the street and disappeared among the shoppers with his bag full of money.

What's more, this lone gunman seemed like quite some character. He didn't bother wearing a mask or any form of disguise and the four CCTV cameras picked up clear images before he blew them out, each one with a different gun; an action which seemed like affectation since he was obviously already on tape. And what a sight he looked! He was wearing jeans and a baggy T-shirt which appeared heavily stained ('dripping blood' according to some eyewitnesses). He didn't walk so much as shuffled; as if every step were excruciatingly painful. But his manner was calmness itself as he munched on a box of KFC and apparently cracked jokes with staff and customers as he waited for his cash.

In fact he escaped with less than five grand. High street banks don't keep much reserve these days and, besides, a Securicor van had made a collection less than two hours before.

At one point, just before he shot out the last camera, it got a distinct snap of his face and it made for a ghoulish picture. His left eye was swollen and distorted and looked like it might pop out at any second. Below that, the flesh of his cheek was puffy and yet somehow . . . well . . . you couldn't make it out from the low grade film.

Of course, you could see his features quite clearly on the DVC footage secretly shot by 'TV personality Ami Lester' (as the papers dubbed her). And this was the best hook of the lot. A minor weather girl, cable presenter and music television VJ (this last, of course, a case of mistaken identity), she'd been working undercover on a pilot for a reality show and, with no apparent regard for her own safety, she'd filmed the whole thing. The media, who always found a joyous onanism in praising one of their own, trumpeted her as some kind of hero.

Naturally the police had taken possession of her camera as evidence and in any case she'd already sold the rights to the footage to one of the terrestrial broadcasters as part of the contract she'd signed within hours of the robbery (in alliance with her production company, TVX). Nonetheless, she was able to release a single frame of the criminal which fully revealed the grotesquerie of his face. Below his popping eye, his cheek was putrescent and scrobiculate, colourless tissue competing with pustules that were moist with yellows and greens. It was this gruesome likeness that accompanied the headlines to every news bulletin and stared out from every front page.

Despite the fugitive's horrific appearance, some readers thought they recognized him – among them a decrepit Catholic priest, and an alcoholic, vituperative poet – but they couldn't say for sure. One, the librarian from a London university, considered calling the cops but at that moment she was distracted by a tinny tune, impossible to pin down, that had bugged her at least weekly in the five years she'd worked there ('Should auld acquaintance be forgot . . .'). An office worker from Kennington actually went through with it. But she was no more certain than the rest since she remembered him through a cloud of Bulgarian wine and could only recall his Christian name anyway.

In the evening following Murray's robbery of the Putney bank, the rest of his former gang met up at Emma and Tariq's. Every one of them felt compelled to do so because of what he'd done and yet what he'd done had also somehow released them from any feelings of responsibility. For this reason and several others the atmosphere among them was very peculiar.

Emma seemed almost somnambulant as she had for a few days now. It was another month before anyone (even Tariq) knew why when she finally acknowledged her pregnancy only by miscarrying. In contrast, her husband was all bounce and bumptiousness; full of half stories of his new business partners ('a major sportswear company' was all he'd say) and full of himself. When, with an absurdly expansive gesture, he threw open the front door to find Tom and Karen kissing on the step, he said, 'And about fucking time too.' And then, turning to the others, he announced: 'Just to let you know, Tom and Kazza have finally got their bloody act together.'

After minutes of simmering, Freya reacted to this by telling Ami that she was seeing Nick Jackson. As intended, Tom overheard and he said, 'Jesus, Frey!' So she looked daggers at him and at Karen and back at him. Only Kwesi and Ami seemed oblivious to the rising tension.

When the news came on TV and its title music played, all of them patted Ami on the back and said things like, 'It's the start of big things. The start of big things. Seriously.' But Ami didn't seem particularly happy about it. Then the picture of Murray flashed up and they were all silenced. For those who'd been at work – Karen, Tom, Tariq and Freya – it was the first time they'd seen its full horror.

Tariq tried, 'Do you think that's make-up?'

But Ami suddenly seemed to snap and her words came out in a rush. 'It's not! I was there! That's exactly what he looked like! And why did he come in without a mask? Freya was going to make him a mask, remember? Where's he planning to go?'

Emma spoke up for the first time. 'I know he's been sick for a while.'

'It's not my fault!' Freya exclaimed.

Kwesi said: 'Fuck. Why did he go through with it?'

'It wasn't for *us*,' Emma said quickly. 'Not for Tariq and me.'

Tom looked between Karen and Tariq. 'It was Murray-fun,' he said. 'It had to be finished.' He sighed and studied the grains in the stripped beech of the floating floor. 'Murray'll be all right,' he began. At first he didn't sound very convincing but he carried on anyway. 'Definitely. You lot don't know him like us three. Murray can get away with anything. You remember Knock Down Ginger?'

'Or the Antiques Trade?' Karen added.

Tariq said, 'Strangers on a Train.' And the other two both started laughing.

'Murray will always be all right. The thing about Murray is
. . . well . . . how long have you got? You never know what's

going on with Murray so there's no point trying, know what I mean? The thing about Murray is he's a chancer.'

'A social terrorist,' Tariq nodded.

'The thing about Murray is he's like a sprite,' Karen said thoughtfully. 'No really. I'm serious. There's something magical about him. He's like . . . I don't know, you know? . . . like the Fonz or something.'

They were all giggling now. 'The Fonz?' Tom said. 'He'll love that. Shit. I could tell you some stories about Murray . . .'

Tom launched into an anecdote from LMT; about the time Murray pretended to be a blind man in the Arndale Centre. Apart from Kwesi and Ami, they'd all heard it before but they listened attentively and packed up at the right moments. Then Karen and Tariq joined in, trumping Tom with anecdotes of their own. Then Kwesi told the one about Der Vollbartclub Von Aachen and they all pissed themselves laughing. Suddenly they were all swapping anecdotes, stories, memories and Murray lived in their telling as surely as he had done for the last decade. Now Ami recounted the day's events – how Murray ate his chicken and shot out the security cameras – and now, recontextualized among selected recollections, they were safe, even funny.

If they knew in the back of their minds that they wouldn't tell these stories often in the future, they didn't admit as much, let alone what that might mean. And when Tom concluded, 'Murray's fine. Murray'll always be fine', they all agreed and they all believed him.

Tom almost believed it himself.

Some months later, Tom and Karen were sitting side by side on their sofa in their flat. It was the last night they would spend there and everything was packed up into huge cardboard boxes with clues scrawled across the side: 'tom's shit', 'kitchen stuff', 'files and things'. With Big-In-Property's help (he wasn't so bad when you got to know him), Karen had bought a small Queen's Park cottage at three and a half times her salary (she was now heading up transport policy since Jared had left for the private sector) and they were moving tomorrow. They hadn't gone into it together partly because they wanted to 'wait and see' and partly because Tom had only been working for TVX (as a researcher on Ami's show) for ten weeks and consequently couldn't get a mortgage anyway. They were sharing a Chinese and had drained a bottle of Pinot Grigio.

For the first time in ages, Tom was thinking about Murray. Specifically, he was thinking about the night they tried to buy guns from Kush and Murray shot him dead. Specifically, he was thinking that this was the last time he'd seen his oldest friend. But Tom still couldn't talk specifically so instead he propounded an abstract and apparently unconnected theory (supported by several seemingly irrelevant examples) that human behaviour was primarily driven by fear of farce.

Unsurprisingly, Karen had little idea what Tom was getting at but she did suspect that he was getting at something before eventually concluding that he was getting at her. She responded spikily and they were soon batting balls of bile at one another until they were both embittered and bewildered by the turn things had taken.

They sat now in silence, side by side. This was a reprise of many evenings they'd shared over the last decade but they'd get through it. They each momentarily wondered if the new house was such a good idea. They each briefly thanked god that they hadn't been able to share the mortgage. Neither of them noticed how quickly their recently romantic reunion had reverted to previous and well-practised patterns of behaviour.

Karen wanted a distraction. She wanted to put on some music but the stereo was already boxed and taped so she switched on the TV instead (the rental guys were collecting it in the morning). They caught the tail end of the news. It was an updated report on a corpse dragged out of the river a couple of months previously. The Met spokesman said the body must have been submerged for at least a decade so police experts had used the latest techniques to create a scale bust of the victim. The editor now cut to this revolving grey plaster sculpture: face on, left profile, back of head, right profile, face on. A young man between the ages of twenty and twenty-three, they said. A free-phone number scrolled across the bottom of the screen and the public were encouraged to get in touch. 'Someone must know this man,' the spokesman concluded.

Tom was sitting forward on the sofa. 'Fuck! Who does that look like?'

Karen gazed grouchily at the screen.

'I said who does that look like?'

The urgency in his voice made her peer a little more closely. 'Huh!' she said. 'Murray.'

'Too right it looks like Murray!'

Karen turned curiously to her boyfriend. His voice was strained, his cheekbones hollowed and the tendons in his neck strung like rigging. 'What's up with you?' she asked. 'That's not Murray. They said he'd been underwater for years.'

Tom looked at her and his eyes were glistening. 'It's the spit of him,' he said.

Karen burst out laughing. 'Sure. But Muz can look like anyone. You know that, Tom. Muz can look like anyone.'

'Right,' Tom smiled and nodded. He shook his head like he was trying to rattle it clear. But now there was an old issue bothering him; one that had pestered him for the last few months and, of course, a decade more besides. He pulled a face that Karen recognized at once. 'Can I tell you something?' he asked.

At long last Tom confronted Karen about Murray's confession; the one that had led Tom to punch him, the first and only punch of his life. He told her that he knew what had happened on their last day at college and it didn't matter but, now that they were back together, he had to clear the air.

Karen said she had no idea what he was talking about so he was forced to explain.

Karen's reaction was not what he'd expected – there were no sighs and no rising hackles. Instead she shook her head so slowly it appeared that she was simply stretching the muscles in her neck. 'Sleep with Murray?' she said. 'That never happened.' And her very manner brooked no argument.

Tom said (pathetically, he thought), 'But why would Murray lie?'

Karen shrugged; a movement so slow that it was as if she were casually loosening her shoulders. 'Why does Murray do anything?' she replied. 'You know Murray.'

Again they lapsed into silence. It was the kind of silence that requires breaking but Karen didn't see why she should say anything and Tom's head was hectic with puzzling. Why had Murray lied? He'd said he'd always look out for them.

Vaguely Tom remembered something he'd once thought; about the clarity that was found in disappointment. Then he remembered an idea he'd had; how people were either prostitutes to their dreams or kept their dreams as retained courtesans. It sounded like a neat construction but he no longer had any idea what it meant. Perhaps he'd lost his clarity. Eventually he realized there was nothing else to do but lean towards Karen and take her hand. 'I'm sorry,' he said and she immediately leaned towards him and rested her head on his chest and stretched her legs out the length of the sofa. He wrapped a protective arm around her but he still wanted reassurance. 'Are we all right?' he asked. He heard what he thought was a sigh and he was momentarily dispirited. But in fact she was just enjoying the smell of him, her nose buried in his shirt.

'Yeah,' she murmured with a devotion he appreciated and, though he couldn't see it, he could hear her smile. 'We're all right. Really. We're fine.'

Of illumination

25

The thugalicious niks are beating them. They dragged them off the transparent, upturned nothingness and beat them with their bats and sticks until they silenced their calls. And they're still beating them – Lewisham6, Gunnersbury, Garrick and Regent. Or rather the indistinct assemblage of flesh, feather, bone and instinct that once gave those names meaning. Why are they doing it? Perhaps it's because us pigeons tried to be more than we are. Or perhaps it's because only humans can be so inhuman and that's the verity.

As for yours truly? I can't scope this scenario any longer and I take a vertical and hightail it away. Imagine! To watch your leader, the peachiest coochie your bead ever set upon, pummelled to a pulp. Can you illuminate such a thing? I can't; not since language now escapes me, words ruffling my feathers as they pass through me and away like the breeze through an autumn ash.

I take a wing west and south and find an overhang on Millbank where I can pause and perch. They say that a pigeon who doesn't clock the sky for too long descends into moonacy. But now I thirst for that and no mistake! What else have I to look forward to? What other hooks upon which to hang my hopes?

To be veritas, it's hardly hyperbole to suggest that nobirdy – neither niks nor pigeons – has ever felt this lonely. For I lack not just the friendship of the flock but even the potential for as much. Dead or dull: all my friends and foes alike. Why should language linger when there's not one geez to gather my gregariousness, no coochie with whom to coo coyly and not even a squib to squawk at? Trust me when I say, I long for oblivion as only a conscious bird can.

I have stopped in this spot for god knows how long. My consciousness is now like breaking waves at a receding tide. The waves still
break and still cling to the shingle like a million fingers even as they
gradually, inevitably, join the great sea. Now, in my moments of
lucidity, I find disturbing details and fearful facts fronting my phyzog. For example, I have just found myself with a squirm in my beak
and wet soil upon my toes. But I recall nut all of swooping for
this squirm and returning to this roost. You can hazard that I'm
disconcertion defined.

The way I scope it, I have enough juice in this bird brain for one
last querulous question and it has to be, 'Why me?' Don't get me
wrong; I haven't fallen all fateful and I'm not directing this diatribe
to a deity with a tremulous timbre to my call. No. I'm serious. I want
to pinpoint the reason and right requires a reason because otherwise
consciousness is no more than a MacGuffin in a motion flixture (and
neither blessing nor wolf at all). Am I illuminating this, clear and
correct? I'm trying, I'm trying . . .

My tongue is tying but let me beak another bash. 'Why' – as in the
question 'Why?' – is consciousness right there. OK? I'm tired now
and I can feel myself slipping and, momentarily, I'll most likely be
shitting on a roof or rummaging in rubbish without even knowing it.
So go think about it for yourselves.

It's dark now and I'm swooping tight to the Thames though I don't
know what for. Instinct and reason? I can barely peep the difference.
Nonetheless I enjoy the uprush from the moonlit white waters that
cools my beads and shivers my breast. I wonder if a state of Content
allows appreciation of even such simple pleasures. Playful like a
squib, I dart beneath the bridges, criss-cross from bank to bank and
fly nineties for a bird's-eye view; like I'm mindmapping London's
artery for the very first time (though, in fact, I know it's the very last).

I'm passing Putney when I clock it – though, to be veritas, it's not
the 'it' that I first clock so much as the black holdstuff, illuminated
by a moonbeam, that nestles in a knotted thicket just below the

south side towpath. For the sake of the heavens, I don't know what decides me to detour (though I confess I've always – always? What does that now mean? – been an inquisitive geez who's not backwards when it comes to burying his beak where it doesn't belong). Certainly I can hear the pipping of my pigeon heart like it might just pop so I figure there must be some expectation of excitement to explain it.

I flutter down on to the mucky bank and my toes disappear up to my feathers in the low-tide slurry and slime. I scope the black holdstuff and I swear I've scoped it before (or one just like it) though my meagre memory won't permit me to pinpoint where. Then, no more than a willow canopy distant, I peep it; this unilluminable thing.

I didn't clock it straight away because it was surrounded by several other species – a starling, three thrushes and a crow – and I hazarded that I'd best not presume on their patch and, besides, what could these backwards birds be beading that would ever interest me? (And aren't I, for all my collapsing consciousness, still the cocky fuckster?) What's more, this unilluminable thing is the same matt mud as the shitty shore and the tide already laps at it and will soon carry it away. Still, now that I've clocked it, I can't contain my curiosity.

I swagger over to my brother birds with bold beads and a suitable strut to my step and they immediately fly away, fearful of my front (for consciousness is not a patch on confidence when it comes to conjuring charisma). So now it's just me and the unilluminable thing and I tiptoe towards it, clucking like a coochie-momma or a gossiping geez. Then a gentle wave from a passing launch breaks over it and turns its top-piece towards me.

Sudden like a thunderclap, I'm shock-stilled with a terror so tangible I can taste it on my tongue, a fear so physical it garrottes my gizzard, a panic so purgative it splatters shit straight from my geez's guts. Am I scared by what I scope? Sure. But scared too by the consequent conclusions that draw themselves up in front of me like the last bridge to my ailing aspirations. Can you follow my flight of fancy? You will; trust me on this.

I'm bead to beadlessness with a savoury's skull (complete with compacted cheek bone) that I can illuminate as surely as it's unilluminable. And as I scope that sagacious socket it gapes like a gate to oblivion where once consciousness comfortably sat in the cerebrum. Do I really need to illuminate the unilluminable? Must I really name that nik? Even if I wished otherwise I cannot stop the two syllables that form on my beak from solidifying into a strangled squawk. 'Mis-hap.' I call it again. 'Mishap!'

I've no time to reflect on this rotting relic, no time to ponder its putrescent stench or to go agog for its festering flesh that dissolves from its frame like the bark from wet wood because, immediately, I'm imaginatively displaced and devolved a decade, a lost lifetime, to be confronted by all manner of pictures on my mindeye. Let me straight-talk: these are not memories as such, more like the spinning celluloid of a motion flixture, coming from the corpse itself, the sprockets spooled from the socket of this peepnik projector. And suddenly I'm a squib again.

I'm a squib again (ten years or maybe, by my feather-brained calculations, even ten centuries ago) and I'm winging it over Waterloo with all the innocence of youth and a numb and nostalgic sensation that must, I suppose, be Content. I'm soaring over Southwark Hall where the student niks strut and shuffle and there's always the choice chance to scope the sweets and savouries dancing around each other like birds around a bird-bath – to be veritas, there's nut all I like better. But today the walkways are deserted and I deduce I'm due a disappointment. Then I clock somebirdy bursting from one of the buildings, striding doubletime. I swoop lazily towards him; more in hope than anticipation of any action. Must I name this nik again? Let's just illuminate him as unilluminable.

Striding towards him is a second savoury you'll ideally identify yourselves; a strapping cue-ball pinxen whose pinxen features I peep as plum purple with some kind of scarcely suppressed rage. Scoping the unilluminable nik's phyzog, I recognize it's all recognition while the hulkster's knows nothing of the kind. For a held heartbeat he holds his position as though ruminating upon a rapid return to the block from which he bounded. But he doesn't; only heaves a hefty breath.

They are just criss-crossing as I position myself on a perch above their heads; a ledge on the first floor. I catch part of what they say but some sentences get gulped by the gusts or the evident emotions of the moment.

'Karen Miller?' throws out the thugalicious pinxen.

Mishap catches that and throws it right back, 'Sorry, china?'

'I'm looking for Karen Miller.'

Several sentences are then buried beneath a breeze and it's some seconds before there's a snatch I can catch. It's the unilluminable nik. 'I'm her boyfriend, china,' he says. 'So what's that to you?' Though his tone's tough like a Tomcat and his voice formally frosty, there's the noisome notion of nefarious violence in the air, no doubt.

It starts to rain and the spit-spots deafen me again. You can fathom how frustrated I am! But beneath the pitter-patter I can still figure what's unfolding before my beads. The cue-ball pinxen's shifty and shirty, all vexed and flexing. Mishap is more motionless but his manner is mocking and his very demeanour a diss. Then the pinxen pushes him hard in the chest and Mishap stumbles a step or two; his arms outstretched somewhere between placation and piss-take.

The unilluminable nik is track-backing fast now. But there's no escape that way, just the tall wall that runs by the river. Whatever Tomcat cockiness was fizzing his phyzog is truly turned out by terror as the enormous pinxen bears down on him. And you can best believe I can hear the thugalicious nik's verbage and it's veritably vicious: 'You think something's funny, you cunt? You think something's funny?' And plenty more besides.

From nowhere, or rather fast and hard from the hip, the pinxen sends a flying fist that connects flush to his foe's phyzog with a gizzard-twisting crunch and crack. Mishap tumbles to terra firma with all the grace of a toppling tree and the pinxen stands over him, jabbing a digit in his direction and burying his boot in his belly again and again. I can hear the unilluminable nik's breath whine and whistle as it's kicked out of him.

'Where is she?' The pinxen has pulled him up and pins him to the wall with a fat forearm against his Adam's apple. The unilluminable nik's thrashing like a sorry squib in a pussy's punishing teeth but he can't loose the lock. 'Where the fuck's Karen?'

'I don't know,' Mishap mumbles. 'I don't know.'

The hulkster hits him hard in the guts and he doubles up just in time to meet a lifting leg that judders his jaw. The pinxen's laughing and it's a sound as cruel as a November northeasterly and loaded with the frenzied fury that displaces a misplaced temper. 'No?' he sniffs. 'You want to go for a swim, you fucker?'

With a single swift shift of his bulging biceps he lifts Mishap clean off his feet and holds him high against the wall so that one hearty heave will deliver him a decent drop to the other side. Now the pinxen's positioned between his thighs with only a massive mitt under each knee holding Mishap fast from free-fall. This is, I scope, not your everyday savoury squabble; not your everyday nik bickering, and I'm attacked with adrenalin and my blood is chilly-chilled.

Other pigeons are pestering my perch for better angles on the action and I'm concerned their coos will drown out the drama below so I take wing and hover high above Mishap's crown. I can hear him whining and whingeing like a swooning sweet, not nearly so frosty as frozen with fear. 'No!' he weeps. 'Oh god! No! Please!' I scope that such a pallid plea for mercy must be lovely to the lugs of this thoughtless thug.

From my lofty position, I can peep both sides of the wall as though they were two frames at the distressing denouement of a morose motion flixture. I scope the tide is just turning low to high and there's maybe two hops of sludge between the brickwork and the washing water. And right beneath where Mishap dangerously dangles, my bead now fixes on a prosaic plank – no tragic timber this – with a big bolt, dark and dangerous, growing from its grain.

Then it happens and I'm watching as if in slowtion. 'Motherfucker!' exclaims the execrable nik as he thrusts Mishap over the edge. He doesn't even stay to scope the fall but shouts and spouts stuff like 'Yeah! Fucker! Fuck you!' – like there's anybirdy to hear him – and then straight away scarpers east; to Waterloo, I hazard. Perhaps he doesn't care to clock what he's done. Probably he doesn't care.

Meanwhile, I peep the body fall and see Murray – 'Murray'; there! With the benefit of hindsight and the fatalism of foresight (perhaps I've no reason left to care. Probably I've no reason left), I've said it – plummet on to the prosaic plank that now plies a poetry of its own. Poetry? Sure. For how else do you wish to illuminate an individual impaled and impassive upon a big black bolt? Way I peep it, you've got to give it some culture, vulture.

I scope the life leave Murray like a sixtysomething savoury catching the last commuter carriage out of this supine city. I hear his wail that only whispers in the wind. I smell the vagaries and vicissitudes of dull destiny that can only dream of death as artifice more than precipice. But you really think I'm thinking more than banal birdshit? Think again and then twice more to be certain. Because this drama's a decade drained, remember, so this is veritably the time before time and thus before language and I can't frame further than instinct and intuition allow.

Us pigeons? Nonetheless we're transfixed and we take to the Thames wall and scope the situation; all cluck-cluck-cluck and coo-coo-coo. It's not like we're jumping to judgements of the peep show we've just peeped. We're not up to such sophisticated suppositions. Clock the scoop and you'll scope, we're no more than an animated audience in the cheep-cheep-cheep seats.

Our patience with this perishing plot is just beginning to evaporate when Murray finally stirs and struggles on his skewer. His phyzog's a gory horror and pink froth foams at his pale peepnik lips. He's making sounds somewhere between groans and giggles – 'uh-huh-uh-huh-uh-huh' – and he's definitely dazed and disorientated; doesn't know what's happened or where he is (sprawled and spread-eagled and kebabed on a bolt at the turning Thames tide). The fingertips of his left hand are lying in the lapping water and he turns his top-piece to clock them and there's that noise again – 'uh-huh-uh-huh'.

Our clamouring crowd of pigeons settle down next to him and circle above him like vultures to be veritas. But there's no insult in our interest any more than there's belief it's our business. No. We're just true London birds who find best success scavenging for scraps, smug in our simplicity and living our lives vicariously and that's the verity.

Being the courageous kind, however, I cannot contain my curiosity – you see? 'Always' *is* apposite after all – and I flutter down to land on his leg. Ha! I've never been so proximate to a peepnik before and I just rest there a tick, relishing the position of my perch. Now, I clock the longest and fattest and squirmiest squirm my squib's beads have ever scoped and it's wriggling out of the mud and over Murray's right mitt. I have to have that squirm! I have to haste to taste its fulsome flesh! Don't diss me. For the sake of the heavens, I'm only a pigeon.

I hop over to Murray's mitt and I peckchop that squirm just as quick as I can, dead down the middle. Trouble is, high on haste, I cut clean through its blubbery body and my beak digs deep into the soft skin of peepnik palm. Murray bawls like a babchick: 'Eeyee!' Imagine! Down on death's doorstep and he still notices a nip from yours truly. But, to give a veritable version, I should illuminate that the heat of his blood is a thrill (as it is ten years on when I chance to taste the same from a sweet's ear one Notting Hill nighttime).

I bounce up to his ribcage that rises and falls with a weird wheezing sound. His phyzog is turned left and scopes the surface of the river that from this troubled trajectory looks like a shrunken horizon that begins at his very bead before stretching to infinity. I'm a geez that follows a gaze and I too scope the savoury skimming the Thames tide in his rangy rowboat. That peepnik peeps us, I swear it, but he doesn't deign to detour. Why's that? Maybe he mistakes Murray for no more than a sack of shit with this pigeon perched upon it, ready to rummage for best bits and the like. Or maybe he mistakes Murray for a streetnik desperado, drunk and despicable, who's done nut all to deserve his duty. Or maybe – maybe – he's no better than us birds with care secondary to the essential selfishness of success (or, indeed, the paralysing perspicacity of disappointment).

For some reason – sympathy or sentiment, audacity or arrogance, or, let's be veritas, for no reason at all – I skip on to Murray's forehead and my pigeon toes are soft on his skull, I swear. He looks up at me and we're bead to bead as simultaneously, a lifetime later, we're bead to beadlessness. In that moment I scope so many emotions fluttering his phyzog but fear festers beneath them all and now (as in right now, as in right this second as words still wait my command) I wish that then (as in back then, as in long ago) I was able to emphasize my empathy to somehow soothe his suffering. But here (as in here in this half-state where nostalgia and narrative collide) I find I can't and instead I scope a drop of Murray's own blood forming on the tip of my beak that still grips the squirming squirm.

What do you figure? To me such symbolism surely seems absolutely apotropaic and I shake my head so that it falls with the pattering rain to land amid the pink bubbles on his lips. What else was I to do? I scope that, when the feathers fly, peepniks and pigeons alike revert to rituals (invoked or invented) and – you know what? – his features flicker with what's not far from a smile. Just for an instant, I'm granted a glimpse of the wolf in sheep's clothing and the blessing in disguise that do drive me to distraction a decade later. But then he's gone and only the idea remains.

Consciousness: it's the construct that concerns me and mine is connected to Murray's as surely as both are now on their last legs; as surely as the unilluminable nik's nature is the purity of peepnik perfection; as surely as empathy is embraced and discarded by peepniks and pigeons alike; as surely as the London Pigeon Wars were a fuss over nothing; as surely as I'm sure it's a capacity that most do their utmost to avoid. Consciousness: now the narrative's played out and I'm trying to treasure the final few moments of my bird's-eye view, I scope it as a concept that's neither one thing nor the other: neither wolf nor sheep, neither blessing nor curse, neither life nor death. But it's all that there is nonetheless.

To be veritably veritas, I feel cheated. You bet I do. But do you figure I'd swap Content for the brief exhilaration of consciousness, the consciousness thereof and the contemplation therefore? Figure again, my friends.

So yours truly finds himself back on the bank of London's great river in the unforgiving pip of the present, with nothing for company but a carcass that will soon be carried off on the timeless tide as the words slip away with a certainty that soothes and stings in equal measure. The wind is rising and I scope the black holdstuff and it's open and the eddies cast cash into the air (blue, brown and purple queens) and over the corpse of consciousness – illuminated for me, at last, as possibility's ghost – like a tickertape parade, all upside down. I don't expect your pity. I'm just a feather-brained pigeon with ideas above my station (out of the weather, in the warmth of Waterloo). I know that now. I don't expect your pity for Murray, either. He was a slick nik skating on this city's surface so smoothly that he barely left a mark. And when the ice broke beneath him, nobody looked for him. How do you illuminate it? Mishap, I tell you. But I do wonder if you peepniks have pity enough for yourselves. Because this could happen to you yet and pity predicates perspective and couldn't we all do with a dose of that?

My last thought is an absurd one: the realization that the corpse of consciousness took a decade to move upstream, against the tide. Figure that as you feel it. Uh-huh-uh-huh-uh-huh. My call comes quick, eager even as it ebbs: 'Consciousness. Content. Consciousness. Content. Content. Content. Content.' And, finally, words fail me.